ANCIENT WINDS

THE PATHWAY SERIES BOOK 3

KRISTY MCCAFFREY

A PATHWAY NOVEL

Ancient Winds

KRISTY MCCAFFREY

Praise for Deep Blue

"An...engaging tale...McCaffrey has clearly done her research... [she] effectively increases the tension every time Grace enters the water; readers will never know what will happen next." ~ *Kirkus Reviews*

"A hunky filmmaker and great whites, what's not to love?" ~ *InD'tale Magazine*

"... a powerful story ..." ~ D. Donovan, Senior Reviewer, *Midwest Book Review*

"A sexy adventure packed with spine-tingling suspense ... and sharks!" ~ Ann Charles, *USA Today Bestselling Author*

"Once I started reading, I couldn't put it down." ~ Robin, *Romancing the Book*

"... a mix of romance, thriller and sharks ..." ~ Donna M. Maguire, *donnasbookblog*

"This book has it all ... danger, intrigue, romance, scientific fact and a fast-paced plot ..." ~ *Love Books Group*

"I truly recommend this great read." ~ *Night Owl Romance*

"... like shark week in a book ..." ~ Rachel H., reader

2019 Write Touch Readers' Award – Second Place in Long Contemporary
2019 Carolyn Readers' Choice Award – Finalist in Contemporary Romance
2019 I Heart Indie Contest - Finalist

Praise for Cold Horizon

"… danger, angst, and drama come to life brilliantly, with characters keenly portrayed and fully developed. A must read for any lover of adventure laced with spicy romance!" ~ *InD'tale Magazine,* a Crowned Heart review

"Blending romance, suspense, adventure, and action, it really was a great thrill ride of a book and one that I gladly recommend. Give *Cold Horizon* a try." ~ *The Romance Studio*

"Cold Horizon will grab you right out of the gate and keep you turning pages as fast as you can to keep up with the action and adventure and suspense! A spectacular story of determination, courage, and love." ~ Ann Charles, *USA Today Bestselling Author*

"What a roller coaster ride! I highly recommend this book." ~ Dixie Lee Brown, author of the Hearts of Valor series

"Full of action, suspense and adventure. Loved this book!" ~ Rebecca Lyndsey, Author/Illustrator of the children's book *Into the Ocean*

"… this novel had me holding my breath! … definitely recommend it!" ~ Jessica Belmont, *Author and Blogger*

"… the imagery was powerful, the characters strong, the setting authentic, and the climb so very exhilarating." ~ *Shalini's Books & Reviews*

"If you're a fan of believable and emotionally gripping romance novels then this is one for you!" ~ Nen & Jen, *bloggers*

2021 National Excellence in Romance Fiction Winner
2020 Carolyn Readers' Choice Awards Finalist
2020 RONE Awards – Second Runner Up Steamy Contemporary

Praise for Ancient Winds

"… intrigue, romance, history, and adventure into an antediluvian tradition … featuring characters that are not just likable but fully drawn …" ~ *The Book Commentary*

"Ancient Winds grabbed me early and dragged me through the jungle right along with the characters …. As soon as I finished the book, I immediately wanted to read it again." ~ Ann Charles, *USA Today Best-selling Author* of the Deadwood Humorous Mystery series

"This book has everything: exotic setting, a strong hero and heroine, side characters who hold their own, humor, adventure, and a hint of the paranormal …." ~ Patti Sherry-Crews, author of *His Unexpected Companion* and *Den of Thieves*

"… a fantastic journey full of suspense, romance and very interesting theories that are actually real theories! Definitely worth a read!" ~ Rebecca Lyndsey, author/illustrator of *Into the Ocean*

"Very original, action-packed plot with wonderful twists and turns woven together with a romantic sub-plot. I rarely give 5 stars, but this one definitely deserved it!" ~ Joystar, reader

2022 Holt Medallion Finalist

Ancient Winds

Cover Design: Okay Creations - okaycreations.com

Illustrator: penny.illustration - instagram.com/penny.illustration

Editor: Mimi The Grammar Chick – merrelli.wixsite.com/grammarchick

Proofreader: Diane Garland – yourworldkeeper.com

Author Photo: Katy McCaffrey – instagram.com/katymccaffreyphoto

E-book ISBN-13: 978-1-952801-03-7

Print ISBN-13: 978-1-952801-04-4

kmccaffrey.com

kristy@kmccaffrey.com

To Ann and Amber
for help on the writing journey.
It's always more fun with friends along the way.
And many thanks for helping me unbungle my writing bungles.

"The future enters into us, in order to transform itself in us, long before it happens."
~ Rainer Maria Rilke

"As soon as I saw you, I knew an adventure was about to happen."
~ Winnie the Pooh

CHAPTER 1

Isla del Sol, Bolivia
September

Tristan paused on the smooth pathway cut through the rocky terrain and spied the man he was looking for. Dimar Castanos. The short, round-faced Bolivian was standing on a hill that overlooked Lake Titicaca, an endless expanse of blue water. The highest lake in the world possessed both beauty and serenity, but the return of Tristan's low-grade headache reminded him again that his body wasn't comfortable at 12,000 feet.

He ignored it as he headed down the well-worn dirt trail toward his target. Later, he would look for a vendor who sold coca leaves, since chewing on them would treat his altitude-induced malaise better than any aspirin.

With a half-circle of tourists huddled around him, Dimar was speaking quickly and with animation. It was how Tristan had found the slippery little bastard—through the tour company *Bolivia Today!* which was run by Dimar and his cousins, Freddie and Pico. Tristan decided the exclamation point on their logo was as pretentious as the three of them, and he was certain the tour company was run with half-efforts and shoddy promises.

A satisfied smile reached Tristan's mouth. The little shit couldn't run now. If he did, he'd go plummeting off the side of the cliff into the lake below.

Dimar spoke in English, his words clipped with an accent. "There are over eighty ruins on this small island. The Inca civilization dwelt here in the fifteenth century, and there were also as many as eight hundred indigenous families who lived in small villages all over the island.

"Isla del Sol means Island of the Sun. Following a great flood, the entire area of Lake Titicaca" —Dimar swung his arm behind him to encompass the lake— "was plunged into a long period of darkness. After many days, the bearded god known as Viracocha arose from the depths of the lake and traveled to Isla del Sol. He commanded the sun to rise, and then he created the first two Incas: Manco Capac and Mama Ocllo. They were the Adam and Eve of the Andes."

What a crock. Like any other conquering people, the Incas invaded the island, and then to solidify their claim over the local people they had created the mythology Dimar was sermonizing to justify their rule. They also, no doubt, sought to link themselves to the Tiwanaku civilization, fifty miles away as the crow flies.

Harold Gatty's voice echoed in Tristan's ears. "Tiwanaku isn't pre-Columbian," his father had said, his eyes alight with his telltale mania. "It's nearly 17,000 years old, a true marker that advanced civilizations have come to Earth."

Yeah, Dad, but radiocarbon dating put the site more reliably around 100 A.D.

Charlie Hartigan—Harold Gatty was his "stage" name—had always waved Tristan away when challenged about his belief in ancient aliens. "You're no son of mine," he would mumble.

Like any good boy, Tristan had desired the approval and acceptance of his old man. And so, although Charlie was gone now, Tristan continued searching for proof that Earth had been home to more than *Homo sapiens.*

However, a belief that advanced civilizations existed on Earth prior to the Egyptians didn't mean it was true, no matter how many crackpots spouted off about it. And unfortunately, that had included his father.

Such was the limbo of Tristan's life, caught between ancient alien theorists and the cold hard facts of science.

"Now," Dimar said, "I'm going to encourage you to spend your time exploring these ancient pathways on your own, and I will meet you back in Yumani where we will settle in for the night at our guesthouse and have dinner."

The tourists began to disperse, and Tristan stepped forward. When Dimar spotted him, his congenial smile slipped away, and his face turned instantly to stone. He spun on his heel and scurried away down the opposite trail.

Tristan quickly cut him off, putting a hand against the man's chest. "Oh no you don't."

"Dr. Magee!" Dimar plastered a fake smile on his face. "What a surprise to see you here."

"I'll bet. We need to talk."

"I'm very busy. I'm working, as you can see. I don't have time to shoot the wind with you."

"It's *shoot the breeze*."

Dimar stopped moving, his cheerful façade melting into a glare. "What do you want?"

Dimar's disdain, while expected, seemed excessive. Granted, the last time Tristan had been down here it had been a bit of a shitstorm. He'd been mixed up in a few shady transactions of pre-Columbian mummies—courtesy of his father and Dr. Conrad Fontana—and Dimar and his slippery cousins had been in the thick of it. The fallout had been both good and bad—his father had been thrilled with the DNA results and had included them in his last book shortly before his death, but the entire incident had estranged Tristan from his cousin Shea, who claimed the entire incident not only unethical, but that the subsequent conclusions were ambiguous and should hardly have been made public. Somewhere during all of it, Dimar had to deal with a slap on the wrist from his government, for which he apparently still held a grudge against Tristan.

"Time to man up and move on, Dimar," Tristan said.

Dimar pinned a ferocious scowl on him. "They fined me, no thanks to you. You here to settle that?"

"Maybe," Tristan hedged. *Not really.* But he knew to keep his goading to a minimum. For now. "I'm looking for Dr. Irene Caridad."

"Who?"

"Don't toy with me."

Dimar clamped his mouth shut, his lower jaw jutting outward.

"I heard she's headed to Rurrenabaque," Tristan continued, "and that you were seen talking to her."

Dimar frowned. "I talk to a lot of people."

"Why is she in Rurre?"

"How should I know."

"Is she going into the jungle?" Tristan pressed.

"A lot of people go into the jungle. It's quite the tourist destination, you know."

"And you know the wilderness better than most."

Dimar released a dramatic sigh. "You looking for a guide?"

"Are you offering?"

Dimar squinted his eyes so quickly that for a moment he resembled a cat poised and ready for the kill. "I'm not going to Rurrenabaque," he hissed.

"Why?"

"I am busy. I don't have to tell you why."

"Afraid of spooks in the Amazonian jungle?"

Dimar huffed. "You take the spirit world too lightly."

Tristan leaned close. "On the contrary. I take it very seriously. I need to find Dr. Caridad. And I'll pay you to take me to her."

"How much?"

"Two hundred American dollars."

Dimar guffawed, not bothering to hide his derision. "You owe me at least five hundred for the shitkick you left me with the last time you came to our lovely country."

"You mean *shitstorm*." Well, fuck. Tristan really didn't want to play into the man's hubris, but he needed to get into the jungle, and Dimar was the best option he had. "Fine. Five hundred."

"Give me the money now and I'll think about it," Dimar said coolly.

Tristan chuckled with little humor. "Wrong again. And what's there to think about?"

"It isn't just spooks I'm worried about. There are poachers, drug people, gold miners ...." Dimar shook his head, fear flashing through his eyes. "It's never a good idea to go milli vanilli into the jungle."

Tristan released a tired sigh. "I wouldn't want to go into the jungle with a lip-syncing band either. And I can handle myself with jungle criminals. And by the way, it's *willy nilly*."

"What?"

Tristan shook his head. "Never mind. Look, I'll meet you back in Yumani." It was the nearest town in the island's south end. "I've got a room at the same guesthouse where you're staying. You can buy me dinner, and we can chat some more."

Dimar's lip curled a bit and Tristan wasn't sure if it were a snarl or perhaps nausea.

"You're not altitude sick, are you?" Tristan asked, hoping to push aside thoughts of his own unsettled stomach.

Dimar shot him a look of annoyance. "It's not the altitude that makes me sick. So be it. I'll meet you later." And with that the man scampered off.

The island wasn't big, and Dimar couldn't escape unless he wanted to abandon the tour group for which he was responsible. Which was possible, of course, but it was late in the day, and Dimar wouldn't be able to get back to catch the 4 p.m. ferry to Copacabana unless he ran. He was stuck here until morning.

While Tristan could have waited to ambush Dimar at the lodging tonight, he had been restless upon arriving at Isla del Sol. Walking had helped to clear his head. And then he'd spotted Dimar, and he couldn't resist letting the man know that he was here.

But now he had a few hours to kill, so it would be a shame to waste it. Tristan decided to do the touristy thing and take in the island, despite that he'd been here before. The day was clear with a bright blue sky, but it was a buzz of anticipation in the air that he couldn't quite put his finger on that had Tristan's nerves humming. *Or maybe it's my throbbing headache and accompanying lightheadedness.*

While he had never considered that he possessed any kind of paranormal gifts, he did have a knack for sensing when he was on the precipice of … something.

Wearing a safari hat and aviator sunglasses to shield his eyes from the sun's glare, he walked the hilly trails, passing agricultural terraces, tranquil beaches, grazing animals, giant eucalyptus trees and cacti. In the distance, magnificent views of Cordillera Real's snow-capped peaks framed the sweeping expanse of Lake Titicaca.

It was paradise.

He approached a rectangular stone enclosure with three holes in the wall from which water flowed. A woman was bent over peering into the water. She kneeled and tried to reach for something.

"Can I help?" Tristan asked.

She glanced up at him. "Well, I seem to have lost my hat. A gust of wind took it right off. I was thinking of climbing on the ruins to get it, but I don't think the locals would appreciate it."

"You'd be right about that. Lemme see if I can help."

He was taller than her and his reach was just enough that on all fours he was able to grab the tan ball cap bearing the slogan GALLOWAY FILMS stitched in block lettering.

"Thank you," she replied as she took it from him, gifting him with a polite smile. She adjusted a pair of sunglasses perched atop her head, shifting the messy knot of brown hair gathered at the base of her neck.

He dusted off his hands and asked, "Are you a filmmaker?"

"No. My brother is. Marine films, mostly."

"Military?"

She laughed. "No, sorry. Underwater. He films sharks and other things."

"Like Jaws?"

She shook water from the hat. "Yeah, like Jaws."

"You sound American."

"California. You?"

"Originally from Mississippi. Are you enjoying your tour?"

"I am, but I'm not on a tour. I came on my own."

"First time here?"

She nodded.

Tristan indicated the structure beside them. "This is the Fountain of the Inca. The Incas referred to the three separate spouts of water as Ama Sua, Ama Kella, and Ama Llulla, which mean, 'Don't be lazy, don't be a liar, don't be a thief.'"

"How prophetic. I was considering being lazy, a liar, and a thief."

"It's a slippery slope once you start."

"I can imagine. Thanks again for your help." With a wave she turned and headed down the path that led toward a lake overlook.

Tristan made his way back to Yumani, passing donkeys and sheep along the way as he entered the small village with houses dotted along the countryside.

A few hours later, Dimar had managed to elude him at the guesthouse, but Tristan easily tracked him down at one of the local restaurants with a spectacular view of Lake Titicaca.

As Tristan took a seat, Dimar grimaced.

"Dining alone?"

"Just keeping an eye on my guests," Dimar replied, indicating the people sitting at the other tables with a wave of his hand.

"Thanks for saving me a seat." Tristan ordered a local beer and a plate of fresh trout. "Have you given any thought to my offer?"

"Offer?" Dimar grunted. "I know it's an order. But sí, I will take you. In two days. Because you owe me that money."

Tristan gave a salute with his beer bottle and took a drink.

"Excuse me," a female voice interrupted from behind Tristan. "Are you Dimar Castanos?"

A glance over his shoulder confirmed that it was the woman he'd helped earlier at the Fountain of the Incas.

"Who's asking?" Dimar said.

"You've found him," Tristan spoke at the same time.

The woman's gaze settled on Tristan. Instead of the earlier polite friendliness, her eyes flashed with a glint of wariness. "We meet again." But she didn't dwell on their brief acquaintance and instead shifted her focus back to Dimar. "I've been looking for you. You've been incredibly difficult to locate." She stepped from behind Tristan's chair and held out a hand. "I'm Brynn Galloway. I'm a friend of Irene Caridad's, and she told me you would help me."

Brynn Galloway? Why did that name sound familiar?

Dimar shook her hand. "Pleased to meet you," he said, his reply nothing more than a monotone. While Dimar could prove elusive to track down, he was never elusive with his displeasure. Apparently, he'd not only been avoiding Tristan but also California Girl with the ball cap from her brother.

"You should join us," Tristan offered, grabbing an extra chair from a nearby table. He couldn't deny that seeing Dimar squirm gave him joy, but randomly meeting this woman who was also looking for Irene was nothing short of the universe showering him with synchronicity.

"Thank you," she replied, her response business-like. "If it's not too much trouble." She sat while saying the last bit, clearly staying whether it was a bother or not.

Apparently, Irene was drawing others into her antiquities side-hustle, and Tristan couldn't wait to hear Ms. Galloway's side of the story. Because, goddammit, he'd protect his own interests at all costs.

But when Brynn Galloway cast a look his way, the flickering candlelight caressing her cheeks and illuminating eyes that made him think of a calculating jaguar, a jolt of awareness caught him by surprise.

His brief encounter with her had showed her to be confident, intelligent, and to possess a dry wit—nectar to his libido to be certain. But he wasn't looking for a quick lay. Been there, done that. Nor did he have time for emotional entanglements. Chasing antiquities on the black market the past few years had effectively hardened him about every aspect of living.

People were greedy, selfish, self-serving. End of story.

At the moment, he had room in his life for only one thing, and that was retrieving what Irene Caridad had so brazenly stolen from him.

If Brynn Galloway could facilitate that in any way, he'd use it.

He extended his hand and said, "No trouble at all. I'm Tristan Magee." A vague disappointment filled him when there was no violin serenade or explosions of fireworks when she touched him.

After a simple handshake, she tucked herself back into her space.

Get your head straight, man. She's just a woman.

While the restaurant ran a generator, it was only for the kitchen. With the candlelight and the full moon highlighting the shimmering waters of Lake Titicaca, the ambiance was downright romantic.

"You Americans are bullies," Dimar cut in, ruining the mood.

"I beg your pardon?" Ms. Galloway replied.

"First him"—Dimar thrust a finger at Tristan—"now you. I'm on vacation."

"No you're not," Tristan rebutted.

"A working vacation." Dimar uttered the syllables with precision. "Isn't that what you Americans do all the time? So you can write off all your expenses?"

"Well, anyway," Ms. Galloway said. "Irene said that she was unable to wait for me in La Paz and that you would take me to her."

"Who told you that?" Dimar demanded.

Ms. Galloway's forehead wrinkled into a lovely look of consternation.

"Don't worry, he's not as dumb as he sounds," Tristan said.

"Are you sure?" she murmured, flashing Tristan a look of amusement before returning her attention to Dimar with a sigh. "As I just said, *Dr. Caridad told me.* In an email."

Tristan chuckled. "Looks like you've got more customers than you can handle, Dimar."

The look she cast Tristan's way no longer held amusement but instead a glint of annoyance. "Who are you again?" she asked.

"A friend of Dimar's."

"You are no friend of mine, Dr. Magee," Dimar said with a beady glare.

Tristan could all but hear Ms. Galloway's brain clicking away as she contemplated her table mates. He asked in as light a tone as he could muster, "Do *you* know where Dr. Caridad is?"

She shook her head. "If I did, why would I have come all the way out to Isla del Sol, which is beautiful by the way but is costing me an extra two days of travel, to interrogate you monkeys?"

"Bully," Dimar muttered.

"I'm not a bully," Ms. Galloway replied, clearly exasperated. "I had hoped to have this resolved as soon as I landed in La Paz, and frankly, Mr. Castanos, your lack of response has been nothing short of rude and aggravating."

Tristan drained the last of his beer. "She's got your number, Dimar."

"Fine," the Bolivian said. "You can come with us. Dr. Magee here is already paying for my services, so I won't charge you." He gloated triumphantly from across the table.

Ms. Galloway gave Tristan an assessing look. "You're looking for Irene as well? And how do *you* know her?"

"That's not important. You're welcome to join us"—he nodded toward Dimar—"if you like."

"Into the jungle?"

Ms. Galloway's innocent question confirmed Tristan's suspicion that Irene had gone off grid. The question was, why? The only answer he could come up with was she planned to sell his artifact, but it baffled him as to why she would disappear into the Bolivian jungle to do it.

"The one and only," Tristan replied, then he remembered how he knew of Brynn Galloway. It was also clear why she was here, whether she copped to it or not.

"I'll bet you're an archaeologist," he said, knowing full well she was. "Why don't you let me buy you dinner? And we can chat."

～

IF IT WEREN'T for the fact that Tristan Magee watched her with a detached speculative look in his eyes, Brynn could almost allow herself the indulgence of meeting a handsome stranger in a strange land, with serendipity her companion as she crossed paths with him not once but twice. And they were both acquainted with Brynn's mentor, Dr. Irene Caridad, professor of Near Eastern Culture and Language at the University of California, Los Angeles.

The grumpy Bolivian man, Dimar, whom she'd been trying to locate for over two days, had departed, claiming exhaustion. She could only hope that he wouldn't disappear come morning, but her dinner companion had assured her that Dimar would follow through on his promise to take them north. All it had taken was a monetary incentive.

Now it was just her and this enigmatic man who watched her like she had something to hide.

So naturally it had to be *him* playing cloak and dagger.

She should have left when Dimar had, but she was famished, and the trout and vegetables and rice, along with the cold beer, were hitting the spot.

"What do you do, Dr. Magee?"

"You can call me Tristan. I'm a physicist."

"And you work in La Paz?"

"No." Having finished his meal, he leaned back in his chair, tossing his napkin onto the table. "You're an archaeologist, but not a Ph.D., at least not yet."

Was it written on her forehead? She craved the legitimacy a doctorate would give her, but lately she'd been feeling less than excited about pursuing it. There had even been a few moments when she'd considered leaving school and getting on with her life.

"I'm thinking these aren't lucky guesses on your part," she said. Irene must have told him. But why? "What exactly is your association with Irene? I've never known her to work with a physicist."

Rather than answer her question, he said, "I read your paper."

That stopped her cold. "What paper?"

"Your master's thesis on the Moon Tablet of Ur."

Brynn was a bit flabbergasted. It wasn't that her work was a secret, but few people perused research projects for light reading unless they needed to reference it in their own work. And she'd written her thesis nearly two years ago. She was becoming more confused by the minute.

"Are *you* an archaeologist?" she asked. She'd only had one beer, but when the waitress returned, she waved off having another. She needed to keep her wits about her.

"No. Just an interested party. And I'm guessing that's why you came."

"I came to Bolivia because of my thesis?" she asked, wondering if the altitude was getting to her. Impossible. She'd recently spent the summer at K2 Base Camp, and since it was situated at 16,000 feet, she was more acclimated than any Bolivian local. "No," she answered her own question. "I came because Irene asked me to."

"And you didn't think it was odd that she asked you to come to Bolivia when your area of study is Sumerian culture?"

It would certainly have given Brynn pause, except that during their email exchanges, Irene had told her that Connie—Dr. Conrad Fontana and Irene's husband—may have found proof of Sumerian habitation in the Americas. They wanted Brynn to be part of the discovery team, and while she was more than a little skeptical, if it turned out to be true, then it would make for one hell of a Ph.D. dissertation topic.

And while her ambition for gaining a Ph.D. had been slowly waning, she would have come anyway. For Gramps. Her grandfather —Domenico Milano, nicknamed "Mico"—had been a passionate hobbyist of all things Sumerian. Brynn only wished he were still alive so she could share her adventure with him, whether it panned out or not.

Since she had little reason to trust Tristan Magee, she feigned ignorance. "Well, I suppose I need to speak with Irene before I jump to any conclusions. But you think this all has something to do with my thesis? If you read it, then you know that it was a boring treatise on ancient metallurgical practices. Also, much of it was conjecture since the tablet has never been found." She didn't mention the more fringe belief that the tablet also contained celestial maps for space journeying and alchemical references to time travel. She hadn't been foolish enough to include that in her final copy.

He nodded. "Never been found. Is that your story?"

She froze, stunned. "What are you saying? Has it been found?" She couldn't hide her excitement.

Tristan's gaze locked onto her. He was a handsome devil with sky blue eyes framed by dark brown hair, and her heart performed an unwanted flutter. Time slowed, and she felt a rush of everything cliché: a sense of rightness, of anticipation, inevitability. As if she and this man had been destined to meet.

And then it was over, and with a flash of irritation she pushed it aside. *Quit acting like a princess who just found the man who would save her. What a load of horseshit.*

"You think Irene found a Sumerian cuneiform tablet in the Bolivian jungle?" she asked. Was this why her mentor had asked her to come?

"Of course not. How the hell would the Sumerians have gotten here? A flying saucer?"

Connie and Irene had conjectured about the global reach of the Sumerian culture, but that's all it had been—a fanciful hypothesis. Brynn had never really taken it seriously. Sumer was an area of land in Mesopotamia, which was essentially modern-day Iraq. A place far away from the likes of here.

"Right," Brynn said, trying to ignore the crackle of annoyance hovering between her and this man. "You're talking about the alien theories regarding the Sumerians, Dr. Magee." She over-emphasized his name, trying to put professional distance between them. "There's certainly plenty of fruitcakes who like to talk about aliens visiting the earth, and especially their link to the region known as Sumer. A flying saucer would explain how they could have brought their precious clay tablets into the Bolivian jungle. I'm afraid I've never bought into such theories."

"Fruitcakes, huh?"

She relaxed her shoulders. "Maybe that's too harsh. My old college roommate Audrey always liked to consider the possibilities of alien technology. She even thinks the Sumerian gods could have been extraterrestrials. And she's not a fruitcake. In fact, she's a miracle."

"How's that?"

Some of the tension from moments ago began to dissolve and the rigidness in Brynn's body released in small increments.

"As a child, she had brain cancer. When she was nine years old, her father took her camping in Northern Arizona, and something amazing happened. She was cured."

"Just like that?"

Brynn nodded.

"And her cancer never returned?" he asked.

"Nope." She knocked on the table just in case for good measure. Now that she had calmed down—Audrey generally had that effect on her, especially in person but it would seem her aura could also reach across continents—she returned to the topic at hand. "Why are you looking for Irene?"

"She stole something from me."

"And you think she brought it here?"

"I do."

"What is it?"

"The Moon Tablet of Ur."

Was this man for real?

A grin split her face. "Holy shit."

CHAPTER 2

Tristan sat in the small ferry that bounced along Lake Titicaca. It was a ninety-minute ride from Yumani to Copacabana, and then a two-hour bus ride back to La Paz. Locating Dimar had been a grade-A pain in the ass, but visiting Isla del Sol had been almost like a vacation, something Tristan hadn't done in years. And how long had it been since he'd enjoyed a candlelight dinner with a woman? Sparring with Brynn Galloway last night had been ... well, fun.

He glanced to the front of the boat where she sat, facing away from him with her nose buried in a book. Her brown hair was caught up into a ponytail, whipping wildly in the wind. She wore sunglasses, khaki pants, and a basic camp shirt.

Such a normal looking female.

So was Irene Caridad. But the older woman was now hauling a delicate clay tablet into the heat and humidity of the Bolivian jungle, and the potential damage to the artifact made Tristan shudder every time he thought about it. But as batshit crazy as this scenario was, he knew that Irene was whip smart and not one to make rash decisions, so ... she must have a damned good reason for what she was doing.

And that brought him back to Ms. Galloway.

If Irene had summoned the pretty archaeologist, then Galloway must be hiding something.

Was she truly unaware that the Moon Tablet had been found? She'd written a thorough analysis on the piece even though *she hadn't had the tablet in hand*. She'd done her homework, relentlessly following up on all mentions of the text in other Sumerian writings, gleaning insights that had impressed Tristan enough to amp up his search for the actual artifact.

Brynn Galloway's research had changed the direction of his life.

He looked at her again. Last night, after telling her of the tablet, she had questioned him further, but as much fun as it was to be with her, he'd extricated himself lickety-split. He really didn't want to say more than he should, and he seemed to have trouble concentrating when faced with her soulful eyes and distracting lips. And when she'd smiled full-on upon hearing about the artifact, he'd nearly fallen out of his seat.

Shit.

This morning, he'd managed to avoid her at breakfast, but she had quickly caught up to him and Dimar at the boat. Fortunately, to her visible frustration, she was unable to sit with him, which was just as well since Tristan suspected she had a lot more questions to ask, and he wasn't inclined to answer them.

When they disembarked at Copacabana, he made his way to a bus, following Dimar and his group of customers. Once aboard, he grabbed a window seat, and Ms. Galloway swiftly settled beside him.

"Good gravy," she huffed. "It's difficult to get a seat together."

"I didn't realize we were together."

"So this tablet is why you're after Irene?"

"I'm only *after her*, as you put it, to get it back, since she stole it from me."

"Where did you get it?" she asked, plowing forward.

He supposed he should've been happy that she'd given him a night free of an interrogation.

"I'd rather not say." He leaned against the window and shifted his hat to cover his eyes, hoping to sleep.

"Was it found in Iraq or Iran? An excavation? An accidental

discovery?" She seemed to be mostly talking to herself at this point. "Has its whereabouts been known for years and hidden from the public?"

When he didn't reply, she went silent, but that didn't last for long. The bus pulled out and she started chatting again.

"Are you certain it's not a forgery?"

Tristan gave up his nap and dropped his hat to his lap. "Well, if I wasn't sure a few weeks ago, I am now that Irene swiped it."

"Why would she steal it? I've never known her to be a thief."

"Look, I'm not here to debate the moral character of Dr. Caridad with you, since I'm guessing you're her friend, but if you're in on this, then tell me now."

Brynn straightened her shoulders. "You think I helped her steal it?"

Tristan waited. Galloway's countenance didn't budge as she watched him. Shrugging, he turned away. Either she was a very good liar, or she really didn't know anything about the piece.

"All right," he conceded. "You didn't help her. Maybe Irene took it because she's a lunatic, and she's managed to keep her mental illness hidden from her family and friends all this time."

"Really? That's your answer? That if a woman does something subversive then she must be crazy?"

"No, sorry. I'm just a bit frustrated. Irene is a smart lady. That's why I don't understand any of this."

"Look, I can assure you that I had no idea the tablet even existed, let alone that Irene had it," Galloway said. "She asked me to come down here to help on an excavation."

"That must be it then," he murmured. "She's gonna plant the tablet here and pass it off as a South American discovery."

"That's quite an accusation. Maybe she has a reasonable explanation. And what if evidence of Sumerian culture *could* be found in the Americas?"

"I've heard this song before."

"Did you get the piece illegally?"

"You think she's acting as a de facto police force against the illicit tradings of Tristan Magee?"

She answered with a silent raising of both eyebrows. He could hear the *duh* as clearly as if she'd spoken it aloud.

"No, I didn't get it illegally. At least, I don't think so." He muttered the last bit. He never purposefully went after hot items, but that didn't mean he didn't stumble across them in the underground antiquities market. He also wasn't about to tell Galloway that he hadn't actually *seen* the piece before Irene got her grubby little hands on it. There was no denying that mistakes had been made during the acquisition process, but Tristan didn't have the stomach to be censured at the moment. Not by this woman.

"So you don't know where it was discovered?"

"All the information on provenance is back in the States." *Kinda.* "I didn't want to travel with any documentation. I'll admit, I really didn't care where it was found, just that it had been found."

"Why?"

"I have my reasons."

"If Irene does have this tablet, why would she bring it down here?" she asked. "She'd never be able to get it through customs. Maybe she doesn't have it with her. Maybe you're wrong."

Tristan sighed. "It wouldn't be the first time."

"What does it look like?"

I don't know. Sensing that Galloway would put his balls in a vice-grip if he admitted it, he hedged. "It's made of clay with cuneiform markings on it."

Thankfully, she ignored the obvious vagueness of his answer and asked, "What does it say? Did you translate it?"

"No. I don't read cuneiform."

A sliver of suspicion flashed through his mind. What if meeting Brynn Galloway hadn't been by accident? What if she was a plant working with Irene, sent as a distraction to slow him down? Was her next move to seduce him?

He scrubbed a hand down his face.

Hell, it just might work.

Determined to head this one off before he started enjoying her company too much, he asked bluntly, "Why haven't you tried to kiss me?"

"What?"

"If you're here to romance me to learn what I know then you're doing a terrible job."

"Gee, thanks. But no, I'm not here to trick you into bed to ply you for antiquity details. Does that even work?"

"I don't know. Let's give it a shot." Damn. He sounded eager.

Red splotched her cheeks. Okay, he had to concede that maybe she wasn't trying to stoke an attraction between them, an attraction that had been there from the moment he laid eyes on her.

"I apologize," he said. "I didn't mean to offend you."

"I've got two older brothers. It takes quite a lot to offend me."

He paused, then made a rash decision to trust her. A little. "I haven't actually seen the piece."

"You mean it was never in your possession?" Her brows knitted together, making her eyes appear more green than blue.

"I was working through a dealer."

"But he sent you a photo, right?"

He resigned himself to how foolish he sounded at the moment. "The transaction went quickly, so no, I never saw one. And then he said he emailed one, but I never got it. Then I learned from a different mutual acquaintance that somehow Irene had swooped in and taken it."

"And you trusted this entire chain of events?" Her eyes widened with what looked like horror. Or mockery.

He bristled. "In a word? Yes. Because if Irene has it, then it's damned well worth something."

Her expression settled into one of contemplation. "I see your point," she conceded. "Anything else you want to share?"

"That's enough. For now."

"Right," she murmured. "Until I sleep with you."

They locked eyes. Her gaze was deliberate and assessing, her fluster a moment ago gone. It were as if she'd seen all the sparks flying between them and had gathered them up, contained them, and was now in control.

Holy hell. This woman was going to be trouble.

He released a low laugh. "If you wanna play, darlin', let's play."

"All right," she replied, her tone business-like. "Let's establish some ground rules."

This should be interesting.

"Are you married?" she asked.

"No."

"Girlfriend?"

"Not really."

"Someone who would come after me with a hatchet?"

"No." A frisson of unease—and dare he admit, excitement?— flashed through him. She sounded serious.

Was Brynn Galloway going to sleep with him?

He'd never had a woman succumb to his charms so quickly.

"Are you married?" he countered.

"No, no, and no." She cleared her throat. "So here's how it will go. Take me with you to find Irene. If she does in fact have the Moon Tablet of Ur in her possession, I'll help you get it back, but you give me exclusive access to translate it. You can get to first base with that."

"First base? You want me to give you all that just to touch your front matter?" He circled his hand in the air to encompass her modest-looking chest beneath the camp shirt she wore.

"I didn't realize you were so romantic," she replied, sarcasm dripping from lips that were now distracting Tristan. All this talk of sex was only increasing his awareness of this woman. "All right, you can touch the back matter too."

His mind blanked. He had always liked the dip in a woman's lower back, and Brynn Galloway probably had a pretty fine one that he could explore in the dark confines of his motel room in La Paz.

"Once I have a complete translation, and therefore proof as to the validity of the tablet, *then* I'll sleep with you."

He was being played. Of course he was. Brynn Galloway had no intention of taking a tumble with him, but for one sweet, delicious moment he had completely bought into it.

He smiled to hide his surprising disappointment, not understanding it at all. He'd only just met her. There was nothing special about her. If he wanted to get laid, he could backtrack to one of those almost-girlfriends he hooked up with occasionally.

But damn. For several seconds, he had to fight to steady his breathing.

Who the hell was this woman?

When he was certain his voice would sound normal, conveying an air of *I don't give a shit*, he said, "Don't worry, Galloway. You don't have to sell your soul to the devil."

"I don't?" Her eyes twinkled with mock surprise. "You mean I don't have to use my sexuality to get what I want? I don't have to let a man dominate the situation and the decisions to be made?"

Ah, hell. He sighed and prepared for the lashing.

"Do you hit on every woman you randomly meet on the street? Or, in this case, at a remote tourist site in a country like Bolivia? What do you think it's like for a woman traveling alone? There's always a little fear underlying everything: that someone will get the wrong idea, that they won't take no for an answer, that they'll try to manipulate the situation to their advantage. You want me to go in the jungle alone with you?" She barked a derisive laugh. "What if Irene isn't even *in* Bolivia, and this is just a trap?"

"Oh for God's sake," he said. "For the record, I don't want you to come with me and Dimar. I never did. And second, I don't hit on strange women I don't know. You, apparently, are the exception. But, believe me, I've realized my mistake, and I promise not to flirt with you anymore."

"That was flirting?" She about choked on the words. "Well that explains why you don't have a girlfriend in tow."

"I don't have a girlfriend along because they're nothing but trouble."

She narrowed her gaze. "Then it's a good thing I'm not trying to *romance* you. I'm here for Irene, whom I consider a colleague and a friend, and I've changed my mind. I'll find my own way into the jungle, thank you. Oh, and one other thing."

He waited.

"If the Moon Tablet does in fact belong to you, and you manage to recover it, then I still want access."

Of course she did.

CHAPTER 3

B rynn couldn't sleep. She tossed and turned on the firm mattress in the motel, light slanting through the window from a street-light. Her room was modest but clean. No television but the internet was pretty good. Wearing flannel pajama pants decorated with Labrador retrievers of various colors and a pink thermal top, she tugged the sleeves down to her wrists. La Paz was cold and the heater in her room didn't quite take the chill from the air.

Going into the Bolivian jungle with Tristan Magee would be lunacy.

She'd told him she wouldn't be accompanying him and Dimar Castanos, but did she have a choice since she currently had no other way of finding Irene? Had the woman really stolen a Sumerian artifact from Magee? If she had, Brynn had to believe there was a good reason. Shouldn't Brynn trust Irene and try to find her?

The only thing Magee had going against him was that Brynn didn't know him. She was usually a pretty good judge of character, except maybe when it came to romance. That was where her radar had faltered. She'd always picked the dangerous guy.

Was Magee dangerous?

Just because his piercing eyes and rugged good looks were an unfortunate distraction, it didn't mean he was dangerous. And it wasn't as if she were seriously going to have a romantic romp with him, despite the conversation they'd had on the bus earlier today.

A sexy vacation tumble.

The thought rose and fell like a murmuration of starlings.

What would be the harm? So said the part of her that was willing to jump first and sort out the details later.

She needed to focus on something else.

Upon arriving back in La Paz, she had parted ways with Magee and Dimar and was determined to find Irene on her own. Magee had let slip that Dr. Caridad had gone to Rurrenabaque, so Brynn had booked an airline ticket to the small town in Northern Bolivia. A bus ride would take hours, maybe days if there were transportation delays. A flight was only about sixty minutes.

She had spent over an hour contemplating what to do once she landed, however. How would she find Irene by herself? Since Dimar claimed to be an astute guide, and Magee would be with him, maybe she could simply follow them.

Good grief. This was turning into a bad movie. If she went into the jungle alone, she could die.

She sat up in bed, flipped on the nightstand light and reached for her laptop, which had been keeping the other side of the bed warm. Why hadn't she thought to do an internet search of Magee earlier?

She booted up her computer and did a quick check of her email, scrolling past anything that didn't look important, but she stopped at a message from her mom. *What is La Paz like? How long will you be staying down there, sweetie?* With everything still up in the air and not wanting to lie, Brynn marked the message as unread so she could deal with it later.

A message from her oldest brother, Alec, caught her eye, so she clicked it open. He had sent a photo of himself with his girlfriend, Dr. Grace Mann—computer scientist, marine biologist, and great white shark whisperer—out to dinner with Grace's sister, Chloe. He captioned it *Since you weren't here, we talked behind your back.*

Brynn snickered. Chloe Mann, along with fellow archaeologist Audrey Driggs, had been Brynn's college roommates at UCLA when they all had been working toward their undergraduate degrees. Chloe, like her sister Grace, had a graduate degree in computer science, but she'd specialized in acoustics with a minor in linguistics. Chloe was determined to break the barrier between human and cetacean languages. If she had her way, people would soon be chatting with sperm whales.

That Alec eventually had hooked up with Grace last year while on an expedition to film her freediving with great whites was a bizarre coincidence, since he had never met Chloe. But Brynn had crossed paths with Grace a few times and liked her. Alec was in deep—that had been obvious to Brynn from the start—and she wondered how long before he planned to make it official.

It would be fun to be related to Chloe in a roundabout way, reinforcing Brynn's belief in karma, or as she had heard someone once say, *"Winks from the universe."*

Having finished checking her email, she typed Magee's name in the search bar. It took only a bit of scrolling before she found him.

Undergrad in Physics from Ole Miss.

Doctorate from MIT.

He'd taught briefly at Columbia University before taking a position at the Applied Physics Laboratory at Johns Hopkins University in Maryland.

His specialty was acoustics and he'd written several papers that were catalogued at MIT. She clicked one, and then another, and then another. All of them dealt with acoustically levitated objects, mostly droplets and air bubbles in water. Interesting but pretty dry reading. Much like her thesis, she thought. But he'd apparently consumed her work with rapt interest. Why? Why did a physicist care about Sumerian cuneiform tablets?

She found another link. It was a newspaper article about Tristan's collection of archaeological artifacts. *Okay, so he's a hobbyist. An Indiana Jones wannabe.* Brynn knew others like him, most notably Gramps. Most of them didn't have the patience for the slow, tedious, and boring work of archaeology, and discoveries were often unglamorous, garnering nothing more than a fist pump followed by years of painstaking excavation before any analysis could be done. It was why these men, and occasionally women, did the collecting without any of the work.

She frowned when her gaze landed on a different reference. She clicked through to another article about a man named Harold Gatty. Recognition niggled at her.

Harold Gatty was known for his wild theories about alien visitations and ancient technologies. And Gatty was Tristan's father.

Huh.

Wow.

Harold Gatty had been the host of a television show for many years that focused on government conspiracy theories that sought to deceive the public that aliens had been here and probably still were. He also had written several books on the subject.

Since he and Tristan didn't have the same last name, she guessed Gatty was a stage name.

Was this why Tristan was trying to obtain the Moon Tablet of Ur? For his dad? But a quick perusal revealed that Gatty had died about a year ago.

Brynn was aware of the fringe theories pertaining to ancient aliens and the Sumerian culture. It all boiled down to the missing link. Mankind jumped from *Homo erectus* to *Homo sapiens* in the blink of a geological eye. Even evolutionists had been unable to explain it, and while there were many theories for such a speedy progression, there were two that sat at opposite ends of the spectrum.

The first, steeped in Christianity as well as other religions, was simple—God created man, end of story. The second posited a genetic intervention, a tinkering of *Homo erectus's* DNA to create *Homo sapiens*. The most likely suspect for this scientific dabbling? Space aliens.

Ironically both theories shared a common thread—those who believed in them relied heavily on faith.

Many of the stories translated from Sumerian cuneiform tablets spoke of a race of gods called the Anunnaki. Alien theorists stated that the Anunnaki were space-faring beings from another planet, but most archaeologists put the stories in a decidedly mythological vein, not unlike the tales of Greek and Roman gods.

While Brynn enjoyed the fantastic conjectures put forth by ancient alien theorists, she hardly believed in them, and it would be professional suicide to pin her work on any of it.

She grabbed her cellphone, checked the time, and called Audrey. She, Audrey, and Chloe Mann had first crossed paths in a linguistics class at UCLA several years ago, and by the end of the semester had decided to share an apartment together. While Brynn was equally close with both, Chloe's undergraduate field of study had been Marine Biology while Audrey's was Biological Anthropology. Hence, she and Audrey knew many of the same faculty.

"Where are you?" Audrey exclaimed. "Are you still in Pakistan?"

Brynn laughed. "No. I survived K2. I'll tell you about it the next time I see you."

"Then where? Are you on a dig?"

"I'm in Bolivia."

After a longer-than-normal silence, Audrey asked, "With Irene?"

If Brynn had thought the delay was in their connection, Audrey's tone disavowed it.

"Yes," Brynn answered. "Well, no. I'm not with Irene at the moment. She asked me to come down, but once I got to La Paz, she was gone. Apparently, she's headed into the jungle, and I'm thinking of going to look for her with some physicist from the States. I need a pep talk. Or at the very least, for someone to know my last known whereabouts before I disappear."

"She's looking for Conrad." It was a statement, not a question.

"All right, Audrey Driggs, you're sounding ominous. Time to spill it."

"Okay, look. I heard something recently and I really wasn't sure what to make of it." Another pause. "Irene did some time in the slammer."

"What? That can't be right."

"Remember that guy Joe in Germanic Languages?"

"Kinda."

"He told me a friend of his remembers seeing a paper clipping of a young Irene involved in some kind of archaeology hoax while on a dig in Turkey."

"Does he have any proof other than this article?" Brynn asked.

"No."

"Then you know better than to engage in idle gossip. C'mon, Audrey. Irene is our friend. And if she was in jail, maybe there's a perfectly reasonable explanation as to why." Echoes of her defense of Irene to Tristan rang in her ears. How many perfectly reasonable explanations was Irene entitled to? This was getting way more complicated than Brynn had anticipated.

"True," Audrey replied. "You're probably right. But be careful, will you?"

"Yes, of course."

Brynn hesitated, thinking of what Magee had told her—an additional damning allegation against Irene. Shit. If there was anyone she trusted, it was Audrey.

She cleared her throat. "Speaking of idle gossip ... Irene has supposedly stolen a cuneiform tablet from the physicist I told you about."

"And you're questioning whether she might have a criminal bent to her personality?"

"I'm not inclined to believe everything some guy tells me, especially a guy I hardly know."

"Hah. You forget that I lived with you for over five years. There were a few guys ..."

"Yeah, yeah. Ancient history."

"Wait." Audrey dragged the word out. "Is the physicist Dr. Magee?"

"You know him?"

"I met him a few times through Conrad and Irene."

"And how did I miss out on this acquaintance?"

Audrey laughed. "He's cute, right?"

That wasn't exactly how Brynn would describe him. Brooding, reckless, conniving.

Compelling.

She shook off her thoughts before she could let them wander into dangerous territory, still remembering the warmth in her belly when they'd had their *sex talk* on the bus.

"I suppose," Brynn conceded. "But is he trustworthy?"

"That I don't know, but I do believe he's single."

"That's not relevant, Audrey."

"What I'm trying to say is—you're an emerging expert in cuneiform translations, and Irene and Conrad could be up to something. Tristan Magee could be trying to romance information out of you. They all might be using you."

First Magee accused her of trying to entice him into her bed, and now Audrey was saying it could be the other way around. This was becoming outlandish. Brynn didn't bother to hide the sarcasm in her voice. "It's always a great comfort talking to you."

"Just looking out for you, Brynn Lucy."

Brynn smiled over the nickname. Her given name was Brynn Lucia, a nod to her Galloway Gaelic roots and her mother's Italian heritage. She decided to change the subject. "How's work?"

Audrey was two years older than Brynn. After graduating last year with her Ph.D., Audrey had moved to Arizona and taken a job as an investigator for a company called Heritage Archaeology.

"It's good, but I'm about to take some vacation days and head up to Northern Arizona."

"Are you trying to find that place where you were healed?"

When Audrey had been five years old, she had been diagnosed with a malignant brain tumor. While chemotherapy had helped keep death at arm's length, she hadn't been expected to live. When she was nine years old, she had gone camping with her dad and her sister in Northern Arizona and had encountered a man in her dreams who ultimately healed her. It had been nothing short of a miracle.

"Maybe," Audrey replied.

"Do you think you can find the location?"

"I'm not sure, but I'm feeling rather compelled to try." Excitement tinged Audrey's voice.

"Did it start with a dream?"

"You know me too well. Is that silly?"

"No, of course not." Audrey had taught Brynn that life was precious and steeped in mystery. "But now it's my turn to tell you to be careful and watch your back."

"Always. I'll be thinking about you in the jungle. I'm going to want to hear all about it."

"You buy the beer, I'll buy the wings," Brynn said.

"Deal."

Brynn hung up and contemplated her next move. She grabbed her phone again and pulled up another number, the one Tristan Magee had given her. They'd exchanged contact information so that later when he returned from the jungle, he could call her. Yeah, like that was ever gonna happen.

He picked up right away. "Magee."

"I'm going with you."

"Who is this?"

"You have caller ID. You know full well who this is."

"I honestly expected you to call sooner."

"I'm glad to prove you wrong," she said.

"About what?"

"About expecting anything from me."

"You're gonna need an airline ticket to Rurrenabaque," he said.

"I've got one. First flight out."

"Then I'll see you in the morning, Galloway."

When it sounded like he was about to hang up, Brynn said quickly, "Hey."

"What?"

"Was Harold Gatty really your father?"

The other end went silent.

"Magee? You still there?" First Audrey, now him. Was her phone glitching?

"Yeah. I see you've been asking around about me."

"It would be stupid not to know who I'm going into the jungle with."

"Did you ask Dimar about his father too?" Magee said.

"He's next on my internet search, but I'm guessing he has a much smaller digital footprint. Why are you looking for the Moon Tablet of Ur? Is it for Gatty?"

She could hear a rustling sound, and she imagined that Magee was lying in bed and had just shifted the pillow beneath his head. He released an audible sigh. "My relationship with my dad was complicated. Maybe when I know you better, I'll tell you about it. But my interest in the tablet began with my mom, although it was sealed by someone else."

"Who?"

"You."

Brynn arrived at El Alto International Airport bright and early, and luckily located her traveling companions without any mishap.

"Welcome to the circus," Tristan said, a gleam in his eye. "Glad you could join us."

At the sight of Magee, wearing a gray fleece pullover to ward off the chilly Andean morning and towering over Dimar, her heart skipped an irritating beat.

"Thanks for letting me tag along," she said, leaving her pack on her back but setting her duffel bag down and rubbing her hands together to warm them. "I hope I have the right gear." She unzipped her lightweight parka enough to give her neck breathing room.

"We will get supplies in Rurre," Dimar said, turning away and heading to the security checkpoint. He wore only a long-sleeved shirt and pants, but he had two stuffed backpacks on each shoulder. Perhaps they were what kept him warm. Or else the chilly weather didn't affect him.

Tristan grabbed her bag with his free hand. "Irene didn't give you any guidance about what to pack?"

She didn't bother to hide her surprise at his chivalrous gesture. "Thank you."

"I can be a gentleman."

"When it suits you?"

He chuckled. "Something like that. I guess you could say I'm trying to apologize for our misunderstanding yesterday."

She fell in step beside him. "Ah, yes. When you assumed I would trick you into bed." *Time to change the subject, Brynn.* "But back to Irene. She said to be prepared for an expedition and that we'd be roughing it. Not a problem for me. I just spent six weeks at K2."

With their long strides, they had swiftly overtaken Dimar, who asked, "What is a K2?"

"It's a mountain," Brynn said. "The second highest in the world, in fact."

"You're a mountain climber?" Tristan asked, surprise crossing his face.

"No." She followed him through security. "My brother Tyler is. I just tagged along."

"Impressive. So the altitude here must be no problem for you."

"You'd be right about that. I can't say the same about the cold, though. I never got used to it there, and I'm not used to it here."

"Don't worry." Dimar placed a pack onto the security belt and removed his shoes. "It's about to get very warm."

"Is that why you're not wearing a jacket?" she asked.

He shook his head and muttered as he went through the checkpoint, "Americans."

She removed her coat and said to Tristan, "Why does that sound like an insult?"

"Because it is."

They made it to the gate, and after accepting a coffee that Tristan had gotten for her—he was being downright gallant—they sat and waited. It wasn't long before they were ushered to a twin turboprop plane. The seats were three across, separated by a narrow aisle. Dimar took the single seat, so she and Tristan crammed together across from him. As Tristan stuffed his carry on in the small bin above them, Brynn slid into the window seat and stuffed her childhood backpack under the chair in front of her. When she'd returned from Pakistan, her other pack had ripped, and she hadn't had time to buy a new one, so she'd been forced to grab this old thing covered in hearts. She hoped it survived the coming journey.

"I hear you know Irene's husband, Conrad," she said.

He settled beside her. "Heard from whom?"

"Audrey, my old college roommate." Brynn buckled her lap belt, her elbow bumping into his arm. "She said she's met you."

"The miracle girl who believes in spacemen?" Magee asked, securing his own seatbelt. "What did she say about me?"

Magee's interest in Audrey filled Brynn with a flash of annoyance. Only one other time had she been jealous of a roommate, and it hadn't been Audrey. Her freshman year, she and Chloe—young eighteen-year-olds reveling in their independence—inadvertently had been pursuing the same guy they had met at a frat party. Thankfully, it hadn't ruined the friendship because Brynn couldn't even recall the heartthrob's name now.

"To watch my back around you."

He grinned.

"And that you were cute," Brynn added.

"Really?" He appeared to consider that bit of news. "I'm sorry I didn't pay more attention."

Brynn shot him a withering glance.

He lifted his hands in a defensive gesture. "Hey, you turned me down yesterday. Just keeping my options open."

"Turned you down? There was never an offer on the table."

He laughed outright.

"I'm glad you find this amusing."

He schooled his features. "You need to lighten up and appreciate the little things, Galloway."

"And what little things would those be?"

"That I'm batting zero with a woman like you."

"And what kind of woman am I?"

He glanced at her, his nearness in the cramped airplane a bit unnerving. "A once-in-a-lifetime one. But I'm guessing you've heard that before."

The hunger in his gaze caught her completely off-guard. It was gone so quickly she convinced herself she had imagined it.

She looked down and tightened her lap belt. "You're so full of shit, Magee." Audrey was right. She shouldn't underestimate this man.

"I did say you could call me Tristan," he added conversationally, as if the awkward interlude hadn't just occurred.

"Let's just stick to Galloway and Magee."

He shrugged. "You were saying something about Conrad Fontana."

The flight attendant interrupted with announcements as the plane's propellers began to whir, getting louder with each passing second.

"He's down here," Brynn said, raising her voice over the steady buzz of the plane, then she looked out the window.

The attendant finished her spiel, and the plane began to taxi to the runway. Brynn took a steadying breath to ease a flash of anxiety. Normally, she didn't mind flying, but she already considered this jaunt to be in her top five of bad flights.

When she finally turned back to Magee, he had lost his congenial demeanor.

"That must be why she came here. She's taking the tablet to him. But couldn't she have snapped a photo and emailed it to him instead?"

Audrey's words came back to her. *Irene had perpetrated a hoax.* Is that what she was doing here? Magee had said as much yesterday on the bus, but Brynn didn't want to believe it.

"She must have her reasons," Brynn said, willing it to be true. "Do you know Conrad well?"

"I thought I did, but after this bullshit he and Irene are putting me through, I'm gonna say the friendship's over."

"How did you meet them?"

"My dad knew them. They went way back. Two years ago, my dad and Conrad came down here on an expedition junket, and my cousin Shea and I joined them. Shea's also an archaeologist. That was the first time I'd spent any amount of time with Conrad."

"What kind of expedition?"

"What else? Looking for stuff."

"Wait a second, do you think the tablet is an alien artifact? Do Irene and Conrad believe that too?"

The pilot came on the intercom, first in Spanish and then English, stating they were ready for takeoff. Once the speech ended, Magee picked up the conversation again.

"It's an artifact made out of clay. I'd like to think space aliens have a more sophisticated technology than that. But the tablet could have interesting references."

"Who were you going to have translate it?"

Magee sighed. "Irene. And Connie. You're telling me neither of them include any of this in their curriculums at UCLA?"

"No."

"And Irene never discussed this with you?"

"No."

"But she encouraged you to write the paper about the Moon Tablet?"

"Yes."

"And you went forth like a dutiful lackey and did her bidding."

Frustration welled up in Brynn. "It wasn't like that. You have your Ph.D. You know what academia is like. It's a give and take, but of course, since she was my advisor, I had to work on a project for which she could give me not only her blessing, but access to pertinent material." She didn't add that Gramps had been enamored of the Moon Tablet and had spoken of it quite frequently. Or maybe he had shared with Brynn because she had been the only one who would listen. Her own family—her parents and her brothers, Alec and Tyler—frequently had that glazed-over look when she had spoken of the Sumerian culture or Grandpa Mico's obsession with it. Eventually, she had stopped.

Magee turned to her. "But you went beyond that, Galloway." Amusement danced in his eyes. "Irene knew you were smart, and you ran with her suggestion. I know Connie and Irene, and that paper had more than their fingerprints all over it. You're good, Brynn. You're really good."

Her face heated at the compliment. No one had ever praised her work with such earnestness. Not her family. Not Irene. Not even Audrey.

Until this moment, she had vastly underestimated how much she craved it.

Once again, she reminded herself how dangerous Magee's innate magnetism could be. And just how easily she could fall for it.

"Thank you." She kept her voice even and professional, and then changed the subject. "I take it you were an only child."

He smiled. "Did you learn that while you were stalking me on the internet?"

"Maybe."

"It's true. I don't have any siblings, but I grew up with cousins."

"Are you close?"

"Shea and I were. Not so sure now."

"Is Shea a boy or a girl?"

"He's the same age as me. Would you call me a boy?" he teased.

Hardly.

"Why aren't you close anymore?" she asked.

"We had a bit of a misunderstanding the last time we were here. It's been radio silence since."

"Maybe you should try to patch things up."

He gave a barely perceptible shrug. "Maybe."

Magee reclined his chair the few inches it would move and closed his eyes. Brynn wasn't sure if he slept or pretended to, but either way she passed the solitude by watching the clouds pass by the window, entirely too aware of the warmth emanating from the *boy* beside her.

They landed on a narrow asphalt runway and taxied to a patch of gravel and broken pavement. To Brynn's surprise, the flight attendant opened the aircraft door and told everyone to disembark. Tristan unbuckled his seatbelt, stood, and grabbed his pack, and then allowed Brynn to precede him. As soon as she stepped down the airplane stairs, the hot muggy air hit her. The elevation of Rurrenabaque, nestled beside the Beni River, was 900 feet. A big change from La Paz at 12,000 feet.

Two small buses awaited, and the passengers were ushered into them like sardines. Brynn was pressed snuggly beside Magee, her own pack on her lap. He struggled to find a comfortable position with his long legs and sweat began to drip between Brynn's shoulder blades. She suspected it had as much to do with the stuffy interior of their vehicle as to her forced contact with Magee. And damn, touching him wasn't altogether unpleasant.

During the short drive, she busied herself with rolling her shirt sleeves to her elbows. They were dropped off in front of a screened-in building painted in yellow. Brynn breathed a sigh of relief as she exited the tight confinement of the bus and entered the structure, greeted by a colorful sign that said "Bienvenidos al destina turistico Rurrenabaque." *Welcome to the tourist destination Rurrenabaque.* Her high school Spanish was slowly coming back.

As they waited for their luggage, Brynn asked, "How did your mother get you interested in the tablet?"

Magee gave her a sidelong glance then looked forward, ambivalence vibrating from him. Was he reluctant to share personal information with her? Or did it run deeper? Was he possibly conflicted about the reason he was pursuing such an artifact?

"My parents didn't always agree about my dad's line of work, but my mom did try to participate. When I was a boy, she would read to me about the Sumerians. She was especially fond of the Moon Tablet."

"So you acquired it for her?"

He cast her a look of surprise, subtle but genuine. "Yeah, maybe I did."

A lawn tractor appeared outside pulling a trailer filled with their luggage. The load was deposited into a roped-off area, and the passengers clamored to claim their belongings.

Dimar waved them outside to a waiting minivan several slots down from the larger tourist buses. A young Bolivian driver greeted them—a friend of Dimar's if their congenial interaction was any indication—and he took them into town as disco music poured from the radio. Feeling as if she were in a 70's time warp, Brynn decided time travel was possible after all. They checked into a rather nice-looking motel with a modest swimming pool and the town of San Buenaventura visible across the river.

Dimar handed each of them an old-fashioned key. "We stay here tonight. Gather whatever supplies you need in town. Tomorrow we will board a boat and head upriver."

"And then what?" Brynn asked.

"We go into the jungle."

"Can't you be more specific than that?"

"We are in the Amazon," Dimar replied, his tone flat and somewhat mocking. "Although you Westerners like to believe that we have some hidden highway of technology, or some magical powers, sadly we do not. Irene dashed off into the jungle believing that I would bring you to her, but she was full of toast and pickles."

"Come again?"

Magee shouldered his pack. "I think he means piss and vinegar."

"That doesn't make any more sense," Brynn muttered under her breath.

"I do know that Connie Fontana is with Solomon," Dimar added.

"Solomon?" Magee bellowed, startling Brynn. "Shit."

With a hand on her chest, she asked, "Who the hell is Solomon?"

Dimar's lips stretched into the fakest smile Brynn had ever seen. "A shaman. I knew you would like that, Dr. Magee."

"You've known this whole time?"

"No. Or I would have enjoyed your discomfort for a much longer time. I learned it as soon as we landed in Rurre."

Brynn shifted her attention to Magee. "What's wrong with Solomon?"

Magee ran a hand through his sweat-soaked hair. "It's a long story. Maybe—"

"When you know me better, you'll tell me," she cut in, nodding for emphasis. She waved him off. "Why would Conrad be with a shaman?"

"Well, there could be several reasons, but I'm guessing there are two," Magee said.

"Such as?"

"One, Conrad's probably using Solomon as a guide, since the man is very knowledgeable of the area."

"So he's a local shaman?"

"Actually, no. He's originally from Peru, but he's been in Bolivia for a long time."

"And what's the second reason?"

"Contrary to what Dimar just said, there are those down here who *do* use magic to find their way. And I'm betting that Irene wants to show the tablet to Solomon."

"You're saying he can read cuneiform?" she asked, incredulous.

Magee pinned her with those piercing eyes. "Your paper was incredible, but it missed one important thing."

"I'm absolutely thrilled to hear your critique, Magee. Do tell."

"The mystical properties of the tablet."

"Oh, for the love of God."

He winked at her. "It's not God I'm looking for."

"I'm sorry to tell you, but all this alien shit is so easily debunked. When I know you better, I'll explain the many ways how. And you yourself said it's just a piece of clay."

Magee stepped close enough that her nose was inundated with the musky scent of man in the tropics. Her body leaned toward him ever so slightly of its own volition.

"Listen, Debbie Downer," he said. "Whether I believe it or not is irrelevant. But I can only guess that Conrad is using Solomon to help with the more esoteric aspects of searching the jungle for proof of ancient civilizations, since he has no love of Solomon either. And he probably told Irene to bring the actual artifact down so he could use it in a ceremony."

Magee's nearness activated all sorts of hormones Brynn hadn't been on a first name basis with since her teenage years. "What kind of ceremony?"

"Have you heard of ayahuasca?"

"Of course." But in truth, she knew very little about it, except that it was some kind of hallucinogenic.

"You can learn some strange shit during these ceremonies."

Forcing herself to take a step back, she sought to get her female parts back in line, not to mention her rapid breathing and wobbly knees. "Like what?"

"Things about yourself. About life's big mysteries."

"Is that why you're down here? Looking for answers?"

"There's only one question that's haunted humans from the beginning of time." His blue eyes put her in mind of a languid ocean, warm sand, and tropical breezes, with both of them clad in little clothing and …

She lifted the nylon material of her shirt away from her perspiration-soaked chest to cool down. "And what's that?"

"Where do we come from."

"And you think the aliens will tell us on a clay tablet?"

A smile tugged at Magee's mouth. "Yeah, I do."

CHAPTER 4

Brynn stashed her bag in her room, changed into a pair of shorts and a t-shirt, grabbed her GALLOWAY FILMS ball cap, sunglasses, and her backpack, and headed off into town to explore. No sense wasting a perfectly good afternoon worrying about Magee's ridiculous claims of a medicine man dialing up some cuneiform tablet and chatting with his counterpart on a distant planet. Every time she thought about it, she laughed. So much for Magee being normal.

He would fit right in with her past boyfriends. They all had had one thing in common—they pushed the envelope, whatever that edge might be. And Brynn had loved it, making her feel connected to something bigger than herself. She had wanted to show her dad she understood his inclination to live on the edge. On the other hand, it hadn't escaped her that those boys were the only ones with enough balls to face Big Jim Galloway.

But while she possessed the same inner Galloway fire that propelled her brothers through their hobbies and professions, she was also trying to please a man no longer here—her grandfather. Grandpa Milano, her mom's dad, had been born in America, but he'd carried throughout his life the remnants of the Italian accent he had picked up from his parents as a child. He had spent his life as a metallurgist, but his true passion had been archaeology. It was an armchair hobby, and

Brynn had spent her childhood at his feet soaking up everything he knew. As much as she had loved the beach and surfing—she'd spent many hours trying to keep up with her brothers and their outdoor pursuits—when it came time to choose a course of study in college there had been no doubt what she would focus on.

I hope you're proud of me, Gramps.

She made a quick stop at the front desk to get oriented, then set off down the dusty road, following the clerk's directions. She passed wood and palm thatch houses before entering the bustle of town, and soon found herself surrounded by restaurants, bars, open-air souvenir nooks, and a multitude of signs peddling tours into the jungle. As people mingled and mopeds sped past up and down the street, Brynn took her time perusing clothing and trinket stalls. Her mother would love this. Not only did her parents travel frequently and widely, instilling that wanderlust in their children, but Lily Galloway was a souvenir junkie, likely a remnant of growing up with a father who collected artifacts. Brynn's childhood home had been filled with memories of her parents' globe-trotting adventures.

Brynn had inherited a bit of the shopping gene as well, so she browsed the colorful wares to her heart's content, picking up a t-shirt and a bandana, along with extra bug repellent for the upcoming journey into the wilderness. Chatting with the shopkeepers revealed that the locals had shortened the town name to Rurre, which she had heard Dimar use, and that mosquitos were called mozzies. The bugs became worse in October, but if all went well, she'd be gone by then. She also bought a hammock, mosquito netting, and a machete.

Eventually hunger led her to a restaurant with plastic chairs and tables draped with colorful cloths. She took a seat and scanned the menu. When the waitress approached, she ordered a plate of empanadas and an orange soda—the staple drink anywhere south of the U.S. border. Grabbing a guidebook from her shopping spree, she began flipping through it.

"Excuse me. Are you Brynn Galloway?"

Glancing up, she was immediately caught by the man's blue eyes. He reminded her of Magee, except that his hair wasn't quite as dark.

"Yes," she replied.

"I'm Dr. Hartigan."

"Do I know you?"

"No. But I believe you're acquainted with my cousin."

She shook the hand he offered. "Your first name wouldn't happen to be Shea, would it?"

~

TRISTAN HAD COMPLETED HIS SHOPPING—NUTS and dried fruit, an extra machete, more bug repellent, and a spare pair of sunglasses since he always managed to break a few when he traveled.

He had knocked on Galloway's door to invite her along, but there had been no answer. The motel clerk told him she had walked into town.

As Tristan shopped, he kept an eye out, finally locating her a few blocks away amidst a throng of people. Rurre was a popular destination for jungle-loving tourists.

Galloway had changed into shorts, and even from a distance he admired her nice legs. He closed the distance between them, but before he reached her, she ducked into a restaurant. As he entered the establishment, he saw her straight away sitting with a man. Already he had competition.

But as he approached her table, recognition hit. "What the hell are you doing here?" he said to the man.

His cousin looked up and eyed him with cool disdain. "Hello, Tristan."

~

BRYNN ABANDONED the knife and fork and grabbed her empanadas by hand. As her teeth broke the golden outer crust, juice from the aromatic ground beef, spices, peppers, and tomato sauce dripped down her fingers. She was forced to wipe them on a napkin before taking a sip of her soda.

Clearly, Magee didn't seem very happy to see his cousin. Equally baffling was that Hartigan was emitting a strong aura of distrust directed at Tristan.

Brynn settled in to watch the show.

The waitress appeared and after a quick glance at the menu, Magee said, "I'll have the fish special."

Hartigan rested an elbow on the table. "Me too."

While the men didn't look the same—Magee's hair was darker, his defined jawline reminding Brynn of a wave jacking up to twice its height after hitting a reef, his gaze filled with both speculation and cynicism—they were similar in build and definitely had the same sky-blue eyes. Must be a family trait.

Having wolfed down half her meal, she took a breather and in an attempt to ignite the conversation she said, "What a small world. Did you both know the other would be here?"

Magee leveled his gaze at his cousin. "No. And why are you sitting with Ms. Galloway?"

"I thought I should introduce myself."

"And that's as far as we'd gotten before you showed up," Brynn said, resuming the attack on her food. As more juice dribbled down her chin, Magee grabbed several of the paper-thin napkins from the holder at the center of the table and handed them to her.

"Thanks," she mumbled past her food, then added, "What are the odds that the two of you would be on vacation in the Amazon at the same time?"

"Vacation, huh?" Shea said.

Tristan shook his head, as if trying to erase his cousin's presence. "Who told you I was here?" he asked, his tone tinged with accusation.

"Castanos."

"Little bastard."

"Not Dimar. Freddie."

"Does it matter?" Tristan huffed. "All the Castanos are little toads."

Shea nodded at the waitress as she delivered two bottles of local beer to the table, then he held his up in salute. "I guess it takes a toad to know one."

"Fuck you, Shea. Where were you when my dad died?"

Hartigan's hard-lined stance slid away. "Yeah, I'm sorry about that. We didn't know how sick Uncle Charlie really was."

"Are you kidding me?"

"No, I'm not. Look, I don't agree with what happened here two years ago, and I made my opinion very clear to Uncle Charlie, but later when I called him to talk about it, he said he was in remission. Believe me, it weighs on me that my last words to him were about that damned book he planned to publish."

"You told him it was filled with lies and mistruths," Magee said.

"Because it was." Shea set his beer bottle on the table.

"You don't know that."

Squirming with discomfort, Brynn wondered if she could drop to the ground and slink away unnoticed while the two men ripped open an obviously raw family wound. She jammed the last of her food into her mouth and readied herself to leave, but as if sensing her distress, Shea shifted gears and turned to her.

"Sorry about that," he said.

"Maybe I should go." She tossed her grease-soaked and crumpled napkin on the table, then stuffed her travel guide into her bag.

"No, we're good."

Brynn didn't believe for a minute that whatever rift existed between the two men was no longer an issue but rather had been shoved aside to be dealt with later. Still, she remained.

"You can't go wrong hanging around Magee," Shea continued. "His survival instincts are legendary." He glanced at Tristan, who had gone silent. "When he was nine, he was in a coma for days, but then just woke up. Lazarus rising from the dead."

Tristan sighed. "Why the hell do the Hartigans always refer to it in biblical terms?"

"It's a helluva family story," Shea replied, laughing.

"What happened?" Brynn asked.

"Tristan and his mother were in a car accident. Luckily, Aunt Ellie was fine with just a broken leg, but Tristan was thrown from the car."

"That's terrible," Brynn said, swept up with concern, but she could tell that Tristan didn't want to talk about it. "Why don't you have the same last name as Shea?"

"My folks weren't together when I was born. Magee is my mother's maiden name. Later, they reconciled, but I kept the name." He swung his gaze to his cousin. "And I think that's enough family history for now."

"Fine," Shea said. "How about telling me why you're both here?" He looked from one to the other.

Magee sat with stiff shoulders and eyes narrowed, staring at his beer bottle, so Brynn was forced to keep the conversation afloat. "We're searching for a woman named Irene Caridad," she said.

Magee didn't waste any time throwing a look of annoyance her way.

"Interesting," Shea said.

Ignoring Tristan, Brynn asked, "Do you know her?"

"Not personally, but I'm acquainted with her husband. I'm trying to track down Pico, who it turns out is with Dr. Caridad. What are the odds?"

Brynn leaned back in her chair, accepting that one tension had simply been replaced by another. "Who's Pico?"

Tristan finally recovered his voice. "He's also a Castanos. He, Dimar and Freddie are cousins." He shifted his gaze back to Shea. "Why are you talking to Brynn?" he asked once more.

Magee's use of her first name was clearly him marking his territory, and if they had been alone, she might have chewed his head off for it, but she remained silent.

"I couldn't pass up meeting *the* Brynn Galloway."

The waitress set two plates of grilled fish before each man, and then hurried away to a table of six.

Brynn frowned. "I'm finding this notoriety I have to be a little disconcerting."

"You're well-known in small archaeology circles," Hartigan said.

"Hmm, thanks, I think. I guess I should make my fan club official and issue membership cards and autographed copies of a headshot."

"Where do I sign up? Your paper on the Moon Tablet was passed around our office."

What the hell was going on? It felt like she had entered some parallel dimension, because obscure papers on little known artifacts were never well-read.

"Why is everyone so interested in my paper?"

Shea laughed. "I'm going to assume you're just trying to throw me off, because you appear far too intelligent not to know why."

"Ah, okay. I get it now. You think I have the tablet."

"Do you?"

"I don't." *But Tristan does. Or did.* She almost said the last part aloud, but a quick glance at the brooding Magee stopped her. It was clear he had no intention of chatting about his involvement with the artifact with his cousin, so she remained silent, but she had no idea why she felt inclined to protect Magee's interests.

She turned to Hartigan. "I simply did my research. There are thousands of cuneiform tablets that have been found, and while a good portion have yet to be translated, I did my due diligence in researching any known references to the texts in other writings."

She had worked damned hard on that paper, picturing Gramps in her head and having fictitious conversations with him. So many times, she had wished he had lived to see her academic work. And now … how he would have delighted in hearing about this most recent adventure, although he would have told her to carry the pepper spray Tyler had given her at Christmas and trust no man's intentions while in the jungle.

She suddenly remembered the journal she had with her gear back at the motel. Gramps's journal. Her grandmother had sent it from Pennsylvania, the package sitting in a pile of eight-weeks' worth of mail that had collected while Brynn had been at K2 during the summer. In her rush to get to Bolivia, Brynn had stuffed it in her backpack without really looking at it. Apparently, Gramps had instructed Gram that Brynn was to receive it on her twenty-fifth birthday, which had occurred last month.

During the long flight down, she'd done a quick perusal and found it filled with cuneiform, but it was unlike anything Brynn had seen before, almost as if it were truncated or some kind of shorthand. She'd concluded that it was nothing more than a mishmash, that perhaps Gramps had been losing his faculties when he'd written it, something Brynn really didn't like thinking about. And since Gram never really had any interest in Gramps's obsession with Mesopotamia nor had any inkling of how to read cuneiform, she couldn't have known that the notebook was most likely worthless.

But now Brynn wondered …. Could it have something to do with the Moon Tablet of Ur? Was it a coincidence that Brynn had received the journal right before coming down here?

A rather ridiculous notion occurred to her: What if her path in writing the paper had been guided by Gramps himself, watching over her from his perch in Heaven, or wherever he might be? The thought was both heartening and fanciful. And Brynn tried her best not to be fanciful.

But sitting at a table with two formidable men such as Magee and Hartigan on the fringes of the Amazon jungle struck her as fanciful in the extreme.

Did you have something to do with this too, Gramps?

"As it turns out," Hartigan said, "I'm looking for Irene's husband, Conrad, because I think Pico has scheduled a powwow with him. Irene was the sponsoring professor on your thesis, wasn't she?"

"Yes." Brynn decided to go for broke. "Irene asked me to come down here. And then I bumped into your cousin." She gave a nod toward Magee. "And that's it in a nutshell."

Hartigan shifted his gaze to Tristan. "Why are you looking for Irene?"

Tristan stretched his legs beneath the table. "She took something from me."

Hartigan paused, then said, "Interesting."

"You sure say that a lot. Maybe get a thesaurus and find a new word. And why are you here, Shea?"

"For a client."

"Who do you work for?" Brynn asked.

"I run a private consulting company that specializes in archaeological issues."

"That's his way of telling you to mind your own business," Tristan said, his tone derisive.

"I'm not trying to be rude," Shea said. "I'm just not at liberty to discuss it."

Tristan grabbed his bottle and took a long drag of beer. "Convenient."

"Unlike you, I happen to care about my professional reputation. And I'd also like to get paid. Loose lips and murky ethics can limit job opportunities."

"Thanks for the lecture, professor," Magee muttered under his breath.

"I'll tell you what." Shea finished the last of his meal and pushed his plate aside. "Since we're family, I'll let you travel with me."

"And why would you do that?" Tristan asked.

"Because I think our endgame is the same. We're both on a path to Conrad."

"Has Conrad and Irene stolen from your client as well?" Brynn asked. How had she never noticed that Drs. Fontana and Caridad were such kleptomaniacs? Was this Pico going to help Irene sell the cuneiform piece?

Tristan leveled his gaze at Hartigan. "We have Dimar. We don't need you."

"That's true." Shea nodded his agreement with an amiable façade, but it didn't take an idiot to sense the very *unfriendly* undercurrent. "But Dimar doesn't know where Solomon is."

"And you do?" Tristan asked.

Shea folded his arms across his chest. "Thanks for the confirmation."

"Shit."

"I wasn't sure if Solomon was involved. But now I am."

Frustrated by the testosterone-fueled pissing match, Brynn said, "Is there some reason we all can't travel together? It seems silly for there to be two groups heading toward the same goal."

"She's right. What are you worried about, Tristan?"

Magee didn't answer but gave a slight shrug. "Fine. Let's all caravan through the jungle together. It'll be one big happy family."

Shea paused while the waitress cleared their plates. "We'll leave at dawn. It was a pleasure to meet you, Ms. Galloway."

"Please call me Brynn."

Shea nodded and stood. He threw enough bolivianos bills on the table to cover everyone's meal. "See you at the dock at sunrise."

There was no denying Shea Hartigan was a handsome devil, but Brynn was more aware of the dour Scotsman beside her, because surely the surname of Magee had Scottish roots. When had she started paying such close attention to Magee's moods?

Once they were alone, she said, "Are you sure you want to travel with him? The disagreements alone will cost us too much time."

Magee flashed her a look of amusement. "I didn't know you were such a comedian, Galloway."

"One of my many hidden talents. So what's up with you two?"

Tristan scrubbed a hand down his face. "Let's talk about something else. I could use another beer." He waved at the waitress. "How about an upgrade from your soda?"

Brynn shook her head. She might be unsure about a lot of things—her relationship with Irene, the state of her doctorate work, the validity of Magee's Moon Tablet—but one was crystal clear. If she relaxed her guard with alcohol, she'd be in Magee's bed before the sun set. And likely long after. Just the thought of it while she was stone-cold sober made her heartbeat ratchet up a notch and her mouth go dry. Who knew a broody Scotsman could be so sexy?

"No, thanks. I'll stay in my lane."

"Suit yourself." Magee ordered another beer.

～

BRYNN SHOULDERED her backpack stuffed with repellent, snacks, local trinkets, and a colorful scarf she planned to give to her mother and followed Magee down to the river, only a few streets away. A wide swath of water cut through the jungle, set aglow by the setting sun, and green hills beckoned on the opposite bank.

She and Magee walked side by side as silence reigned, the balmy air surrounding them like an outdoor sauna.

"I've never been in the jungle before."

Magee looked down at her feet, clad in hiking boots. "You have good footwear. That's important. There could be mud and bad weather, but mostly it will help if you step on a snake."

"I figured as much. You don't think we'll see an anaconda, do you?"

"It's possible."

Brynn wasn't sure how she felt about that. "I'd prefer a sloth. I heard there are restaurants around here that serve monkey and turtle, which makes me love PB&J sandwiches all the more."

"You're gonna hate jungle cuisine then."

She waited for him to elaborate.

"Peccary head roasted over an open fire," he added.

She grimaced. "I'd better pack extra granola bars."

"Don't knock it. After cooking the head for hours, you can rip the flesh right off the face with your teeth."

She winced. "Gross." Time to change topics. "So you've been down here before?"

"Yeah. I'm a jungle rat. I hope you're prepared."

"For what?"

He stopped at the water's edge and gazed at the gently flowing current. "To either love it or hate it. If you hate it, you'll be so miserable you'll never return again."

"And if I love it?"

"It'll become a part of you and will sing in your blood, calling you home, and overtaking your dreams. Much of the rainforest has been decimated by loggers and farmers wanting to tame the land, to make a quick buck, and poachers have hunted species to near extinction, but despite that, it's the richest and rawest ecosystem in the world. Nothing compares. It's the literal heartbeat of the earth. Saving it should be on everyone's mind."

The buzzing of flies and the musty smell of vegetation and river water couldn't mask the palpable magic of the place. It was the never-ending cycle of life, but she sensed something more. A drumbeat of something distant. Perhaps the Amazon *was* the veritable heart of Mother Nature.

"When were you down here?"

"Aside from two years ago, I spent a summer near the Bolivia-Peru border when I was sixteen with my dad and Shea."

She raised an eyebrow. "Looking for aliens?"

Magee's lips tilted into a cryptic half-smile and he flashed her an assessing look. "There are lots of unexplained things in this world. It's human nature to want to unravel them."

Before she could reply, he continued, "Initially we lived with a group of missionaries, but eventually my dad argued with them. Or maybe it was the other way around—God and aliens don't really go hand-in-hand. Then we ended up with a band of indigenous people and lived in their village for several weeks."

"Were they one of those remote groups that had never seen any outsiders?"

"No. They knew of the outside world. They just chose to remain apart from it. It was pretty rustic, I'll grant you, but it was the best summer of my life." His face took on a wistful expression. "Combing the jungle every day, Shea and I learned to hunt and to track, but mostly I enjoyed watching the animals—howler monkeys, peccaries, blue and yellow macaws, giant anteaters. There are river otters as big as bears. And then there are the ones that take your breath away when you encounter them—black caimans, jaguars, massive anacondas."

"You've seen all that?" Brynn tried to keep the concern from her voice.

"Are you afraid, Galloway?"

"Of course I'm afraid. I'm not an idiot. I've heard the stories about the jungle swallowing people up, never to be seen again. I have a healthy appreciation for what I'm walking into."

The rumble of laughter from Magee smoothed over the edges of her nerves, mimicking the way she'd always felt when facing the surf along with a bunch of boys. It was a combination of wanting to show she was as good as them and a heady desire to simply be one of them. Why did they get to have all the fun? She had always relished proving she could hold her own no matter what the waves threw at her. It hadn't always been pretty, but the tenacity she'd learned back then had proven useful later in life. She'd certainly leaned on it while living this past summer at K2 base camp, one of the most inhospitable places on Earth.

"I'm not backing down," she added.

"I'm glad to hear it." His gaze caught hers, and a frisson of awareness passed between them. She broke the contact and looked back to the river, resisting the invisible magnet in her chest urging her to get closer. She didn't need a steamy fling with a man she barely knew.

Expectancy hung in the air, and not just between her and Magee. She both feared and held in awe the primal world beckoning just beyond the shores of the Beni River, its life force pulsating around them.

In the jungle, everything would be stripped bare.

She couldn't wait to get started.

CHAPTER 5

The following morning, Tristan was up before first light. A knock on Galloway's door presented him with a half-asleep woman in a loose t-shirt and gray running shorts, only one eye cracked open and her brown hair tussled.

She was too damned cute.

"Good morning," he said. "I wanted to make sure you were awake."

"Thanks," she mumbled. "Give me ten minutes and I'll be ready."

"If you're that fast, we can grab a quick breakfast downstairs."

She gave him a thumbs up and shut the door.

True to her word, she was dressed and ready to go, duffel bag in hand and her backpack slung over a shoulder, ten minutes later. It was too early for the kitchen to be open, but Tristan had wrangled bagels, jam, and coffee from one of the housekeepers who slept on the premises.

Galloway drank her coffee black, but Tristan loaded his with enough cream and sugar to take away the bitter edge.

"Want some caffeine with your sweets?" Brynn said as she cradled her cup with both hands, spending equal time drinking and inhaling the aroma.

"I don't really like the stuff," he answered, skimming a week-old

English newspaper he'd found in the lobby. "I just drink it to look cool."

She started eating her bagel. "That's what every young man says: I'm not gonna drink vodka and smoke cigarettes to look cool, I'm gonna drink a cup of joe."

He grabbed his cup by the rim, took a sip, and said under his breath, "Smartass."

She grinned. "At your service."

Dimar arrived looking annoyed.

"We go," he huffed. "Since you make me travel with Freddie."

"But he's family, right?" Brynn asked, popping the last of her bagel in her mouth.

Dimar spun away and said over his shoulder, "He's my black-balled cousin."

Tristan stood and grabbed his bag. "You mean black-listed?" he asked.

"Maybe he means black sheep," Brynn added, wiping her hands of breakfast crumbs on her pants as she rose to her feet.

"Or maybe his balls really are black," he added for her ears only, enjoying the subtle smell of flowers and soap as he leaned close to her.

Brynn smirked as they went outside and piled into the beat-up old van Dimar had waiting for them.

"Such luxury accommodations, Castanos." Tristan slid next to Brynn on a bench seat.

Dimar climbed into the driver's seat, which squeaked in response, then slammed the door with a hard bang, causing Brynn to startle. "You're lucky I found anything," he grumbled.

He was probably right. Most of the town was navigated by scooters and motorbikes, and it wouldn't have been much fun trying to get down to the dock with all their gear, most of which Dimar had packed in the back.

As the crow flies, they weren't far from the water, but the drive managed to take a good twenty minutes since the dock was three miles downstream.

Shea greeted them when they arrived. "Good morning, jungle rats. Ready to go down the rabbit hole?"

"Ready as I'll ever be," Brynn replied, smiling at Shea and handing over her bag. Hartigan set it in the small boat and then helped Brynn on board as she ducked her head to miss the tin roof overhead.

Tristan bristled over his cousin's obviously amped-up charm.

Dimar faced the other Bolivian who was stacking the bags and boxes that had been transferred from the van to the back of the boat. "Freddie."

"You can bugger off, Dim," the man said, his face taut with defiance.

Where Dimar was clearly descended from the indigenous Bolivians, the *originiarios*, progeny of the pre-Hispanic cultures, Freddie was taller, looking like a remnant of the Spanish infiltration three hundred years ago.

"I can't believe you two are cousins." Magee didn't bother to hide his skepticism.

Dimar dismissed Freddie with a wave of his hand. "He is from the dark side of the family."

Brynn donned her ball cap and said, "I think you mean the bad side. Not that I'm agreeing with him," she said to Freddie, quickly backtracking. "I'm Brynn. It's really nice to meet you."

Freddie smiled and shook her hand.

"His mother married my mother's brother, but his mother's father was a loser from the south and no one knows who his parents were. He married his mother's mother, but she should have thrown him out, and then he got her pregnant."

Brynn knitted her eyebrows in an obvious look of horror. "This is sounding incestuous."

Tristan sighed. "Don't worry. I've a feeling he tripped over his words." Then he said to Dimar, "Does any of it really matter now?"

"You don't like your cousin." Dimar pointed at Shea, who grunted in response as he cleared a path to the seats in the front of the boat.

"True," Tristan agreed.

Without looking up, Shea flipped him off.

Tristan grinned. "You can't pick your family, but you can pick your fights."

"All right," Brynn cut in. "Can we try to get along? If not, I'll dump you all in the river and head into the jungle alone."

Everyone got settled, and Tristan grabbed a seat beside Galloway. Freddie fired up the motor and they were soon puttering upriver as the sun rose, the jungle coming alive with bird song, the mist hovering above the water aglow with slanting rays of light.

As the sun crept higher, they chugged along the wide river at a steady pace, passing through sky-high gorges and dense, deep green forests. There were kingfishers and herons and several caimans in the water. They saw fishermen in wooden canoes, logging boats, and the riverside camps of nomadic fishing families.

"It's so beautiful here," Brynn remarked. "And so thick with life."

Tristan settled against his pack, content to enjoy the view, Galloway notwithstanding. She was proving to be a bright spot among a plethora of irritations—Irene's theft, Shea's annoying presence, having to rely on the mercurial moods of Dimar.

It was late afternoon when Freddie guided the boat to a wooden dock and a group of people appeared, greeting them in a local dialect that Tristan knew relied heavily on Quechua, predominately found in the Andes region but introduced a few centuries ago by missionaries. As the people clamored to sell bushels of bananas to the new arrivals, Dimar waved them away.

"Gather your stuff," he said. "We will sleep here tonight. Tomorrow we walk."

Brynn lifted her duffel bag from the boat and set it on the dock. Tristan reached for it.

"What are you doing?" she asked.

"I thought I'd carry your bag for you."

"That's nice, but I can do it myself. I don't need to owe you anything."

Dimar snorted. "Women's liberation. Bolivian women don't do it. I wish they did. Want to carry my bag?"

"No," Brynn answered succinctly. Tristan chuckled.

A young man wearing loose-fitting trousers, a stained buttoned-down shirt, and sandals approached and exchanged words with Dimar, who then motioned to Tristan, Shea, and Freddie to climb the stairs to a wood-planked building with a corrugated metal roof. All the buildings near the river were on stilts due to periodic flooding.

"The men will bunk here," Dimar said. "There is a small hut for Ms. Galloway." He waved her to follow him, and said over his shoulder, "Freddie will find help to unload the boat supplies."

Tristan suspected Dimar had brought more than was needed for their trek. He no doubt planned to barter for items.

The humid, late-afternoon air hung thick inside the one-room accommodations. Tristan and the others put their gear on cots, then everyone exited the building.

Dimar returned sans Galloway and looked at Tristan expectantly. Tristan pulled several bolivianos from his pocket to pay for their lodging, such as it were.

BRYNN SETTLED INTO A SMALL HUT, but it was clear that many other people lived in it. While she was given a narrow mattress on the floor off to the side, there were also three hammocks strung around the room with mosquito netting hanging loosely above each one. In fact, Brynn would have to sleep partially beneath one. She stowed her gear as a young, bright-eyed Bolivian woman entered.

"I am Milenka." She held out her hand, which Brynn shook.

"I'm pleased to meet you. I'm Brynn."

"I hope you will be comfortable here tonight."

"Yes, of course." Brynn glanced around. "I hope I didn't take someone's bed."

"No, no. It will be me and you here. My sisters also stay, but they are not here now. They go upriver."

"You speak very good English."

Milenka smiled. "Thank you. Most Tacana people know English. We go to Rurre a lot. And even La Paz sometimes."

"What do you do out here?"

"We farm. And some raise cattle. And tourists are here sometimes. Dimar and Freddie and Pico bring them."

The mention of the Castanos cousins caught Brynn's attention. "Have you seen Pico recently? He was traveling with an older woman named Irene Caridad."

Milenka nodded. "Yes. She was here. But they are gone now."

"Do you know where?"

"Hard to say exactly, but Dimar and Freddie will find him. Miss Irene gave me this." Milenka held up her wrist, revealing a delicate gold bracelet with ocean-themed charms hanging from it.

"That's very pretty."

"Are you hungry?"

Brynn nodded.

"Good. I will return soon and take you to dinner."

And with that, Milenka left Brynn alone. Although it was muggy in the hut, Brynn organized her things and lay down to rest on the mattress covered with a thin blanket. She soon fell asleep.

TRISTAN SAT at an outdoor wooden table across from Shea. Several villagers, including children, milled around, obviously intrigued by the newly arrived tourists. Freddie and Dimar appeared, speaking abruptly to one another in Spanish. Clearly the two weren't getting along.

Tristan sighed.

"Some things never change," Shea said.

They had dealt with the hotheaded Castanos cousins the last time they were here.

A little boy brought each of them a bottle of soda pop.

"Thanks." Tristan smiled at the youngster.

Switching to English, Dimar said, "I cannot travel with him." He jabbed a stubby finger in Freddie's direction.

"You cut her loose, Dimar." Freddie pursed his lips tightly.

"Where is the code of men?" Dimar sat down beside Tristan so hard the bench shook.

Brynn arrived, looking half-asleep and a bit disheveled, and Tristan immediately nudged Dimar away. "Get lost." He waved Brynn over as Dimar glared at him and stood up.

Behind her was a Bolivian woman, and as soon as Dimar's gaze landed on her, his scowl deepened, but Freddie's pinched face relaxed.

As Dimar and Freddie began arguing in a local dialect, Tristan didn't have to guess at what was happening.

Once Brynn settled beside him, Tristan leaned close and asked, "Who's that?"

"Her name is Milenka. She's my roommate and has been helping me get around."

Milenka jumped into the raucous conversation that included finger pointing and waving of arms.

"What's going on?" Brynn said, alarm evident in her eyes.

From across the table, Shea replied, "Love triangle."

"I think we know why Dimar didn't want to come into the jungle." Tristan handed Brynn his soda.

With gratitude in her gaze, she took a long drink, after which she asked, "Should we do something?"

At that moment, however, Dimar stomped off and Freddie clasped Milenka's arm and guided her away.

"Relief at last," Tristan muttered.

Several young girls surrounded them, glancing at Brynn and giggling.

"You seem to have groupies," Shea said.

Brynn leaned to the side to dig something out of her trouser pocket, bumping into Tristan. Her ponytail whipped into his face, making him aware that he'd been watching her too closely.

She retrieved a pack of sugar-free gum and handed it to one of the girls. "You can share it."

Her gift was met with a bevy of toothy grins. An older woman waved the youngsters away, then returned with plates of food.

Talking ceased as they dug into the rice, beans, and fried plantains.

The girls filtered back, each chewing a piece of the gum and laughing. Brynn made silly faces at them as she ate.

"This is really good," Brynn said. "I didn't realize how hungry I was."

When they were finished, Dimar reappeared and they all moved to a campfire. Brynn stuck close to Tristan as they crowded onto a bench, several of the locals joining them.

"So I've noticed a lot of ants everywhere," Brynn remarked.

Pressed against her, Tristan said, "You need to behave yourself."

"Why?"

"They punish people by tying them to the fire ant tree. The bite is so poisonous that if you were left for more than half a day, you would die."

"Splendid. Thanks for the tip."

Tristan looked past Brynn. "Everything okay, Dimar?"

The Bolivian mumbled something unintelligible.

"I'm sorry about Milenka," Brynn said, her tone quiet, almost soothing. "Were you together a long time?"

"Long enough."

"And she's dating Freddie now?"

Dimar's shoulders sagged and he huffed in obvious frustration. "I told her I didn't want to be tied down, and she immediately falls into Freddie's charms."

"You mean she fell into Freddie's arms?"

"Whatever."

"If you weren't exclusive, then you can't really blame her, can you?"

Dimar's expression turned feral.

"You're getting way too involved." Tristan's hot breath tickled her ear.

Brynn glanced at him, her face mere inches from his. "Just trying to help."

He arched a brow. "Fire ants, remember?"

"Discussing relationship troubles could get me lynched?" she whispered.

"You don't want to meddle in this. You'll regret it. I promise."

"Fine." She crossed her arms, and then said, "How did your father get caught up in ancient alien theories?"

He supposed he asked to be on the serving platter now that he'd turned her attention away from Dimar's love life.

"You can blame that on our grandfather," Shea said, sitting on the other side of Tristan. "He was a cartographer."

"What's a cartographer?" Dimar asked.

"Map maker," Tristan replied. "He loved to share his knowledge of ancient maps. One in particular was the Piri Reis map from the 1500's that had accurate depictions of Antarctica."

"Why would that be important?" Brynn asked.

"Antarctica wasn't discovered until the 1800's."

"That got Uncle Charlie to thinking that those early cartographers had access to other maps," Shea chimed in, "like maybe from the Lost City of Atlantis. And surely those maps had been made by aliens from outer space, because otherwise how would the proportions be so accurate?"

"Uncle Charlie was Harold Gatty?" Brynn asked, confirming her earlier conclusion that they were one and the same person.

Tristan nodded, and said, "His real name was Charlie Hartigan. His public persona was Gatty."

"Why did he use a stage name?"

"My mom insisted."

"Aunt Ellie didn't want the notoriety that she seemed to sense was imminent," Shea said.

Tristan leaned forward, elbows on knees. "And the more he pursued his passion of alien occupation of the earth, the more I suspect she wanted to protect me."

Shea shook his head. "You just never wanted to be part of the family, Tristan."

"The only one I have a problem with is you."

"What are we pursuing here in the jungle?" Dimar cut in, his tone impatient. "Dr. Irene was very secretive, and when I handed her off to Pico, he wouldn't say anything either."

Tristan was inclined to say nothing, but Brynn spoke up. "Did you see what she carried with her?"

"No."

"We think she has a Sumerian cuneiform tablet."

"And that's all we know." Tristan slanted her a look of censure.

She flashed one right back at him.

"What is Sumerian?" Dimar asked.

Brynn answered. "The Sumerians were a group of people who lived about five thousand years ago in Mesopotamia, an area that includes Iraq, Syria, Iran, Kuwait, and Turkey. They're considered to be responsible for the dawn of civilization. They developed the lunar calendar, and organized time into hours, minutes, and seconds, which of course led to the invention of clocks, telescopes, and map-making tools and charts." She nodded toward Tristan. "Your grandfather can thank the Sumerians for his profession."

She continued, "But it's also believed by some that the Sumerians were influenced or guided by a race of beings called the Anunnaki. They worshipped them as gods and wrote many stories about them. But some people, such as Dr. Magee and his father, don't believe they were just fanciful tales. They think they were true."

"What if the Anunnaki were astronauts visiting from another planet?" Tristan said. "The Sumerian culture was very advanced. Where did that knowledge come from?"

"I take issue with the fact that humans were too dumb to figure any of this stuff out," Brynn said. "You have to remember that early scholars—those stuffy white men who practiced archaeology in the 1800's—had an innate bias. They believed that any non-European simply wasn't smart enough. It colored how they presented their findings in places like Africa and Persia. When you speak of advanced societies, it usually entails an understanding of the stars and the seasonal cycles of the earth, and surely there was at least one genius among the humans who could figure it out." She held up a hand. "And before you start talking about the amazing ancient structures that have been built—the pyramids, the intricate stonework of the

Incas—remember that all that was needed was a dedication to the cause and a knowledge of simple geometry."

Tristan nodded. "True. But what if you're wrong?"

"The words of a religious acolyte. It all comes down to faith, right?"

"Not necessarily. But why can't both be true? Ancient man was intelligent, and he had help from the stars."

"Occam's razor, Magee," she said.

Dimar frowned. "What is that?"

"The simplest solution is most likely the correct one," Shea offered. "But even that's used in too simplistic of terms. The true application of Occam's razor is that simpler theories are easier to deal with than more complex ones because they're easier to test."

Brynn frowned in Shea's direction. "Are you on Magee's side?"

Shea chuckled. "Yes and no. Uncle Charlie believed in the complexity. I have no idea if he was right or wrong. And now Tristan is trying to prove him right, but I believe the complexity will do you in, cousin."

Tristan straightened his back and ran a hand through his hair. "So I shouldn't try? That's bullshit in my book. Knowledge and innovation are pushed by the bold."

Shea laughed again. "You were never humble, even as a kid."

"It's not arrogance," Tristan countered. "It's bullheaded curiosity. And you know it's a Hartigan trait, because you have it too."

"Tell me more about these Anunnaki," Dimar said.

"Certain scholars believe," Tristan said, "that the Anunnaki were ancient extraterrestrials that came from a planet called Nibiru, or some have called it Planet X, and that this planet is in our own solar system but with an elliptical orbit that takes it far from Earth for thousands of years at a time. Nibiru was dying, so the Anunnaki came here to harvest gold, which could be turned into a dust that could then be injected into their planet's atmosphere to protect them from deadly ultraviolet rays. They used the humanoids that were present on Earth as slave labor, genetically manipulating them to make them better and more intelligent. We're the result."

Silence ensued, and then Dimar howled with laughter. "That's the most ridiculous thing I've ever heard."

Maybe. Critics had been deriding Harold Gatty for most of Tristan's life.

"It all boils down to the missing link theory, which isn't really even pushed anymore," Shea said.

Dimar raised his hand like he was a school child. "I know what that is. There's some skeleton out there that connects us to the monkeys."

"It's more the idea that man leaped from Cro-Magnon to *Homo sapiens* too quickly," Tristan said. "Why haven't we found intermediary evidence? Alien theorists believe it's because we had genetic help with that transition. Hence, there is no missing link, which explains why we never found one. We also know that RH negative blood only showed up 35,000 years ago, and many purported alien abductees have that type."

"Then where are these Anunnaki now?" Dimar demanded.

"Gone," Tristan said. "But they left us behind."

"Uncle Charlie used to say," Shea said, "that since we know there is at least one planet in the universe with life, and on this planet life is everywhere, then we can extrapolate that life in the universe is possible."

Brynn smiled. "That's a very elegant way of phrasing it."

Dimar stroked his chin, his expression contemplative. "So I could be descended from a god."

Tristan didn't bother to hide his sarcasm. "The impeccable irony of the universe."

CHAPTER 6

In the early morning hours, Tristan roused himself from a deep slumber. His dreams had been filled with jungle sounds, aliens from the sky, and Brynn Galloway telling him he was crazy. He sat up and pushed aside the mosquito netting covering his bed. Dimar, Shea, and Freddie were still sleeping, although Freddie had arrived so late that it was obvious he'd been with Milenka. Shea had switched beds to separate the feuding cousins.

Tristan ran a hand through his hair, trying to shake the last remnants of sleep loose. He went to his duffel bag—hanging from a hook to avoid ants—and grabbed a clean shirt, which he quickly changed into, and his toothbrush. There was a makeshift sink just outside the hut with water available. He didn't want to smell like an unbathed sumo wrestler.

Galloway flashed in his mind. No, he wasn't cleaning up for her. And he sure as hell didn't care that she didn't believe him about the Sumerians and the Anunnaki.

Once he felt more presentable, he headed into the makeshift mist-filled village. He wasn't even sure what the settlement's name might be. Villages came and went in the Amazon, especially along rivers such as the Beni, and the only certainty was that nothing was certain.

The sun had risen but the thick forest canopy kept it hidden, blocking its shafts of sunlight for most of the day, so the world revealed itself in a palette of muted gray and shades of green.

The loud screech of macaws echoed around him and the eerie call of a howler monkey forced his gaze upward. The annoyed male—the large testicles swinging from his nether region were a dead giveaway —puffed his chest out and began throwing sticks and leaves at Tristan. When Tristan held his ground, the monkey gave up and went back to eating a piece of fruit, but Tristan couldn't help but feel the animal's disgust at having to deal with a 6'2" human interloper.

The clammy aroma of wet soil, dew-ridden leaves, and detritus surrounded Tristan, and he stopped to view and inhale the spectacle. The Amazon jungle was a living, pulsing thing, and a longing for it slammed into him.

He'd missed it. He'd never realized just how much until this moment. And it wasn't just the place, but the connection—something ephemeral and impossible to describe, like a piece of his soul that had gone missing.

His breath quieted, and his heartbeat slowed. Like a mother, the jungle accepted his return, offering instant forgiveness.

He walked across the compound, passing mostly makeshift huts and a smoldering outdoor cookfire.

When an older woman, short and plump, her bosom filling a bright pink dress, caught sight of him, she waved him forward, smiling and insistent. At least she was clothed. The deeper they went into the jungle, the less the indigenous people wore.

The aroma of cooking food and coffee started a rumble in his belly. There were three wooden tables present, so Tristan guessed she ran a restaurant of sorts, likely for the tourists who passed through. She badgered him into sitting and a younger girl brought utensils and set out a bowl of sugar.

Just as he started digging into a plate of fried eggs and potatoes, an old man entered the hut.

It couldn't be.

"Pepito?"

Releasing a bark of laughter, the old man's eyes became nothing more than slits. He stepped closer and Tristan was amazed that he had hardly aged, his dark skin still smooth. Pepito had to be well into his nineties.

"Tristan Magee," the Bolivian said with a thick accent.

Pepito sidled forward, and Tristan stood just in time to grip the man's forearm and engulf him in a hug.

"I didn't know you were here." Happiness filled Tristan as they both sat down across from one another.

The older woman tittered and brought Pepito a plate of food and coffee as well. Pepito said something to her in his language, and she giggled and gave Tristan's shoulder a friendly swat of her hand.

"You thought I was dead," Pepito said to Tristan, as if reading his mind. "But not yet." He paused to eat his food, and Tristan did the same.

"I hear from the jungle express two days ago that there are Americans in the jungle, and I knew it was you, so I walked here to see you."

Tristan paused. "Two days ago? We entered the jungle yesterday. Is the jungle express psychic?"

Pepito chuckled, leaning forward and saying in a low voice, "The jaguar told me."

Pepito had always spoken of the jungle as if he were one with it, as if he sat in a room with all the animals and the plants and the sky and the rain. Everything was connected, he would say. Tristan had been sixteen years old when he'd first met the old man and at the time, he'd simply thought Pepito was loco, a little like Tristan's own father. But maturity had tempered that sentiment. If a man saw magic in the world, did that make him crazy? Tristan was beginning to think not.

"What else did the jaguar tell you?" Tristan asked.

"He said there is a woman."

"The last time you said that, I got into trouble with that local girl." Tristan tried to keep his tone light, but his shoulders tensed anyway. It wasn't a local girl he was worried about; the one who flashed to mind had brown hair and a killer smile, and was immune to both his charm and his bullshit. *Brynn.*

Pepito laughed. "*Sí, sí.* You were a handsome young man from a foreign land and that chica could not resist you." Tristan knew he referred to the young local girl from so long ago, but his thoughts lingered on Brynn. "You are pushed from the inside. A restless boy. And now a restless man. But there is a woman here. With you."

"Did the jaguar spy her?"

"No. Ruben told me." He flicked his head toward a hut somewhere out there.

Tristan relaxed. Pepito was messing with him.

"What's your angle, old man?"

Pepito gave him a questioning look.

"What do you want?" Tristan clarified.

"I want to meet her."

BRYNN AWOKE, feeling rested and clear-headed. She'd slept deeply, which surprised her. It had only been a few days, but maybe she was getting her jungle legs. Only a month ago she had been in one of the coldest environments on Earth, and now she was deep in the Amazonian rainforest. Excitement filled her. She did love an adventure.

She arose quietly, discarding her dirty t-shirt for a clean one and giving her armpits a quick sniff test. A bit of deodorant would do the trick. She felt around in her duffel bag until she located it.

Nearby, Milenka slumbered in a hammock, a chrysalis waiting to become a butterfly, currently fending off the overtures of two men. The Bolivian woman didn't snore exactly, but the sound of her steady breathing made Brynn wonder if folding oneself into a hammock each night promoted good sleep. She would know soon enough, since Magee had informed her they would all be sleeping in the hanging contraptions once they entered the jungle. Because of snakes, he'd said.

Lovely.

Brynn could tolerate a lot of discomfort and knew how to blend in and be one of the guys—two older brothers had toughened her emotional hide, and her time on the competitive surfing circuit, especially during her teenage years, had taught her fortitude and a finely-tuned ambition. She knew she could handle seeing a snake, but she feared if she happened to step on one then all bets would be off. She'd start squealing like a pig.

Not on my watch, she vowed.

A glance at her trousers confirmed they weren't too dirty yet and could therefore continue to be worn, probably for days. How long would they be in the jungle? She was hoping only a week at most. But she had spent nearly two months in Pakistan over the summer, so perhaps that timetable was too optimistic.

She could hear Gramps's voice as if he were standing beside her. *Journeys of the soul take however long they need to take. And life itself is the ultimate journey.*

She crept out of her hut. An early-morning mist hung in the air and the forest hummed like a mother singing to her child, *welcome home, welcome home.* Life, green and verdant and lush, surrounded the settlement in overwhelming abundance.

There weren't many villagers up and about yet, but the ones who were smiled and nodded a greeting. Not wanting to intrude, Brynn gravitated to the boundary between jungle and settlement, lured by the squawks, calls, and whistles that beckoned.

She was greeted by giant trees and draping vines and birds fluttering above, her senses on Mother Earth overload, and she didn't see the giant brown creature blocking her path until the last second.

Startled, she came to an abrupt halt. The beast swung its head to look at her, its head tapering down to a long pointy nose. A giant fluffy tail swooshed behind it, and the cutest eyes watched her. Then, a nightmarish metamorphosis took place as the creature reared to its hind legs and waved the most impossibly long talons at her, reminding her of Edward Scissorhands or Wolverine.

Oh shit.

Stumbling backward, she slammed into someone and strong hands gripped her upper arms. "Anteater," Magee whispered into her ear. "Very dangerous."

He began guiding them slowly backward while the creature huffed out menacing noises. With Magee's proximity, sweat began running down Brynn's back. When they had moved about ten feet, Magee pushed her behind him, never taking his eyes from the animal, which hadn't moved.

Clasping his bicep, a piece of granite disguised as muscle, Brynn peeked around Magee. "Why are they so big?" she asked.

Magee wrapped his arm behind him and around Brynn's waist as he continued to push her backward.

When they had moved another ten feet, Magee's stance seemed to relax. That's when she saw the machete in his right hand.

"Oh God, were you going to kill it?"

Magee turned and grabbed her hand, hauling her along. "Don't loiter, Galloway."

She had to run a little to keep up.

"And yes, I was going to kill if it came after you." His voice was edged with irritation, almost anger.

"I'm sorry," she said. "I had no idea. I didn't go far."

He stopped and faced her, releasing her hand. "No, I'm sorry. I should have been very explicit with you. Don't go walking in the jungle alone. Ever."

Brynn bristled at his condescending tone, biting back a retort.

"Adult anteaters can kill a full-grown man," he continued. "You saw those talons. One swipe across your abdomen and your guts are spilling all over the jungle floor."

"That's terrible. How do they protect the children here?"

"The kids know better. You have a machete. Where is it?" He looked down the length of her body.

"With my gear," she said quietly.

"Keep it with you at all times." He watched her as if he had more to say, then turned and continued down the path to the village.

Brynn hustled to keep up, casting a final glance over her shoulder. The anteater had turned and was walking away.

~

TRISTAN SOUGHT to calm his nerves at the makeshift village restaurant where he'd had his breakfast not twenty minutes ago. He had introduced Brynn to Pepito, and now they were exchanging pleasant small talk at a separate table.

She could've been killed. What had she been thinking, wandering around? Didn't she have any sense?

Pepito had insisted on meeting her and had shooed Tristan off to go find her. After confirming that she wasn't in the hut she shared with Milenka, he had developed a suspicion that she'd gone exploring. It's exactly what he had done the first time he'd been here that summer with his dad and Shea. And he'd ended up in a worse predicament when a pit viper had dropped onto him from a tree branch.

But thankfully, this morning, the villagers had quickly realized what was happening as he'd stalked around looking for her and had pointed toward a pathway. Brynn was in the jungle.

Finding her facing off with a giant anteater had been surprising since the creatures didn't usually come so close to human habitations. But one constant of the jungle was never to presume anything.

He kept glancing at her as she smiled and chatted with Pepito, and then she accepted a plate of food from the Bolivian woman. The older man leaned close to say something, and Brynn immediately locked eyes with Tristan. She'd caught him staring at her, and he couldn't look away fast enough to feign innocence. Her brows furrowed and she returned her attention to Pepito.

Shea arrived. "We have a problem."

"Just one?" Tristan responded.

"Freddie and Dimar are gone."

"What do you mean they're gone?"

"Milenka left about an hour ago, apparently to see her sisters upstream, and Freddie decided to go with her. And then Dimar left too. I'm told Milenka will return tomorrow, so we can only hope it will spur the return of our boys."

"Perfect," Tristan muttered.

"Then it's settled." Pepito's voice boomed across the hut.

"Pepito?" Shea exclaimed, so engrossed in telling Tristan about the loss of both of their guides that he'd been unaware of the man's presence until now. "It's great to see you." He clasped the older man's hand.

"I am graced to see you both, my American comrades. That settles it."

"What's that?" Shea asked.

"You will stay one more night."

Tristan clenched his jaw. "It seems we have no choice." Unfortunately, they couldn't go into the jungle without Dimar or Freddie.

Pepito took his seat once again. "There is someone you all need to meet."

"Who's that?" Shea asked.

"An elder who also has just arrived from a village many days' walk from here. It is a divine coincidence."

Tristan crossed his arms over his chest. He had some idea where this was going. "A medicine man?"

Pepito would neither confirm nor deny the question, giving a look of comic relief.

"Still a slippery bastard, aren't you, Pep? I'm not doing a ceremony."

A toothy grin spread across Pepito's mouth. "But Brynn has agreed. And you should accompany her. Shea, too." He acknowledged all of them, then said, "I am no bastard. And now that you have time, I will tell you my family line."

Tristan suppressed a groan. Not only must he now endure an ayahuasca ceremony, he was about to be forced to listen to a Pepito recitation of his family lineage, which the old man claimed ran back to the dawn of civilization in South America. Tristan had endured both before, and nothing good had come from either.

CHAPTER 7

B rynn crossed her legs and waited, a robust smell emanating from a pot on a small cookstove in the corner of the hut. It offered a natural essence, as if it were a soup made of dirt and bark and leaves, but at the same time it periodically triggered Brynn's gag reflex, which she suppressed by taking focused breaths through her mouth.

The shelter they occupied wasn't on stilts since it was further away from the river, so she, Tristan, and Shea sat directly on the ground. This seemed significant, since Brynn had always heard that shamanic ceremonies could send a person off into worlds not as solid, or as real, as the one humankind inhabited. But maybe all anyone experienced was a dream, or a self-induced imagining. Still, it seemed safer to be anchored to the solid ground of Earth, even if that connection was only through her butt cheeks.

She could hear her brothers' voices from when she was young. *Are you afraid of the bogeyman, Brynn? We think there's a ghost in your room, little sister.*

Like any older siblings, Alec and Tyler had done their fair share of picking and needling to gain the upper hand with her. But she hadn't been that little girl for a long time now … so a shamanic ceremony in the Amazon wasn't something she would cower from. And come Thanksgiving, she'd have a story to tell around the family dinner table. She's pretty sure neither of her brothers had ever ingested ayahuasca. She pushed aside what her parents would say. They had always encouraged her to broaden her horizons, but they would surely frown upon this. Drugs were never part of that equation.

To Brynn's surprise, the shaman was a woman, and Pepito was so respectful of her that Brynn peered at her more closely, wondering if she was something more than human.

But she appeared quite ordinary with a round face, flat nose, and two long black braids spilling down her back. She wore a blue skirt, white blouse, and sandals, and a fancy hat sat atop her head, streaked with dirt and sweat.

Pepito introduced her as Miss Carla, who smiled as she removed her hat, and the deep creases of her wrinkles revealed her age. How did the woman keep the gray from her jet-black hair? Perhaps Bolivian shamanesses didn't need anything as mundane as hair coloring and instead used magic to enhance their beauty regimen.

As Pepito and Carla conversed in some amalgamation of Spanish and other local dialects, Brynn felt again that warm feeling for Pepito, as if he were a jungle grandfather of sorts. It made her miss Gramps even more.

It had been clear within five minutes of meeting Pepito that the man held great affection for both Tristan and Shea, and she could only guess this was why the two cousins had finally agreed to participate. She was told the three of them had met years ago in Peru when Tristan's father had come to the jungle looking for clues to ancient civilizations. Extreme adventuring at its purest.

As Miss Carla checked the pot and its brewing contents, she grinned and laughed with regularity. Brynn decided she wanted to age this way, possessing a palpable energy and zeal for living.

According to Tristan, the contents of the cookpot had been boiling all day and contained various bundles of the ayahuasca plant, a drug outlawed in the United States, but perfectly legal to use in Bolivia.

Tristan leaned over and whispered in her ear, "I forgot to tell you that this plant is called La Purga. Wanna know why?"

"I know why." She eyed the empty bowls Pepito had placed before each of them. It was the only part she wasn't looking forward to.

"I prefer to think of it as psychedelic tea," Shea said from the other side of Brynn. She was sandwiched between the two Hartigan cousins. "It's time for a magical mystery tour."

"If it's any consolation," Tristan said, "drinking it can clear you of worms and intestinal parasites."

Brynn stared at him.

"Because of the vomiting and diarrhea," he added helpfully.

"Thanks for the tutorial." She clamped down on her mounting anxiety. Maybe this wasn't such a good idea.

Appearing to sense her unease, Tristan patted her hand where it rested on her knee, the gesture meant to be friendly, but her skin still reacted to his touch as if he had branded her, sending a warm tingle clear to her shoulder.

"Don't worry," he said, his eyes flashing, "I'll still like you afterward, despite the puking and the runs."

She averted her gaze, afraid he might be able to see how much he got to her at times, swallowing past the dry lump in her throat.

Miss Carla ladled scoops of liquid from the pot and handed a tin cup to each person.

"The plants were harvested just this morning," Pepito said, "and have been boiling all day. The proper prayers were said and offerings given. Drink."

"Bottoms up," Shea said, making fast work of his portion.

Brynn paused to sniff the brew. It only filled a quarter of the cup and had the consistency of thick coffee. "It looks like mud."

Shea wiped his mouth with the back of his hand. "Just pretend you're drinking a garden."

Tristan knocked his back as if it were a shot of tequila. In a strained voice he said, "The Garden of Eden."

Brynn took a steadying breath and managed one small sip. The liquid rolled across her tongue like she imagined motor oil might, if drinking motor oil were something she aspired to accomplish one day. Bits and pieces of plant matter and bark coated her tongue.

Blech.

Miss Carla's bright gaze watched Brynn. "All," she said, bringing an imaginary cup to her mouth and tipping it back.

Bolstering herself, Brynn closed her eyes and quickly downed what remained in her cup.

What disgusting shit.

She coughed, blocking her mouth with the back of her hand.

Pepito offered a canteen of water, which helped to push the plant chunks down her throat, although the oily film remained on her tongue.

Her face puckered, and she didn't bother to hide her distaste.

"Be calm," Pepito said, translating for Miss Carla, who walked back and forth, her vividly blue skirt swooshing in rhythmic response. "The shield of everyday life will be removed, and you will see the world beside this world. It will be filled with spirits that are not normally seen. Plant spirits, animal spirits, the pulse of the earth. There will also be bad spirits. Take care and be strong. For most people, it is a very personal experience of inner growth. Many purge their sins. Do not fight the process. Do not be afraid."

Brynn tried her best to focus on Pepito's voice, but the sound faded into the background. She looked at Tristan beside her. He sat calmly, his arms propped casually on his crossed legs, his gaze forward and focused on … *something.*

Without warning, her stomach cramped, and a wave of nausea crashed over her.

Attempting to stay in control, she breathed deeply, sweat breaking out from every pore on her body. The churning in her abdomen was quickly becoming a maelstrom, and she wiped her shirtsleeve across her forehead. She had always hated getting the stomach flu as a child. She hated vomiting more than anything. She hated any semblance of helplessness ….

Oh God. She really was gonna puke in front of Magee.

Lurching forward, she emptied what was in her stomach into the bowl, which wasn't much thankfully, since they had been instructed to fast for most of the day.

As she remained hunched over, an incessant buzzing filled her ears. In the background, as if at a distance, Shea or Magee, or maybe both, retched.

Regret began to fill her thoughts. The college boyfriend she had professed to love, only she hadn't. The time in high school she lied to her father so she could sneak out with her friends to drink beer at the beach. The time in middle school when she had chickened out during an opportunity to kiss her crush—what was his name?—but she'd told her friends that she'd done it anyway to save face. When the boy confronted her, she had laughed it off but there had been genuine hurt in his eyes, which she had pretended not to notice. The time in fourth grade when she stole nerdy Gina's purse during a field trip because her friends had dared her. Later, she hid it elsewhere on the school bus and never admitted her guilt, leaving Gina in tears and the teachers disappointed in whomever had done it.

Brynn wanted these thoughts to go away.

I never meant any of it. I'm sorry.

Gramps. He had passed away suddenly seven years ago when Brynn had been a high school senior. She had thought she had more time with him, skipping her sojourn to Pennsylvania that year. She had assumed she would see him at Thanksgiving or Christmas, but instead they'd lost him right before Halloween. The remorse and the grief made her chest hurt, and she rubbed at it, trying to assuage the very real physical pain.

I'm sorry, Gramps. I'm so sorry.

Something seemed to move in a dark corner of the hut. Brynn squinted, trying to focus. Barely visible, a dark shape materialized with glowing eyes and pointy ears.

Whoa.

"Is that a vampire?" she muttered.

There was no response to her question. She blinked again and the creature was gone.

More movement. Some kind of furry beast with a long snout.

Sweet Mother of God, it's a werewolf!

Another blink and it disappeared. Brynn scowled. This was ridiculous. She didn't believe in scary, mythological creatures. They existed only in books or movies. She was imagining this. It was all a dream.

A rush of longing to be a better person filled her.

I should tell Mom and Dad how much I love them. I should offer to watch Alec's dog, Grace, more often when he must be away on a filming expedition. I should make more of an effort to get to know his girlfriend, the other Grace.

Her brother obviously had a thing for females named Grace, whether they were human or canine. Did he realize it?

Her body released a loud snorting guffaw, startling her, and she quickly slapped a hand over her mouth, embarrassed. Although she sensed the others in the room, she could no longer see them, so hopefully they hadn't heard her. But maybe she had scared off Dracula and the American Werewolf from London with her noisy vocal reactions.

Her mind went back to wandering, locating every trail that seemed to end in regret.

I should visit Audrey in Arizona. I keep saying I will, and then I never do. I should go diving with Chloe. When she invites me, I'm always busy. She studies sperm whales, for crying aloud. How neat is that? What's wrong with me? They were my best friends in college and I never see them now. Am I a good friend? I could be better. I could be so much better.

Fragments of a William Wordsworth poem arose in her thoughts. *For I would walk alone, under the quiet stars ... the ghostly language of the ancient earth.*

Miss Carla, her face soft and ethereal, gently wiped a cloth across Brynn's mouth and helped her to lie back. Brynn tried to smile and say thank you, but she couldn't seem to locate her body in time or space. She had no idea if any of her body parts moved at all.

Close your eyes.

Had Miss Carla spoken? Strange, because Brynn hadn't heard her speak a full sentence of English.

Had it been Gramps?

She was in a crowd of people who spoke a foreign language. As the scene became more fully formed, and she felt more present, the Grand Bazaar in Istanbul materialized before her. The language echoing around her was Turkish, and she was nine years old. She had come to Turkey with Gramps, just the two of them, for an adventure. But on this morning, he'd had a business meeting, so she was accompanied to the great shopping mecca by a Turkish girl named Sefa that he'd hired to look after Brynn. Sefa was seventeen years old, and Brynn had thought her so worldly with her beautiful long hair, dark complexion, and English tinged with an exotic accent.

They milled through the indoor shops that offered all types of colorful wares: sparkly brooches; antique Turkish rings with emerald stones; vintage pocket watches; mirrors; snuff boxes; sandals; grand carpets. There were historical maps and globes, paintings and hookahs and backgammon sets. It was overwhelming.

"What do you wish to buy?" Sefa asked.

Brynn clutched the lira bills in her hand that Gramps had given to her. She was thinking a scarf, because that seemed practical, and she wondered if she had enough for one in silk or even cashmere. But now that she was here, her interest was expanding like a flower basking in sunlight, and she desired something more special than a piece of clothing she could easily find back home. But how did she convey that to Sefa?

Sefa looked down at her and laughed. "I have an idea," she said, clasping Brynn's hand and tugging her through the crowds, only stopping when she reached a small café. Or maybe it was a deli. Brynn wasn't certain. Brynn tucked her money into a pants pocket, not wanting to waste it here. She wanted to make sure she had enough for her special souvenir.

Sefa spoke to the girl behind the counter in Turkish, and soon Brynn was ushered to a back room where an older woman greeted them and bade them sit at a round wooden table.

"Do you drink coffee?" Sefa asked.

Brynn shook her head.

"Would you like to try some?"

Brynn shrugged, too tongue-tied to ask Sefa what was happening.

The older woman placed a small cup filled with a thick brew atop a saucer. She indicated with a wave and a nod that Brynn should drink.

Bolstering her confidence, Brynn brought the cup to her lips. The liquid was strong and pungent, with a muddy consistency and a bitter taste, but it wasn't altogether unpleasant. She continued to sip the beverage while Sefa spoke to the old woman.

When Brynn was almost done with her drink, Sefa said, "Leave a bit of liquid at the bottom, then swirl it around with the coffee grounds and quickly turn over the cup onto the saucer."

Brynn did as she was told, the cup clanking loudly against the plate.

"Now," Sefa continued, "wet your finger with your tongue, then place it on the bottom of the cup and make a wish."

Brynn thought for a moment, then did what Sefa had said, silently wishing for a grand revelation of something archaeology-related for Gramps. Part of the purpose of this trip was to acquire trinkets and artifacts for Gramps's collection back home. Wouldn't it be great if Brynn found something for him?

Sefa smiled. "We must wait for the grounds to cool."

The older woman brought them a plate with two pieces of baklava, and Brynn sank her teeth into the flaky, sweet pastry, gobbling it up in no time and licking her fingers clean.

Finally, the old woman sat in a chair beside Brynn and lifted the coffee cup, turning it over, and then stared intently at the contents.

She was silent for so long that Sefa finally said something.

The old woman fixed her gaze on Brynn, a look of curiosity on her face, making Brynn uncomfortable. She spoke in Turkish, so Sefa had to translate.

"She says that she has never seen this before. You are connected to the past. The ancient past."

Her words didn't really mean anything to Brynn, so she politely remained quiet.

"I told her you would like to buy a souvenir, one that has meaning to you. She says you are on the right path because you have been drawn here to a specific item."

"What is it?" Brynn asked, hopeful. She imagined something rare and beautiful awaited her.

The old woman stood and indicated for Brynn and Sefa to follow. She led them out of the coffee bar and into the throng of customers, her stride confident and swift. Both Sefa and Brynn had to run in fits and starts to keep up. When the woman finally entered a shop at the end of the walkway, she went immediately to a shelf covered in an array of dusty statues, ashtrays, and magnets. Searching the items, she plucked one up and handed it to Brynn.

It appeared to be a ring, but the gold-plated opening wasn't round but square. Surely, it wouldn't be comfortable to wear. Even worse, atop it was a tiny replica of a cylinder with markings in an unappealing shade of dark brown. Brynn thought the writing could be cuneiform, a subject that Gramps was obsessed with, so she supposed he would like it.

Resigning herself to her fate, her shoulders slumped. She wasn't about to argue with this fortune-telling Turkish woman, and she didn't want Sefa to think she was an ungrateful tourist, but the ring truly was the ugliest thing Brynn had ever seen. But she had to concede that perhaps it was meant for Gramps and not her, and who was she to question the hand of providence, a subject about which her grandfather frequently spoke. She smiled her thanks to the old woman, who nodded in finality.

The transaction didn't take long, and luckily Brynn had enough money, since it was obviously a cheap knock-off of some older and more ancient relic. When she presented it to Gramps later, his enthusiasm surprised her. He translated the markings on the tiny cylinder, saying they indicated a female name: Ninsun.

Dressed in rumpled khakis and one of his favorite colorful Havana shirts, Gramps handed the souvenir back to her. "You should keep it, Bee."

He was the only one who called her that. Some thought it was a shortcut of her first name, but the full nickname was Bumble Bee, a reference to her high energy as a child.

"It called to you," he continued. "It's yours."

Brynn suppressed a grimace as she took the ring. She should have just gotten a pretty scarf and been done with it, but she'd been too shy to speak up when Sefa had taken her to see that Turkish woman, hoping that something magical would happen. Embarrassed by the entire incident, Brynn stayed quiet, accepting this was to be her only memento from her trip to Istanbul.

"Maybe the past is touching the future through you," Gramps had said.

As soon as he'd spoken, a tingling started at the base of her skull and crept higher, encompassing her entire scalp. Strange. Her brows bunched up as she earnestly asked, "How?"

He shrugged. "I don't know, but it's an intriguing thought, isn't it?"

"Have you ever had the past touch you?"

He laughed. "I believe I have."

"Really? How?"

"In dreams."

Brynn tried not to show her frustration. Why did adults talk in circles?

He laughed, hearty and proud. "A true Milano woman, smart and perceptive. Just like your mother and your grandmother." Then his expression became serious. "There's something else on the cylinder," he said, pointing to the ring in her hand. "Why don't you work on translating it."

"Do you know what it says?"

"I do. One day when you decipher it, we'll see if we match."

The scene shifted and Brynn was now in a bright sunny meadow. Squinting from the intense light, she spun around so fast that a wave of dizziness hit her. A glance down at her feet revealed they were clad in toddler-sized tennis shoes. A child's laughter beyond drew her attention.

The boy ran to a tree and stopped. He had to be about six years old. Tyler?

Oh God. When she was just five, her brother Tyler had disappeared from their aunt and uncle's ranch in Telluride, Colorado, while the two of them had been playing alone. He'd been lost for eighteen hours and had almost died. Her parents had been distraught, and Brynn had always felt it was her fault.

"Tyler! Tyler!" She ran after him, but he never looked back, just kept going into the woods.

"No! You'll get lost," she screamed. "Stop!"

But he didn't hear her, and by the time she got to where she had seen him, he was gone. Absolutely gone. She stopped, unsure what to do.

Mommy and Daddy will be so upset. They'll be so mad at me that I didn't stop him.

She started to cry.

Brynn's point of view shifted so that she was now standing beside her younger self. Unable to watch herself suffer, she knelt down, looking at a side view of Brynn-the-child, her youthful features scrunched into painful sobbing.

"Shhh," Brynn said. "It's okay."

Brynn sensed that she couldn't physically touch her child-self, but some connection had taken place because child-Brynn had stopped crying, although she continued to look forward.

"It's not your fault. Tyler will be found."

Peace settled into Brynn's chest, like a gently flowing stream, but then a flutter of movement among the pine trees caught her attention.

Was that a man?

~

BRYNN OPENED HER EYES. She lay on the floor of the hut, a dim light illuminating the ceiling. Beside her was Magee, sleeping. Shea too.

Her head pounded. She gingerly pushed to a sitting position. Pepito was gone, but in the corner sat Miss Carla, leaning back, her eyes closed.

Brynn rubbed her forehead and glanced at Magee. He didn't look comfortable on his back, his face turned away from her, his mouth slightly open as he slumbered in an unsteady rhythm.

Miss Carla opened her eyes and nodded; her mouth quirked into a knowing smile.

Brynn didn't say anything, feeling a deep exhaustion in her bones. She pushed to her feet and waved to indicate she was leaving, then she departed the hut. The darkness enveloped her and she wished for a light, but she'd left her flashlight with her gear. She hoped it wasn't a fatal mistake. Doing her best to remember the path back to her accommodations with Milenka, she eventually made it to her bed. Her roommate was still absent, so Brynn sighed with relief to have a bit of privacy, probably the last she would enjoy for a while. She dug a bottle of ibuprofen from her pack, took two tablets, and settled herself into bed, trying to ignore the headache pounding behind her eyes until the medicine could kick in.

The memory of that time at the Grand Bazaar had been so clear and precise, as if watching a movie, but the encounter with Tyler had been more disorienting, as she apparently had been switching focal points between her younger self and herself today. And it had been different than what actually had happened.

She and Tyler had been playing a game, and when he hadn't come back, she had sat by a tree for a long time, not worried but annoyed. She hadn't told her aunt and uncle that her brother was missing until more than two hours had passed. Because honestly, it hadn't seemed like it was a problem.

But later, when there had been a frantic search for Ty, with lots of people helping, along with the arrival of the police and the sheriff and her distraught parents flying in from California as soon as they could, that's when Brynn had realized something terrible had happened, and somehow, she should have stopped it.

She had carried that pain, that regret, that shame, her entire life. And for some strange reason, it was now gone.

But what about the movement of something, or someone, just beyond her senses? She never recalled a man present with her in the wilderness, and as far as she knew, there hadn't been anyone involved in Ty's disappearance. Her brother had simply wandered off on his own. She pushed aside the ripple of uneasiness that accompanied the recollection. Her imagination was obviously in overdrive from the ayahuasca.

CHAPTER 8

Tristan poured a second cup of steaming coffee from a pot the local restaurant lady had left for him. She still wore the same pink dress from yesterday, resembling a plump flamingo set against the deep greens of the surrounding foliage.

With his elbows propped on the table, he sighed as the strong brew began cutting through his monstrous headache. It was just after dawn according to the watch on his wrist, a trusty all-purpose all-weather thing, but it was still quite dark since sunlight had a hell of a time penetrating the jungle canopy.

No more fucking ayahuasca. God, he'd hated it the first time he'd done it, and he hated it now. Both times he was right back in that hospital bed, his nine-year-old self in a coma following that car accident with his mother. And the vision … the one he'd rather forget. The one that the ayahuasca kept returning him to …. He scrubbed a hand down his face. Rather than acknowledge the fear that he'd carried since a boy, he latched onto the anger. Being pissed off was preferable to dwelling on the bogey monsters of the past. He'd only participated because he hadn't wanted Brynn to be alone.

When he'd awoken, she was gone so he'd made his way here. Shea had wandered off to sleep or shower or whatever. He guessed Brynn had done the same.

The look Miss Carla gave him when he'd departed had been filled with knowing and compassion, but he resolutely shut it away and didn't look back.

Brynn walked in and sat down across from him, wearing a navy linen t-shirt that hugged her athletic frame, cargo pants, and hiking boots. Her brown hair was pulled into a ponytail, revealing a clear and focused gaze. She was a breath of fresh air, all energy and purpose, while Tristan was crawling out of the depths of what felt like the ultimate hangover.

"Good, you're here," she said, grabbing a cup and pouring some coffee. "Is there any food?"

"You can eat?"

"I think so. I'm starved actually." She took a sip then smiled as she caught sight of Flamingo Lady, who walked over to them. Through broken English and gestures, Brynn placed an order for breakfast.

He spoke when they were alone again. "You're awfully chipper."

"I feel amazingly good."

"That's nice. Did you learn the secrets to the universe?"

"No. And there was entirely too much remorse happening in the beginning."

The corner of his mouth lifted in a smirk. "Yeah. Makes you feel a little shitty, huh?"

She nodded. "But this morning I feel lighter, as if a burden has been lifted. I don't know why. What a strange experience. I relived a childhood trip to Istanbul with my grandfather in which I purchased this ugly trinket of a ring. I haven't thought of it in years."

"Where is this ring now? Maybe it's important."

Brynn shrugged. "I don't know. I don't remember."

"Is your grandfather still alive?"

She deflated a bit. "No."

"Then maybe he was trying to visit you, tell you something."

"You think so?" Her face brightened with anticipation as a plate of eggs, rice, and ripe papaya was placed on the table before her. "What about you? What did you experience?"

He waved a hand in front of his face as if batting away the memory. "A whole lot of nothing."

"That bad, huh?"

He made a grumbling noise.

"It's okay, you can tell me when you know me better." She happily filled her mouth with food.

Her comment punctured his sour mood, releasing some of the steam from his irritation over the ceremony. He released a ghost of a smile and stared at her a smidge longer than polite society allowed.

He'd never had much use for polite society anyhow.

BRYNN WALKED THROUGH THE JUNGLE, single file behind the men. Earlier, Dimar and Freddie had returned without Milenka. She had remained with one of her sisters. Neither of the men spoke to the other, and Brynn had followed Tristan's lead and not questioned them. They needed to get going since, according to Tristan, the rainy season was just around the corner, and they wanted to be well and gone from the country before the downpours began.

The jungle was an eruption of sound and little sunshine, but Brynn decided the shade was preferable to direct sunlight. The humidity, however, was still so thick that within minutes sweat trickled down her face and along her back. She slid her childhood pack off one shoulder and removed her hat, then hooked it to a carabiner hanging off the side. She pulled a handkerchief from her pocket and used it to wipe her face, repeating the action every few minutes.

She was in decent shape, but after several hours of trekking she was gasping for breath and longing for something stronger than water. At a rest stop, Magee seemed to read her mind. He walked back to her and pulled a baggy filled with powder from a shirt pocket.

"Give me your water bottle," he said.

She handed it over. He unscrewed the lid and added a few tablespoons of the powder, tightened the lid and gave it a good shake.

"Kool-Aid?" she asked.

"Electrolytes. You're losing too much salt in your sweat. Water will never hydrate you enough."

"Thanks." She took a long drink of the fruity-tasting water and didn't mention that she'd brought along electrolyte tablets, which were stuffed somewhere in her pack. In truth, she'd forgotten about them, making her wonder if she was already dehydrated and making poor decisions.

After a brief rest, they kept going. There was no cellular service here, but Brynn pulled out her cellphone to take photos as they trekked. She had an extra battery pack, and she estimated she could get three, maybe four charges out of it before it too went dead.

Tree branches frequently rustled and Brynn found herself looking upward more and more to catch a glimpse of the perpetrator. Mostly monkeys. Their brown bodies scurried back and forth, their long tails usually the last thing she saw. A cacophony of birds filled the air, and twice Freddie stopped to point out a snake slithering through the nearby underbrush or looping around a branch.

Unnerved, she clamped down her reaction.

"Not poisonous," he had said.

When they saw the third snake, she paused. It bobbed its head and watched her. Was it as curious of her as she was of it? It was so trusting, for certainly there were humans out there that would try to kill it.

As if in response to her thought, Freddie said, "Many guides use this path for tourists. The animals are accustomed to seeing humans."

Brynn continued taking photos and an occasional video, until after a time, she realized she was alone. Had she fallen behind? She hurried forward to catch the group before they got too far ahead, but after several minutes, there was no sign of them.

She paused to regroup, the rhythmic sound of her breathing filling her ears. In the stillness, the sounds of the jungle became louder: the birds, the screeches, the rustle of branches overhead, which she hoped was monkeys and not a snake, or snakes. She wiped her kerchief across her forehead, glancing at the tree trunks and the thick vegetation. She was still on a path, if the cleared brush and branches were any indication, and a footpath was visible. She was certain there had been no fork in the trail that she might have missed.

At least, she didn't think so.

Had she passed the trail the others had taken, oblivious to her error?

Indecision crept slowly into her chest.

She made a wide scan of her surroundings, intently focusing on every possible side trail. To her dismay, she suddenly saw them everywhere.

Her heart took off at a gallop.

Shit. Shit. Shit.

Was she lost?

This was outrageous. A scan of her watch indicated she had been with the group not forty-five minutes ago. How could she have gotten so far off-course? Why hadn't one of them come back for her?

Calm down, Brynn.

She needed to stay put, because surely they would return when they noticed she wasn't with them. And hadn't Freddie said this was a touristy area? Someone would stumble onto her.

But she could help things along. For ten minutes, she yelled for help, until her hoarse throat and ringing ears forced her to stop. With no response—not even the sound of voices in the distance—her shoulders sagged in defeat.

Locating a log, she brushed off a few ants and sat. She pulled her water bottle from her pack and took a sip, then stopped. She should ration it.

She waited for three hours, filling her thoughts with mundane activities to pass the time and keep her anxiety at bay. Should she spend Thanksgiving with her roommate Audrey in Arizona? Would her parents be going to Hawai'i for Christmas, and should she go as well? Or should she return to Istanbul and continue deciphering cuneiform tablets at the *Arkeoloji Müzeleri?* She loved the cosmopolitan and vivacious city once known as Constantinople, with its historic mosques, mouth-watering food, and one of the oldest covered markets in the world—the Grand Bazaar. The very place that Sefa had taken her to see that fortune telling woman who then encouraged her to buy the hideous ring. She wondered again where the trinket had gone. She should ask her mom when she returned to the States.

Her mind returned to the vast Sumerian collection of tablets at the Archaeological Museum in Turkey, a place that always had been comfortable to her, but since she'd likely spent too much time away from school already, she should probably stick close to home. Still, those tablets were her best bet at finding a topic for her Ph.D. dissertation, especially if this wild goose chase prompted by Irene and Conrad proved unfruitful, and possibly even criminal, in the end.

Worry gnawed at her. Maybe she shouldn't have come. Maybe she was wasting time better spent on her studies. And yet …

She'd met Magee, and through him a spark of her grandfather had come back to her. She imagined that Gramps had been like Tristan when he was younger, although more responsible. But had he really been? Her grandmother had told stories of their travels, even dragging Brynn's mother, Lily, along when she was young. They had made yearly pilgrimages to Italy to see family, and afterward would travel to places like Egypt, China, Mongolia, India, and Nepal.

As the day began to wane and the light became gray, Brynn watched the ants.

They were everywhere. Big ones, small ones, black ones, brown ones. The most fascinating were the leaf-cutters, marching in a straight line, the beginning and ending points known only to them. Each one carried atop its back a portion of a tree leaf that it had chewed away, marching it back to their lair. Did they eat them? Or do something else with their booty?

Such industrious little buggers.

Or were they hurrying before night fell?

With that sobering thought, panic began a new campaign to overwhelm her.

Should she have kept going, just like the ants? Had stopping doomed her somehow?

No. *No.*

She allowed the jitters in her belly one brief dance and then wrestled the ball into a tight knot, where it sat, hard and tense, in her abdomen.

It was better to remain in one place. It would make it easier for her to be found.

Tyler hadn't done that. When he had been lost, he'd started moving almost immediately, and had never stopped.

But he had been six years old. A child, making naïve and ignorant choices. He was damned lucky to have lived.

She was smarter than that.

Dammit, she was trying to justify being smarter than a young boy.

Why hadn't they found her yet?

Doubts swirled in her mind like dust devils. Maybe she was nowhere near where she had lost the group. Maybe those few minutes of rushing to catch up had hopelessly steered her off course.

How appallingly easy it had been to get disoriented.

She inhaled a fortifying breath. It was time to take stock of her supplies.

She opened her pack. She had a hammock and mosquito netting. Magee had insisted she carry her own and now she was grateful for his edict. She had water fortified with electrolytes in her canteen. About ten ounces, she estimated. If she took a sip or two every hour, she should be able to stretch it into tomorrow.

What if no one comes tomorrow?

Ridiculous. Logic told her she couldn't be that lost. No sense grabbing worry too soon.

She had food—a bag of dried fruit and nuts and two granola bars. She wasn't hungry—the stress ball in her gut made sure of that—so she would save eating for later. Her most important chore was getting the hammock secured before nightfall. Even though she had a headlamp, she didn't relish mucking about in the dark, mostly because of the snakes. Whether poisonous or not, she didn't want to accidentally step on one.

She spent several minutes hunting for a space between trees that would accommodate her hammock, all the while keeping a close eye on where she had been sitting all afternoon, not wanting to make her situation worse by straying too far. On a whim, she lifted her machete and made a mark on the tree to the left from where she had been sitting. She would use this to orient herself in the morning, worried that she might awaken and be confused about which way to go. Because if no one came for her, she couldn't remain here indefinitely.

She had a compass, which she could use to return to the village from where they had started. She was certain they had been walking north away from the river. All she had to do was trek in a southerly direction. Buoyed by that thought, she strung her hammock, took care of bathroom duties, and then climbed into her bed, zipping it over her. At least she was protected from the bugs during the night.

For the longest time, she listened to the native sounds, an ancient language that called to something deep in her bones, certain she'd never be able to sleep.

Brynn stepped back, shocked by the crowd of people in the jungle. They were all around her.

What's going on?

She didn't speak aloud, but they must have heard her.

You can see us? *they asked.* Can you help? The door is closed.

She came suddenly awake, unable to shake the sensation that she wasn't alone. Were there others beyond the fringes of her very limited vision? Fear coiled in her limbs and a sense of foreboding nudged her.

How long had it been? Lost in the darkness of the jungle, both time and space stretched into nothingness, but a glance at her watch told her it was only 10 p.m.

She froze. Something was out there.

A puff of air brushed her left ear.

Oh God.

Another puff of air. And then a growl. Her nerves fired from head to toe.

It had to be a jaguar, or a puma, or a panther, or whatever the hell they called them down here. And it was right next to her.

With her muscles locked into a painful inertia from the awkward position of lying in a hammock, she doubted she could move with any swiftness. The jaguar was so perfectly adapted to the jungle, and

Brynn had no illusions about her own abilities—she was a clunky addition to the environment, a weak link this predator would dispatch with little emotion.

As the cat moved past her, mesmerizing emerald eyes framed by rich black fur locked onto Brynn's stunned gaze. The cat lifted its head as if catching a scent, then turned and walked away, the jungle swallowing her up.

Holy shit.

A light bobbed in the distance. For a wild moment, Brynn wondered if it were a fairy, a primeval Tinkerbell.

"Brynn!"

Thank God. It was Magee.

She released a breath she'd been holding. "I'm here," she answered, her voice shaky.

∾

OVER A CAMPFIRE, Dimar brewed a pot of strong coffee to accompany a hastily made dinner of canned tuna and rice. Despite the late hour, Tristan decided Brynn could use the sustenance, and unfortunately they didn't have decaf.

When he'd realized several hours ago that they'd lost her, the worry in his stomach had gone from mild to clenching as the day had worn on. Now that he'd found her, he was filled with equal parts gratitude and anger. He was relieved she wasn't hurt or worse, but at the same time he had to curb the urge to yell at her to be more careful. He didn't need her death on his hands.

But it was obvious she wasn't up to hearing it. For now.

And then there had been the embrace. She had scrambled out of her hammock and without hesitation had hugged him, burying her face in his shoulder and whispering her thanks over and over. Before he'd thought better of it, he'd held her just as close.

He could still feel her in his arms, the fierceness of the contact still burning his skin despite the barrier of clothing.

He was so fucked.

Despite the late hour, Tristan brought a hot cup of caffeine to her, kneeling beside her where she sat in a foldable camp chair. Shadows beneath her eyes and the weary slant of her shoulders spoke of her exhaustion.

"This should help," he said.

"Thank you." Her fingers brushed his as she clasped the cup and took a sip. "The elixir of life," she added, a ghost of a smile on lips that were slowly gaining color, although they still appeared too pale by lamplight.

"What the hell happened, Galloway?" he murmured. "We almost lost you."

"You did lose me." She cradled the cup close. "Somehow I took a wrong turn. When I realized what had happened, I stayed put but it was probably too late by then. How did you find me?"

"We've been backtracking every trail all afternoon. You need to keep up."

"I realize that now. I was going to use my compass in the morning to find my way back to the village where we started."

"If you were lost anywhere else in the world, that might be a sound decision, but compasses don't work in the Amazon. Something in the environment wreaks havoc on magnetics. Don't ever trust one."

She raised an eyebrow. "Now you tell me?"

He was glad to see a spark of the old Galloway slowly returning.

"I guess you passed the initiation."

She grimaced. "Men and their initiations. I had one of those at K2 as well when I fell into a crevasse."

Panic wiggled her ass in Tristan's chest. "Are you trying to die?" he asked, his tone bordering on accusatory. Hell, maybe she was. He didn't like it.

"No." Her face screwed into a defiant expression.

"Then pay more attention."

Her eyes narrowed, her thankful countenance disappearing.

He should clamp down on his irritation, he really should, but he couldn't seem to stop the words from coming out of his mouth. "If you're going to compare disappearing in the jungle to being trapped in an ice cave, then don't. The Amazon is worse."

"You don't say?" Brynn replied, her response pithy and breathless and filled with mockery. "Then I suppose I shouldn't tell you about coming face-to-face with a jaguar."

"You saw one of the cats?" Dimar exclaimed, ceasing his work setting up camp and coming to stand behind Tristan.

"Yes. Big and black and the greenest eyes I've ever seen."

"A cat just walked right up to you?" he demanded, his voice thick with disbelief. "Right here, where we're sitting?"

Brynn lifted her coffee for a sip and said into her cup, "Yes, Dimar." She flicked her gaze between Tristan and the Bolivian. "Or would you both like to call me a liar now too?"

Dimar huffed off.

"I'm not your enemy, Galloway."

"Well you're not exactly my friend right now."

Her statement deflated some of the stiffness in his back and shoulders. "You're right. Sorry." He stood but remained close to her.

"Why is Dimar so upset?" she asked.

Shea grabbed a cloth and lifted the coffeepot off the fire, then poured himself a cup. "He's just jealous. Many locals believe seeing a jaguar is special, almost sacred. You've barely been in the jungle a few days and you've already encountered one. You're upsetting the natural balance, Brynn."

"Why doesn't that surprise me." Tristan crossed his arms and took up a sentinel stance as Brynn's protector.

"How did you fall into a crevasse?" Shea asked, taking a seat on the opposite side of the fire.

"I spent an afternoon ice climbing, and I fell on the way back to camp."

Shea leaned forward, his elbows on his knees and watched her through the flames. "How far?"

"I don't know, maybe twenty feet. I was roped to two other people, which likely saved my life."

Dimar reappeared and asked, "What happened with the cat?"

"She sniffed my left ear."

"She?" the Bolivian demanded. "How do you know?"

Brynn shrugged. "It's a fifty-fifty guess, right?"

The look of envy in Dimar's eyes was a sight to see.

"Face it," Tristan said to the man. "You're not worthy enough to meet one."

Dimar's glare was razor sharp. "Tomorrow, we need to make tracks. Already we are behind schedule. Do you think I want to spend weeks guiding you monkeys?"

Brynn huddled closer to the fire. "That's my line, Dimar."

"Down here, we're all monkeys," Tristan said.

THEY TREKKED for the whole day. Brynn fell into robotic movements, feeling secure about not getting lost again, especially since she was in the center of the line of men. She'd decided not to mention anything about the people she'd seen in her dream, or vision, or whatever it was. Dimar was being a grouch about the jaguar, but she suspected he'd be downright terrified if she told him she had been visited by spirits. Could that have been what they were? Seemed best to keep it to herself.

Dimar, Freddie, Shea, and Tristan each took turns hacking a path with their machetes. By late afternoon, her fatigue grew, but she didn't say anything, knowing that her earlier disappearance had slowed everyone down. She'd spent a childhood traipsing after her two older brothers, and she knew the reputational cost of complaining, so she'd learned a long time ago to stuff it down.

As the light was waning, and Brynn was having trouble keeping her eyes open, they came upon a clearing and the remnants of an abandoned campsite. Everyone spread out to inspect it. Brynn dropped her pack and sat on a log beside the ashy remains of a campfire.

Dimar paced around while Tristan scanned the perimeter.

When Tristan's gaze landed on her, he said, "We'll stay here tonight."

Brynn silently acknowledged him and rose to set up camp.

Magee strung his hammock near hers, saying, "In case any jaguars come by tonight. You seem to be a magnet for animals."

Shea dropped a pile of wood near the fire pit. "I guess that's why she's with you."

Tristan gave a derisive laugh while Brynn hid her sudden embarrassment by concentrating on unpacking the food bag. Was it obvious she liked Magee?

The object of her occasional random steamy thoughts moved closer, brushing against her as he took the bag from her. "You look like death walking, Galloway."

Charming. The voice in her head didn't hold back the sarcasm. Magee's charisma was only matched by his abrasiveness, prompting Brynn's burgeoning good feelings for him to slide away.

It was just as well. Mooning over him was getting distracting. She'd had relationships based on nothing but sex, but she was ready for something more solid, and every feminine instinct she had told her Magee wasn't that man.

"Thanks," she said, not bothering to hide the edge in her voice.

Freddie and Dimar prepared a dinner of rice and beans, and as they were finishing their meal, a rustle in the darkness startled everyone. Brynn shot up from her chair, knocking her mostly empty plate to the ground, while Tristan and Dimar grabbed machetes. A figure emerged—bedraggled, sweaty, and dirty—carrying a pack.

Irene Caridad.

CHAPTER 9

B rynn sat beside Irene while the woman gulped down water and scooped piles of rice and beans in her mouth like a ravenous dog. She looked dazed and exhausted, and after Brynn's experience of being lost, she could appreciate the panic that Irene must be dealing with. Still, Brynn's anger was swiftly rising to a boil.

"Are you all right?" Brynn asked, narrowing her eyes, trying her best to fake a little congeniality. She pushed a breath through her nose so her irritation wouldn't be audible.

Irene wiped the back of her hand across her mouth, taking a break from her food, and tucked her shoulder-length hair behind one ear. The normally straight strands were matted with sweat, the gray streaks against the black standing out more than normal. "Yes. It's fortunate I found you all." She turned to Brynn. "I'm glad you made it."

No thanks to you. Instead, Brynn said, "Is it true?"

"Is what true?" The look in Irene's gaze was so genuine that Brynn felt a twinge of remorse for launching so quickly into accusation-land.

"Did you steal from Magee?"

"Steal what?" Her face pinched into further confusion.

Until now, Tristan had been sitting on the other side of the fire alongside Shea, Freddie, and Dimar with a blank expression reminiscent of a statue, the orange glow of the firelight illuminating the wall of men.

Raising a brow, Tristan's tone was eerily quiet. "Is that how it's gonna go, Irene?"

But Brynn wasn't fooled by his calm façade. Censure emanated from him like a pulse wave. His gaze was dark and unflinching, and it was obvious he was pissed.

Irene set her empty plate on the ground and wiped her hands on her dark pants, then raised her eyes to his. "I'm not sure what you're talking about."

He narrowed his eyes. "The Moon Tablet of Ur."

A flash of recognition crossed her face and then was gone.

"Where is it?" he pressed.

"What makes you think I have it?" Irene countered, but Brynn knew she lied. She had spent enough time with her mentor to know when the woman was rattled, no matter how well she was striving to hide it. "And why on earth are you interrogating me like some criminal?"

"Because you are. The tablet is mine."

"No, it isn't."

"Says who? You?"

Irene sat straighter. "Yes. I bought it from a proper dealer."

"Bullshit. Do you have papers?"

"I don't have to defend myself." She pressed her lips together. "This is ridiculous."

"It is ridiculous," he continued, "because I'm guessing you don't have papers, or the ones you possess are bogus. Because that piece is mine. It was stolen before I could take possession and then, oddly enough, sold to you. I'm really disappointed, Irene, because I thought you vetted your purchases better than that."

Irene went silent, frowning into the fire.

"Dog got your tongue?" Dimar finally said.

Everyone looked at him, but no one bothered to correct his mangled phrase.

Irene took a deep breath. "All right, look. I did buy the Moon

Tablet, but I didn't know it was stolen. *My apologies, Tristan.*" The last part was said with a flourish and a definite hint of sarcasm.

"I don't want your apologies. I just want the damned tablet, so hand it over please."

"That might be a problem. I don't have it anymore."

"What a surprise," Tristan deadpanned.

"What happened?" Shea asked, cutting in.

"When Dimar wasn't available, I booked Pico to guide me."

"You knew I wasn't available," Dimar rebutted. "You refused to wait until I was."

"You were a bit helter skelter with your schedule," Irene said. "I couldn't wait indefinitely."

Dimar rolled his eyes. "You Americans and your rigorous scheduling. And I am no Helen Keller."

Shea added more wood to the fire. "Where is Pico now?"

"He abandoned me."

Tristan scoffed. "Did you manage to piss him off too?"

Irene leaned forward and clasped her hands together, revealing dirt-rimmed short fingernails. "Fine. I'll tell you what I know. Last night we ran into a group of men who I believe might have been poachers or drug runners, or maybe gold-diggers. There was an argument and somehow Pico managed to escape with the pack that had the tablet in it. One of the men must have hit me, because I woke up much later, alone and lying in the dirt." She touched her hairline and winced. "I've got a big welt."

Brynn leaned closer to have a look, wondering if Irene had fabricated the whole incident. But there was indeed a raised bump on the woman's forehead. "It doesn't look bad," Brynn said.

"Oh good." Relief filled Irene's voice. "Thankfully, the men left some of our gear, so I had a bit of water and food. I went in search of Pico, of course, but I must've gotten turned around."

"Please tell me the tablet is protected from the elements," Tristan said.

"It is. It's in a specialized briefcase, cushioned and sealed."

"You're lucky those men didn't kill you," Freddie said, darting his eyes at Dimar beside him. "Milenka's brother said there is a group we need to watch out for."

"What kind of group?" Brynn asked.

"You're such an idiot, Freddie," Dimar exclaimed. "Rigo is *in* the group. He runs with those Russians, the Mamani brothers."

"There's Russians down here?" Brynn was becoming more confused by the minute.

"I think he means ruffians," Magee muttered. "As for Rigo and the like, there're always men out here doing what they shouldn't."

Concerned, Brynn looked from man to man. "Should we call the police or something?"

"Do you see any local police stations around here?" Magee indicated the jungle lying in wait just beyond the firelight. "Don't worry, I can handle it." He looked at Shea. "You packing?"

"Of course."

"Packing?" Brynn echoed. "Meaning you both have guns? Is that necessary?"

"Yes," Magee and Shea answered at the same time.

"I'm afraid they're right," Irene said. "Not only because of criminals, but the animals, and even some of the indigenous people can be dangerous too."

Were they all crazy to be out here? Maybe. Probably.

"Why did you haul the tablet down here?" Shea asked Irene.

A slight pause. "I wanted to show it to Connie."

"Then bring a photo." Tristan's tone was laced with obvious rancor.

Shea resumed his questions. "How'd you get it into Bolivia?"

Irene's face took on an expression of defiance. "You know how I got it in."

"How?" Dimar asked, displaying a wide-eyed and curious demeanor that Brynn couldn't believe was real. She almost laughed aloud. Everyone was behaving as if they were fighting over a stash of diamonds. Good grief. As much as she loved and revered ancient artifacts, in reality it was only a clay tablet.

Shea cast a disparaging look at Dimar and said, "Well, if we're all gonna play stupid, then my money is on a well-placed bribe." He turned back to Irene. "But let's return to why you needed to bring a Sumerian cuneiform tablet into Bolivia."

"I wanted Conrad's help in deciphering it."

"I call bull again," Tristan said. "You were planning to bury it, weren't you?"

"That's a rather bold accusation," she retorted. "The real answer is rather mundane. I haven't been able to reach Conrad for over three weeks now. I could've brought a photo, but I was excited by the piece, and sometimes there are faint markings that can't be seen on photographs. It's always better to view the actual piece."

Tristan tilted his head slightly. "Then wait for him to come home, for God's sake."

"I had to act quickly," she said.

"Why?" Brynn asked.

"I thought the tablet wasn't safe if I left it." She looked at Brynn. "And you still hadn't returned from Pakistan, so I couldn't leave it with you. It seemed best that I bring it with me."

"Were you being threatened by anyone?" Shea asked.

"No," Irene answered, "but the Moon Tablet has been sought for quite some time. Eventually others in the archaeology community would learn I had it." She shifted her gaze to Tristan, silently making her point.

"I knew because you scuttled my deal. And I'd already paid for it."

"Then you should request a refund."

"You're hilarious, Irene. And so much for the tablet being safe, since you've now lost it."

She sighed. "Yes, that's been unfortunate, but I don't think Pico will damage it. He kept asking me about it, and I suppose what little I did tell him made him think it was valuable, so that's why he grabbed it when he ran. My guess is he's going to still take it to Conrad."

"Aren't you concerned that he abandoned you and pretty much left you for dead?" Brynn asked, incredulous. "He doesn't sound like a decent person."

"Hey," Dimar interrupted, clearly affronted. "Don't talk about my cousin that way." He pointed at Irene. "He probably did look for her, but she went wandering off. That's not his fault."

Irene held up a placating hand. "It doesn't matter. It's all water under the bridge now. Let's just move forward."

Remembering what Shea had said in Rurre about Pico being involved with stolen artifacts, Brynn asked, "What if Pico isn't taking the tablet to Conrad? What if he's decided to keep it for himself?"

Irene frowned. "Why would he do that?"

"To sell it," Shea answered.

"But if Tristan is correct," Irene said, "then it's been stolen twice over."

"So you're admitting to your theft," Tristan said.

Irene's face pinched into a scowl. "I truly didn't know about your deal, Magee. But I can't make you believe me." She pushed hair away from her face. "I fear that if you're right and Pico does sell it, he'll probably do so for far less than it's worth."

Shea shook his head. "Even a few hundred dollars would be a goldmine to him."

Dimar crossed his arms, puffing out his stocky chest. "We are not criminals. Not like Dr. Caridad and Dr. Magee."

"I'll not be grouped with the likes of Irene," Tristan retorted.

"So you're saying every deal you've ever made has been on the up and up?" Shea accused.

"Okay, stop," Brynn said. "We're not getting anywhere. How can we find Pico?"

"I still think he'll make his way to Conrad," Irene answered. "Is that where you were headed? To find Connie?" She looked at each man in turn, and finally at Brynn, who nodded. "That's good. Will you take me with you?"

Tristan raised a brow. "Planning to steal more stuff?"

Before the two of them could argue any further, Brynn asked, "Irene, have you translated the tablet? What does it say?"

Irene's gaze reflected the firelight. "I tried a quick pass, but I quickly hit a dead end. It's not standard cuneiform. We might need to cross-reference with Akkadian, but I'm not even sure that's the answer. It's odd really, unlike anything I've seen before. It's almost like a cuneiform shorthand."

THE SHADOWS EBBED and flowed with the quiver of each crackling flame as Tristan watched Irene and Brynn chat about his tablet. He was finding it hard to believe that Irene had no idea that she had purchased a hot artifact. And what about Brynn? Was she really on his side or just pretending to be?

While Brynn initially had displayed an edge of anger toward her mentor, now they were like a couple of teenagers discussing boys on a Friday night. He had become accustomed to his distrust of Irene, but it was now clear he hadn't believed that Galloway would truly work against him.

And why? Because he wanted her.

Lust had a knack for sucking intelligence right out of his brain.

But there was something else far more insidious than a carnal craving for the woman sitting opposite him. In short, he *liked* her, far more than a steamy jungle rendezvous warranted. He admired the agility of her mind almost as much as the curve of her hips. Hell, maybe more. He couldn't recall the last time that had happened. And it had him stupefied.

Shit.

He was in it up to his knees.

"Have you heard of Harold Gatty?" Irene asked Brynn.

Brynn flashed a glance at Tristan before answering. "Yes, I know of Magee's father. Please don't tell me that you also believe that space aliens came to Earth and wrote all about it in the Sumerian tablets?"

"Not all tablets, but yes, we do believe there are clues in some of them."

Brynn's dark brows crashed toward each other. "Just how long have you and Conrad been looking for proof of alien technology?"

"I think our interest went back to college when we began dating. We heard Carl Sagan lecture about life beyond the stars, and we were hooked by the idea. Conrad initially studied pre-Columbian artifacts but later he came over to my discipline when the Sumerian culture started revealing some interesting things. We've always kept this part of our research separate from our teaching duties, however."

Skepticism crossed Brynn's face. "Worried about the fallout?"

Tristan suppressed a smile. Irene and Brynn might have a secret something between them that would undoubtedly bite him in the ass later, but it was also clear that Brynn was bothered by Irene's apparent interest in life beyond the stars. Had they never discussed this before?

"Well, yes," Irene said. "We did need to keep our jobs, so we took great care. We have bills to pay like everyone else. But we indulged our interest whenever we could, traveling and studying and seeking out artifacts that might shed light on it. If we could have a break-through—a real one—then we'd throw all our work behind it and share it with the world."

"Just because people believe that evidence points toward other-worldly interventions doesn't make any of it true."

Galloway's words buzzed in Tristan's ear. His father had sought validation, hadn't he? And now Tristan wanted to give it to him, no matter how ludicrous the old man's theories might have been.

Irene took a deep breath. "All I can say, Brynn, is there's so much on this planet that we don't understand, so why can't that expand to the heavens? Surely you've heard of the panspermia theory."

Brynn nodded with resignation, like a mother humoring her child's outrageous proclamations. "Humans were seeded from outer space."

"The simplest version is there was life on Mars at one point, and then that life was transported via space rocks to here."

"Fire and brimstone on early Earth." Brynn maintained a poker face. "That's a pretty standard theory."

"Or another is that the asteroid belt was actually a planet that destructed in some way, and before it did the inhabitants made their way to Earth."

"And the Sumerians may have documented this?" Brynn asked.

"Possibly." Irene turned to Tristan. "But Gatty had more … interesting ideas, didn't he? There's a story that he met with a high-level agent with the U.S. Defense Intelligence Agency who supposedly told him that his job was to monitor three different extraterrestrial groups that are *still living on Earth*. The technology we seek could be right under our noses."

Brynn's eyes widened ever so slightly. "And where are these aliens supposed to be living?"

"Inside mountains and caves and in the deep ocean."

Shea shook his head and chuckled, his disbelief obvious. "How convenient." He turned to Tristan. "Did you ever hear about this meeting?"

Actually, yes. The idea of it had given Tristan nightmares as a child. But he shrugged in response, not really wanting to delve into a topic that was as heated as religion or politics.

Irene continued, "The man told Gatty that the aliens sometimes took DNA, sperm, and other bodily samples from humans, and that the aliens themselves resembled humans. Is it so hard to believe that otherworldly beings might have created us, or mutated a version of early man to make us into what we are today?"

"No, it's not that hard," Shea admitted. "But most people believe that God created us."

Irene lifted her chin, reminding Tristan that she possessed a keen intellect. She had to be in her sixties, but she had aged remarkably well, the fine skin around her eyes wrinkle-free. "What if they're one and the same," she said. "And God so loved man that he created man in the image of himself."

"Or we created God to be the image of *ourselves*." Shea loved a good philosophical debate. It was intensely annoying at times. "Just as we've imagined aliens to resemble us. It's human nature. Like attracts like. We need to understand the unknowable by putting a familiarity to it. It helps humanity stay sane."

"You're related to Gatty, right?"

While Shea had been with Conrad two years ago during the South American expedition, he'd never before met Irene.

"He was my uncle."

Paddy, Shea's father, had worried that maybe his brother, Charlie, or Harold Gatty, had been afflicted with an undiagnosed mental condition. Tristan wondered if Shea hadn't believed that as well. He could ask, but truthfully, he really didn't want to know.

"You're rather cynical in both directions," Irene said, her gaze assessing. "The Magees were a devout Irish Catholic family. Despite that, Tristan believes."

But that wasn't entirely true. "Not quite," Tristan said.

"Oh? But you hunt these relics down with more tenacity than even Conrad."

Galloway watched him, her stoic demeanor faltering a bit, and for a moment he caught a glimpse of … curiosity. Perhaps a flash of hunger. Or maybe that was his own wishful thinking.

The light of the campfire revealed the soft contours of her cheeks and lips. An impulse burned in him to drag her back to Rurre, hole up in a motel room, and let his only care in the world be the peaks and valleys of her body.

The scenario was immensely appealing.

The problem, of course, was Galloway's likewise keen intellect. He shouldn't be surprised that Irene had recruited her, however unknowingly. Or maybe it wasn't unknowingly. And that was the second problem.

He'd come too far to let everything he was working toward be shot to hell because he had a hard-on for the wrong woman.

"I'm more interested in the science," he said. "I think there may be more practical answers to the questions you're asking, Irene."

"Okay. Then why can't we both be right?"

"What science are you talking about?" Brynn asked.

"Acoustics," he said. "Sound. Much of the extraterrestrial theories hinge on the idea that many of the ancient structures we've found around the world could never have been built through simple human ingenuity. So naturally, there must have been help, that the gods of Sumeria, and later of Egypt must have been aliens. And other cultures have similar historical references, but I've always thought there were more plausible explanations."

"Scientific ones."

"Yes," Tristan answered.

"Then why are you so interested in the tablet that Irene took?" Brynn's voice was quiet but her intense gaze all but scalded him.

"Because he's trying to straddle both worlds," Shea said, "while he looks down his nose at everything. You thought your old man was full of shit. And he probably was, so you take the high road of a physicist that everything can be explained. But you also want proof, if it's out there, that Uncle Charlie had been right all along."

"Thanks for that insight into my psyche. Should I believe that people such as the esteemed Dr. Irene Caridad and her equally learned husband, Dr. Conrad Fontana, are deluded as well?" While the statement wasn't entirely untrue, he still let sarcasm coat his words. "There are thousands of people, if not more, who buy into this stuff. People who came to my dad with stories and proof—or what they believed to be proof—validating theories he ascribed to. Everything from aliens having been here for eons to the idea that every technological advancement we've had has been reverse-engineered from recovered crashed spaceships. Lasers, microchips, fiber optics. Even Kevlar. It all came from the little green men. I think I'm the perfect person to pursue this. I'm not a fanatic believer, and I'm not a disbeliever either."

Shea snorted. "The entire movement is propelled by *argumentum ad ignorantiam*."

Tristan knew where his cousin was going with this; they'd had this discussion many times.

With a look of consternation, Brynn said, "I'm afraid my Latin is a little rusty."

"Argument from ignorance," Irene translated.

Shea continued, "It's the idea that if there is no logical terrestrial explanation for how the pyramids in Egypt came to be, or the Nazca lines in Peru, or the giant statues on Easter Island, then the theory that they must've been built by big-headed bug men has to be true."

"We're not all mindless idiots," Tristan said.

"No, we're not," Dimar chimed in, puffing out his chest. He leaned close to Tristan and asked in a low voice, "How *were* those things built?"

Tristan ignored him.

"What about that Russian woman," Shea continued, "whose name I can't remember, who had been a pilot and had been married to a cosmonaut? She wasn't an idiot, but later she claimed that Leonardo da Vinci, Jules Verne, and Ray Bradbury were alien mediums, although I'm guessing she never met any of them in person." His voice rang with skepticism. "It's not a matter of intelligence, really. Maybe more wishful thinking gone rampant. She claimed to have seen Bigfoot as well."

"I believe in Bigfoot," Dimar said. Freddy nodded in agreement. "There are monsters in the jungle too. I never thought there might be outer space bugs, but you have never seen some of the beasts around here. It would curl your tongue."

"I think you mean curl your toes," Brynn said, then her expression softened, and she looked at Tristan. "It's okay to want to do right by your father."

Her sudden compassion had him wishing his father still lived so he could introduce the two of them. Over the years, he had brought few girls home to meet the old man since Harold Gatty's inability to tone down his outrageous assumptions about UFO's and government conspiracies naturally had made him a potent social repellent. Tristan had had no desire to have it rub off on him. But for some odd reason, he was certain Brynn could have handled his dad.

"Have you ever heard of hyperdiffusionism?" Brynn asked him.

"No, Shea never bounced that one off me."

"I had to pick my battles," his cousin replied.

"It's the hypothesis that certain historical technologies or ideas originated with a single people or civilization before their adoption by other cultures," she said.

"And it's a sound one," Irene said flatly.

Brynn stared at Irene, and even in profile Tristan could tell that Galloway was momentarily stunned.

"No, it's not," Shea argued. "It minimizes the contributions of great civilizations such as the Celts and the Maya and the Romans. It implies they were given their culture by someone else."

"Why is that so difficult to believe?" Irene asked. "Every advancement has learned from the one before it."

"I'm confused," Brynn said. "I took your class in Forbidden Archaeology. You made us trace the idea of a 'mother culture' back to Plato's Atlantis. You made us read that outrageous book *Species with Amnesia*. You gave every indication that this train of thought was dangerous. And wrong. Are you saying you lied?"

"Brynn, I don't have to believe something to teach it." Irene's voice held equal tones sternness and exasperation. "The course was a requirement. And if you recall, we proved that there was transoceanic pre-Columbian contact between the Vikings and the Americas."

Dimar smiled and nodded. "Like Thor. I saw that movie."

Shock plastered Brynn's face. Tristan felt for her. It was terrible to be disappointed by one's elders. It had happened so many times with his dad that he'd lost count. But while each incident had lessened in disappointment over time, they still managed to carry the sharp pinch of an unwanted bee sting.

"The root of hyperdiffusionism claims that the earth was home to a single advanced civilization," Shea said. "Through its destruction, it gave rise to all the recognized early cultures—the Sumerians, the Egyptians, the Olmec. But there's no way around the idea that diffusionism is a highly racist ideology."

"Is that what you're accusing my dad of?" Tristan shot back.

"No. Uncle Charlie was many things but not that. It just helps to understand where this idea of aliens seeding the earth *really began.*"

"Maybe we can all agree to disagree," Irene said.

"What about your lecture on mummification?" Brynn said. "You yourself said it was a slippery slope to presume that the Egyptians must have traveled to the Americas since people here, as well as many other locations around the world, also practiced the ritual."

"But we don't know that," Irene said. "Maybe the Egyptians *did* travel. Or since they were tied to Mesopotamia and the Sumerians, maybe it was those civilizations that traveled. That's why Conrad and I are here. To search for that proof."

Brynn's face took on a shade of disgust as she said, "And by default the fact that the Sumerians were linked to the Anunnaki obviously confirms alien contact. That's bullshit and careless science. Culture isn't contagious. You taught me that."

"Brynn's right," Shea said. "Similarities arise because the same adaptive traits across civilizations are needed to survive." He prodded the fire again with a stick, sending orange-firefly sparks into the air. "'Extraordinary claims require extraordinary evidence.' Carl Sagan said that."

"And that's what we're all searching for," Irene said. "We don't need to argue. We're all on the same page."

"I suppose you agree with the flat-earthers too," Brynn said, her voice hollow.

"What is that?" Freddie asked.

"Exactly what it sounds like," she said. "There's a movement going on that we've been lied to about the roundness of our planet and that it's actually flat. They base it on such things as the Chicago skyline is visible from Michigan on a clear day. If the earth were curved, that wouldn't be possible."

Surprise overtook Dimar's face, and in an angsty tone he asked, "Is this true?"

"No," Tristan, Shea, and Brynn answered all at once.

Shea added, "They believe it all—that the moon-landing was a hoax, the space station is a hoax, satellites that connect our phones and our nightly entertainment are hoaxes. It gets ridiculous after a while."

Brynn stared into the fire. "It's proof that our ability to be connected the wide world over can be used against us. Anyone can say anything and post it online. If they're persuasive enough, people will start to believe it."

Tristan bristled. "Again, I must reiterate that I'm not an idiot. Isn't it better to have someone with a scientific background exploring these ideas? Leave emotion out and just stick to the facts."

Shea raised an eyebrow. "Can you do that?"

"Of course I can." But inwardly Tristan wasn't completely certain. Still, he'd never cop to it.

Shea smirked. "It's not a lie if you believe it."

"How profound," Tristan said, not bothering to hide his derision.

"It's not profound," Brynn said. "It's a quote from George Costanza on *Seinfeld*."

"Good catch," Shea said with a smile.

Dimar released a bark of laughter. "Ahh. Art Vandeley. Good show."

"Naturally, you would relate to that character." Tristan shook his head. "Since he was a lazy opportunist."

Dimar's face hardened. "I'm not lazy."

Freddie rolled his eyes. "Well ..."

"I read a few of your papers about acoustic levitation," Brynn said to Tristan, thankfully changing the subject.

"I'm honored."

"I thought it was the least I could do since you support my academic work so enthusiastically."

"And your thoughts?" he asked, genuinely curious.

"It's obviously important work, especially in atmospheric chemistry, but it can hardly be extrapolated to the pyramids."

He watched her intently and waited. "And?"

Shea interrupted. "And she wants to know if you proved that the pyramids were built by moving the large stones with sound levitation."

Tristan shrugged. "It's certainly a possibility, but I think it more likely a lot of men worked really hard. I also think the architects had a basic understanding of math. Building ramps to move the blocks is basic trig, as Brynn previously mentioned. The same is true at places like Macchu Picchu and Tiwanaku here in Bolivia. They simply had very skilled craftsmen, not supernatural help."

"But what prompted them to build such places in the first place?" Dimar asked, rejoining the conversation after his brief pout. "Something from above must have told them."

"Perhaps," Tristan said. "Or maybe they like nice things."

"Well, I think it's exciting," Irene said, beaming. "We could be on the cusp of discovering something fantastic."

"Is that why Conrad is in the jungle?" Brynn asked. "Do you think there's something fantastic to be found down here?"

"Connie was here two years ago, and ever since he's wanted to continue looking for the secrets the jungle surely holds. You know what I'm talking about, Tristan. You've been here with your father a few times in the past, haven't you?"

He nodded. That summer so long ago, he'd slogged his way through thick growth and scary terrain in search of … that elusive something his dad was determined to find.

"Tristan and I were sixteen years old the first time," Shea said. "I think Uncle Charlie brought us along more as slaves to haul his gear, but it did make me want to be an archaeologist."

"I thought it was because you were obsessed with the movie *Jurassic Park*," Tristan said.

"Definitely a favorite, and I did toy with the idea of paleontology, but in the end, I was more interested in ancient peoples."

"Officially you never found anything," Irene said. "But what about unofficially?" Her gaze flicked between the two of them, a speculative gleam in her eye.

"We did come across a few things," Tristan conceded, then sighed. "But honestly, it was probably pre-Columbian. Right, Shea?"

"Thinking back on it now? Yeah."

"The thing about my dad is that for all his crazy ideas, for all his passionate fervor for the existence of something beyond Earth, he was innately curious."

"About what?" Brynn asked.

"Where do we come from? Why are we here? What's our purpose?" Grief nudged him. Despite everything, he still missed his old man sometimes. "Harold Gatty made people think. He gave them a sense of wonder and hope for what might be out there. And there's nothing wrong with that in my book."

CHAPTER 10

The next day they followed Irene into the jungle. She claimed she could lead them back to the site of her and Pico's encampment, so they could investigate for any clues about where Pico might have gone. Dimar had argued that they should avoid the spot, but Tristan doubted the perpetrators had stayed put. Still, he kept his gun in his waistband for easy access just in case. Shea did the same.

He trailed Irene, Galloway behind him. He hadn't had a chance to speak with Brynn yet regarding the state of her allegiance, but the conversation he'd overheard last night between the two women after everyone had gone to bed had given him a sliver of hope.

"Tell me more about the tablet," Brynn had said.

"It was just as I said," Irene replied. "I couldn't decipher it, although I didn't really put forth much effort before coming down here."

"Do you have a photo?"

"No."

"Why not?"

"In the rush to get down here I forgot. I thought I had time, but don't worry. Pico will get it to us, and then you can look at it."

"You don't have any proof of the tablet at all?" The disbelief in Galloway's voice had been crystal clear.

He'd lost the thread after that when the women's voices had descended to inaudible whispers.

Thankfully, Irene still had her own hammock in her gear since they didn't have an extra. If anyone would have been forced to relinquish their sleeping quarters, Tristan had been prepared to upvote Dimar, but the truth was Tristan would've volunteered himself. He wasn't about to be labeled a selfish ass in front of Galloway, her loyalties notwithstanding.

It was just as well he was positioned between the two women as they moved along a somewhat cleared jungle pathway, giving him the best way to keep an eye on both. He didn't need them getting lost. Or dashing off for a secret powwow.

By late afternoon, they came to a small clearing with debris and food cans strewn about.

Shea slid his pack from his shoulders and set it on the ground. "At least they're environmentalists."

"Was this your campsite?" Tristan asked Irene as he shucked his gear and unsheathed his machete. She nodded. He made a sweep of the area, Shea also doing the same.

Tristan frowned when he spied Dimar and Freddie standing frozen along the perimeter. "What the hell is wrong with you two?"

"I don't like this place," Dimar said.

"Why?" Shea asked.

"Dead snake." He pointed to an area covered with dense foliage. "Anaconda."

Shea grimaced and walked away.

"It's getting dark, and trekking at night is dangerous," Tristan said. "This is as good a place as any to set up camp."

Dimar shook his head in obvious disagreement, as Brynn and Irene took a peek at the remains of the snake; from what Tristan could see, it was nothing more than a decaying carcass of what looked like a large reptile. But the size of it …. Tristan couldn't help but be impressed.

They set up camp, with Dimar oscillating between angry glances directed at Tristan and nervously scanning the surrounding jungle. Late-day sunlight slanted through the colander-like canopy.

Dimar retrieved a pouch from his pack and began sprinkling a powder along the edges of camp.

"What are you doing?" Tristan asked.

"Protection."

"From what? Anacondas, or maybe aliens?"

"Everything."

BRYNN WAS RELIEVED to learn that a small creek was nearby. While Shea unpacked gear, and Dimar and Freddie glanced around nervously, Tristan offered to accompany Brynn and Irene. With his gun in his waistband and a machete in hand, she was happy to have him along. While she looked forward to washing off the layer of crusted sweat that had taken residence on every part of her body, Dimar's response to their choice of habitation for the evening wasn't making her feel any better.

Aware that nightfall was imminent, Brynn hurried along the path behind Irene, wishing to be back at the campfire when true darkness fell, and the creatures of the night could see them far better than they could them.

Screeching from the canopy startled Brynn. "What is that?" she asked, exasperated.

"Monkeys." Tristan kept stride beside her. "Howler probably."

"Are they aggressive?"

"They can be. They're very territorial, but if you stay clear you'll be fine. They won't hunt you down." He threw her a wicked grin. "Well, mostly."

"You're no help," she grumbled, stumbling against him. He didn't push her away and she struggled to get back on the path without pawing him too much. Had she turned into a territorial monkey, letting the world know she had her sights on Magee?

Ridiculous.

As soon as they came to the water's edge, Irene knelt and began her ministrations, but Brynn came to an abrupt halt, staring at the scene before her.

A late afternoon haze illuminated the trees, and vines draped the landscape like flowing silk. Birdsong filled the air, and blue butterflies danced along the unseen air currents. The scene was right out of a prehistoric movie, and the cinematographer had surely earned every penny of his salary.

In this surreal environment, the abundance of life bordered on miraculous, making Brynn feel small and yet honored to bear witness to such richness. She inhaled the heady aroma of composting earth and wondered if she had finally stumbled across paradise.

In barely louder than a whisper she said, "Just when you decide it's hell trekking through the jungle ...."

"The elixir of life." Tristan's deep voice rumbled through her, causing her to shiver a bit. So odd, considering the thick muggy air and the never-ending sheen of sweat that covered her skin.

Reluctantly she broke the spell, and seeking space, she moved about ten feet away. She needed a break from the constant companionship of the group. Of *him*.

The exhaustion she had been holding at bay flooded her limbs, and she began to think about curling up in her hammock and going to sleep. The jungle was a relentless companion, offering intense, exquisite communion at the price of reaching one's personal and psychological wall every damned day.

Brynn wasn't out of shape, with either her stamina or her emotional muscles, but Amazonia was pretty much kicking her butt.

Magee disappeared from her peripheral vision, so she quickly unbuttoned the placket on her camp shirt, peeled the fabric from her arms, and set it on the ground. She would keep her black sports bra on, so no chance of Magee catching a looksee.

She went down to her knees and scooped water into one hand, rinsing her arms and neck, and then her face, and ending with an underarm splash. She debated applying deodorant, but considering the buzzing mosquitos she instead dug the bug spray out of her bag, spritzing a bit here, there, and everywhere.

She sighed and sat back on her rump, taking a moment to relax, listening to the soundtrack of the wilderness filled with chirps, whistles, buzzes, and screeches. She barely registered the soft, subtle sliding sound behind her until a sense of danger tickled the nerve endings along her spine.

She glanced over her shoulder.

Holy shit!

There was a giant snake piled right behind her.

She gulped down a breath, smothering the scream clawing to get out.

With eyes wide, she stared at the beast, every muscle in her body taut and itching to run. Desperately she held that impulse in check, since reacting like a lunatic might make things worse.

The monstrous thing was coiled on itself—its dark green skin dotted with yellow triangles. Its head rested in the middle and there was no doubt it was watching her.

Her heart sledgehammered painfully in her chest.

God. Oh God. Is it an anaconda? Of course it is, you idiot!

Calm down. Deep breaths.

I can do this. Irene and Magee are just over there. They'll come to help.

Years ago, she had visited a facility that kept nearly every snake in the world, including pythons, rattlesnakes, pit vipers, cobras, and the most venomous snake in the world, the inland taipan of Australia. They had also had an anaconda—a ten-footer, small compared to the one she currently faced, but still impressive. The staff had let the reptile out to visit with the public, allowing the snake to sprawl her massive body across the linoleum tile. Brynn had been fascinated by the creature's docility and inherent shyness.

The snake had been trying to escape to a corner to hide, a natural inclination when confronted with too much stimulus or too much danger. Brynn had reached out and touched the cool, rubbery texture of her skin.

But did this wild creature before her feel relaxed or threatened? Perhaps it possessed a different kind of confidence than a captive snake would, a trait shaped by the fact that it was at the top of the food chain and probably knew it.

Its black, beady eyes watched her, and its tongue flicked in and out.

Had this magnificent and terrifying creature ever interacted with humans? Did it consider Brynn a threat? Or couldn't it care less about her?

Brynn's eyelids fluttered as a bead of sweat slipped from her forehead into her right eye, causing it to sting. She swallowed hard, certain the snake could hear it. *Please don't be annoyed.*

"Are you done?" Tristan asked from a distance.

The green reptile immediately swung its head to the side and began to uncoil, moving to the left.

The same direction as Brynn's escape route.

Shit. Shit. Shit.

Brynn sat perfectly still, her back straight, her legs crossed, and her head turned at a crick-inducing angle. She watched with dread as the snake's head moved out of her line of sight, which had been on the edge of her vision to begin with. Panic squeezed her chest.

Move. She needed to move. Why was it so damned hard?

With another impossibly loud and painful swallow—her neck muscles were so tense that her throat had all but closed up—she slowly swiveled her head to the left to see where the snake was going.

She squeaked out a gasp as the snake's head moved beside her left leg. The movement behind her could only mean it was uncoiling, possibly trapping her. Her only means of escape was forward, directly into the creek. But water was their domain. She'd be jumping right into the beast's lair.

A clump of hair that had escaped her ponytail partially blocked Brynn's view, vibrating with the trembling of her body. She wanted to call out to Tristan or Irene for help, but she feared any noise would startle the snake to move faster. For now, its body inched along, slow and steady.

Did it intend to slither right on by? Or would it trap her in a life-squeezing coil? Even if Tristan came, would he be able to help, or would it be too late?

She was about to spring into action when Tristan's quiet voice said, "Don't move."

Then, to her horror, he dropped to the ground and grabbed the snake's head. The creature responded immediately, shooting straight for the water, knocking Tristan's hands from it. As he tried to wrap his arms around the snake's body and hold it back, Brynn was flung face first into the pond by the backend of the now-flailing body that was all hard muscle. She threw her arms out to break her fall, screaming until her face hit the water, which filled her mouth and nose, choking her. She fought like a mad woman to stand, but the entire weight of the snake's body had her pinned. The fight to survive gripped her with a frenzy.

Suddenly, the weight was gone, and Tristan hauled her upright. Coughing and wheezing, she pushed wet hair from her face, but her fingers dripped with something slimy. And it had a God-awful odor.

Tristan stared at her, his mouth ajar.

"What is it?" Her hands froze. Had the snake somehow bitten her? Was she missing a chin or maybe an ear?

And then Tristan burst out laughing.

What the hell?

"Mind telling me what's so freaking funny?" she demanded, her voice quivering, trying not to gag over the smell.

He confirmed what she was beginning to suspect. "You're covered in snake shit."

"Are you kidding me?" Galloways didn't indulge in self-pity, but at the moment Brynn didn't care as her gag reflex made another pass.

Tristan stepped forward. "I'd suggest closing your mouth. It's a lot gooier than normal."

"And what exactly is *normal*?" she asked from the corner of her lips, speaking as if she were a ventriloquist. Her voice had jumped to an annoyingly higher octave.

He nudged her to turn and face the water again. "Well, most snakes poop like you and me, hard and in chunks."

"God, you're gross."

He placed a hand on her shoulder, but she resisted when he tried to push her down.

"Says the woman covered in feces. C'mon, it's all right. Kneel down. We need to get this off you, because right now you've got me beat in the gross department." He coughed, clearly struggling with the putrid aroma himself.

"What if it comes back?" But she went to her knees anyway.

"It won't."

She leaned forward and tucked her head as he started sluicing water into her hair, slowly ridding her of the disgusting goop.

"It's all your fault for jumping on the damned thing," Brynn yelled up at him, trying to keep streams of water from going into her nose.

"I'm sorry. I really thought I could catch it."

"Catch it?" She closed her eyes as water and God-knew-what-else ran in rivulets down her face and into her ears. She spit before speaking again. "Why in the world would you want to do that?"

His ministrations got a little rough and she had to steel herself from getting pushed back into the water.

"To measure it, of course."

"Well, of course."

Irene's voice came from the left. "What happened? Is Brynn all right?"

"She's fine. But we need some soap to cut through this. And she's gonna need a change of clothes."

"Brynn, is your stuff back at camp?" Irene asked.

"Yes." She had brought only a small bag filled with the barest of toiletries to the creek.

"I'll go grab something. Be right back."

Still unable to sit up, Brynn waved a hand behind her. "My shirt is over there."

"Umm, no. It's in the drink. The snake must've dragged it in."

She heard a plop on the ground. He must have pulled it out of the water.

"Anacondas are beautiful animals," Tristan said. "How did you manage to sit right next to it and not see it?"

"I have no idea," she moaned, as Tristan's big hands spun her around so he could splash water on her rear end, repeatedly patting her buttocks.

"Are you spanking me?"

"Would you like me to?"

"You're impossible." She sat back, combing fingers through her wet hair to push it away from her face since her ponytail holder had disappeared. "I think I can do the rest myself." She wanted to remove her bra and rinse it out, but she wasn't in the mood to give Magee a free show.

He didn't move. "Do you believe Irene's story?" he asked.

She was taken aback by the sudden change in subject and the laser focus of his gaze.

"I'm not sure. There's a lot I don't seem to know about Irene and Conrad. I'm a little shook, to be honest. I thought she had integrity." She wiped water from her nose again. "Can I believe your story?"

"I'm a bastion of integrity."

"Yeah. I forgot." She heard Irene approaching. "Can we talk about this later? In private?"

A ghost of a smile tugged at his mouth, crinkling the edges of his eyes. "This is as private as we're likely to get for a while."

She couldn't be sure, but she thought she heard more than regret about not being able to converse discreetly. The speculative look in his eyes made her think of a bare-chested Magee, roving hands, and hunger that had nothing to do with food.

He stood.

Glancing around, she asked, "Are you sure the snake won't come back?"

"Despite their fearsome reputation, they're fairly shy creatures. He or she is long gone."

Magee walked away as Irene appeared with clothing and a bottle of biodegradable soap. Brynn took the items then turned away and removed the rest of her clothing. She scrubbed herself down with the soap along with washing her hair twice. Irene made herself useful by lathering and scrubbing Brynn's soiled clothes.

Brynn dried herself with a small towel, and then changed into the clothes that Irene had brought.

"Was it a giant anaconda?" Irene asked.

"I don't know. I suppose it was about twelve feet long. How big can they get?"

"I've heard there are some that can be over twenty-five feet long."

"Sweet mother." Brynn swayed for a moment, feeling a little queasy. "I guess I'm lucky then."

At Irene's questioning look, Brynn added, "There would've been a lot more shit from a bigger snake."

CHAPTER 11

After Brynn and Irene returned to camp, Tristan went back to scout the area where Brynn had encountered the snake. Shea joined him.

"I'm beginning to think Brynn is some kind of Amazon whisperer," Shea said. "A jaguar and now an anaconda."

"Don't forget the anteater." Tristan stopped at the creek's edge and rested his hands on his hips. "That's the only one I thought might actually hurt her."

"Dimar's gonna shit himself over this."

"Well, the snake certainly did," Tristan said, scanning the water and mangroves for any movement. The visibility was terrible as night descended, high-pitched howls and shrieks filling the air as the jungle animals prepared for a night of hunting.

Shea laughed. "Brynn's taking it well. Especially since you never told her about your propensity for snake wrangling."

"She's a tough girl." That fact made Tristan inordinately proud. "And as for the anacondas, it's like a first love. You never quite get over it."

"I've never known you to pine for a woman."

"I don't." Unbidden the thought filled his head: *Except maybe Galloway.* "But all bets are off when it comes to those snakes."

"You're a strange one, Magee. If we weren't related, I doubt we'd be friends."

"We're friends?"

Shea shook his head in mock disgust. Tristan was glad for the near darkness so that his cousin couldn't see the grateful smile that had crept onto his face. Their estrangement the past two years had weighed on him.

The adrenaline from earlier had finally dissipated and he was beginning to feel a little spent. He'd been shocked to find Galloway sitting less than five feet from a good-sized anaconda, but her composure throughout the ordeal had been impressive. It was why he'd thought he might have a chance of detaining the snake. His friend, Jack, would have appreciated any measurements and markings.

"You think we'll see Jack tomorrow?" Tristan asked.

"Maybe. I haven't been able to contact him, but that's not too out of the ordinary considering his outpost is deep in the Bolivian jungle. I think he moved here just to avoid phone calls."

Jack Montgomery was a biologist who spent much of the year at a research facility he had helped build. He hustled for funding, brought in other scientists, grad students, and the occasional paying tourist, and conducted research of the animals and ecosystems that existed in the Amazon. Tristan and Shea had met him two years ago, not long before their relationship had gone to shit.

"We should at least try to check in with him. He may have useful intel."

"We're not spies, Tristan."

"No? We chase thieves. We try to recover stolen artifacts. Sometimes we're spies."

"Well, I prefer consultant. And I'm not of a mind to risk my life for a trinket or two."

"Why are you really here, Shea?"

Shea paused, night fully closing in on them. "More mummies are leaving the country."

"It's not me," Tristan shot back.

"I didn't say it was. But Fontana's been in the country all summer."

"You think it's him?"

"Maybe."

"Who hired you?" Tristan asked.

"The Bolivian government. So there won't be any backroom deals this time if you get into trouble."

Tristan snorted. "Of course not, oh right and honorable Sir Shea. Someday you'll be backed into a corner and your scruples won't be able to save you."

"Life doesn't always have to be lived with a *screw you* attitude."

"You weren't Harold Gatty's son." The words caught air before Tristan could stop them. A heaviness settled that had nothing to do with the humidity.

"No, I wasn't." Shea's voice was quiet and filled with something akin to compassion.

But Tristan wasn't looking for pity. Changing the subject, he asked, "Why would Conrad be sneaking mummies across the border?"

"I don't know. Is he looking to continue Gatty's work?"

"I didn't think Conrad was an alien theorist disciple, but I'm not so sure after talking to Irene. She's as bad as my dad was, so maybe Connie is too."

"People do weird stuff for weird reasons. And what about Brynn?"

Tristan frowned. "What about her?"

"Irene invited her down. Is she really an innocent bystander?" Shea said aloud what Tristan had been mulling over these past days since meeting her.

"You know as much as I do about her," he replied. "But for what it's worth, I don't think she's involved in anything illegal. She's got a conscience that would rival yours."

Shea smiled. "I'll take that as a compliment. But you're still an ass."

"Stop with the praise. It's gonna go to my head. How're Sara, Rose, and Ben?" Tristan asked, referring to Shea's siblings and Tristan's remaining cousins.

"They're well. Rose is pissed that you never come around to dinner with the parents anymore. She thinks you're an ass too."

"All right, I think we've established that."

"Mom and Dad would love to see you."

It had been two years since he'd seen Uncle Paddy and Aunt Anna, and he'd be lying if he said he hadn't missed them.

"Maybe I'll come for Thanksgiving," he conceded.

"That would be great, but I won't say anything to Mom just yet, in case you flake out. She'd be thrilled and would start planning all your favorite dishes."

Shea's mother, Anna Mancini Hartigan, was Italian and a damned fine cook. Just thinking about her homemade gnocchi or creamy Panna cotta dessert was enough to make Tristan's mouth water. "I'll come," he said, and silently promised that he wouldn't let them down.

As they walked back to the clearing where they had set up camp, Shea said, "So if Galloway isn't part of the Irene and Conrad scheme, would she be fair game? That is if she doesn't have a boyfriend."

Tristan's moment of bliss split apart like broken glass. "You want to ask her on a date?"

"Why not? She and I seem to have a lot in common."

The newly-sprouted warm and fuzzy feelings for his cousin fled in an instant, and his jaw ached as he clamped down on his knee-jerk response, which was basically—*she's off limits*.

Shea chuckled. "Calm down, Romeo. I'm just kidding. Man, you should see your face. You look about ready to kill me."

Tristan glared at him. "Not funny."

"Hell yeah it is. I think you've finally met your match. Get ready to start pining."

BRYNN SAT HUDDLED near the campfire. Night had fallen and with it came the snapping of twigs, the rustling of bushes, and the sounds of scurrying, a melee of ingredients to set her nerves on edge. She braced herself against the trembling of her body, which had slowly overcome her in the last hour.

She wasn't normally a person who frightened easily, but her mind wouldn't stop dwelling on the fact there was a boatload of creatures out there, waiting, ready to kill.

The bugs, the spiders. The snakes. Poisonous ones like vipers and bushmasters and lanceheads. Dimar had been kind enough to name them for her.

This place was a living nightmare.

She shuddered and cupped her mug close, staring at the fire while the others talked around her, fearing that if she spoke, she'd spill her growing terror for all to hear. She needed to hold her own here. Clinging to her pride was the only thing giving her motivation at the moment.

"Don't worry, Brynn," Shea said, startling her from her trance. "The snakes don't want to eat you."

"Says the man who didn't face one today," she muttered.

"Point taken." But his gaze offered compassion, lessening her anxiety. "Did Tristan ever tell you about our summer down here when we were in high school?"

"Peccary head roasted over an open fire," she whispered.

"He *has* told you."

She responded with a silent raising of her eyebrows and an attempt at a smile, but she suspected it looked more like an agonized grimace.

"So Uncle Charlie was my dad's younger brother, and I think you know he was also Harold Gatty, self-professed and self-taught expert on UFO sightings."

"Is there any other?" Tristan asked. "It's not like you can go to college for such shit."

"True," Shea said. "Anyway, Uncle Charlie was always a little different. He came to the Amazon because, like most places, there were unexplained things down here, and he wanted to investigate."

"No," Tristan cut in, "he came down to get high on ayahuasca and pump the shamans for information. He seemed to think they could corroborate some of his theories. Factual science wasn't his thing."

The derision in Magee's voice surprised Brynn. By all accounts, Magee was on a hunt to vindicate his dad, but apparently, he harbored some bitterness about it.

"Whatever his reasons," Shea continued, "it was an amazing opportunity that Tristan and I jumped at. While Uncle Charlie was busy with his stuff, Tristan and I decided we would see the real Amazon, so we asked one of the locals—a boy name Shingo—to take us into the wilderness."

"What happened?" Brynn asked.

"He took us in a *peque-peque* upriver, which was a small boat with a motor. For a few days, we stayed at a village and each morning, Shingo would take us into the jungle to look for creatures. There are places known as colpas, which are basically salt licks. Animals congregate there because nearly every living creature needs salt to live. He took us to one and it was like nothing you've ever seen, with over a hundred blue and yellow macaws hanging out. We stayed for hours observing them.

"But we really wanted to see an anaconda, we wanted to become *anaconderos*. Anaconda men. So we begged Shingo to take us to an old man we'd heard about that might know where the giant anacondas lived. Shingo didn't want to, but we bugged him long enough and he finally threw up his arms and said okay. We had to go further upriver to a farm where an old man named Alejandro lived. He was sitting outside his house, barefoot in filthy clothes and there was quite an odor to him. He had to be about ninety years old and didn't speak great English, but through Shingo we learned that he'd been living near the river his entire life. When he was young, he had transported goods by canoe, and he had come into contact with many tribes, some friendly and some not-so-friendly.

"He knew the language of the local Indians—called the Ese-Eja—and he'd seen many jaguars and giant anacondas, and even some species that were still unknown to science. When he was young, he had undergone an initiation that included a shaman sewing the nerve from an electric eel into his forearm, which would guarantee strength and virility for life, and which made him a native among the tribe."

"Lovely," Brynn said.

"He told us of an anaconda he'd seen once that was so big it was eating an adult tapir. They're like giant pigs. He said the snake was this round." Shea touched his fingertips together and created a huge circle with his arms. "He claimed there was a place that had forty-foot snakes."

Brynn shuddered. "So the horror movies weren't wrong. Did you go there?"

"We wanted to, but he wouldn't give us the location. He said it was too deep in the jungle and much too wild for a pair of *gringo* boys. He didn't want us to get killed. So he sent us to a different place where he said we'd still find snakes."

"And did you?" Irene asked.

Tristan shook his head and took up the story. "No. Instead, Shea decided he'd stash some meat in his pack."

"It was a gift from Alejandro's wife," Shea said. "A hunk of peccary meat that had been wrapped in a plastic bag. I didn't really want it, but I didn't want to be rude."

"Yeah, well that nearly cost us our lives."

"How?" Brynn asked.

"We hiked all day," Tristan said, "so had to camp out that night. We had a small tent and all three of us crammed inside. Shingo told us we should put our packs outside the tent, but Shea didn't want ants to get on everything, so he kept it with him. Sometime during the night, I awoke to strange sounds coming from outside the tent. A kind of dragging noise. I had a very bad feeling, but very cautiously I unzipped a tiny bit of the front flap and was greeted by multiple pairs of red eyes."

"Monsters," Dimar whispered.

Tristan nodded. "Yep."

Brynn stopped breathing and stared. "What were they?"

"Black caimans," Tristan replied. "A type of river crocodile."

"What did you do?"

"They had us surrounded, clearly having caught the scent of the rotting meat in Shea's pack, so I quickly grabbed it and threw it to them."

"And did they leave?"

"Not quite," Shea said. "Shingo and I woke up, and when we realized what had happened, we couldn't believe that Tristan had given them the meat. Because now they expected more, and we didn't have more. But Shingo reassured us that they were ambush predators, so if they'd wanted to kill us, we'd already be dead. They were checking us out."

"Living dinosaurs," Tristan said, his voice tinged with awe. "Our very own Jurassic Park moment."

"Shingo convinced us that we had to scare them off," Shea said. "So after much soul-searching, and pathetic whimpers every time one of the beasts stepped closer, we all burst from the tent, yelling and waving our arms like madmen. It was all or nothing."

Irene laughed. "Did it work?"

"All of them fled into the river," Tristan said, "except one. Shingo said she was a female. She was huge, maybe twelve or thirteen feet, and she held her ground, staring at us. We all immediately quieted down, and we watched her for a long time. She could probably sense our beating hearts. I always wondered if she was trying to decide which one of us to eat."

"My money was on you, since you still had rotten-meat-stink clinging to you," Shea said.

Tristan lifted a brow. "Were you gonna sacrifice me?"

"It was a passing thought, but then the big lady turned and disappeared into the water. We couldn't believe what had just happened, and immediately went back to Alejandro to tell him the story."

"And he told us we were full of shit," Tristan said.

"He didn't believe you?" Brynn asked.

"No," Shea said. "But it didn't matter. We know it happened. But we never found the anacondas."

"So this was why Magee all but grabbed that snake earlier?" Irene asked. "To make up for missing out the last time?"

Shea laughed. "It's the one that gets away that always haunts you."

Irene leveled her gaze at Tristan. "Were you planning to kiss her?"

Tristan looked at Brynn. "Maybe," he said, a speculative gleam in his eye.

She froze, then looked away with an air of nonchalance she was far from feeling.

"So close," Tristan murmured.

Shea continued, "Uncle Charlie was always searching for proof of extraterrestrials, but isn't the world we have pretty amazing on its own?"

"It was his religion," Tristan said.

"Well, I loved him anyway."

"That's because he wasn't your dad. All I ever wanted growing up was normal."

"Is that why you're so normal now?" Shea shot back.

"Fuck off," Tristan muttered under his breath.

"Normal is overrated," Irene said. "And why should we all be sheep in this world? Your father was a wolf. And so are you, Tristan."

Brynn scratched her scalp beneath her wet hair since nothing dried quickly in the jungle. "I hope it's my imagination, but I can still smell snake shit."

Irene turned to her, empathy in her gaze. "I'm afraid it's not your imagination, dear."

CHAPTER 12

The sauna engulfed Brynn as they trekked into the jungle the next morning. At least, that's how she thought of it. She imagined she was sweating out impurities from the snake incident the night before, so she happily embraced the perspiration.

But the bugs. It was unreal. Although the mosquitos weren't bad yet, there were still enough that she had bites on her arms and legs, despite that she mostly wore long-sleeved shirts and pants. She seemed to have more itchy welts today, so the mozzies must have gone to town on her last night when she had stripped down to wash away the anaconda feces.

She tried not to think about the disgusting secretion. One day it would be a funny story. But not yet. Instead she focused on every goddamned thing that flew around her: the buzzing things, the flying things, the jumping things. Beetles, green bugs, blue bugs, clouds of multi-colored flies. There were squirming white grubs that proliferated in dead foliage. So many birds. Lizards. Frogs. Millipedes.

And cockroaches.

The deeper they went and the more Brynn witnessed, the less she wanted to sleep amongst all of it. She had no doubt that if she died, her bones would be picked clean of flesh in less than twenty-four hours. Thank goodness for the invention of hammocks.

But the trees were magnificent. Dimar knew his vegetation and shared his knowledge, inching up her respect for him. There was the Brazil nut tree, with an eight-foot-wide diameter that reached to the top of the canopy, offering constant shade while at the same time trapping the humidity below.

"The air up high is more refreshing," Dimar said. "Less thick, like it is down here."

Brynn began repeatedly gazing upward with longing, envious of the monkeys and birds that could so easily access the upper branches.

Smaller trees held a banana-looking fruit, and some even had brightly colored orchids. Vines draped themselves everywhere and spongy mosses covered tree trunks. Ferns in all shades of green curled and nestled everywhere, forming delicate arches into a land of exquisite beauty.

They hardly needed to search for alien life elsewhere. It was all right here in the Amazon.

Brynn walked beside Irene, her fingers hooked in the straps of her heart-covered pack. "There's been mention of a man named Solomon. Do you know him?"

Irene wiped a handkerchief across her forehead, her hair pulled into a ponytail. "I don't but Conrad does. He's a shaman of high reputation, and Connie was very impressed by him, so he knew he had to find him again."

"Why?"

"The man has many contacts. And he offers other services of the more arcane kind. We don't want to leave any stone unturned."

"What does that mean?"

Irene at least had the grace to look chagrined.

Brynn helped her out by asking, "Supernatural, right?"

The annoyance changed to consternation. "It's not that simple, but I guess that's one way to label it. It's more like he can help with a glimpse into another world, another time."

Brynn tried not to sound condescending, but her voice betrayed her anyway. "Time travel? Are we trapped in a badly-written sci-fi movie now?"

"Don't be so judgy, Brynn," Irene admonished, giving her a side-long glance. "I know you better than that."

Brynn's frustration boiled over. She had always liked Irene, had trusted her, practically placing the eggs of her academic career in Irene's basket. But now she was hurt and angry that her mentor might have lied to her, might have used her. Might be using her now.

Was she overthinking it, blowing it out of proportion? Or were Irene and Conrad shysters? And what did this mean for Brynn's own career in archaeology? She feared she needed to extricate herself from them and soon, before whatever they were up to rubbed off on her somehow.

"I'm not so sure I know you anymore," Brynn said.

Irene reached out to clasp Brynn's elbow as they walked side by side. "I know this is a lot to take in. I wish I could've told you about it in our living room back home with a glass of Chardonnay and a tray of cheese, making it a grand afternoon of shared interests. But I'm glad you're here. I truly am."

The genuine yearning in Irene's voice caught Brynn off guard. And the woman was clinging to her as if she were at sea. Maybe she was.

Up ahead, Magee and Shea broke the trail with their machetes. What were their motives? While Brynn wanted nothing more than to trust them, it would be foolhardy at this point. Growing up in the surfing culture along with two older brothers had taught Brynn to have a strong backbone, especially when faced with the wants and desires of others.

But Brynn hadn't been careful this time, having succumbed to the charm and magnetism of Irene and Conrad. There was no doubt that she'd wanted to find someone who could appreciate the Sumerian culture the way Gramps had. Being with them had reminded her of her childhood.

Her gaze landed on Magee again. He'd removed his hat and his dark hair was wet from perspiration along the nape, his sweat-stained shirt stretching across his broad shoulders. Her displeasure over him trying to capture the anaconda instead of rescuing her was starting to dissipate. A quietly plotted revenge was the better way to go.

Although getting Magee covered with snake shit would probably make the man inordinately happy.

As Magee cleared a pathway, Brynn couldn't help but feel she was following him into more than just the jungle. Both he and Irene were searching for something. Which one should she follow? Which one should she believe?

When Brynn had announced to her parents that she planned to study archaeology at UCLA, they had tried to talk her out of it. Just because she was fascinated by Gramps's hobby, it didn't mean she should give her life over to it. Her dad had wanted her to major in the sciences, or maybe even try her hand on the pro surf circuit, but she'd doubled down with her innate Galloway stubbornness and told them she wanted to narrow her focus to Near Eastern Language and Culture studies—or what everyone in the department called NELC. She had immersed herself in mastering languages such as Sumerian, Akkadian, Assyrian, Hebrew, and Aramaic, along with the difficulty of translating cuneiform tablets, of which she'd already had a huge head start. Gramps had started teaching her cuneiform when she was ten.

When one of her first digs was to ancient Mesopotamia—modern-day Iraq—her dad had been soundly against it. It had taken many discussions to convince him to let her go, and Irene had been a big part of that. She'd managed to win over Lily and Jim Galloway, and that first excavation with Irene had been one of the most amazing trips Brynn had ever been on.

She owed her mentor so much. But how long should that debt be paid? How much loyalty did Irene deserve from Brynn? Would chasing after evidence of space aliens bolster Brynn's career?

Hardly. This was a fool's chase.

Maybe she should have taken up professional surfing after all.

TRISTAN HALTED; a small leopard watched him from ten feet up the trail.

"We're close to Jack's, right?" he asked Shea.

"I think so."

Tristan relaxed. "Then that cat isn't wild."

Dimar stepped beside him. "It's an ass-a-lot."

Tristan frowned. "A what?"

"I think he means ocelot," Shea muttered.

A man wearing a baseball cap, shorts, and knee-high rubber boots appeared beside the cat.

"Jack!" Tristan yelled.

"What the hell?" As Jack walked toward them, the cat fell in step behind him, watching with an alert wariness, its long, black-striped tail twitching back and forth.

He shook Tristan's hand and then Shea's. "Didn't expect to see you two."

"You're not an easy man to get a hold of," Shea said.

"And it was a little last minute," Tristan added, and stepped aside. "This is Irene Caridad and Brynn Galloway. Ladies, Dr. Jack Montgomery."

Jack removed his hat, revealing dark-blond hair that had grown too long. The whiskers on his cheeks bore a burnished hue against his tan skin. "Pleased to meet you both." He clasped their hands, and then positioned the ball cap back into place.

"I think you know Dimar and Freddie."

"I do." Jack nodded toward the men. "Where you headed?"

"We're looking for Irene's husband," Tristan said. "Dr. Conrad Fontana."

Jack thought for a second. "Doesn't ring a bell."

"We think he might be with Solomon. And we also believe that Pico is headed that way."

Jack hesitated. "Okay. I might have some info. We're not far from the compound. Why don't you all come in for lunch?"

Tristan nodded. "Appreciate it."

The ocelot, which had been hanging back, was now sniffing near Brynn's foot. The medium-sized cat was impressive-looking with a mottled black, white, and tan hide, a white underbelly, and round ears. The inherent strength in the animal was easily visible, but from the front he resembled a housecat.

"Is he yours?" Brynn asked, extending a hand so the animal could sniff her fingertips.

"Of a sort," Jack said. "He was caught in a snare several months ago. I rescued him and nursed him back. He's free to leave, but he keeps hanging around. I call him Reggie. He doesn't usually have an interest in other people, but he seems to like you."

"Brynn has a knack for attracting wild friends," Tristan said.

"Is that why she's hanging out with you?" Jack raised an eyebrow, then turned to lead them to his conservation outpost.

The ocelot remained on Brynn's right side, so Tristan took up sentry on the left.

"He's sweet," she said.

"Sweet is a relative term down here. He could probably rip your throat out while you slept if he wanted to."

She cast a disparaging scowl at him. "Do you like ruining moments?"

He grinned. "It's my specialty."

"You're just jealous because I'm a jungle whisperer, and you're a disgruntled physicist."

He flinched. "Ouch. The lady has claws."

They rounded a turn in the path, revealing a building with a thatched roof surrounded by several smaller huts.

"This is quite a setup." Appreciation rang in Brynn's voice.

Tristan had to agree. Montgomery had built himself a little wilderness getaway.

"What do you do down here, Jack?" she asked.

"In simple terms, I catalog the jungle," he said. "It's difficult to help the ecosystem and the creatures in it if you don't understand it."

"How did you get started with this?"

"I came down years ago on a high school trip and was hooked, so I studied biology and as soon as I could save enough money I came back and have been here ever since."

"How long ago?"

"About five years now. Long enough to buy this piece of land and build this facility."

"They actually sell plots this deep in the jungle?" she asked.

"There's always somebody with their hand out when it comes to the government," he replied. "The proverbial law of the jungle." He pointed to two men sitting on an open porch. "That's Dr. Emmett Brown. He teaches environmental science at Stanford. And beside him is Garrett Chu, his grad student."

The two men stood and shook hands all around but soon excused themselves. A young Bolivian man appeared with an armful of plantains.

Jack clapped him on the shoulder. "This is Yerko. He's my right-hand man."

"Pleased to meet you," Brynn said.

"We've got a few extra mouths for lunch," Jack said to him. "Can you whip something up?"

Yerko smiled and nodded. *"Sí."* He ducked into a room that if Tristan remembered correctly was a kitchen, Dimar and Freddie following him.

Jack offered everyone a cold beer. "Fridge runs on propane. It's a luxury I can't do without."

Tristan relaxed into a hammock-like chair, while the ladies sat on a wooden bench. Nothing like a cold-brewskie on a hot day. He opened a can and took a long drink.

"It's sure nice to have visitors," Jack said, then lowered his voice. "Dr. Brown and Garrett are very anti-social."

Shea settled into a woven chair. "Isn't that why you live in the jungle? To get away from people?"

Jack laughed. "Yeah, mostly. Suits me most days. But Yerko doesn't know anything about American football. I need someone who shares my passion."

"Then stop rooting for the Patriots, and maybe you'd make some friends." Tristan didn't bother to hide his disdain.

"You need to give up on the Saints, Magee. Get behind a team with some teeth."

Tristan made a face of mock disgust. "I'm gonna be nice since you gave me a beer. I'm sure each one is a precious commodity."

"Enjoy it because that's the only one you're getting out of me." He nodded toward Brynn. "But you can have as many as you want."

"Thanks," she replied. "I take it you don't have a wife down here?"

"Nope. Not many takers, I'm afraid."

The ocelot rubbed his head on Brynn's leg. She smiled and scratched behind his ears. "At least you have Reggie."

Jack laughed. "He's as happy as his last meal. But he's obviously got his sights set on you. I hope you don't mind."

She never took her eyes from the animal. "Not at all." She cooed and even made a kissy face.

Tristan sighed. Damned cat was hogging all the attention.

Jack shifted his focus to Tristan and Shea. "So you're down here looking for Solomon?"

"And my husband, Conrad," Irene cut in.

"I haven't heard of a man called Fontana, but I'm hearing chatter that Solomon has been traveling with a tall American."

"That's him," Irene affirmed.

Jack acknowledged her with a nod, then said, "They're looking for Innadaltu."

A myth Tristan's dad had sought the last time he was down here. "Isn't every kook?" Tristan said in a low voice.

"Watch your tongue, Tristan," Irene admonished him. He wasn't sure if she was scolding him about Conrad or his dad.

Brynn ignored the exchange, asking, "What's Innadaltu?"

Shea offered an answer. "There's long been rumors of places in South America where a shaman could access other realities and dream worlds, and perform special ceremonies. Myths claim the one here is called Innadaltu. Some believe it's a type of portal."

Brynn lifted a brow, her tone surprisingly even and matter of fact. "Does Conrad believe it's a phone to call E.T.?"

Tristan gave a humorless laugh. "That's what my dad thought."

"Did you find it?"

Shea shook his head. "Solomon didn't know, or else he purposely led us astray."

Tristan looked at his cousin. They hadn't discussed it at the time, especially since Shea had left early, but Tristan had often wondered the same.

Irene's face pinched with concern. "Why would he do that?"

"To keep the spoils for himself?" Tristan shrugged. "Who knows."

"So you're saying he's been yanking Conrad's chain for weeks now?" Irene demanded.

Tristan felt little pity for Fontana. "Your husband is a big boy, Irene. I'm sure he can handle Solomon."

She went quiet but clearly was still fuming.

"Well, I think you'll find them, or some clue to them, near Turtle Village." Jack leaned in the doorway to the kitchen and said, "Dimar, you know where that is?"

The Bolivian came to stand in the entranceway. "Yes, I know it."

"How far is this Turtle Village?" Irene demanded, rejoining the conversation.

"About thirty clicks," Jack replied.

Confusion flashed in Dimar's eyes as he folded his arms across his chest. "What does that mean?"

"It's about twenty miles," Tristan answered.

Hope blossomed on Irene's face. "That's not too far."

"Maybe not on a wide-open prairie," Jack said. "But in the jungle, it'll take you about three days."

Irene swung her attention to Dimar. "Can you get us there?"

The man's eyes fluttered in some type of eye-roll.

Tristan stared at him. "Are you having a seizure?"

"No. Of course I can take you there. But it's going to cost more."

"Bullshit. Why does it cost more?"

"Because that's a dangerous area. Just ask Freddie. He knows."

"Are we talking drugs dangerous?" Tristan asked.

"I think he means more of a spiritual danger," Jack offered.

Tristan narrowed his gaze at Dimar. "We have to pay you more because you're afraid of ghosts?"

Dimar pinched his lips together and nodded vigorously.

Irene waved a hand. "It's fine. I'll take care of it."

Tristan shook his head in defeat. "Then that bill is all yours, Irene."

Yerko nudged Dimar aside and indicated that lunch was ready—a pot of beans, rice, and tortillas. Everyone gratefully dug in.

CHAPTER 13

Brynn couldn't sleep and found Tristan sitting by a small fire near the main building. With elbows on knees, he was hunched forward, his gaze intent on the flames as shadows ebbed and flowed across the angles of his face. He sported a few days' growth of whiskers and his dark hair was curling along the collar of his shirt. The wilderness was slowly consuming them, making them wild in the process, or maybe it was simply the jungle stripping away societal barriers and laying them bare. Brynn suspected, however, that Magee had never paid much attention to such niceties.

"Communing with aliens?" she asked, keeping her voice low so as not to disturb the others who might be nearby. Tristan had been right —privacy was in short supply.

The glint in Tristan's gaze conveyed annoyed amusement. And maybe something else. The tug in her belly was immediate, and she all but lifted her nose to catch his scent. For a moment she let herself revel in everything male that was Magee: muscle, strength, and possibly the biggest aphrodisiac for her—irreverence.

He motioned for her to sit as he said, "Well, if you consider talking to Dimar interacting with something not of this world, then the answer is yes."

She took a seat, leaving the one between them empty. Wouldn't want him to get the wrong idea.

"Sometimes I have trouble sleeping in the jungle," he said.

"Is that a sleeping aid?" she asked as he took a sip from his canteen.

He replaced the lid. "Nah. Just water. Can you play backgammon, Galloway?"

"Yes. I used to play with my grandfather."

"I'll be right back."

He disappeared, and then returned with a mini version of the game. He unfolded the board and proceeded to set it up on the empty chair between them.

"Why backgammon?" she asked, helping him organize the pieces in the glow of the firelight.

"It was my dad's favorite. Did you know it's one of the oldest known board games?"

"I do. They've found evidence of it in Mesopotamia. Maybe it was a gift from their alien benefactors."

"The dice were made from human bones, so no alien intervention likely."

"You do know your artifacts."

"I try." He handed her a die, his hand brushing hers. "Need a refresher on the rules?"

"Nope, I'm good," she replied, pretending his touch hadn't left a burn mark.

They each rolled a die—a 5 for her and a 3 for him. She won the toss, so went first, moving one piece five spaces and another three.

"What do you know about Thoth?" Tristan asked as they continued to take turns rolling the die and moving pieces toward their home board.

"Interesting you should ask. I read a book about him while I was in Pakistan."

"No paperback novels for you."

They both leaned forward to better see the board in the firelight, but Brynn couldn't deny she liked the excuse to reduce the distance between her and Magee. There was certainly an energy between them, and it chased away her fatigue with a flush of anticipation.

"I like a good fictional adventure just like the next person, but I was curious."

"About what?"

"The idea that Thoth, an Egyptian deity, might have originated from something earlier."

"Sumerian you mean."

"Yes."

"A woman after my own heart."

He forced one of her pieces to the middle bar. She rolled and easily moved it. As the game progressed, however, that would become more difficult.

"Have you read the Emerald Tablet?" Tristan asked as he threw the dice carefully onto the narrow gameboard.

"Yes."

"What did you think?" He moved two pieces and handed her the dice.

"That it was the actual words of the Greek god Hermes and the Egyptian god Thoth? Umm, no." She took her turn. "It was written in Arabic sometime in the sixth century or perhaps a bit later."

"But who knows what it was based on." Despite the tiny board, Tristan was surprisingly adept at moving the miniature game pieces.

"So you think the Moon Tablet might be the precursor to the Emerald Tablet?" she asked.

"It did inform your thesis, didn't it?"

"Partially," she said with great care. She worked hard to avoid any woo-woo science in her work, since it could have discredited all of it. "But since you've read my paper, you know that I didn't include any references to the Emerald Tablet, nor the fact that Thoth stated that humans were gods in the making."

He grinned at her last statement. "I get it. But what about off the record?"

"As above, so below. Every kid learns that in Sunday school. And it was never clear in the work—at least the translation that I read—that the philosopher's stone could be created."

"The Emerald Tablet was about transmutation. You offered a compelling argument in your paper that the Moon Tablet was fundamentally about metallurgy."

"We finally agree on something," she said wryly. "What a shock."

He made his move on the board. "I think you're beginning to like me."

"That's not what I said. Anyway, metallurgy isn't magic or outer space nonsense. It's a science that has been developed over time through trial and error."

She took her turn.

"Maybe," Tristan said.

"I'll grant you that later interpretations of the Emerald Tablet indicate a more supernatural slant," she conceded.

"You mean religion."

"I mean connecting the soul to divinity and to creation itself, not just of individuals but also the world. And that's where I think we're both out of our league. Unless you have a Theology degree as well? It didn't show up in my internet search."

"No degrees in divinity. And I'm kinda flattered that you investigated me like some P.I."

"I won't lie. You're very entertaining, Magee. But I want to point out that while you read my paper like it was some kind of bible to follow, I can assure you it's not. Please remember that I was unable to corroborate the transcription that I hypothesized with the actual tablet, which can sometimes have broken or damaged cuneiform symbols." She paused, her brow raised in a questioning stare.

"I already told you I don't have a photo of the Moon Tablet, but maybe Irene has one sewn into her trousers."

"It's so very odd that neither of you took a picture. Maybe I should offer to wash Irene's clothes so I can search the lining."

"Or you could frisk me for it."

She leveled her gaze at him. "Believe me, if I wanted something from you, I wouldn't have to frisk you for it."

For a brief moment, jungle sounds filled the soundtrack of their pseudo-date. A sexy grin slowly spread across Tristan's mouth. "Damn," he murmured. "I gotta watch out for you."

She returned her attention to the game board, trying to push aside the weighted attraction to this man that seemed to run thick in her veins.

"I must reiterate," she said, attempting to shift to more neutral ground, "that the conclusions in my paper must be taken with a grain of salt. At the time that I wrote it, Irene said my conjecture was fine since the work wasn't headed for journal publication anyway."

"Such a cheerleader," he said, then added, "That must have stung."

Yes, but she didn't say it aloud.

"Don't sell yourself short, Brynn."

"I'm not trying to." She sighed in frustration. "You're smart, Tristan. There's no doubt about it. So please stop pulling these theories out of your ass. People want so desperately to believe in this stuff that they ignore the obvious. Have you actually watched all the crazy UFO videos floating around the internet?"

"Have you?"

She pressed her lips together. "Maybe."

He chuckled softly. "You *are* curious."

"I never claimed I wasn't. But the videos are accompanied with commentary by the armchair photographers that's filled with the most outrageous conjecture. Do you know how much space debris there is orbiting the earth? Most of these theories are bunk. They have logical explanations."

"Okay, I'll grant you there's a lot of wild stuff out there. Remember, I lived with my dad when he was in his heyday. These people came to our house. They had dinner with us. They told us incredible things. When you hear enough of them, you start to think there might be something to it because not every last one of those folks was delusional. In fact, some seemed quite normal."

Brynn landed the last of her checkers on her home board—which Tristan had yet to do—so she prepared to start removing them. She was gonna win.

"When studying ancient cultures," he continued, "researchers like you ask the same question—what if? That's all I'm doing here."

"You like the game."

"Backgammon? It's all right."

"That's because I'm winning. No, I mean you like chasing stuff. You like the challenge."

His gaze went dark, igniting a fire in her belly. "I think you like a challenge too, Galloway."

Her mouth went dry. "Can I have some of that water?"

He handed her the canteen. She took a sip and made a split decision to open up to him. "My gramps was more than a hobbyist. He was a disciple."

"Of Sumer?"

"Yes. One of the reasons I decided to study Assyriology and Near Eastern Cultures was because of him. If reincarnation is real, then he surely lived back then. His obsession with it, his depth of knowledge, his passion for collecting—it was incredible. Not that I realized this as a child. I thought he was eccentric. He and Gram lived in a small town in western Pennsylvania, and I loved visiting them. They had a beautiful red brick house that sat on a hill, a peaceful and magical place. He kept his collection in the lower level with a door that led outside, and I often took pieces out on the grass and played with them until one day my horrified grandmother caught me." She smiled. "Gramps told her it was okay. I think I was the only one in the family who had any interest in his stuff, and I became not only his favorite grandchild but his constant shadow."

Tristan had stopped playing, listening intently. "What kind of stuff did he collect?"

"He had a mathematical tablet that approximated the square root of two. He had tablets written in Sumerian, Akkadian, and Hittite. Some had magic spells or recipes. But he also had a love of ancient musical instruments."

"Such as?"

"Lyres and harps and dulcimers. My favorite was the lute. I was always strumming away on it. I wasn't very good, but I didn't care."

"Self-taught."

She laughed. "Definitely."

"Where is all this stuff?"

"It's with Gram. She still lives in the house. I'm guessing you'd like an introduction."

"Does she want to sell any of it?"

It had yet to come up in the family, but the thought had crossed Brynn's mind more than once. "Maybe. Probably."

"Don't worry, Brynn. I'd do right by her."

"Maybe you would," she said, but it didn't matter. If her grandmother wanted to sell the collection, Brynn would be there every step of the way to make sure Magee, or anyone else, didn't take advantage of her. "But there is one thing I'll never part with. Gram recently sent me a notebook while I was in Pakistan that belonged to Gramps. He'd left instructions that she was supposed to send it to me when I turned twenty-five."

"And when did that happen?"

She wrinkled her brow. "The package arriving? I'm not sure. I guess around August twelfth."

A small smile tugged at his lips. "Is that your birthday?"

"Yes."

He laughed.

"What?" she asked.

"My birthday's on August twelfth as well."

"Huh. What are the odds?" Or was he pulling her leg?

"Actually, there's a 99.9 percent chance that you'll have a birthday match with someone with only seventy people present."

"But there's only two of us," she pointed out.

"Which makes it a remarkable coincidence. I guess we'll have to celebrate together next year. I hear you're a surfer-girl. Maybe you could teach me?"

"I'm not sure I'd have the patience," she teased, tamping down the flare of happiness in her belly from his casual words.

His eyes danced with amusement, then he shifted the conversation back to neutral ground. "So what's in the notebook?" he asked.

"Notations, information, drawings, leads on pieces." She paused. "It also contained glyphs."

"Cuneiform?"

She nodded.

"Anything of interest?"

She shrugged. "I can't translate a good portion of it. But the Sumerian language has been dubbed 'the Sumerian Problem' in some circles."

"How's that?"

"Sumerian doesn't fit into any of the major linguistic groups in Mesopotamia at the time. Everyone else spoke Semitic languages—Hebrew, Arabic, Assyrian—but not the Sumerians."

Magee grinned. "Alien language?"

"Or more likely that the Sumerian people migrated from somewhere else, far away."

He sighed. "Spoil sport. Have you shown the notebook to Irene?"

"No." She looked at him expectantly. "I'm hoping you'll keep this in confidence."

"On my honor."

"So you profess to have honor?"

His smile reached his eyes. "I'm not such a bad guy, Galloway."

"I never said you were."

As Tristan added more wood to the fire, Brynn asked, "Have you been completely up front with me?"

"More than you know." Before she could decipher his response, he continued, "Are you thinking what I'm thinking?"

Her eyes snapped to his. *About us taking a tumble?*

"Irene's motives," he said.

She released a pent-up breath, feeling both relieved and sheepish that her thoughts kept wandering off into naked Tristan land.

"You might be right about her bringing the tablet down here to hide it," she said, trying to get her head back in the game. "I spoke to Audrey before we left La Paz."

"Your defy-the-medical-odds college roommate?"

She nodded. "She told me she'd recently learned that Irene may have been involved with archaeological hoaxes in the past."

"No shit?"

"Shhh." She ducked closer to him, bringing her nose within inches of his. "It's all a bit of hearsay right now, so again, lock it in the vault."

His gaze glinted with defiance.

"Seriously?" she said. "You just agreed to keep my confidence on the other thing. What makes this different?"

"Because it's a helluva juicy secret, that's why, and if it's true then Irene is a two-faced liar."

Her jaw locked in frustration. "Keep your voice down," she pleaded. "We don't know this for certain, and I'm not about to run around flinging accusations without any proof."

"What flippin' more proof do you need?" he scoffed. "She brought the damned tablet down here to plant it."

"Maybe." She sighed. "Probably. Except you would've known once it was discovered."

"Yeah, but since she claims to have had no knowledge of my place in the buying line, that wouldn't have occurred to her."

"But it's all changed now."

"Hell, yeah."

She glanced around to assure herself they were alone. "Are we safe?"

Magee chuckled. "You think Irene is going to murder us after burying the tablet?"

"It crossed my mind," she hissed in a whisper. "It would be so easy to dump us out here, and simply claim that we became lost. I was *already* lost. That happens all the time, right?"

"You watch too many movies. But if it makes you feel any better, I'll make sure that Irene doesn't kill you."

Hearing him say it aloud made her realize how ridiculous it sounded.

"How ironic that you're shooting down *my* conspiracy theories," she said. "I thought they were your bread and butter. Why are you so difficult sometimes?"

The grin on his face literally made her heart miss a beat. Shit.

"You really *do* know me. I'm touched." He held up a hand. "Okay, okay. I'll try not to mention Irene's criminal past over morning coffee. But if she baits me, I make no promises."

"Fine." She examined the game board. "Ready to finish this?"

"You itching for a victory?"

She rolled the dice. "It became clear early on that I'd beat you."

"Just when I think I couldn't like you more, Galloway, you prove me wrong."

She gave him a look of exasperation, but in truth she basked under the backhanded compliment. She probably shouldn't trust Magee any more than she'd trusted Irene and Conrad, but one thing was certain —Magee was a lot more fun.

"But don't count me out yet," he added.

The roguish grin was back, and for one brief moment she almost invited him into her hammock.

CHAPTER 14

Tristan finished packing his gear, then joined everyone on Jack's porch. He hadn't had the most restful sleep and the reason greeted him with a cup of coffee and a "good morning." He watched Galloway retreat over the rim of his mug.

Trying to distract himself from the woman who had invaded every dream he'd had during the night, he shifted his attention to Irene. She was speaking with Dimar and Freddie, and Tristan watched her through a lens of suspicion. People accused him of being underhanded, but he'd never stooped to tricking the world at large. On that thought, however, an image of his dad flashed in his head. How many truths had Harold Gatty distorted to keep his belief system alive? Was Irene simply doing the same thing? And would it be considered wrong if one day the hypothetical theory—that aliens had visited Earth or were currently visiting—was proven to be true? Would the shenanigans of Irene Caridad, Conrad Fontana, and Harold Gatty be forgiven? And shouldn't Tristan himself be included in that dubious group?

Jack handed him a hand-drawn map. "I've marked where I think you'll find Solomon and Irene's husband."

"Thanks."

Shea finished his coffee. "We'll try to come through on our way back."

"The welcome mat is always out," Jack said.

"Appreciate it." Tristan shook Jack's hand, as did Shea.

Brynn approached. "Thank you, Jack." She clasped his hand as well.

They shouldered their packs and the group headed out.

AFTER A LONG DAY OF TREKKING, Brynn was relieved to hang her hammock as Freddie and Dimar set up camp. Her muscles ached not just from the all-day trekking but also from the scuffle with the anaconda two days ago. She looked forward to crawling into her hanging bed and going to sleep. But first, food. She set her pack on the hammock and hoped little critters wouldn't make their way to it.

On second thought, leaving it here probably isn't a good idea.

She snatched it up and approached Tristan who was bent over organizing a cookfire. "Where would be a good place to leave this?" she asked.

"If your food and snacks are sealed up, it should be okay on your hammock."

She nodded, and then stilled. Tristan stood up, his back straight, and he seemed to sense the same thing she had.

"Someone's here," she murmured.

Magee grabbed his machete and moved to the edge of the clearing, and she followed. She peeked past his shoulder as he inspected the border that separated them from the jungle. Fresh footprints were visible.

A rustling in the vines to their right had Tristan rushing forward. "Don't move!"

"Are you gonna cut me, Tristan?" an elderly man asked, holding his hands up in surrender, but his grin quickly defused the flash of fear that had coursed through Brynn.

Magee's shoulders sagged as he lowered his weapon. "Sono-fabitch, Solomon. Are you trying to get yourself killed?"

TRISTAN SAT beside Brynn as everyone gathered around the cookfire, the night having darkened to an inky, endless void. Had Solomon brought the darkness with him? Tristan wouldn't doubt it. The old shaman had accepted the food that Freddie had offered and was now steadfastly consuming it.

Before he could question the man, Irene beat him to it. "Have you seen Conrad? I thought you were with him." She'd only just been introduced to him but had quickly discarded a friendly demeanor.

"I was." Solomon scooped the last of his rice from his bowl, then handed it to Dimar.

Dimar scoffed as he took it. "I'm no damn doctor maid."

"Nursemaid," Shea corrected, poking at the fire. He had become the unofficial fire maker, a role he'd had when he and Tristan were boys, running amuck in the woods of Mississippi.

Dimar stood in a huff and went to wash the bowl in the makeshift kitchen he and Freddie had set up.

Solomon placed his hands on his knees, his arms straight. "Now that I have found you, I can take a moment to rest."

Solomon hadn't changed. He wasn't tall, but his lanky body was all angles and geometry, which Tristan had always thought strange, because shamanic travels involved moving forward and backward in time, shifting locations on a whim, trusting in a person's intuition, in their ability to recognize symbols and spirits and all things that made no sense in this world. In the world of physics, Tristan had always envisioned a shaman with the flowing curves of infinity, defined by a sideways "8," the world all but folding back on itself.

"I've been with Dr. Fontana," Solomon said, his gaze settling on Irene. "Glad to finally meet Mrs. Conrad. We've been expecting you."

"That's good," she answered. "Then why are you here? Did you come for us?"

Solomon shrugged, his expression one of nonchalance. This was the Solomon Tristan remembered, a mercurial man who tended to dabble in both the dark and the light. He was also a liar.

"Planning another sting, Mr. Voodoo?" Tristan asked.

"What is a 'sting'?"

Tristan released a humorless laugh. "I'm not buying this innocent act."

Dimar took his seat again, snickering with laughter, his eyes shining with glee. Apparently Dimar didn't like Solomon either.

"Did you know that I'm originally from Peru?" Solomon countered, raising a dark eyebrow. Despite his age, whatever that might be, he had the energy of a teenager, like he was plugged into the outlet of the universe. Shit, maybe he was.

Tristan nodded, impatience edging his voice. "Yes, you've mentioned it more than once."

"I grew up near the Madre de Dios, a big river much like the Beni. My father was a shaman, and a worthless, shitty human being."

His fireside audience stilled, everyone clearly shocked by this random confession. Solomon had never been an over-sharer, so Tristan wondered what his game was.

"So you might surmise," the old man continued, "that my education as a shaman was tainted. But far from it. Instead, I have always conducted myself with one philosophy—you get what you ask for. And because of my father, I have always felt it was my duty to balance good and bad, to restore harmony wherever I can. To walk on the wild side."

"You get what you ask for?" Tristan repeated, incredulous. "The last time I was here, you threw me, my dad, and Conrad to the wolves. You're a snake."

Solomon puckered his lips, scrunched his eyebrows together, and stared at the fire. "Is that the narrative you've been telling yourself?"

"I don't mean to interrupt," Brynn said, "but what's going on?"

"Yes, boy, tell us what's going on in your angry heart," Solomon demanded, suddenly filled with brimstone and fury.

In the past, this smoke and mirrors shit had scared Tristan into submission. That and the fact that his dad had revered Solomon and his otherworldly abilities, a love that Harold Gatty had managed to instill in Conrad Fontana. From there, the three of them had played a wicked game of archaeological negotiation.

But that was then. Now, Tristan refused to be cowed by the man.

"Fine. For those of you that may not know the whole story"—Tristan indicated Brynn and Irene—"here it is in all its glory. Two years ago, Shea and I came down with my dad and Conrad. Dimar, Freddie, and Pico were our guides. We were in the same area we are now. Conrad and my dad had been friends for a while and often spoke of what could be hidden in the Amazon.

"My dad would've loved to have found little green men living the good life down here, but in truth he was more interested in possible evidence of advanced technology. There were rumors of places where odd symbols had been found, and Conrad believed they might be cuneiform. If found, maybe it would prove that Sumerians had traveled around the world more than five thousand years ago.

"For three weeks, we all traipsed around following local folklore clues but found nothing. We were also searching for you." Tristan looked at Solomon. "Dad was adamant that we find you."

"I remember," the shaman responded. "We had stayed in touch over the years." But his tone didn't convey a long and deep friendship. Tristan's heart sank a little further in his chest. Why did he care so much what Solomon thought?

"As I recall," Shea said, "you didn't want to help us, but the villagers insisted."

"They were persistent." Solomon glanced at all the men. "You all were. It was clear you needed a level head."

"And that was you?" Tristan muttered.

"Of course it was. The villagers were too starry-eyed by the presence of Harold Gatty. They had learned of his fame and believed he would bring tourism dollars to them. They were ready to throw out the welcome mat."

Tristan ran a hand through his sweat-soaked hair. "What was wrong with that?"

"I know the answer," Dimar interrupted, "and it's three words: exploi-tation."

"That's one word." Tristan shifted his focus back to Solomon. "But you led us to a valid site."

"No, he didn't."

"No, I didn't."

Dimar and Solomon spoke at the same time.

"Are you saying it was fake?" Shea asked, his tone disbelieving. "There was a cave, wall markings, and some evidence of past habitation." He looked from Brynn to Irene, as if trying to help them see that he couldn't be so easily duped. "We found mummified remains buried with pouches and bags and small clay jars. There were all sorts of smaller paraphernalia like sandals, beads, and feathers."

"I'll admit," Solomon said, his voice somber, "my goal was to lead you to a place that was of little value in order to protect the communities in the area, but I was surprised when I got there. It turned out to be a good site after all."

Tristan failed to hide his disdain. "You're not making much of a case for your shamanic abilities, old man."

"I'm not a prophet."

"God help us if you were."

"Yes," Solomon continued, "my initial motive was to mislead you, but then the mummies were located and Conrad and Gatty became obsessed. But not you, Shea. You abandoned us."

Aggravation flashed across Shea's face. "I didn't abandon you. Conrad and Uncle Charlie were adamant about removing the mummies for transport out of the country."

"For what purpose?" Brynn asked, her expression serious as she listened to the exchange with laser focus.

"DNA testing. Not only were they violating the law and likely to get into trouble with the Bolivian government, removing the mummies would damage efforts at classification. And don't even get me started on how easy it is to ruin the testing with cross contamination from modern DNA. I pleaded my case, but none of you would listen. I wasn't going to stick around and be a part of that."

"What happened?" Brynn looked from Shea to Tristan to Irene to Solomon.

"Look," Tristan said, "Conrad was certain they could move the mummies and get the clearance required to transport them to the States. It was never anyone's intention to break the law." He turned to Solomon. "What I can't figure out is why you arranged to have the mummies sent to La Paz only to turn us in to officials once we got there?"

"What?" Solomon's face displayed what appeared to be genuine surprise. "I didn't turn you in."

"They told us you did," Tristan pressed. "I had to pull strings to get out of it, not the least of which was agreeing to locate an Incan collection on the black market, a shit job if there ever was one. If it wasn't you, then who?"

Solomon's gaze settled on Dimar, who barked out his defense. "Oh no. It wasn't me."

"So you got the mummies out?" Brynn asked.

"No," Tristan said. "But Conrad managed to smuggle a different one, right, Irene?"

"I have no comment," she replied.

That was bullshit. Tristan had been forced to come up with fake papers for that one to protect his dad, and he'd leaned on his mentor, Marina Kallis, to do it, angering her as well. He was beginning to realize that Conrad was as slippery as his wife.

"So you used *that specimen* for the DNA test," Shea said.

Tristan knew this would only raise Shea's ire more, but so be it. "Yep."

Luckily, Brynn kept the conversation flowing before Shea could erupt again. "What were the results?" she asked.

Shea spoke before Tristan could answer. "The remains were not from an autochthonous Native American maternal lineage."

Dimar's mouth froze in an open position. "Huh?"

Tristan translated. "They came from somewhere else."

"The most probable location being Europe thousands of years before," Shea added.

Brynn frowned. "They weren't indigenous to the region?"

"Like I said, I find the results to be highly suspect, but this is what Harold Gatty reported in his final book that was published just before his death. I called him and tried to talk some sense into him, but he wouldn't listen. I didn't realize how sick he was. I'll always be sorry that the last conversation I had with him was in anger."

Tristan still couldn't fathom that Shea hadn't known how ill his father had been. Surely someone in the family would have told him. But even Shea's father had barely made it to see his brother before Charlie Hartigan passed. Had Tristan's dad truly downplayed his illness to everyone but his wife and son?

Dimar crossed his arms. "What did he say in his book?"

"He took his typical strong stance," Tristan answered, acknowledging his father's stubborn pride, "that the mummy results showed proof the Nephilim tribes, which were part human, part supernatural being—the literal 'sons of God' and 'daughters of men' according to Genesis in the Hebrew bible—had not only traveled into Europe but had also crossed to the 'New World.' And that world was here in the Amazon."

"It was conjecture on a grand scale," Shea said. "Even for Uncle Charlie. I wouldn't have a problem with his book if he would've just labeled it as fiction. I know it still brings income to your mother, Tristan. I'm not trying to tear down his legacy, just make it a little more honest."

"Really?" Tristan countered. "'Cause it sure as hell sounds like you're ripping that legacy to shreds."

Shea shook his head and went silent.

Tristan looked at Solomon. "I guess all we can do now is let it be ancient history. We need you to take us to Conrad."

Solomon shrugged. "I am busy."

"Doing what?" Tristan mocked. "Walking around the jungle?"

"You always were a rude boy."

Shea huffed, saying, "On that we can agree."

The tension seemed to dissipate, although Tristan didn't appreciate that it was at his expense.

"If you must know," Solomon said, "I decided that Conrad and I could not work together. So I left."

"What?" Irene's expression flashed with panic. "You've left him alone?"

"He has a man with him. A helper."

"You need to take us to him."

Solomon was nonplussed by Irene's fervent demand. "I am also looking for that twit Pico," he added in a conversational tone, as he settled his gaze on first Dimar and then Freddie.

The Castanos cousins exchanged a perplexed look.

"We don't know where he is," Freddie said.

Solomon tilted his head. "He was supposed to bring more supplies."

"He was with me," Irene said. "But we became separated when we were beset by ruffians. He ran off. I'm sure he's making his way to you and Conrad. We should return to Conrad's location immediately."

Shea poked at the fire, creating a flurry of sparks. "What kind of supplies was he bringing you?"

Solomon's face relaxed into a bemused expression. "Shea, my boy. I've missed your straight-A integrity. You think I'm dealing in dirty artifacts."

Shea lifted his gaze, his face glowing orange from the firelight. "Are you?"

"There are two sides to every story. Black and white. Good and evil. My nasty father and myself."

Shea sighed. "And you still like to evade questions."

"Will you please take us to Conrad?" Irene entreated once again.

Silently, Solomon seemed to consider it. Finally, he said, "Okay. I can do that."

Tristan narrowed his eyes. "And just like that you change your mind."

Solomon didn't rise to the bait. "We are human beings. We change our minds. What is so wrong with that? Why did Pico run off?"

"Irene said the men who took her had guns," Dimar said. "Pico was lucky to escape."

"So was I." Irene's voice was tinged with annoyance. "Since he left me behind."

"Who were these men?" Solomon asked.

"I don't know," Irene said. "There were four of them. I'm guessing drugs, or maybe they were looking for gold. They could've been poachers, but they didn't have any large bags to transport animals."

"There is a problem with the gold miners," Solomon said. "We try to avoid them if we can. I don't think they will find where Conrad is, since it's high ground. The search for gold tends to be lower." He shifted his attention to Dimar. "You're on the wrong trail. Did you know that? Are you lost?"

"I'm not lost," Dimar rebutted, clearly affronted. "We saw Jack. He told us to come this way."

Solomon nodded. "The American. I like him. And why are you here, Tristan?"

"Pico has something that belongs to me."

"What?"

"An artifact that's come all the way from Iraq."

Solomon nodded. "I have heard of it."

"From whom?" Tristan asked. "Conrad?"

"No. The light people."

"What are the light people?" Brynn asked.

"There are others always around us." Solomon encompassed the surroundings with both hands raised. "Through our spiritual travels, we can interact with them."

"Are they here now?" Dimar demanded.

"They are always here."

Dimar grumbled something in Spanish that was no doubt a swear word.

"They won't hurt you," Solomon added.

Dimar looked uncomfortable. "So you say. But you don't know. And all sorts of strange stuff happens out here."

"I may be a man of the spirits," Solomon said, "but I am also of the real world. We are in the jungle. For those not experienced, it is dangerous." His gaze went from Brynn to Irene. "We should all stay together."

Irene leaned forward, curiosity shining in her eyes. "Has Conrad found anything of interest?"

"That's a question for him. But he has spent much time searching. I'm sure he's eager to see you."

Then Solomon shifted his gaze to Brynn, his eyes lingering with speculation. "But you. They are very interested in you."

"Who?" Brynn asked.

"The light people."

CHAPTER 15

Trailing the group, Brynn walked beside Magee, feeling surprisingly good. It was welcome after days of fighting fatigue and dehydration. Her body was finally acclimating to the steamy climate and robust terrain.

Wait. Was she thinking about the jungle or the man beside her?

Her attraction to Tristan was now a constant background hum, and while she hadn't necessarily gotten used to it, she had learned to ignore it. Sometimes. Occasionally.

Truthfully, when she was tired, and her temper ran just shy of grumpy, she indulged her imagination, wondering how Magee would feel beneath her hands, his mouth on hers, his gaze clouded with lust …. Shit. She fanned herself. The temperature was hot enough without her mind adding on another ten degrees.

"Your shaman friend isn't what I envisioned," she said.

"What did you expect?"

"More … presence."

Tristan chuckled. "You thought he would be grander than life."

She dodged a leafy vine. "Maybe more eerie. He seems quite normal. Although I'm not sure if I should be looking over my shoulder for these *light* people." She thought of her dream when she had been lost, right before the jaguar had appeared beside her. She'd been surrounded by … *others*. And what had they said? Something about needing her to open a door for them. She was about to tell Tristan about it, then thought better of it.

"Yeah, that was kind of a strange comment, even from him," he said.

"Should I be worried?"

"I'm sure he'll be able to sort it all out for you in a ceremony."

"More ayahuasca?" Brynn groaned. "I know you weren't trusting Solomon when you first saw him, but what about now?"

Tristan's face pinched into a grimace. "Maybe he didn't turn us in. Maybe I've been harboring a grudge that shouldn't be. Wouldn't be the first time."

"You're not an optimist, are you?"

"My dad … and other things … burned that out of me."

Shea slowed his pace ahead of them and said to Brynn, "Do you wanna know how you can tell how depressed Tristan is?"

She nodded.

"First, he listens to John Denver. Then, he'll move to Barry Manilow. If he gets to the Carpenters, he's a goner."

Tristan muttered something under his breath.

Shea continued, "If you hang around him long enough, his melancholy tunes will come out."

"How about I just like the music?" Tristan said. "From an acoustical point-of-view, Karen Carpenter's voice is nearly perfect. They all are, really. And *Copacabana* is a great song."

Shea began whistling the tune, and Brynn sang along under her breath about a girl named Lola. Solomon waited for them to catch up, then added in a deadpan tone about Lola's showgirl status. The absurd moment continued as the shaman and Shea continued trading lines from the song. Solomon even started dancing.

Brynn turned to Tristan, who wore a disgusted scowl. "Apparently, your love of Barry Manilow isn't much of a secret if a shaman in the middle of the Bolivian jungle knows about it," she said.

Shea and Solomon continued with the songfest, and Brynn couldn't resist joining in—they sang *I Write the Songs* and *Mandy* before moving on to John Denver's *Rocky Mountain High* and *Thank God I'm a Country Boy.* They ended with a rousing rendition of *Rainy Days and Mondays* by the Carpenters. Shea knew a lot of the words, but it took Tristan's participation to really bring the songs home. It certainly helped pass the time, since it was a long day of hiking through the jungle. It reminded Brynn of childhood visits with her grandparents in Pennsylvania. Gramps had loved to sing in the church choir and had taught her many of the songs. She was no Karen Carpenter, but Gramps had always praised her singing voice, even going as far as teaching her vocal exercises. One tonal set in particular brushed her memory. She hadn't thought of it in years.

IN THE AFTERNOON, they followed what Brynn guessed was a tributary of the Beni River. She sensed they were deeper in the non-civilized world as animals no longer hid from them. Two harpy eagles watched the terrain like sentinels, visible on the branches of a leafless tree. A rotund tapir with the face of an anteater and as large as a donkey swam by before making a quick getaway into the forest. A large, shaggy animal drank from the river's edge. According to Tristan it was a capybara, the world's largest rodent. It reminded her of a guinea pig she'd had when she was a child. The pet's name had been Tom Jones, courtesy of her mother, since *She's A Lady* was apparently her dad's ode to his wife.

As they came to a small settlement, children bounded forward wearing t-shirts and shorts, and similarly dressed adults greeted Solomon with a familiarity that spoke of friendship. While the village was in a remote location, the modern clothing indicated contact with the outer world.

Solomon introduced them to a short man named Eduardo. "They are the Tacana people," he said. "They have invited us for dinner, so we will sleep here tonight."

"Is this Turtle Village?" Brynn asked.

Solomon silently agreed.

Brynn and Irene were guided to a spare hut while the men were sent elsewhere, and everyone stashed their gear and hung their hammocks. They reconvened at the center of the village in time for dinner. Sitting beside Tristan at a wood-hewn table, Brynn strove to appear grateful as the first dish arrived.

"That's not what I think it is, is it?" she murmured quietly.

"Yep," Tristan answered, pulling one off the skewer. "Beetle larvae. It's not too bad." He popped it into his mouth.

She didn't want to be that team member that was too picky, but … *shit*. This was high on her disgusting meter. Steeling herself, she slid a giant worm off the stick and quickly put it in her mouth before she could think twice about it.

She couldn't hide her grimace when it touched her tongue.

Chew, dammit. Chew quickly.

Crunch gave way to a gooey inside.

Oh God.

She repressed a gag and quickly swallowed.

Tristan grinned. "I like the nutty undertones."

The only response she could muster was a noise indicating her agreement since she feared she might upchuck at any moment.

When Tristan offered her another one, she waved him off. "Getting full," she said, barely choking the words out. Not the truth, but she was rapidly losing her appetite.

Suddenly the upper canopy came alive with movement. There had to be at least a hundred monkeys above them, screeching as they scampered and swung from tree to tree.

Tristan glanced upward. "I guess they want some appetizers."

"They can have mine," Brynn offered.

She watched with awe as the lean and agile capuchins gathered together, followed closely by the tinier squirrel monkeys.

The Tacanas waved them off, but the monkeys remained, refusing to budge. Brynn guessed they were staying for dinner.

Her hunger was renewed when several women brought plates of fish, which tasted vastly better than the beetle worms. Brynn dug into the food, which was served with a side of boiled potatoes.

Once the meal ended, the monkeys dispersed, and everyone moved to sit around a fire. Solomon began to translate the conversation, although some of the villagers spoke a bit of English.

"This is an old story," Solomon began. "It is to be shared with newcomers such as yourself. A very long time ago, the universe was made. First came the water, called Namu. It gave birth to the earth, called Ki, and the sky, called An. They mated and had a son named Enlil. Enlil ruled the earth. Then the water and the sky had a son named Enki, and it was Enki who created man."

Brynn exchanged a confused look with Irene, who sat across from her, then said, "Where did they learn this story?"

Solomon asked one of the Tacana men, then translated, "It has been shared for as long as anyone can remember."

"What's going on?" Tristan asked her.

She looked at Shea instead. "Wouldn't they have a cosmology that was more pre-Columbian?"

"That would be expected," Shea replied. "But since information can be shared so easily today, they could certainly learn other creation stories. Did you recognize the one he told?"

"It's a Sumerian telling," Irene answered. "Right down to the names."

Shea considered the implication. "That's a strange coincidence."

"Most creation stories are similar," Tristan said.

"True," Shea said. "To a point. I'm not familiar with what the Tacana would normally believe, but Incan mythology revolves around the creator deity Viracocha. If I remember correctly, he created everything—the universe, the sun, the moon, etc."

Solomon nodded. "Yes. We have stories about Viracocha. But the one I told you is the oldest and the most important to the Tacana people who have lived here."

"You mean just in this area?" Brynn asked.

"Yes."

Did that mean …

Tristan jumped her thought. "If this place has been steeped in this mythology, there must be a reason why."

Brynn pinched her eyebrows together. "I know what you're think-ing. There must have been a Sumerian here a long time ago and he or she told them the tale. But think about it. That would have had to be somewhere between two and three thousand years ago. I don't know how old the Tacana are, but I would venture to say not that old. And somewhere in the last four hundred years Christianity arrived in the Americas, overlaying many local religions and shaping them accord-ingly. The story Solomon just told likely would not have survived. So how did it? Are they pulling our leg?"

"You can't rule out the obvious," Tristan conceded.

"I'm touched."

"By what?"

"That you might agree with me that they learned it from someone else. And that it was very possibly recent."

"No," Solomon interrupted. "It is a very old story. They didn't read it on the interweb."

Irene held up a hand. "Wait a minute. What did Jack call that portal that everyone is looking for?"

The lightbulb that went off in Brynn's head blinded her. "Of course. *Innadaltu*."

"The word is probably corrupted from something else," Irene said.

Together she and Irene went back and forth on possible phrases, until they both erupted simultaneously with, "Ina Nanna Daltu!"

Everyone stared at them.

With excitement, Brynn said, "It's Sumerian."

"It means 'The Moon Door,'" Irene added in a rush.

One of the village men smiled and nodded. "Innadaltu."

"Is it around here?" Brynn asked.

Another nod, but despite several rounds of questioning, they weren't able to get the exact location.

Still, the infiltration into this remote area of Amazonian Bolivia of so much Sumerian culture was truly bizarre. What could it possibly mean?

When she voiced this aloud, Tristan smirked and said, "My vote is E.T."

Brynn couldn't completely shake her skepticism on the subject. She puffed out a weary sigh. "And we're back to disagreeing. It was sweet while it lasted, Magee."

"The Devil's greatest art is to make us believe that he does not exist." Solomon's voice took on an eerie emphasis, sending a chill down Brynn's spine, as everyone stopped and stared at the shaman.

Brynn was about to ask what he meant, when he added in a lighter tone, "I read that somewhere."

Regardless, it carried a whiff of prophecy to it. She was beginning to appreciate Tristan's ambivalence toward this man.

TRISTAN HAD SLEPT SURPRISINGLY WELL. The Tacana village had been warm and welcoming, the food had hit the spot, and he had been lulled to sleep by a chorus of chirps and trills and caws. In the morning they'd had a breakfast of ripe papaya, sweet bananas, and strong coffee. After saying farewell, they had set off into the jungle and Brynn had been quite mesmerized by the markings on a tree as they left the outskirts of the settlement. She had pulled out her cell-phone, fired it up since there was no reason to keep it on round-the-clock with no service, and snapped several photos.

"What is it?" he had asked, the others already moving on without them.

"It's strange." She pointed at a marking carved into the bark. "It looks a lot like cuneiform." Her voice held disbelief.

"Can you decipher it?"

"Off the cuff? No. The markings seem ... off. I don't want to slow us down, so I'll study the picture later."

All day they traveled. Tristan suspected they were nearing Conrad's camp because Solomon insisted on not stopping despite that darkness had eventually enveloped them. Using flashlights, Tristan remained vigilant for wild animals, especially since Galloway had a knack for drawing them to her. He was relieved when they finally came to a campfire with the shadows of two men sitting near it.

"Conrad!" Irene pushed past Tristan and ran into the arms of the taller one.

"Irene?" He wrapped her into his embrace. "I've been worried about you."

Leaning back to face him, she said hastily, "I know. It's a long story, but we finally ran into Solomon and he showed us how to find you."

When Conrad raised his eyes to the rest of them, Tristan could sense the man's annoyance as Irene stepped back.

"Always nice to see you, Connie," Tristan said, not bothering to temper the mocking edge to his tone, although he did shake the man's hand.

Conrad appeared to ignore the jab and greeted Shea and Brynn. "I didn't expect so many old friends." He looked at Solomon. "Come back to apologize, did you?"

"I couldn't very well let your friends, *or your wife*, wander around the jungle, could I? Wouldn't want them to die or anything."

"Well, I'll deal with you later."

A ripple of censure filled the air, but Solomon shrugged it off and made his way to the fire, sitting on one of the vacated stools.

"Rigo, come and help my wife," Conrad demanded.

A young Bolivian man stepped forward.

"Rigo?" Dimar asked, squinting into the darkness.

"Yes," the man answered.

"Why didn't Milenka tell me you were here?"

Freddie dumped his pack near the fire. "Because she's not your girlfriend anymore."

Dimar's back stiffened. "That's because you stole her."

"Don't tell her where I am," Rigo said hastily. "She thinks I'm in Lima. She didn't want me going back into the jungle."

"What's going on?" Tristan asked.

Freddie answered, "Rigo is Milenka's brother."

"Is Pico here?" Irene asked.

"No," Conrad replied. "Why?"

"He took the artifact from me and ran off. I was certain he would bring it here."

Conrad sighed. "Well, shit." He gave an impatient wave forward. "All right, everybody come on in. Might as well make yourselves at home."

He reached for Brynn's pack, but Tristan intervened. "She came in with me."

"Really?" Conrad looked at Tristan with a suspicious glare.

"Irene didn't wait for me in La Paz," Brynn said. "I had to find another way. Tristan and Dimar were available."

"I didn't realize you knew one another."

"We didn't," Brynn said. "We met at Isla del Sol almost two weeks ago."

"Never underestimate the power of kismet," Conrad said, his voice warm and chummy.

Tristan didn't bother to hide his scowl. "This isn't a friendly visit, Fontana."

Conrad chuckled. "It wasn't necessarily cordial two years ago, but I'd thought we'd become friends."

"Your wife stole something from me. On your behalf, apparently. And I had to come all this way to retrieve it."

"Is this true, Irene?"

"According to Tristan, he'd already purchased the tablet before me," she replied, sitting on one of the canvas stools that Rigo had put out. "However, I had no idea."

Conrad swung his gaze to Tristan. "Well, there you go. It was a misunderstanding, and it would seem the person you have a beef with is the broker."

"Thank you for explaining it to me," Tristan deadpanned.

"When we find Pico, we can address this further."

In the muted firelight, Tristan didn't miss the quick frown that Irene threw her husband's way. Clearly, Irene had no intention of addressing it further.

Hell. He was going to have to steal the damned thing back. There was always a stumbling block when he tried to do the right thing. "What if Pico's dead?" Tristan added.

Dimar's chin snapped up. "Pico is dead?"

"No," Conrad answered, his voice firm, and took a seat. "Pico knows the jungle as well as you boys do. Everyone talks about the Castanos cousins and what good guides they are. I have every confidence he'll turn up." He turned to Irene. "How did Pico get the tablet?"

"We were attacked, Conrad." Her voice was threaded with panic, and Tristan had to concede that it sounded real as she explained what had happened.

Conrad reached over and took her hand, concern written plainly on his face. "My God. Are you all right?"

She nodded. "I'm so glad we found you."

He gently lifted a palm to her cheek and leaned close, whispering something to her. It was clear that Conrad was devoted to his wife. No wonder she was willing to do the nasty work of thievery and smuggling for him.

Since there were no more chairs, Tristan sat on his knapsack beside Brynn. Rigo poured everyone a weak cup of coffee, which surprisingly hit the spot, chasing away the fatigue of the day.

Tristan looked at Conrad. "Are you going to tell us why you're deep in the Amazon and in sudden need of a Sumerian artifact?"

"Well, since you've come all this way, I'll show you tomorrow," Conrad replied. "I've learned that it's best not to visit the site during the night."

"Why?" Brynn asked.

Tristan chuckled. "He's talking about spooks."

Conrad fixed a pointed stare at Tristan. "You don't want to mess with the spirits."

"The *wrong* spirits," Solomon said. "I tried to tell you, Conrad."

Brynn shifted her attention to Fontana. "What exactly have you found down here?"

His eyes shone in the firelight as his gaze circled the group. "You won't believe it," he said.

With his attention sufficiently snagged, Tristan sought to keep his voice level. "Try me."

"Proof that links Sumerian culture to the Amazon Basin."

CHAPTER 16

Brynn looked at the man sitting across the fire. Conrad Fontana had always been a quietly imposing professor. He was tall with a muscular physique he honed with a devotion to the gym. He could be intimidating, and many students had found him less than personable. Some were openly afraid of him, but Brynn hadn't ever felt that way. Growing up with her dad—Big Jim Galloway—who had a larger-than-life persona, as well as his brother, Uncle Simon, and her two older brothers who were always reaching for the dangerous and daunting in life, she was accustomed to males of this sort.

Having just been to Turtle Village, it was clear *something* was going on down here and that somehow it was related to Sumeria, but the skeptic in her kept whispering that there had to be a plausible explanation. So, on the heels of that thought, Conrad's bold pronouncement caused a knot to form in her stomach.

Screeches echoed from the jungle, along with buzzing noises and the rustling of branches. When there was a crunch of underbrush, a frisson of unease raised gooseflesh on Brynn's arms and down the back of her neck.

What lay in wait in the dark was almost as frightening as the path that Conrad was proposing, a path that was likely littered with subterfuge and ill intentions.

Irene and Conrad were really going to do this. They were going to lie to the archaeological community. They were going to lie to the world.

Freddie had departed to set up his hammock, so Tristan grabbed his stool and settled beside Brynn, his leg touching hers from hip to thigh. It was an overt move and Brynn welcomed it, leaning into him, accepting the refuge he offered.

Taking a steadying breath, she said, "There have been theories of contact between the Asian and European continents and South America prior to the arrival of Christopher Columbus, but most of these have been debunked because the artifacts found are often not as old as first proposed. I don't mean to sound pedantic, but I learned that from Irene."

Shea chimed in. "There have been inferences that languages are similar—there was speculation that the Zuni language in New Mexico was linguistically similar to Japanese—but there's simply not enough proof to say there was contact."

"But what if there was?" Conrad said. "Don't forget about the Fuente Magna artifact."

Brynn sighed. "That's very controversial."

Conrad nodded. "Yes, but that doesn't necessarily mean you should dismiss it."

"Remind me again about that one?" Tristan asked, shifting beside Brynn but keeping his thigh in contact with hers.

Conrad spoke before she could. "It's a stone bowl that was found near Lake Titicaca in the 50's, and it features cuneiform markings. There are many who believe it was Sumerian."

"The problem," Brynn said, "is that details of the bowl's excavation are nonexistent. Simply going off the markings isn't enough to say where it was from. It could've been planted, and likely in this century, not five thousand years ago." She paused. "What kind of proof have you found, Dr. Fontana?"

Conrad gently took hold of Irene's hand and lifted it to his lips, dropping a kiss behind her knuckles. "We've found a place the locals call Innadaltu."

Solomon muttered in a different language under his breath, and Brynn was certain it contained obscenities. So, the shaman hadn't wanted Conrad to find the place.

"It's a strange site." His smile was almost serene, his eyes glowing with delight. "You won't believe it, but I'm glad you're all here. I've been struggling with the markings, but they're definitely cuneiform." Conrad released Irene's hand and draped his arm around her shoulders.

"It seems highly improbable," Brynn said, shaking her head. She barely stopped the next words that threatened to tumble from her lips. *We're onto you. We know it's a hoax.*

"Is it?" Conrad asked. "I'll grant you, I've only been here a few days, but it's not like anything Amazonian, that's for certain."

"They must be fake," she replied. *And created by you. Or someone else.* Perhaps the same person or persons who influenced the occupants of Turtle Village. The same ones who may have planted the Fuenta Magna bowl decades ago.

"I understand your skepticism, but I'll show them to you and Irene in the morning. Maybe you both can make heads or tails of it."

Exhaustion kept her from arguing further. There was nothing to be done about it anyway. At least, not for tonight.

"Have you been down here all summer?" Shea asked.

"Yes," Conrad answered.

"And you only just found this ruin?"

"Yes. You know how it is. Rumors abound. Indigenous tribes have fables that must be meted out. But I'd first heard the story about Innadaltu when we were all here last time." Conrad stood and helped Irene to her feet. "We might as well get some sleep. It'll be snug, darlin', but I'm happy to have you here finally."

Irene released a bashful laugh, and Brynn hoped the camp wasn't about to get an earful of a Conrad and Irene love reunion.

The couple disappeared into the darkness, a small flashlight in Conrad's hand showing the progress to their hammocks. And they each had their own hammock. There was no reason to share, except that they'd been apart for months. Somewhere in her gear, Brynn had a set of foam earplugs, the type airlines passed out in First Class. She really ought to dig them out, if only to drown out the incessant buzz of the night jungle.

Dimar, Freddie, Rigo, and Solomon stood and with barely mumbled *goodnights* they departed, the darkness swallowing them up.

"Anybody have any tunes?" Tristan said quietly. "'Cause I really don't want to listen to Connie getting his jig on."

Brynn released a tortured groan as she leaned forward, covering her ears with her hands. "It's like being trapped with your parents in a hotel room," she whispered.

"I might still have some juice in my cellphone," Shea said, digging the device out of a buttoned pocket along the side of his tan pants. "Care for some AC/DC?"

"Play it, man," Tristan said.

The hard beats of *Back in Black* began.

"Have either of you ever heard of Percy Fawcett?" Brynn asked.

"Yeah," Shea replied. "He was a British explorer who came to the Amazon several times in the early 1900's. He eventually disappeared, never to be seen again, probably killed by an indigenous tribe."

"He came down here looking for a lost city," she said. "A city that was eventually found."

"It was said he shot a 62-foot anaconda." The pride in Tristan's voice was hard to miss.

"Why do those snakes keep getting bigger with every story I hear?" Brynn asked in exasperation, trying to calm the bone-deep fear it invoked.

Shea glared at Tristan. "You always were the worst part of a camp out."

Tristan chuckled. "Don't worry. Snakes that big would be very private creatures, hiding away in the deepest recesses of the jungle and never having contact with humans. I didn't mean to scare you," he added for Brynn's benefit.

"You didn't," she lied.

Shea shifted his attention back to her. "What were you saying about Fawcett?"

"Right," she said. "He believed that a complex civilization had lived down here at one time. He called it the Lost City of Z. When it was identified a few years back, it truly *was* magnificent, but it was certainly not evidence of aliens."

"Your point, Galloway?" Tristan said.

She had already voiced her concerns to Tristan earlier, but not Shea. She plowed ahead, keeping her voice as low as she could and still be heard over the hard beats of the music. Brynn was beginning to think the AC/DC band members had come to the jungle to hone their voices—they quite complemented the primeval noises.

"I'm skeptical," she said. "Either Conrad is completely misreading the signs and symbols, which I find hard to believe since he's no idiot and is quite good in his field, or I have to wonder if this *find* of his is an elaborate forgery."

"Very possible," Shea agreed.

"Or maybe," Tristan cut in, "it's the first definitive proof there was contact with other parts of the world along with one of the earliest civilizations ever documented."

"Contact like that might have gone back to the first or second century," Shea said, "but what you're proposing is more than two thousand years before that."

"Why is it so farfetched?" Tristan countered, and Brynn was beginning to suspect that he liked to argue for the sake of arguing, since he had somewhat agreed with her earlier theory that Irene and Conrad were executing a hoax. "You're in the jungle right now," he said, his gaze on Shea. "You can see how easily it swallows up evidence of anything."

Brynn frowned. "But don't you think something like this would've been found by now?"

"Well, Tristan is somewhat right on that count," Shea said. "Who knows what the jungle is hiding. They might never have found the City of Z without lidar."

Brynn knew about the laser measuring system. Using an airplane, the apparatus could map terrain that was inaccessible on foot and covered in jungle canopy. It had revealed the outline of the vast City of Z, which otherwise would have remained hidden.

"So we should get some lidar out here?" she asked.

"Maybe," Tristan replied.

"Why is no one stating the obvious here?" she asked, lowering her voice which forced Tristan and Shea to bring their faces closer to hers. Shea also turned down the volume of the music emanating from his phone.

"And what's that?" Tristan asked.

"Conrad, and possibly Irene, are committing a hoax."

"I agree," Shea said without hesitation.

Brynn contemplated the fire. "If it's true, then I don't understand the endgame. Are they doing it for fame and fortune?"

"They want to legitimize it," Tristan said.

"What, exactly?" she asked.

"Those that believe in the alien intervention theory, at any level— whether it be little green men abducting people in their flying saucers, or that aliens were kept and dissected at Area 51 in Roswell, or that a long time ago aliens tinkered with the DNA of Neanderthal man to create the humans we know today—have all been labeled as fringe crackpots. Crazies. Did you ever think that such accusations were done on purpose?"

"Government cover-ups?" Brynn tried to make her question light-hearted, but Tristan didn't look amused.

"Not necessarily governments," he said.

Shea chuckled. "Secret societies. It's like sitting around the dinner table with your dad."

Tristan glared at his cousin. "You can't tell me it doesn't tweak your interest."

"Look," Shea said. "It's fun to imagine. It makes for chilling books and scary movies, but the reality is that life on Earth is difficult and slow, and creatures come and go, and there's no grand design to any of it."

"Don't say that to your Catholic mama," Tristan retorted.

Shea sighed. "I try to keep my divine doubts to myself."

"Look, maybe this is a hoax," Tristan continued, "but what if there's a bigger picture? Conrad may be trying to lay the groundwork to protect future work. Real, actual finds."

Brynn was appalled. "You sound almost proud of what they might be doing. A lie is still a lie."

"Sometimes misdirection is necessary for the greater good. The world isn't always so black and white, Galloway."

Her temper flared. "The world is what we make of it. So how about filling it with some integrity?"

Tristan held up his hands as if warding off her attack. "Hey, don't shoot the messenger. I'm not saying it's right. But people do stupid, questionable, and ridiculous shit all the time. Quit acting so shocked that Connie and Irene are possibly executing a gigantic lie to further their careers."

"What careers?" Brynn demanded in a strangled whisper. "This will ruin them and possibly me in the process. What can they be thinking?"

"They're believers." Shea's tone held a grimness to it. "Just like Uncle Charlie. They may be manipulating discoveries and data for their own agenda, but at the end of the day they simply believe that alien intervention must be true, and they're damn well gonna find evidence of it, even if they have to unscrupulously doctor a site to find it."

Tristan tensed beside her, and Brynn turned to him, a sudden realization settling over her. "Is that what your father did?"

"Any proof is good proof," he said quietly, running a hand down his face. "That's what the old man would say."

"Uncle Charlie was a modern-day shyster," Shea said. "And he was driven by his convictions." After a pause, he added, "That made him a dangerous combination."

Tristan released a thick, heavy sigh. "Maybe." He glanced up at Shea. "Stop painting him as some kind of monster."

"You knew he had a screw loose, Tristan. It's why you studied physics instead of joining the family conspiracy business. You knew it was fucked up."

Tristan lifted his chin, his eyes flashing. "Yeah, I knew it. But no one has the right to tell someone that everything they believe is bullshit."

Brynn understood. It was getting harder to ignore the sharp pain in her chest when she thought of Conrad and Irene. She had studied with them, believed in them, and now it was all shot to hell. Or was it?

"What if we all agree to have an open mind?" she asked.

Shea and Tristan both looked at her. She shifted her gaze between them.

"Tristan's right," she said. At Shea's furrowed brow, she added, "To a point. Progress is never made without taking chances. Perhaps I've been too swift to condemn Irene and Conrad. Maybe we need to leave a little room open for the impossible to shine through. Honestly, I've been worried about all the work I've put in at school, that if my professors are proven to be hucksters, then I'll be guilty by association. But maybe we're here to be witnesses." She settled her gaze on Shea. "Just like you were two years ago."

"I didn't ask to be," he rebutted.

"Just like I don't want to be right now," she said. "But maybe we have to stop worrying about our own personal shit. We can't always choose the circumstances we find ourselves in, but we can choose how we view our role in all of this."

The flames of the fire displayed their primal dance, lighting the way through the dark.

Tristan turned to her, and she returned the sparkle igniting in his eyes.

"Or in the words of the Carpenters," she added, "we've only just begun."

CHAPTER 17

The next morning, after a breakfast of black coffee, powdered eggs, and tortillas, Brynn fell in line with the others and followed Conrad down a narrow trail hugged by jungle on either side.

She was down to her last clean t-shirt and hoped that later she would be able to rinse out the dirty laundry that filled her duffel bag. Who was she kidding? Clothing would never dry in this humidity, and she'd end up with a mix of body odor and mildew.

A Kobayashi Maru, as her brother Alec liked to say, referencing an old Star Trek film. It was basically a no-win scenario. In the movie, cadets in the military program were required to go through the Kobayashi Maru simulation, only there was no way to beat it. It was meant as a measure of leadership skills. However, the iconic character Captain Kirk cheated and reprogrammed the computer so that it was possible to complete the mission. He didn't like to lose. Alec didn't like to lose, either. Neither of her brothers did, really.

But Captain Kirk is a fictional person, and sometimes there really is no solution.

Which brought her back to her enticing body aroma. She wasn't smelling like roses. Not that anyone else was, so why should it matter, but a woman had to have priorities when it came to hygiene.

Brynn didn't think she had a problem with losing. She'd certainly lost many a surfing competition when she was on the youth circuit, although she had always been driven to keep up with Alec and Ty. She'd definitely worked hard for the college degrees she currently possessed—an undergrad in Middle Eastern Studies with an emphasis on Sumerian and Akkadian languages, and a master's degree specializing in Sumerian cuneiform. She'd been determined to study and learn Akkadian, since it would complement her already strong knowledge in Sumerian, courtesy of her gramps. It had been odd, really, how much he had stoked her childhood curiosity in a five-thousand-year-old language.

Akkadian was an extinct language spoken in ancient Mesopotamia until it was replaced by Aramaic around the eighth century B.C. It was the earliest attested Semitic language and used cuneiform script, the same as Sumerian, although the two languages were unrelated. But if Brynn had learned anything from Grandpa Milano, it was to do your homework, to learn beyond that which was required of most.

A memory surfaced of her ten-year-old self sitting at the kitchen table in her grandparents' house in Pennsylvania.

"Will you give me a hint, Gramps?"

Her grandfather had been teaching her to decipher cuneiform, and he had several books open to photographs of clay tablets. She chewed on the end of a pencil, her brain hurting as she tried to translate the symbols before her, the result a mishmash of letters and words scratched on a piece of paper.

"No," he said as he washed and dried the dishes he had used to serve a lunch of tuna fish, cottage cheese, and freshly-sliced peaches.

"Why not?" She gulped down the last of her milk. "Mrs. Campbell always gives us hints during math class."

"She shouldn't. Hints will only teach you to memorize patterns. Don't let anyone ever tell you that the struggle isn't worth it. Even if your answers are wrong, you're learning to *think*. That's more valuable than me giving you the right answer *right now*. When you're older, you'll understand. In fact, you told me so."

Brynn's face pinched into a frown. Of late, Gramps had been saying some strange stuff, not the least of which was when, about a year previously, he had determined that she would spend part of every summer with him and Gram, and during that time he would teach her the symbols and writing of ancient Mesopotamia.

Despite the fact that none of her friends had any idea what she was talking about, Brynn had found it rather fun, if only to spend time with her grandfather.

"Then I'm gonna need some brain food after that old-people lunch," she had teased.

He hung the dishtowel on a rack and smiled. "Your grandmother's homemade chocolate chip cookies coming right up …."

A pang of longing pierced Brynn, and she stumbled on a tree root.

"Easy." Tristan's hand reached out to steady her.

They came to a small clearing and fanned out around Conrad as he knelt down. "We'll need to crawl a bit." He disappeared on all-fours into a tunnel hollowed out in the foliage.

Irene followed. Brynn would have hung back, but Tristan motioned for her to go next. She dreaded encountering any creepy-crawlies lying in wait. With hope, the noise from Conrad and Irene would scare them away.

Brynn was glad she'd worn pants since the ground was not very forgiving. Branches scraped her face and arms as she moved slowly forward. She paused to sneeze, her nose overwhelmed by the musty smell of moist soil and thickly covered shrubs. Scrambling, she was relieved when she finally emerged from the tunnel and was able to stand. She crowded onto a ledge jutting from a rocky hillside.

"Is this part of a ruin?" she asked, reaching out to touch one of the stones.

"Yes," Conrad said. "We need to climb now."

Gramps was wrong. The ability to parse out a pattern was a handy skill in archaeology. She ran her fingers down the manmade structure and smiled at Tristan beside her. "Earth to Major Tom."

He returned her grin. "Who says David Bowie wasn't an extraterrestrial?"

Although a bit steep in parts, there were good footholds and Brynn had no trouble ascending, but with the rising sun and thickening humidity, she was soon drenched in sweat, rivulets repeatedly stinging her eyes.

When they reached the top, she pulled a handkerchief from her pack and wiped her forehead and face. Tristan took a drink of water from his canteen, then passed it to her. She gratefully took a swig, then handed it back.

Now that they were on top of the hill, she could see it was as over-grown as down low, but Conrad made his way to a blue stone enclosure. It was carved into the mountainside, featuring a doorway without a door and a notched platform that might be used for an offering.

Brynn touched the smooth surface, stunned. "How did this get here?" It was huge and obviously shaped by someone, or many some-ones, and clearly not from a local quarry.

Tristan dropped to a crouch. "It's a type of granite. Bluestone, if I'm not mistaken. It probably came from the Andes mountains."

Brynn stared down at him. "How the hell did it get here?"

Tristan's knowing smile gave his answer. *Extraterrestrial help.* "Bluestone contains a crystal that has excellent piezoelectric qualities," he said. "It's also magnetic."

"Are you saying it's a beacon?"

He shrugged.

Irene stepped forward, perspiring profusely, and said to Conrad, "How on earth did you find this?"

"It was Rigo," Conrad said over his shoulder. "I do believe Solomon was trying to keep me from here, which is why I eventually sent him away."

Solomon hadn't accompanied them this morning, instead remaining in camp.

"Why would he do that?" Brynn asked.

"I think he believes I'll desecrate the site," Conrad answered. "But, of course, he's wrong."

"Is he?" Shea cut in. "Isn't that what you and Charlie did the last time we were here?"

Conrad stopped and faced Tristan's cousin. "With the mummies?"

He appeared sincere. "We moved those according to protocol. You were here. You saw it. We had government approval."

"Until you didn't. Then you sneaked one out and proceeded to mishandle it."

"That's your opinion, Hartigan. We were conducting a scientific study."

"Is Solomon worried about looting?" Brynn asked.

"Perhaps," Conrad answered. "It's why I didn't let Dimar and Freddie accompany us."

Brynn's brows knit together. "Couldn't Rigo just tell them?"

"I suppose. But he assured me he wouldn't."

"We should leave this place now!" Solomon's booming voice startled them all. They spun around to face the shaman, who was breathing heavily, having obviously followed them.

"I've already been here several times," Conrad replied. "Nothing bad has happened."

"This is a sacred place, used only by shamans. We should not be here."

"Calm down." Conrad emphasized his words with his hands. "We're just looking around. That's all I've done so far."

Solomon paused as if considering his words, then he gave a slight shake of his head, as if doomsday was upon them. "There can be spirits here. Dangerous ones that are best left undisturbed."

"What's the purpose of the bluestone?" Brynn asked.

"Shamans use such places as doorways into other dimensions."

"Then we'll be okay," Tristan said. "None of us are medicine men except you. We won't be dabbling with the spirits."

Solomon placed his hands on his hips, taking what looked like a warrior's stance. "We will do a ceremony."

"No," Tristan moaned. "No way."

Solomon glared at him. "It's not up to you. You all must be cleansed, or you will pollute this place. I'm afraid I must insist."

As Tristan muttered swear words under his breath, Brynn made a mental note to ask him why he hated the ceremonies so much.

"I'm sure that would be okay," Brynn said, trying to diffuse the standoff. Besides, she guessed that Irene really wanted to have a chat with the spirits—she had said as much, although she'd planned to have the Moon Tablet on hand for it. But maybe the ceremony would still work anyway. Not that any of this was scientific, but Brynn was curious enough to go along for the ride. For now.

"Yes, fine," Conrad said. "We'll do it."

Everyone nodded except Tristan.

"Tomorrow then," Solomon said. "I'll start getting everything ready." He turned and left them.

Tristan ran a hand through his hair. "It's a waste of time."

"But we might learn something useful," Irene said, then looked at Conrad. "Is there more here?"

He nodded and took them around the large granite altar. Behind it was a cave entrance. Conrad pulled a flashlight from his pack, as did Tristan. Brynn had a small one in her pocket, which she switched on.

They were able to walk inside but Conrad, Tristan, and Shea were forced to hunch over due to their height. As they entered the chamber, Brynn scanned her flashlight along the side walls, but there were no substantial markings. When Tristan stopped suddenly, she bumped into him.

"Sorry." She leaned around to see what they were looking at.

Conrad lit two kerosene lamps that hung from a bolt in the wall, while Tristan and Shea continued scanning the area with their flashlights. On the back wall, an array of symbols became visible. Brynn pushed around Tristan in the tight quarters and came shoulder-to-shoulder with Irene. They both stood stock still.

"It's cuneiform," Irene whispered, "just like on the Moon Tablet."

Scanning the symbols, Brynn masked her growing excitement—or was it anxiety?—from those around her.

Could it be?

She'd have to study and compare the markings to be certain, but they looked awfully similar to those written in the notebook Gram had recently sent her.

A shiver rippled through her.

Gramps had somehow had access to these truncated glyphs.

TRISTAN STOOD at the granite altar with Conrad and Shea. While Conrad had taken photographs of the markings inside the ruin, Irene and Brynn had stayed back to investigate further. They were so entranced, in fact, that Tristan was pretty sure they didn't notice the men leaving.

Shea ran a hand down the smooth granite face. "You finally did it. You linked the Amazon to Mesopotamia."

"I know you were a skeptic," Conrad replied.

"And you're a tenacious bastard." Shea looked at him, his gaze definitely frosty. "If it's true."

"You calling me a liar, Hartigan?"

"You said it, I didn't."

Conrad's face hardened. "I didn't forge those markings."

Tristan raised a hand to cool down the standoff. "All right, all right. It's worth investigating, which is why I'm guessing you brought Irene down here. And why she brought Brynn. You suck at Sumerian, Conrad."

Conrad arched a brow. "And you're completely illiterate in it."

"True. When we find Pico, you can return my artifact, and I'll be on my way."

An amused smile ghosted Conrad's mouth. "You sure you don't want to stay? If we'd only had Rigo back then, we would've found it sooner. It's what your father had been looking for."

Tristan remained silent, not wanting to rise to Fontana's bait.

Conrad continued, "It's about more than proving there was contact between the Asian continent and the Americas going back five thousand years, although that's a mind-blowing narrative for the history books. But there's something else."

Tristan narrowed his eyes. "What?"

"The ancient winds of time are revealing technology primitive man didn't possess. Not the Romans, the Egyptians, not the likes of Plato or Aristotle or even Isaac Newton, though not for want of trying."

The glint in Conrad's eyes reminded Tristan why they'd had a falling out two years ago. The man was a smooth-talking but ever-abrasive asshole.

"We're close. I can feel it."

Shea crossed his arms. "To digging up more mummies and desecrating the dead?"

"If the mummies prove to be something more than human, then yes. But it's more than that. It's about transmutation."

"The Philosopher's Stone," Tristan muttered, his conversation with Brynn echoing back at him. "Are you saying it's here?"

"I'm very interested in what's written on those cave walls," Conrad said. "And Irene was bringing the Moon Tablet because we believe it might be the key to all of it. The symbols for both appear to be similar."

"Is that why you had Brynn write that paper?" Tristan asked. "To help you prove that the Sumerians knew how to turn lead into gold?"

"Yes, Brynn's thesis lays some important groundwork about the metallurgical abilities of the Sumerians. But it's more than that. Symbols and rites that accompany metallurgical operations bring an active collaboration between man and nature. It was a type of cosmic embryology to transmute metals. The Philosopher's Stone would supersede time. It would contain opposites, reconciling the Dark and the Light."

"What the hell are you talking about?" Shea asked, incredulous.

"I'm talking about the transmutation of man and the Cosmos. It's more than UFO sightings, and government conspiracies, and meteorites that might contain an amoeba of bacteria. It's about a breadth of knowledge that was gifted to us from the stars."

Shea raised an eyebrow. "And you think that's *here*, in this cave?"

"Well," Conrad replied, "we're going to find out, aren't we?"

Tristan laughed, and said, "You gotta go big or go home, as my dad would say."

Shea turned and walked away. "You're all fuckin' nuts."

CHAPTER 18

Brynn wolfed down her dinner, then grabbed her pack and dug out her grandfather's journal. She probably should have scanned and backed it up somehow before lugging the paper journal into the muggy jungle, but it was too late for that now. She hadn't realized how important it might be until she'd seen those markings in Conrad's cave today. They appeared eerily similar to Gramps's handwritten notes. But she would need to study them to be certain.

Brynn had always held the belief that Gramps was simply an armchair enthusiast, that his translations and conclusions were nothing more than the musings of a hobbyist. And so she hadn't really taken him too seriously, despite the fact that he had instructed her well when he had taught her cuneiform.

But now … she was being forced to rethink just what her grandfather had been. According to her mother, Lily Milano Galloway, he had loved to travel, and he had frequently taken his wife and daughter on journeys to the Asian and European continents, saving his vacation days from his job as a metallurgist at a roll foundry so they could travel for several weeks at a time. Brynn's mom had clambered through ruins from China to Egypt, an exotic childhood filled with the wonders of the world.

But was it possible that Gramps had been more than a mere traveler? In addition to the cuneiform glyphs that made no sense, Gramps had also included sections about many of his sojourns to gather knowledge and acquire artifacts. And honestly, his tenaciousness had bordered on reckless, if many of his recountings were to be believed. As a child, she'd had no clue of the risk her grandfather had taken at times for the information he had amassed. Had Mom and Gram ever realized how dangerous his hobby had been?

And the irony wasn't lost on her that Magee reminded her of Mico Milano, or that Brynn's own blood sang with the same stubborn interest in the ancient world.

Wanting to make the most of the waning daylight, Brynn found a place tucked away from the group, dug the notebook out of her pack, and began scanning through it for clues.

"Is that it?" Magee asked, startling her.

"Quit sneaking up on me."

He dropped to her level, kneeling. "Better me than Connie or Dimar."

Her gaze locked with his, and she was struck by the intense blue of his eyes, like a cloudless sky or a baby's blanket. It must be the light, she thought. Or some inner fire announcing he was sent by the gods.

"You do look a little suspicious over here hiding," he added, sitting down beside her. "You still thinking this place is a hoax?"

"Do you?" she countered.

His dark brows lifted, smoothing the fine lines at the corner of his eyes. "My dear sweet Brynn. You're starting to sip the Kool-Aid."

"If it's a hoax, it's a damned complicated one."

"Why?"

She indicated the notebook in her lap.

"Your grandfather?" Tristan asked. "The symbols match?"

"I've only made a cursory pass, but yes, it appears that some do. But he doesn't offer a straightforward translation."

"Are you sure what he wrote is legit?"

Her frustration rose quickly, reaching a crest in less than a second.

"You're seriously asking me this? The man whose father touted the existence of little green men?"

"Look, you don't have to convince me that my dad manipulated information for his own agenda. I'm just asking what kind of man your grandfather was. Passionate idealists can play massive head games."

"Is that how you think of your father?"

Tristan narrowed his eyes. "Even in the deepest web of lies and fabrications, there's almost always a kernel of truth."

"I suppose."

"It's that truth I'm after."

She inhaled a lungful of air, pungent with jungle life and a hint of musky man beside her. It would be so much easier if she didn't like Magee.

"I have no reason to believe that Gramps lied about any of his findings or research," she said steadily.

"You don't think it's possible he came down here and found this place?"

She shook her head. "No."

"Have you considered that *he* could have planted the glyphs?"

"He didn't!" She took a breath to let the white-hot anger his question had ignited dissipate. "Gramps wasn't like that. And as far as I know, he never came to South America. He was always more interested in Europe or Asia."

"Maybe he invented them and showed them to someone else, who then came down here and had a scribble-fest."

"Not everyone is a con man." She really didn't like thinking that her Gramps could have been involved in something shady, even if it were without his knowledge.

"Are you sure your grandfather wasn't ever down here?"

She eyed Magee. "You really think *he* made the markings?"

"His own personal Sumerian sub-language, spreading it around the world to help conspiracy theorists everywhere."

Feeling unmoored from a life she thought she knew, she said, "I don't know. I don't recall him talking about South America. I guess I'd have to ask my mother." Could Gramps have made the markings in the cave? It was an unbelievable hypothesis. "I just don't think that's a viable conclusion, Magee."

"Yeah, I'll admit it's stretching things a bit. But if you have to prove the contents of this site are valid, you'll have to release your grandfather's notebook, and you can bet your ass you'll get questions like these."

"So you're trying to help me?"

"Of course. I've got your back, Galloway. Unless you're the forger." He watched with the tenacity of a fox playing with its prey.

"You're such an asshole," she uttered under her breath.

He grinned. "But I think you like me anyway." He nudged her shoulder with his. "Don't worry. I don't think you did it. You wear your integrity like a badge of honor. The rest of us aren't even close."

"Except maybe Shea," she said, wondering why he was letting her off the hook, since he had no reason to believe she *wasn't* in on the possible scam. Honestly, she had the most damning evidence of all— Gramps's notebook.

"Shea always was a little goody-two shoes."

She sighed. "There's nothing wrong with that."

"No, I suppose not." He levelled a hot gaze on her.

A flush of heat that had nothing to do with the steamy jungle rolled across her skin, igniting a new wave of perspiration. And hunger for Magee.

"I guess there's no hope," she murmured.

"So fatalistic, Galloway."

She understood his meaning. They were talking about them. As a couple. And all the naked acrobatics that went with it. Instead of confirming it, however, she said, "I'm going to forever smell like a sweaty monkey."

A slow grin spread across his tantalizing mouth, a mouth she'd envisioned kissing far too often in the past few days. "I don't mind. I've often wondered what it would've been like if we'd met under different circumstances," he said.

"Cleaner, maybe?"

"But a lot less fun."

She shook off the spell that Magee could cast over her just with a look. "I really thought you'd be doing cartwheels through camp over all of this," she said, nodding in the general direction of the portal of Innadaltu.

"Let's just say I'm a little skeptical. Conrad is convinced there's proof here that will help him turn lead into gold."

"What?"

"He's looking for the damned Philosopher's Stone. Even I'm not crazy enough to think it's in the Amazon. And philosophy and alchemy aside, turning lead into gold has already been accomplished. Nothing magical about it, just a shit-ton of energy is needed. But he seems to think the Moon Tablet will offer some clues, so we need Pico to show up and present us with it—which I'm beginning to suspect is more and more unlikely—and then you and Irene can work your translation magic."

Brynn frowned. "Did you tell him about this notebook?"

"No," Tristan said quietly, his eyes softening. "I have no intention of giving him a leg up if I can help it."

"Thanks."

"They're all nutjobs here, Brynn."

She released a quiet laugh. "Including you?"

"I never claimed to be normal. But I was counting on you to be."

"Thanks. I think." She took a quick gulp of water from her canteen. "Can I ask you something?"

He nodded.

"Why don't you want to do Solomon's ceremony tomorrow? What are you so afraid of?"

The easy rapport they'd been sharing vanished, as Tristan threw up a wall that was all too clear.

She wasn't deterred. "What did you see when we were with Pepito and Carla?" she asked. That first shamanic ceremony felt like a life-time ago, and Brynn missed Pepito's warmth and general good humor, and the obvious fondness the elderly Bolivian had for Magee.

Tristan looked away, stretching out a leg.

"It's happened before, hasn't it? You keep having the same vision." She wasn't sure why she kept pressing him, except that something told her it was important. And she'd opened up to him about Gramps and the notebook. It wasn't that she thought she deserved equal treatment; it was more that she had a craving to know Magee better. To understand him.

She stared at his profile. "C'mon, Magee. Tell me."

He gave her a sidelong glance, then started picking up small stones and throwing them at a tree trunk about ten feet away. "You know about the car accident when I was nine. While I was in the coma, I had a vision of figures emerging from a white light, standard stuff I guess, except that my mind was filled with scary stuff like aliens and UFOs and abductions. My dad, you know. So it's not a huge leap that I was a bit terrorized. I thought I was being visited by extraterrestrials, that they'd come to take me away. And maybe they did take me and I don't remember, but then it was over, and afterward I got better. My dad even said it was a miracle, since I came out of a coma the doctors thought I never would." He paused. "Logically, I know it was likely some kind of dream or hallucination but buried deep in my amygdala is a fear I couldn't shake then, and which I seem to relive at inopportune moments—such as a shamanic ceremony. In plain terms, I'm terrified the aliens will come back for me." He laughed, a bit unsteadily. "There you have it. Tristan Magee's Fears 101. And when we were with Miss Carla, I was right back in that hospital room."

"Did you see the vision?"

"Yes, in all its horrifying glory."

"Have you tried to speak with one of them?"

He frowned. "I know you're trying to offer therapy, but I don't need it."

"I'm saying, maybe next time—if there's a next time—maybe try talking with one. Ask what it wants. If it does want you for medical experiments, then at least you'll know."

"Gee, thanks. That would really put my mind at ease."

"It's not you today that needs to be put at ease, it's your nine-year-old self. You need to reassure that piece of yourself."

He blew out a breath. "Maybe."

A commotion drew their attention. Solomon came into camp with another man who looked a lot like Dimar.

"Is that Pico?" she asked.

"The one and only." Magee stood, adding in a low voice, "You better stash that notebook."

She did, then grabbed his extended hand. He hauled her to her feet, and she snatched up her backpack to keep it close.

Pico sat on a stool and peeled off his own pack, dropping it to the ground.

Tristan rushed forward as if Pico had just manhandled a glass plate. "Easy."

Pico jumped to his feet, his thick black hair damp with sweat. "Get away." Then his eyes widened with recognition. "Tristan?"

Tristan stopped short of grabbing the man's belongings. "Nice to see you again, Pico. Now, hand over the clay tablet you're carrying, and we'll never have to see each other again."

Pico wiped his broad nose with the back of his hand and shifted his gaze to everyone standing in a circle around them. His stained t-shirt and trousers had seen better days, and Brynn noted that he resembled Dimar's short stature more than Freddie's lanky build.

"I guess you didn't expect such a jolly reunion," Tristan added.

Brynn was certain she saw a sneer on Pico's wide lips when he looked at Magee. A second later, however, his face was impassive, his dark eyes giving away nothing.

Tristan smiled, but it was far from congenial. "All your best buddies back in one place."

"Do you have it?" Irene asked Pico.

The man's shoulders sagged as he once again sat on the stool and placed his hands on his knees, shaking his head. "I don't."

"What do you mean you don't have it?" Tristan demanded.

"I had trouble and I lost it."

Tristan swore under his breath, then said, "Where?"

"Yesterday." His gaze landed on Rigo. "It was your friends who attacked me."

Rigo froze, his eyes wide.

Conrad turned to the man. "Who is he talking about, Rigo?"

"I'm sorry they attacked you," Rigo said to Pico, "but I had nothing to do with it. They probably thought your artifact had value. They'll try to sell it."

"Who?" Conrad repeated.

"The Mamani brothers."

"Where will they go?" Tristan asked.

Rigo shrugged, although his frame was taut, tense. "Rurre, probably. There's a buyer there."

Tristan said to Pico, "We'll leave in the morning and you'll help me find them."

Pico slumped on the stool. "I cannot. I'm so tired. I need water and food."

As Freddie brought both, Brynn said to Magee, "I could go with you."

Tristan looked surprised. "I'm not asking you to."

"And I need her here," Conrad said. "Irene has confirmed that the markings in the cave are irregular. She needs Brynn's help."

"And you should stay," Tristan said to her. "This is important to you."

But she didn't want him to leave. It was as simple as that.

"If they're going to sell the piece," Rigo said, "it will take a week or more to make the arrangements."

"We could leave in three days then," Pico said around a tortilla filled with rice and beans stuffed into his mouth. "I will help you then."

Conflict warred on Tristan's face.

"I'll work quickly," Brynn said. "I could go with you in three days." She sounded desperate, so cautioned herself to dial it back.

"Can't stay away from me, can you?" he said quietly.

No. She allowed a smile to tug at her lips.

With so many watching their exchange, she felt inclined to cover up her true motive. "Not you. It's the Moon Tablet of Ur I'm after."

But the glint in his gaze told her he knew she was lying. She did want to see the tablet, but she didn't want this adventure with Magee to end. She hoped she didn't come to regret this.

"All right," he agreed. "Three days. Then we move out."

CHAPTER 19

Tristan awoke to the predawn trills of birds in the canopy above the camp. A scan of the ground beneath him revealed no snakes, spiders, or anything else he wouldn't relish stepping on, so he rolled out of his hammock, his shoes still on. It often didn't seem worth the effort to take them off, since something squishy or with a stinger could find its way inside.

A glance at Brynn in her enclosed hammock showed her sleeping. He thought about waking her, but he suspected she was exhausted, so he let her be.

He passed Shea, Dimar, and Freddie slumbering with various volumes of snoring. Solomon and Pico were missing, but the shaman had set up camp separate from the *gringos*, as he called them, so Pico must have joined him. Apparently, Dimar and Freddie preferred the *gringos*, no doubt because their paycheck came from them.

He found a well-trodden path and was soon rewarded when he came upon Solomon's camp. The shaman was awake, tending to a cookfire, the knuckles on his hands bulging more than Tristan had remembered. The knowledge pressed into him with an uncomfortable urgency. There was never enough time.

He really loathed endings.

And goodbyes.

"Come and sit," Solomon said, waving him forward. "Now that we've cleared up that I didn't cave to the authorities as you have chosen to believe all this time, we should catch up on missed news."

Pico was asleep nearby, nestled into his hammock like a *humintas*, a Bolivian tamale. Tristan could easily eat ten or more of the tasty corn and cheese concoctions in one sitting.

Settling onto a wooden stool, he said, "I didn't realize you and Pico were such pals. You did call him a twit a few days ago."

"We get along." Solomon offered an appeasing smile.

"I guess Pico lost your supplies."

"No, he didn't." Solomon pulled a pharmaceutical bottle of pills from his pocket.

Another pang of anguish sliced through Tristan. "Are you sick?"

Solomon shrugged. "Aren't we all a little sick? Only one thing is for certain—the bodies we occupy will one day fail us. No sense dwelling on it."

Tristan cleared his throat. "Is there anything I can do?"

"No."

When Tristan had met Solomon that first summer he'd been down here—sixteen years old and filled with hubris and risk-taking—the man had seemed otherworldly, brimming with a life force that seemed to make his eyes see things others couldn't. Tristan's father and Solomon had engaged in grand arguments about unseen worlds and the very nature of reality, and Tristan had been somewhat awed by how the shaman had stood up to the famous and somewhat crackers Harold Gatty.

But like most things in his life, Tristan's connection to Solomon had slipped away over the years in a sea of self-interest, both Solomon's and his own.

To hide the flare of unexpected emotion clogging his throat, Tristan looked at the stool he sat upon. "Did you make this?" he asked.

"Yes. It is good to create something useful. You should try it."

The comment thawed Tristan's melancholy mood. Solomon scooped out fried plantains from a pan on the cookfire and placed them on a plate, then he handed it to Tristan.

"Thank you," Tristan said, and he began gingerly to eat the hot food with his fingers.

"This place is sourced high," Solomon said.

"What does that mean?"

"There is an energy here that whoever built the ruins must have known about."

"Probably." Tristan didn't dispute that, but it was of little use to him. "Are you going to tell me it's related to your light people?"

"Perhaps. And perhaps in the wrong hands, it can be abused."

"Are you talking about my dad?"

Solomon shrugged. "You want so much to bring validation to your father, and yet you mock what he sought."

Hell, maybe. Weary from the battle of trying to stay one step ahead of those who would try to hold him down, hold him back, whether it be Conrad and Irene or a client who wanted a piece and held him by the balls by paying too little for it, for testing Tristan's integrity by making him justify some of the murky deals he'd made in the past—it was all a stain on his soul.

Brynn.

She had sparked something in him. The need to be better. The need to maybe let go of the tether that still held him bound to his father, even in death. To face his childhood fears.

"You want me to do the ceremony." As Solomon watched him intently, Tristan caved, but only a little, and said, "I'll think about it."

Solomon clapped him on the shoulder. "You're thinking. What a vast improvement."

"Smartass," Tristan muttered under his breath.

Solomon's eyes flashed with amusement, but as he looked away a cloud of worry overtook his expression.

Thinking it was about the old man's health, Tristan didn't ask. Some things were better left unsaid.

～

When Tristan returned to the main camp, Brynn was gone. He had a feeling where she might have gone, so he grabbed his pack and quietly slipped away, tracing their steps from yesterday back to Innadaltu. He found Brynn sitting against the blue rock altar, her eyes closed.

"Hey," he said.

She cracked an eye and greeted him with a smile. "How did you find me?"

"It was either this or you'd wandered off to powwow with a sloth."

"Close encounters of the wild kind. I have to admit that I'm beginning to prefer the animals over our camp mates."

"I hear you." He let the simple fact of being with her fill him with calm. "I hope it doesn't include me."

Her smile widened, and she roped his heart without even trying. "You're the wildest one of them all," she said.

He removed his pack and sat beside her, craning his neck to look up at the monolith. "So, what do you think?" *About this outrageous ruin deep in the jungle. About us.*

"Can you feel it?" she asked quietly.

"What?"

"The hum. Press your back up against it."

He did as she said, the vibration slight but definitely there. Pushing his increasingly persistent desire for her aside, he reached for his pack and retrieved two items.

"Why do you have a compass?" Brynn asked. "I thought you said those don't work down here."

"It's not for navigating." He crouched and faced the rock, aiming the compass at it. It spun wildly. "Interesting." He lifted the other device. "This is a Tesla meter. It measures magnetic fluxes in the environment." He took a reading. "Hmm, this is interesting as well."

"What?"

"The rock is reading twenty times higher than the surrounding environment. It might explain your buzz."

She stood and faced the granite altar, hands on her hips, and started humming Manilow's *Copacabana*. Pausing the song, she asked, "Why is there a door that goes nowhere?"

"Maybe the light people use it, Lola."

She laughed at his nickname for her, taken from the song, then became contemplative again. "Maybe the light people use sound to travel through it."

"You're starting to sound like Solomon."

"Did you decide to do the ceremony?"

As he walked around the perimeter with the Tesla meter, he said, "Maybe."

"What if we sing?" she suggested. "When I was young, Gramps sang in his choir and taught me vocal exercises. There was one in particular he had me practice over and over. Maybe I could create some kind of resonance."

Tristan laughed. "Knock yourself out. You don't have to convince me that acoustical properties can do magical things."

She began humming a series of tones, increasing the volume with each repeat of the sequence. It lacked musicality but put Tristan in mind of the tone generator he had used in his lab work while still in school. Brynn had a strong, clear voice, and she seemed to fall into a rhythm as she shifted along the frequencies.

There was no grand result, no opening of the door that really wasn't a door, or a flash of light, or a glowing aura. However, Tristan felt something, a humming that seemed to flow through him, vibrating in the marrow of his bones.

Brynn stopped, and the spell was broken.

She sighed. "Well, it was worth a try."

"A RE YOU MENSTRUATING?" Solomon asked.

"No," Brynn answered, as did Irene, who sat beside her.

"That is good."

"Why?"

"You would be more visible to spirits, and therefore more open to attack."

"Swell," Brynn muttered, but she felt oddly secure sandwiched between Irene and Tristan, who had agreed at the last minute to participate. Maybe she could hold his hand if his shamanic journey became too much.

Shea and Conrad were present, along with Dimar, Freddie, and Pico rounding out the group. The ceremony proceeded much the same as the one with Pepito and Carla, although they were outside this time in Solomon's small encampment, sitting in a circle around a fire that offered respite against the coming darkness.

Brynn's stomach wasn't altogether calm, but the brew that Solomon had made was somehow less bitter and smoother on the palate, and thankfully she didn't vomit this time. It still tasted like a bowl of wet dirt, but Brynn had to guess there was skill in making the drink, and perhaps Solomon had refined his own blend to something easier to ingest.

She lay back and just as she drifted off it dawned on her that they were all reclining on the jungle floor. She was about to ask Solomon to guard them from the wild things of the forest, but her mind slipped away to that ethereal place between waking and sleep.

She stood in the clearing, as did everyone else, but the light was muted as if they were in a psychedelic painting. She swung her gaze to Tristan and tried to reach out to him, but he turned and walked to where the jungle began, only he couldn't get past it. Banging his fist on some unseen wall, he yelled Solomon's name.

This was different than the last ceremony, and an unmistakable malevolence hung in the air. Was she sensing the bad spirits which Solomon had spoken of? Brynn stepped back and approached the invisible barrier. She began to hum, as she had at the blue granite portal earlier, but this time the vibration could be felt from her throat clear down to her hand. When she placed her palm on the barrier, it split with a crack, causing her to jump back. Searching for Tristan, she moved toward him, but he suddenly winked out and disappeared. What the …?

With a jolt, Brynn opened her eyes. Blinded by sunlight and lying on a hard bench, she cast a hand across her face, but the bobbing motion made the effort ineffectual. Sitting upright, she found herself on a boat, wooden and old-fashioned with white cloth sails. It swarmed with the hustle and bustle of people. The men—some with chest-length curly beards—wore long tunics draped with a swath of fabric hanging from one shoulder. The women wore similar clothing but in brighter colors—red, blue, and yellow—and their hair was tucked into side buns and adorned with headdresses, their ears showcasing golden hoops.

The vibrancy of the scene buzzed around her, making her lightheaded. A glance down showed that she was adorned in the same clothing, a pretty maroon silk that was edged with delicate embroidered designs. She smoothed a hand across the fabric, amazed by the texture.

A man shooed her along, so she stood and exited the boat. With slightly wobbly legs, she walked along the ramp to the dock. Lifting the long hem of her tunic, she peeked at her shoes and gazed appreciatively at the bejeweled design of the flat footwear. Very cozy. Very comfortable.

She moved along with the crowd, unsure of her destination. She most certainly had traveled *somewhere*, and she marveled at the authentic immersion. It was like a dream, but more. And she hadn't simply journeyed to another continent; she was fully convinced she had traveled *somewhen*.

Time travel. Fascinating.

She passed by vendors selling jewelry adorned with flower motifs, a melee of deep lapis lazuli and gold. There were colorful clothing stalls and barley beer for sale.

She stopped abruptly. The signage wasn't in English, and she was reading it quite easily. A clamor of barking dogs played a background beat to the crowded marketplace.

Sumerians valued dogs.

She spun in a circle, viewing the busy shopping area in a new light. *I'm in Sumer.*

Was the river beyond the Euphrates or the Tigris? The ancient land of Mesopotamia was situated between the two.

"Pardon me," she said, tapping an older woman passing by. At the woman's confused expression, Brynn quickly pivoted and spoke again in the Sumerian dialect. The woman appeared bemused by Brynn's stumbling attempt using a version learned in modern-day Los Angeles, but she nonetheless answered the question.

"We are in Ur," she said.

Brynn was about to ask what year it was, but anything the woman said would mean little since the people here certainly didn't follow a modern timeline. Instead, she said, "Who is the King?"

"We have been blessed with King Shulgi, who has most recently succeeded the great King Ur-Nammu."

Brynn thanked the woman and did a quick calculation in her head. If she remembered correctly, Ur-Nammu's reign ended around 2030 B.C.

She stared at her surroundings with renewed interest. Men and women and children of varying ethnicities—European, Asian, and African—mingled with the local Sumerians. During this period, Ur—located in today's southern Iraq—was considered one of the largest cities in the world and quite cosmopolitan. Sumerians were great traders. And Brynn was here. Right now.

She hardly dared to breathe.

This was fantastic. She was living every archaeologist's dream.

Drawing in a gulp of air, she released a laugh combined with a silly grin, and began moving through the crowd, both excited and awestruck.

When she finally emerged on the opposite side of the marketplace, she stopped abruptly and stared. In the distance was a temple, a stepped pyramid of great height. Known as The Ziggurat of Ur, it originally had been built by King Ur-Nammu in 2100 B.C.

Her eyes filled with tears of joy.

While she had visited it once with Irene, what stood in the future was much different than this one—taller and grander due to the addition of the upper layers by the Babylonians in the 6th century

B.C. This one wasn't as pretty, but it encompassed the original construction, and that drew Brynn more than any shiny façade might.

It was thought to have been over thirty meters in height, but it appeared to be much less, although the girth remained true to the foundation studied in the future. The monumental staircases were present, three in all—a main one in the front and one on each side. That feature had apparently remained intact.

Brynn knew it was unlikely she would be allowed to ascend—it was reserved for High Priests and Priestesses—but for one singular moment she imagined making the climb to the sacred chamber at the top.

As she approached the famous temple, her gaze roved over the mud bricks used for construction. If only she had a camera. A young woman approached, smiling, and took Brynn's arm, guiding her to a room at the base of the pyramid. Brynn didn't feel threatened, so remained silent. Stepping into the darkened interior, Brynn strained to adjust her vision. The girl entered behind her and pushed the wooden door closed.

Flickering candlelight illuminated several worktables. Atop them were clay tablets and seated before each one was a young girl holding a reed and making the slatted markings of the cuneiform language.

Brynn gasped, then quickly shut her mouth and simply gaped.

"I have brought her," the girl said, her diction Sumerian but the translation flowed smoothly in Brynn's mind.

A dark-haired woman with an olive complexion emerged from the shadows, wearing a white gown trimmed with gold. "Welcome. I have been hoping for visitors. I am Ninsun."

Ninsun?

That was the name on the ring that Brynn had purchased in Istanbul all those years ago when she had traveled with Gramps.

"Do I know you?" Brynn asked.

The woman contemplated the question with a bemused expression. "Not yet," she murmured. "I do believe this is our first meeting. Come, sit and let us speak of important things."

She led Brynn to a table in the back. Once seated, a girl brought a plate of what looked like apricots and a pitcher of liquid.

"Am I really in Ur?"

Ninsun nodded, pouring Brynn a drink. "And you are from across the sea. You live in a vast forest, thick and wet."

"Bolivia? Oh, no. I'm not from there. I'm just visiting. I come from a place called California. It touches the ocean and is very beautiful."

"And you're from a future time?"

Brynn hesitated. "I believe so." She reached for her ceramic cup and took a sip. Red wine, and it had a flavorful undertone. If this was simply an elaborate dream, it was a richly detailed one.

"I've been hunting the future for some time now." Ninsun took a sip of her drink. "An entryway recently opened, and I invited you."

"So I'm time traveling?"

Ninsun arched a delicate brow. "You seem surprised."

"I am. I've never done anything like this before."

"But you have the light around you, like others who can do this. The portal you came through has been closed for some time, but it recently re-opened. And it was you I saw on the other side."

Had it been my singing? An instruction that had come from Gramps …

"Why do you seek out others in this dreamworld?" Brynn asked.

"The world is so much more than what we see. There are other ways to travel the pathways of knowledge, which is why I decided to explore the future. I have a question. Maybe you have the answer."

CHAPTER 20

Tristan rubbed a hand at the back of his neck, feeling a bit confounded. "You time traveled?"

"Yes." Brynn sipped her morning coffee, her eyes bright. "It sounds crazy, but it felt so incredibly real."

Tristan had awoken sometime during the night with Brynn snuggled against him, and although it was nice, he had dragged himself up and had gotten her to her hammock, then he'd quickly crashed into his. With dawn well past, everyone was now sitting around the fire clearing their heads, eating boiled potatoes and canned chicken for breakfast while sipping a strong dose of caffeine.

"I don't think you're crazy," he said. "It's me you're talking to, remember?"

Her gaze filled with gratitude, and she said quietly, "I think maybe I owe you an apology for being so skeptical about some of your theories."

"You're forgiven." He went back to picking at his food. His stomach was still a little lopsided from last night's ceremony, but he was somewhat consoled by the fact that Dimar looked like hell. He wondered what kind of journey the Bolivian had encountered. Pico and Freddie appeared to be in better shape.

"Since you went back to Sumer, did you find out what those truncated symbols in the cave mean?" Conrad asked.

"No," Brynn replied, but Tristan wondered if that were true. Conrad didn't know about the notebook Brynn possessed from her grandfather.

"You actually believe you were in Ur in 2030 B.C.?" The disbelief on Irene's face was hard to miss.

Brynn released an excited huff. "It's hard to describe. It was like a dream but so much more."

Tristan was transfixed by her flushed cheeks and almost giddy excitement, letting it chase away the cold chill of his own journey, which had put him right back in that damned hospital.

Irene's face softened. "What happened?"

"I met a woman who called herself Ninsun. She oversaw a group of girls writing in cuneiform, and she asked me several questions."

Shea poured more coffee into his cup then replaced the pot on a small wire grill that covered the fire. "About what?" he asked.

"Basically, it was about metallurgy."

Conrad set aside his empty bowl. "Some believe the Anunnaki—the gods of Sumer—came to Earth to mine gold, and they used the Sumerians as slave labor."

"Well, Ninsun failed to mention any of that." Brynn's voice held a hint of dry sarcasm.

"What did you tell her?" Conrad asked.

Brynn shrugged. "I talked about my grandfather, who lived in Pennsylvania and was a metallurgist."

"Was?"

"He passed away suddenly from a stroke my last year of high school." Brynn took a swallow of coffee, but Tristan doubted she needed the stimulant. She was fairly buzzing now. "Ninsun showed me some of the tablets her girls were working on."

That caught Irene's attention. "What did they say?"

"They were transcribing city-state rules, for the most part. But she did show me one tablet that she said was in honor of Nanna. He was the god of the Moon," she added for everyone else.

Irene's eyes widened. "Did you see the Moon Tablet of Ur being made?"

Brynn paused. "Maybe. I'm not sure. That's not what she called it. But I did take a peek over her shoulder to see what it said."

"And?" Irene demanded.

"Since you had the actual tablet in your possession, you would know better than me, but it appeared to be an alchemical treatise with various symbols. I think I might have seen one for gold and silver, and maybe salt and sulfur."

Tristan shifted his attention to Solomon, who had been strangely silent during the conversation. "So what do you make of Brynn's journey?" Tristan asked. "Did she really time travel?"

Solomon seemed to struggle to come out of whatever stupor he had sunk into. "It takes great skill," he said, raising his gaze to Brynn. "This ancient woman came forward and pulled you back to her, but you—" his dark brows crashed together "—have a strange aura around you. Tell me about your childhood."

"What do you mean?" Brynn asked.

"Did you have strange encounters when you were a child?"

"Like ghosts?"

"Perhaps," Solomon conceded. "But what about coincidence? Did you know things before they would happen?"

Brynn emptied her cup but thankfully didn't reach for more coffee. Tristan would have stopped her since she had started shifting restlessly on her camp stool.

"Well, there was this one time when I was five that my brother became lost. Tyler was six and we were playing in a meadow at our uncle's house in Colorado. He disappeared for eighteen hours before he was found by a local man, miles from where we had started. I didn't know this until recently, but my mother said that the following morning when he still hadn't been found that I told her where he was. She said it was eerie, really, how accurate my description had been of the area where he had been found."

"But you don't remember doing this?" Tristan asked.

She shook her head. "No. I was very young. I do recall feeling sad and scared that he would die, and that somehow it would have been my fault because I'd been the last person to see him."

"Any other incidents you can remember?" Solomon prodded.

"Not really. But my grandfather and I always had a close relationship. He taught me cuneiform when I was a child. Come to think of it, he would often say that time wasn't linear. To be honest, I really didn't know what he was talking about." She looked at Tristan. "I haven't had a chance to ask, but did your journey go any better this time around?"

"It was about the same."

Her gaze filled with compassion. "I'm sorry."

Solomon leaned forward and said, "Tell us."

As everyone fixated on Tristan, he reluctantly explained what had happened when he was nine years old and had nearly died.

"Why did I not know this?" Solomon huffed.

"Maybe because he's been hiding it," Dimar moaned, finally joining the conversation. "He knows something is chasing him. Maybe it's aliens, or maybe it's demons. And he's brought them here." His voice cracked on the last sentence in an obvious display of panic, and he went back to rubbing his forehead.

Tristan didn't appreciate Dimar's little freak-out, since it set off a chain reaction of his own personal triggers. He started to sweat, so he wiped his shirt sleeve across his forehead, trying to will his heartrate back to normal.

Brynn touched Tristan's shoulder, startling him. When he looked into her eyes, he saw concern. Then she released him and turned to Solomon. "Can ayahuasca reshape memories?"

"Perhaps," Solomon replied, his tone bordering on noncommittal.

Annoyed by the shaman's aloof demeanor, Tristan asked, "Don't you have anything more to say?" They'd done the damned ceremony for him. The least he could do was guide them through the end result.

Solomon considered the question, then sighed. "Of course. I prefer to think of the journeys as opening doors. Doors that were shut, but now you can enter those rooms where experiences lie, and you can remember them."

"Well, my journey was more pedestrian," Conrad said. "I fought the gold miners." He released a satisfied smile. "And I do believe I won. We shall keep our territory for now." He turned to Irene. "Tell them about your journey."

"I guess I had an experience similar to Brynn, except that I believe I met with people who lived here in the jungle at some point in the past."

"Did you learn anything?" Brynn asked.

"Just that I believe this cave, or maybe it is a portal, I don't know, has been here and in use for some time, maybe hundreds of years."

When Dimar grimaced again, Solomon said to him, "Why don't you tell us about your experience?"

"It was dark and there were creatures with glowing red eyes, and then a giant anaconda ate me."

Aghast, Brynn said, "That sounds terrible."

Dimar ran a hand across his face, shaking his head. "I thought this ceremony was meant to calm the spirits. I would say it's been the opposite."

"Getting eaten by a snake isn't necessarily a bad thing," Solomon said. "In fact, it can be quite transformational."

"Just ask Brynn." Tristan nodded in her direction. "She wrangled an anaconda and lived to tell about it."

Dimar shot him an angry stare. "Don't lecture me on monsters. You're being chased by aliens! What if they come to get you and take me instead?"

"Well, hell," Tristan said, warming to the idea. "I didn't know that was an option. I'll keep that in mind if the space dudes do show up."

"Look," Conrad said. "The only threat around here are the drug runners and the gold prospectors. And I believe my journey was showing me how to handle them."

Dimar made a dismissive sound and rolled his eyes.

"Shea," Brynn said. "What about you? What happened on your journey?"

Shea shifted in his seat, almost squirming, which surprised Tristan. Not much rattled his cousin.

"What's wrong?" Tristan asked.

"Well, it's funny you brought up that incident when you were in the hospital. I went back there too. You probably don't remember because you weren't awake, but I was allowed to visit you once in the hospital. During my journey, I saw Uncle Charlie. He told me we've been looking in the wrong place."

"What do you mean?" Conrad asked.

"That we should turn our eyes inward rather than looking to the stars."

Conrad frowned. "Then you were speaking to an imposter. Right, Solomon?"

Solomon didn't answer right away, then he finally said, "Sometimes what you're looking for is right in front of you the entire time. You must shift your perspective to see it."

"Maybe the Anunnaki didn't come here for the gold," Conrad said. "Maybe they came for an entirely different reason."

Tristan finished his coffee. "Such as?"

Conrad shrugged. "I don't know. Maybe they were simply explorers, curious about the universe. Maybe they left their technology here on Earth when they departed."

"Such as metallurgy?" Brynn said.

Conrad nodded. "We think lead was used even before copper. There are traces of it as far back as 8,000 years ago in Iraq."

"And you think they taught us how to turn lead into gold?" Irene said.

"Is the formula on the walls in the ruins?" Dimar asked. His eyes darted back and forth between Irene and Brynn. "Can you translate the process? And give us each a copy?"

"I hate to tell you, Dimar," Tristan said, "but it's not a big secret turning lead into gold, it just takes an enormous amount of energy."

Dimar wasn't deterred. "Perhaps your aliens know a shortcut."

"The atomic number of lead is 82, and for gold it's 79, so three protons need to be removed to change it. This can't be done using chemicals, and the amount of energy needed is on the order of a nuclear reaction."

"You're just trying to confuse me with your scientific jargon."

"Okay, here's something easier to understand. In the 70's, a nuclear facility in Siberia turned the lead shielding of an experimental reactor into gold. By accident. But there's no way in hell you're gonna do it out here in the jungle with a crucible and a hot fire."

Dimar puffed out his chest. "Strangers speak the truth in fiction."

Tristan's brows crashed together in a vee. "Are you speaking in tongues now?"

"I think he means that *truth is stranger than fiction*," Brynn translated.

Irene sighed. "I doubt the markings in the cave will tell us how to build a nuclear reactor and make ourselves some gold." When Conrad was about to interrupt, she held up a hand to silence him. "I know, darling, that you would wish it otherwise. But we still might learn something important. Brynn, let's get up there and study the cuneiform markings more. Conrad, leave the glyphs to us. Besides, didn't you say you'd found something?"

This was news to Tristan. "What?" he asked.

"I found evidence of a burial on the other side of the portal rock."

"Please tell me you're not about to desecrate another site." Shea's tone bordered on insolent.

"Of course not," Conrad said. "I just want to do some preliminary work, gather enough information so we can get the site protected for more extensive work later. It will help to get the Ministry of Cultures and Tourism to authorize this dig on a grander scale."

Shea remained silent, a muscle in his cheek twitching.

Would Conrad try to smuggle whatever he found out of the country? Tristan doubted Fontana would be able to get around Shea. Still, Tristan wouldn't put it past him to try. They'd need to keep an eye on him.

"Why the hurry to get the site validated?" Brynn asked.

"There are factions that want to turn Bolivia into the energy powerhouse of South America," Irene said. "There are two proposed hydroelectric mega-dams to be built on the Beni river, but the generated electricity wouldn't stay local, it would primarily be exported, and to add insult to injury, it would submerge places like this, affecting dozens of communities and displacing thousands of people. It would destroy Innadaltu before it could be fully investigated and understood."

Tristan could almost hear the gears clicking in Brynn's head, because he felt it too. As angry as he was at Irene for leading him on this absolute goose-chase for one clay tablet, he had a grudging respect for her desire to protect the area from Dimar's three-letter word—exploitation.

"Dr. Caridad isn't wrong," Solomon said. "We need to protect the way of life down here. From every avenue of evil."

"If we could make our own gold, it would solve everything," Dimar chimed in.

Tristan didn't bother to hide his sarcasm. "As long as we're pursuing a realistic goal."

"There is a Buddhist fable," Solomon said, "of a group of blind men each describing a different part of the same elephant. They each capture an important part of the animal, but none know the complete animal."

Tristan looked at the shaman. "Since when have you been studying Buddhism?"

"It's a hobby."

"So are you saying we're the blind men?"

"I'm saying that there's always a bigger picture. A bigger story. We are players in it, even if we can't understand our role."

Tristan raised a brow. "Trying to dumb it down for us?"

Solomon finally cracked a smile. "Whatever works."

CHAPTER 21

B rynn lifted the flashlight and examined the writing on the cave wall again, while Irene worked quietly beside her. The slightly chilled air was a welcome relief from the heat of the jungle. Echoes of conversation from Conrad, Shea, and Tristan filtered to them from a different arm of the cave, but it was unintelligible as they worked on unearthing what had turned out to be a mummy. It was delicate work since this climate would likely leave it in very fragile shape.

Brynn had already photographed the glyphs with her cellphone while Irene had held up a light. Not the best way to document, but it was all they had at the moment. Now, Brynn was examining for pigmentation and strokes. She still hadn't mentioned Gramps's notebook.

"This truncated cuneiform only exists on this northwest wall," Irene said, "which indicates it may have been written all at once, or at least during a compressed period of time."

"But how old is it?" Brynn murmured, more to herself.

"Well," Irene said, "while we obviously can't use comparisons to known writings in this region, I don't think that will matter much."

"Why not?" More and more Irene's propensity to abandon sound archaeological protocols was leaving a bad taste in Brynn's mouth.

"Because it's so far outside what we would expect to see here."

"Exactly, Irene." Brynn was still buzzing from her shamanic journey with Ninsun, knowing deep down that the experience had been real, but it still didn't explain these markings in the Bolivian jungle. The hint of a headache was beginning to form as Brynn's logical mind shifted into overdrive trying to explain it all. Still, one possibility continued to jump out. "Even you have to admit that this could be an elaborate forgery." One that her grandfather might have been wrapped up in, which left a heavy weight on her heart.

Irene snapped her gaze to Brynn. "Are you accusing me?"

Brynn released an audible sigh, but she was more pissed-off than anything. "What the hell are you and Conrad doing?" Brynn whispered. "It's bad enough that he was involved with the mummy theft with Tristan's father. But this writing doesn't make any sense down here." And it definitely didn't make sense that it existed in her grandfather's notes. "When you release this, you both are gonna go through the fire professionally. You have to know that." The question was—did Brynn want to go through those flames as well? She could walk away now. Never say anything about the notebook.

Caught in the aura of the flashlight's beam, a flicker of uncertainty crossed Irene's face before shifting to one of resolve.

"All right, look," Irene said. "I won't try to convince you that faking a site has never occurred to Conrad or me."

"Because you've done it before, haven't you?" Brynn blurted.

Irene's dark eyes widened in surprise.

Brynn shifted the flashlight to her other hand. "There's been talk back at school."

"Ah, I see. Well, I suppose if I tried to defend myself, you wouldn't believe me."

"Depends on the defense. I've always admired you, Irene. It's hard to live in a world where I don't." Emotion clogged Brynn's throat.

Irene paused, pushing back a stray clump of hair that had escaped her ponytail. "I'm sorry for not being more upfront with you. I imagine you're talking about a dig in Turkey at the start of my career.

It's true, there was some … unprofessionalism at play … but I'm not a criminal."

"Did you plan to bury Tristan's clay tablet in this cave? Is that why you hauled it all the way down here?" Her tone was now somewhere between a whisper and a desperate plea. Damn. Brynn really thought she had a handle on her emotions regarding all of this. Apparently, she didn't.

The glassy look in Irene's eyes told Brynn that it had been *exactly* what Irene had been planning.

Brynn refocused on the glyphs. Everything was pointing to the fact that Conrad had obviously doctored these, except for the weird coincidence of Gramps knowing about them.

Brynn turned to Irene. "Did you know my family before I came to UCLA?"

"No. Why?"

"You'd never met my grandfather?"

"The one who taught you cuneiform? No, Brynn, I never met him."

Brynn had told Irene about Gramps in broad strokes over the past few years but nothing more. While her grandfather had amassed a large collection of Sumerian writings, histories, and tablets, he hadn't been a scholar, so Brynn had downplayed her connection to him beyond the love and affection a granddaughter would have for her grandfather.

Now, however, the irony wasn't lost on Brynn. She had thought Irene and Conrad were the experts, the true authorities, but maybe it had been Gramps all along.

I'm sorry for doubting you, Grandpa Mico.

"Look," Irene said. "All of this is legitimate, despite how it might appear. And I know that Conrad will take great care in excavating that mummy, so that we can use the positioning and layers of remains to help us date this cave. And later, we can use infrared spectrometry. I found some indication of more standard cave art over there." Irene indicated the wall behind her. "There are handprints and hunting scenes. This falls in line with other rock art found in Bolivia and is dated to 7000 B.C. I wouldn't say that the cuneiform glyphs are that old, but at least we know there was activity here as long ago as that. It means this cave has been in use and accessible for thousands of years, which I find remarkable. But what we really need to do is decipher these glyphs."

"I agree," Brynn replied. *And I plan to do just that.* "I'm going to take a break first and get something to eat." Brynn reached down to grab her backpack.

"All right," Irene said. "I'm going to stay a bit longer."

"Let me know if you find anything."

"Of course."

Irene reached out and pulled Brynn into a hug. At first, Brynn resisted but then allowed herself to sink into the warmth of the gesture. Maybe she was a fool to believe Irene, but she still cared about the woman.

Brynn exited the cave, the sound of the men reaching her, but she didn't stop to chat. She wanted to spend some time looking at Gramps's notebook, and she didn't want to waste the small bit of privacy she had carved out for herself. She made her way back to camp and settled in at a small table that Rigo had set up. She was facing the path that led to the cave, so she would be able to see when everyone returned. Solomon and the Castanos cousins weren't here, and Rigo was sleeping in his hammock.

Brynn pulled a blank pad of paper from her pack so she could take notes as she studied the photos of the cave on her phone alongside her grandfather's notebook. But when she tried the pen she had grabbed, it didn't work, despite several scribbles to get it going. Hoping she had another to write with, she began searching her backpack, digging through the main pocket. When that didn't turn up anything, she moved to the zippered pouches. Her fingers felt something odd buried deep at the bottom of one. When she pulled it out, she gasped.

It was the ring from Istanbul!

Shocked, Brynn stared it. She hadn't seen it in years, not since returning from that trip. This was the backpack she had taken on that journey when she was ten years old—the ring must have been in there the entire time. It was still as ugly as she had remembered, but now she felt nothing but fondness for it. She could almost feel Gramps beside her.

As she turned the small scroll anchored at the top of the ring, she studied the cuneiform symbols, faint but still readable. She'd been unable to decipher the markings all those years ago, but she was more well-versed in the language today. She ought to be able to now. There were three lines of script, and as the meaning became clear, her heart slammed against her chest and she froze, barely daring to breathe.

NIN.SUMUN

BR.NN

M.CO

Oh my God.

Ninsun.

Brynn.

And the last one.

Mico. Her grandfather's nickname.

TRISTAN STOOD BACK and held up a small spotlight, illuminating the mummy that he, Conrad, and Shea had spent the better part of the day uncovering. He wiped at the sweat on his forehead with the back of his arm. Although it was much cooler in the cave than outside in the jungle, they had for the last hour been digging hard to clear a space around the perimeter of the mummy. They could do this only after Shea had spent several painstaking hours checking the boundaries to be certain they wouldn't inadvertently damage another mummy. While Shea had done that, Tristan had helped Conrad carefully clear away the dirt covering the skeleton. They had only removed a thin first layer, and in the process Tristan decided that archaeology work was tedious, muscle-straining, and well … boring.

Conrad and Shea were bent over, closely examining what they had exposed.

The skin on the skull, tight and leathery-looking, appeared freeze-dried. And there was hair on the scalp. So much hair. Tristan didn't remember the other mummies from a few years back possessing such luxurious locks, although this one had hair matted with dirt.

He shifted, a little unnerved. The face, with its hollow eye sockets and hole for a nose, looked macabre, like something out of a haunted house. And Tristan feared the mummy was of a young person, making his stomach churn. It was hard to imagine the mindset required to take the life of children to appease imagined gods. Maybe that was why believing his father's theories of creatures from outer space suited him better than a nebulous set of deities that would encourage such atrocity toward children.

"It's so odd to find mummies this far in the jungle," Shea murmured. "The conditions are too wet and humid. And why was this one inside a clay pot?"

Tristan had wondered the same thing. While the ceramic container had since collapsed, it was obvious that the body had been entombed in what appeared to be a large vase.

"There's been recent evidence in Iraq of mummies buried this way." Conrad's voice echoed off the surrounding walls.

"Sumerian?" Shea asked.

"Probably not." Conrad leaned on all fours to examine the find closer. "Mesopotamians didn't practice mummification, so the find is probably dated somewhere around 500 B.C. But why the same type of burial here?" He pulled a tape measure from his gear and measured the corpse. "Five feet one inches. It appears to be a female. The cave has done a good job of staving off jungle rot."

"It would appear so." Shea shook his head in apparent disbelief. "They must have used salt in the embalming process to hasten desiccation. It's been documented near the coast of Chile and the Andes Mountains."

"The skin appears intact, but I wonder if the organs have been removed."

"You planning to extract her to find out?" Shea asked.

"Yes. It would make it much easier for analysis. And look here." He pointed at a type of matting that surrounded the body. "Sumerians did this with the lower classes. What if a Sumerian had traveled here and made those markings on the wall, and then interacted with the locals? Perhaps there was an exchange of ideas?"

Shea crouched near the skull. "What about the ceramic casket?"

Conrad shrugged. "I don't have an answer for all of it."

"But a little DNA analysis might tell you whether this girl was human," Tristan said. "Or something else."

Conrad chuckled. "You sound like your father, Tristan."

"Removing this mummy is a bad idea." Shea shined his flashlight into the macabre face of the skull. "We don't have time to do it properly."

Conrad's eyebrows shot up. "Who's in a hurry?"

"You've already been down here for weeks," Shea said. "Are you planning to stay longer? The rains are coming, and it's going to be a wet, hellacious mud bog down here soon."

"Which is why we should remove little Sumerian Suzy as soon as possible," Conrad said succinctly.

Shea shot to his feet. "Fuck, Conrad. You may as well film the whole thing on your cellphone so you can release it as soon as you get back to the States. 'Alien girl found in South America.' You know you'll need permission from the Ministry of Culture."

Conrad smiled. "I've already got it."

"What?" Shea frowned. "How?"

"I wanted to avoid what happened last time, so I took my time in cultivating the right connections. Contrary to what you might think, Shea, I'm not trying to do something illegal. I can get the mummy out without resorting to bribes."

In the glow of the lamp, Shea appeared skeptical.

"Please tell me we're done," Tristan said, turning away from the mummy. He didn't particularly like hanging out with a two- or three-thousand-year-old dead girl who might not have been human. Besides, it had been a long day, and he was beat. Thankfully, Conrad agreed.

As they exited the cave, they came across Irene, who said, "Brynn's already gone for the day."

Conrad remained to talk to his wife, so Tristan and Shea made their way back to camp. A quick check showed Brynn to be napping in her hammock, so Tristan decided to do the same. As the setting sun cast the jungle into dark shadow, Tristan closed his eyes, only intending a twenty-minute nap.

CHAPTER 22

B rynn was dreaming.
But it was so real.

Sitting in an anteroom in the Ziggurat of Ur, Brynn could see through a doorway where several girls in white garments hunched over clay tablets with wedge styluses in their hands.

Brynn turned to Ninsun, who sat across from her. "What are they working on?"

"They are writing the City rules in both Sumerian and Akkadian."

Brynn knew of the close relationship that had developed between the Sumerians and the East-Semitic Akkadians, creating a strong cross-over influence between the two languages, and a Rosetta Stone for modern archaeologists to decipher cuneiform with confidence.

"But you wish to know more about"—Ninsun waved her hand between the two of them—"this, don't you."

Brynn nodded. "It would seem that we've met before."

Ninsun smiled, but her expression was one of amused tolerance. "Yes. This is our second meeting." Her voice held the tone of stating the obvious.

Brynn shook her head. "I know that. What I mean is have there been other … encounters besides these two?"

"Perhaps. Time is more fluid in the space we are in right now."

"I found a ring with your name on it that I acquired many years ago. My name and my grandfather's name are also on it, written in cuneiform."

Ninsun's gaze shifted and glazed over. "I see." After a pause, she raised her eyes. "You told me of your grandfather's skill with metals. It would seem that we do indeed visit with him." She stood. "Shall we go?"

"What?" Brynn jumped to her feet. "I'm afraid he's dead."

"A minor inconvenience, I assure you."

Ninsun took Brynn's hand and for a moment Brynn experienced an unsettling disorientation as the scene around her morphed and changed, like an array of cheesy special effects from a low-budget film. As a wave of dizziness accosted her, she closed her eyes and waited for the nausea to pass.

When she dared to open her eyes, she gasped. They were in her grandparents' house in Saltsburg, Pennsylvania, standing in the lower-level hallway that led to her grandfather's room of collectibles. As she slowly approached the entranceway, Gramps's familiar form became visible, sitting at one of his tables, faced away, and peering down at a collection of rusted, metallic artifacts.

Was it really him? Was he really alive? Or was this all part of an elaborate dream?

Ninsun came to stand beside Brynn as they both stopped in the middle of the room. It was much as Brynn had remembered from her childhood. While this area was at the basement level, there was a door that led to a driveway and sunlight poured in through several windows, brightening the space. A fireplace and couch made it warm and cozy in the winter when snow blanketed the land, and Gramps's many collectibles were nicely displayed on several tables positioned along two walls. There were also statues and the occasional plant taking residence on the floor. It was honestly one of Brynn's favorite places in the world. And even more so with the man slowly turning around to face them.

Gramps's gaze shifted from Brynn to Ninsun and then back. *He can see us.* His hair wasn't quite so gray, and his face bore a smoothness that told her he was younger than she had ever remembered. It would appear they had traveled back in time.

"Hi, Gramps," Brynn said.

His eyes sparkled with delight. "What is this?" he said.

"It's a little hard to explain," she said, "but I've come to visit you. This is Ninsun. And brace yourself—she's from Mesopotamia."

"Did your grandmother slip something into my morning coffee?" he asked, his tone wry. "She always said my imagination would do me in one day."

"I'm sure it was cream and sugar today, just like always. It's good to see you." The pain of the loss of him sliced through her and tears welled in her eyes. She wiped at them and smiled. "I've missed you."

A shadow crossed his gaze. He cleared his throat. "I can see we're in some new territory here." He lifted a hand. "Don't say anything more about ... me. Or your grandmother." He recovered a semblance of his good humor. "Some things are better left to God."

Realizing her error—that she may have inadvertently told Gramps about his own death—Brynn glanced at Ninsun, who still hadn't spoken. But the woman traveler from the past remained silent, not offering the rebuke Brynn was certain she deserved.

Brynn turned back to her grandfather. "How old am I right now? In this time, in your time."

"When I spoke to you this morning on the phone, you were still a very precocious five-year-old, if not in great distress." His brows fell toward his nose and true pain pinched his face. "Tyler is missing. Is that why you're here? Has something happened to him?"

So today was the day after she and Tyler had been playing in the woods at Uncle Simon's ranch where Ty had wandered off and disappeared.

"No. And he's okay," she replied in a rush before she could think better of it. "They'll find him by the end of today." She described exactly where he would be located, to hell with ruining the past.

Gramps's shoulders sagged with relief. "Praise God for that. Your grandmother and I were planning to fly out first thing tomorrow. It will be nice to be going for a reunion and not ... something else." He took a steadying breath and looked more intently at Brynn. "So, you're from the future. How old are you?"

"I'm twenty-five."

"Extraordinary. How are you doing this?"

Ninsun stepped forward and now spoke, using a dialect of Sumerian. "There are other pathways that can be used if you know them. I'm pleased to meet you, Domenico Milano."

"You can call me Mico." Her grandfather's use of the language was quite good, surprising Brynn.

"And you may call me Ninsun. I am from the City of Ur, and I understand you have knowledge of the science of metals."

"Ur." A smile tugged at his lips and his voice held a tinge of awe. "Fascinating. And yes, I'm a metallurgist."

"Then I wonder if I might ask you a few questions?"

As Gramps and Ninsun began speaking of the chemical properties of copper, Brynn was drawn to the scene through the window, so she left the room and went outside. She supposed she should stay and soak up the exchange that was so wild and out-there that no one would believe her, but her desire to be outdoors overtook her.

She walked to the back of the house, taking in the green grass and the lush trees of summertime. Her grandparents' home sat on a hill overlooking the Kiskiminetas River, and she and her brothers had spent many balmy summer evenings running around on the lawn chasing fireflies.

Across the street was a private, all-male boarding high school—The Kiski School—which Gramps had rallied to get Alec and Tyler to attend, but in the end the area had lacked one important aspect—waves. Her brothers were surfers, and both had wanted to stay in California. If Brynn had been a boy, however, she would have jumped at the opportunity to attend. It would have been worth it to see her grandfather every day.

Should she tell her mom about visiting Gramps in the past? Lily Galloway was fairly open-minded. She might even be happy to hear about a moment in time—*somewhen?*—that included her father. Brynn decided that the next time she was with her mom, preferably after a nice meal and a bottle of wine, she would tell her about this.

When Ninsun found her, Brynn knew immediately that it was time to leave. A flutter of panic filled her chest. *Gramps.*

He had come outside and now he opened his arms to her, but as Brynn stepped into his embrace, they seemed to hover just beyond the other.

"What a shame," he said, "that this doesn't work better. You're a beautiful young woman, Brynn, and I couldn't be prouder of you."

"The cuneiform—"

"I know. Or rather, there's much I don't know. And frankly, I don't want to. But I'll look after you in this timeline. I'll make sure I teach you so that you're ready for the future."

Brynn wanted to say more, but Ninsun indicated that it was time to leave.

"I love you, Gramps." She tried to smile through her tears.

"I love you too, Bee."

~

BRYNN CAME AWAKE WITH A START.

Bee.

In the gloaming of twilight, she rolled out of her hammock and immediately went to her notebook. *It couldn't be that simple.*

Using the nickname Gramps had used for her—Bumble Bee—she set about deciphering the glyphs in Gramps's notebook using a flashlight as she huddled over the small table. Peripherally, she could smell the dinner that Rigo was preparing, the aroma hinting at a pot of beans.

As she cross-referenced her preliminary translation with the photos from the cave, she was able to form a semblance of sentences. Where there were gaps, she guessed. Eventually she unlocked the entire code, and she roughed out a translation.

It was a paragraph. Written to her. The goosebumps came immediately.

. . .

My dearest Brynn,

This connection to you is beyond my understanding and it was limited, which is why I'm leaving this clue for you. I was able to dictate this to a Tacana girl by learning Quechua. I think I visited her a long time ago. Ninsun showed me that you would find this place. She taught me the toning that I taught you to open the portal, which you will need to do. This time loop requires it. And the advancements of the Sumerian people? Let's just say that you and I play a small but significant role in that.

I don't know my fate, but I sense that I leave before your grandmother. Please look after her, as well as your mother.

I love you, Bee.

Grandpa Mico

P.S. You will believe Ninsun controlled our visits, but it was you.

For a moment, she closed her eyes and basked in the essence of having her grandfather nearby. If this were a hoax, it was beyond elaborate.

Her heart pounded, and she suppressed a sob.

How did this work? Was it possible that Gramps had been skipping through time during Brynn's childhood? And why hadn't he told anyone? Or at least told her, since he'd obviously interacted with her future self?

The answer came immediately. No one would have believed him. Especially not ten-year-old Brynn. She would have thought him a bit loony, or a bit eccentric, but she wouldn't have been convinced. Would she?

But now, it was beside the point. Gramps had known he had needed to keep this a secret. At least until he could tell Brynn. And this was how.

Had he developed the shorthand? Is that why it was written in his notebook? Then why hadn't he included a translation? She had to acknowledge that it would be very Gramps of him to make her work for it.

It would appear the time traveling had been nothing more than an exchange of information. Obviously, Gramps had given Ninsun advanced metallurgical data which she had likely introduced in her time period. If so, the Sumerian's advancements weren't necessarily alien-borne, but future-borne. From humans, just like them.

It was such an intriguing idea, if that's what had truly happened.

Now what? Should she show this to Irene? Reluctance pulled at Brynn. What was the point? Irene might actually accuse Brynn of forging everything—the notebook, the writing in the cave, hell, maybe even the Moon Tablet of Ur that none of them could seem to hold onto.

Her decision was made. She would keep the translation to herself.

CHAPTER 23

Tristan awoke from his nap and spied Brynn huddled over her grandfather's notebook in the glow of a flashlight, wholly immersed in her work, so he let her be and instead followed the path that led from their camp to Solomon's. But as he neared, he sensed something was wrong and stopped in the shadows to wait.

About twenty feet away, Rigo—looking agitated—was engaged in a tense conversation with Solomon, whose jaw was set in a look of annoyance.

"They demand to speak with you," Rigo hissed, loud enough to reach Tristan's ears.

Solomon turned his face slightly, enabling Tristan to hear his response. "You know that's not wise. I do not wish to be seen with them. Especially now. There are too many others around. It makes no sense."

"They won't like your answer." Rigo shook his head, then said, "I need to check on dinner." He spun away toward the path to the other camp.

Tristan suppressed an impulse to show himself and demand to know what was going on as a sour feeling churned in his gut. He'd wanted to believe that Solomon had changed, that he really did care about what was happening here. That he had cared about Harold Gatty. That he had cared about Tristan.

But something about this didn't seem right, and Tristan knew his gut responses were generally right. Solomon was up to something. Somehow Rigo was involved.

That meant it was a Bolivian thing. While he would have liked nothing better than to return to Brynn, he went in search of Dimar, finding him sitting by the main fire.

Tristan sat beside him, asking in a low voice, "What's the deal with Rigo and the Mamani brothers?"

Dimar shrugged. "How should I know?"

"What about Solomon? Do you see him much?"

"He is usually north most of the time. But he does come to these villages at least once a year." Dimar sighed. "We are not all criminals, Dr. Magee. But the Mamanis … they like to force their bellies around."

"Come again?"

"They push around."

"You mean throw their weight around. Does Solomon work with them?"

Dimar shrugged again. "Why not? They bribe very well. But don't worry. Solomon isn't their leader."

"Who is?"

"There is talk, but I know nothing for certain."

"What kind of talk?"

"That they are led by a woman." The derision in his voice conveyed his low opinion of that possibility.

"But you've never been bribed by them, or this woman?" Tristan asked.

Dimar's gaze sparked with defiance. "Of course not. But you have to be careful out here. Sometimes you have to play on both sides of the bridge."

"You mean fence."

Brynn came to sit by him, looking rather distracted. He leaned into her nearness, enjoying whatever physical contact he could get. When this was all over, he planned to take her on a real date, and see where this simmering attraction might take them. "Everything all right?" he asked.

She nodded. "Yes, of course."

He didn't believe her but didn't press further since Shea, Irene, and Conrad had entered camp, followed by Solomon, Freddie, and Pico.

As everyone prepared to eat, Tristan's senses went on full alert when Rigo pointed to one pot for Brynn, Tristan and Shea, and a different one for the Castanos cousins. Something wasn't right.

"Why did you make two dinners?" Tristan asked.

With an earnest look on his face, Rigo said, "I didn't have enough supplies for everyone, so I made something separate for them." He indicated the Castanos boys.

"What's going on?" Conrad asked.

"I don't like the dinner," Tristan said. "I'd rather eat that." He pointed to the other pot bubbling with what looked like a stew.

Tristan didn't miss the flash of annoyance in Rigo's eyes, but the young man quickly recovered and indicated for Tristan to take what he wanted. "Help yourself."

Tristan scooped the stew into a bowl, then filled a second bowl with the beans from the first pot, which he handed to Rigo. "Eat this."

"What are you doing?" Conrad asked.

Tristan held Rigo's gaze. "Just making sure the food is edible."

Looking like a cornered dog, Rigo took the bowl and scooped a bite into his mouth. When he didn't fall down dead, Tristan had to concede that perhaps he'd been wrong in his suspicions. Still, he made sure Brynn ate the stew and not the beans.

Rigo hadn't tried to poison them.

Later, Dimar brought out a jug of *chicha*, a fermented drink made from the yucca plant, which he passed around. Everyone poured a bit into their cup. Tristan had had *chicha* before, but this one was especially sweet, and too late he realized he had let his guard down.

And that was the last thing he remembered.

～

BRYNN SAT across from Ninsun in the Ziggurat of Ur.

"The dream of the alchemist is to create life," Ninsun said. "That which was, will be again. That which is, has already been. Life is abundant and circular, and traveling through time is possible, in this way that we are doing right now. It has always been so. It is a skill locked inside humans. They need only remember."

Brynn awoke with a jolt, her cheek resting on the ground and the aroma of dank dirt filling her nose. A muddled confusion soon gave way to comprehension. *Still in Bolivia, not Mesopotamia.*

Carefully she sat upright, her temple throbbing with a dull headache and her mouth feeling as if it had been stuffed with cotton balls. She licked her lips to restore much needed moisture.

A gray haze hung over the now-dead campfire, and snoring alerted her to the unconscious forms of Tristan and Shea nearby, both sprawled on the ground as if it were the most comfortable of beds. Her aching back said otherwise.

What the hell happened?

The last thing Brynn remembered was sitting around the fire, eating dinner, although ... Tristan had been acting strange about that. He'd insisted she only eat the food from one cookpot and not the other. And then they had downed some *chicha* ...

Was the beverage really that strong? Had they all passed out like drunks after only a few sips? It didn't make sense. She had no recollection of falling into an inebriated state. It was as if one minute she'd been savoring the sweet drink ... and the next minute she was here. And somewhere in between she'd had a conversation with Ninsun.

Was she going mad in the jungle?

Quite possibly.

Another glance around caused her to suppress a shudder. Just how many bugs had crawled over her? How many snakes had checked them out? Her hand flew to her hair, and she blew out a relieved breath when she confirmed that no animal had defecated on her.

Praise the small victories.

She stood and made her way to the two men, noting that no one else was around. A bad feeling took root.

It took her several minutes to rouse Tristan, who appeared far groggier than her even with the addition of water from a canteen she'd located, and then Shea.

"I knew it," Tristan said, nursing what appeared to be a colossal hangover.

"Knew what?" Shea demanded, dark circles under his eyes as he struggled to climb out of his own dazed state.

"Rigo poisoned us."

"Is that why you were so weird about dinner last night?" Brynn asked.

Tristan gave a barely perceptible nod as he sat on the ground, digging the heel of one hand into his eye, clearly trying to pressure-point his way out of his hangover. She shuffled over to him on her knees, positioning herself behind him, and rubbed his temples with her hands.

His shoulders slumped. "Thanks." His voice held gratitude and relief. "I thought he'd do it in the food, but the little bastard added it to the *chicha*."

Brynn dropped her hands to Tristan's shoulders and started digging in, eliciting a groan from him. "I thought Dimar brought the drink," she said.

"She's right." Shea stood and started rummaging through the gear that was strewn about. "It wasn't Rigo, it was Dimar. But why?"

Tristan scanned the campsite. "Everyone's gone, right?"

"It looks like it," Brynn replied. "But I only just woke up. Maybe they're all at the cave."

"Is there stuff missing?" Tristan directed the question at Shea.

"Why would they drug us to steal from us?" she asked. "They've been with us all along. They could've stolen anything at any time."

Brynn dropped her hands as Tristan pushed to a standing position, then he pulled her to her feet. They joined Shea in scouting the camp as well as Solomon's quarters and the cave. Most of the gear was gone as well as the people. And the mummy had been dug up and removed.

"We've been had by all of them?" Brynn asked, trying to wrap her mind around this extreme betrayal. "Frankly, I find this …."

"What?" Tristan prompted when she paused, a permanent scowl on his face since they had begun their search. "Shocking? Unimaginable?"

"Well, yes, those things, but it's more than that. Don't you find it strange that it was so coordinated? That they would all do this behind our backs. That they would all leave us face down in the dirt?"

"The beauty of human nature," Tristan added, hardly sugar-coating it.

"All right, Mr. Gloom and Doom," Shea said. "I kind of agree with Brynn. There's more going on here than the fact that everyone appears to be in on some massive grift."

Tristan planted his hands on his hips. "So what do you think it is?"

"I don't know, but we're definitely wasting time. Conrad's gonna take another mummy out of the country, and I don't believe for a minute that he's got the proper permissions. I need to stop him."

"I'm not going with you," Tristan said.

"What do you mean?" Brynn asked.

"I'm guessing Conrad is headed out of the country, same as two years ago. He needs to get that mummy back to the States before anyone notices. I'm still after my tablet. I'm going after Solomon and Rigo."

"Why them?" Brynn asked. "They didn't have it."

"I've got a feeling they know who does."

Brynn looked from Tristan to Shea and back again. "Okay, how do we start?"

CHAPTER 24

The jungle was alive with night sounds, and it was more than a little unsettling. Tristan scratched his arm, then his wrist, then his neck. He was covered in mosquito bites. He reached into his pack and rummaged around until he found a flashlight.

Lightning flashed, illuminating the shadows of the jungle as brightly as if it were daytime. Without a pause, thunder boomed. He knew what was coming. He cursed. He'd lose whatever trail Solomon and Rigo were leaving behind, but he was loath to stop.

The tracks Tristan had found went southeast, and he'd been certain they'd belonged to Solomon, but now doubt was setting in. Maybe the *chicha* had scrambled his brain. Maybe he was following random footprints.

Sonofabitch.

The rain came down in buckets. More like bullets. Tristan kept going but the jungle quickly turned into a muddy bog. Each time a lightning bolt lit the area up like a light bulb, Tristan flinched, then he jumped again when a crack of thunder boomed less than a second later.

But there was no place to stop. They needed higher ground, so he kept going. He and Brynn wore slickers, and a steady waterfall streamed off the brim of his hat.

Sunrise happened at some point but was severely muted by the canopy of trees and the dark clouds hovering low in the sky. At least he could see a little better and no longer needed his flashlight.

Sometime later, he came to a fast-flowing river.

But it couldn't be the Beni. They must be on some tributary. Shit. He knew better than to use his compass. And whatever trail he'd been following was now completely gone.

～

THE RAIN WAS RELENTLESS, and Brynn wondered more than once if Tristan truly knew his way. But he seemed so driven and kept moving forward, so she continued to follow.

Despite the canopy above, the rain came down in sheets, producing poor visibility. In fact, she couldn't see Tristan up ahead. Her foot caught on an exposed tree root and she fell, and continued slipping in the mud when the ground sloped downward. With growing fear, she clawed at the ground to stop her momentum.

With a jerk, Tristan grabbed her foot and yanked her into the base of a tree where he had anchored himself with his legs.

As she clutched at the protruding limbs, she yelled over the rain, "Thank you."

He pointed just beyond them. "You almost went in the river."

She squinted and could just make out the swiftly flowing water. That was close. Her heart slammed into her chest.

"We'll wait out the storm here," he said.

"And then what?" She had started shaking all over.

"And then you're not gonna like what comes next."

～

BRYNN STARED AT MAGEE. "You must be insane."

"You said you're a surf girl. This should be no problem for you."

She returned her gaze to the river. The rain had stopped, but despite the slicker, her clothes were still wet, leaving her skin chilled.

Thankfully, her body-wide trembling had stopped, but a shiver ran through her as she watched logs and downed trees getting pushed along in the water. Big ones.

"Was this your plan all along?" she asked.

"No. I thought I knew where we were going, but I got turned around. It's actually fortunate to have found a river."

"Is this the Beni?"

"I don't think so. It's too narrow. But it'll reach the Beni at some point. We're lost, Brynn. This is the best way to become unlost."

"Have you done this before?"

"Once."

"And how did it go?"

"I'm still alive, aren't I?"

"That doesn't make me feel better."

Her heartbeat echoed in her skull, like an internal ticking clock. Counting down the minutes until her death.

Magee's solution was to ride the logs down the river. What had taken them days to trek by foot would now take only hours to get them close to the Beni, and from there they could make their way back to Rurrenabaque.

"You're just surfin' the logs, Brynn."

She took a steadying breath. "But what if you fall?"

"You can't."

Because then, of course, the river would swallow them up, and they would drown.

"You can do it," he said.

"What if we wait for someone to find us?"

"There's a limited window when the river will flow at this capacity and get us where we need to go. There's no guarantee anyone will find us."

She heard everything Magee didn't say—they were lost, possibly life-threateningly lost, and they needed to act to save themselves. They needed to be decisive.

"Okay," she said quietly.

She removed the slicker and her hat, and then double knotted the shoelaces on her boots. Pulling her hair back, she tied it in a tight ponytail to keep it out of her face.

They both made sure their gear was packed as securely as possible. After cinching her pack to her back, she pumped her arms above her and in wide circles to make sure she had as much range of motion as possible.

"Ready?" Tristan said.

She nodded. "Ready."

They gingerly went to the edge of the riverbank, but not fully into the water, taking care to avoid getting swept away by the current. It was difficult to gauge how strong it was near the embankment since the rain had turned it into a rushing maelstrom.

Single logs floated past, followed with clusters. Some were close, some were far.

They waited and watched, trying to get a feel for the velocity of the water and what it would take to leap atop one of the floating trunks. Finally, Tristan signaled for her to get ready.

A log about three feet across came near.

"Now!" Tristan yelled.

He leaped, and then Brynn jumped. If she'd hesitated, she would have missed the opportunity and she didn't relish the idea of being on a different tree than Magee.

Lying on her stomach, she hugged the log, her legs clenched to keep her attached to her new boat. They took off down the river.

Tristan pushed himself up and Brynn carefully did the same, worried that any jostling might cause the tree to spin and flip her right off. But it seemed stable as it rushed along in the water. Brynn began to feel steadier and straightened up a bit more. Tristan glanced over his shoulder.

"What do you think, Lola?"

"I think I'm staying on my ass, thank you very much."

He let out a whoop, and Brynn released a shaky laugh, barely letting herself enjoy the exhilaration of flying along the waterway like a ride at an amusement park.

An extremely dangerous ride, she reminded herself.

And that danger quickly became apparent when they rounded a bend and a logjam appeared in the distance on the right side.

"What now?" she yelled.

"Now we jump."

Shit.

Tristan moved from straddling the log to his hands and knees, and Brynn did the same. There was no time to argue or tell him no. A log appeared to their left, and Tristan jumped over to it. Brynn quickly did the same, wobbling and nearly falling in the process, but she managed to keep her balance.

Treat it like a surfboard. She had a strong core from surfing—time to start using it.

She rode the new log and luckily it stayed in the current at the center of the river, taking them further downstream. When it got dicey, with a possible entanglement imminent, they jumped from log to log. Brynn envisioned she was riding a wave in California or Hawai'i, and her body naturally responded, her strength revealing itself.

Exhilarated, she stopped feeling afraid and instead marveled at what she was doing—riding a river through the Amazon jungle. She relished telling her brothers.

As if on cue, the rain came again, along with electric shocks of lightning and ear-splitting thunder. She huddled on the log they currently occupied, Tristan in front of her, squinting into the melee coming down on them. Time slid away. They easily could be in the ancient past when dinosaurs roamed the earth, and every living thing was at the mercy of the elements.

Visibility dropped to zero. Tristan was nothing more than a faint gray shadow in front of her.

The log slammed into something, throwing Brynn over the side. The weight of the water sucked her down and she fought frantically against it. Breaking the surface, she gasped for breath.

"Tristan!"

She couldn't see past the logs pressing against her. She shoved hard against one and it spun away from her, the effort causing her to choke on a mouthful of water. Another giant trunk came toward her, and she backed up enough to avoid it crushing her. Searching for a hand hold on any of the logs, she tried in vain to cling to one, but her hands kept sliding off the slippery surfaces.

Finally, she spied an extruding branch and grabbed it. Thankfully it held. She wanted to rest, but any minute another log might slam into her from behind, possibly knocking her unconscious or crushing her skull.

With sheer determination, she fought to haul herself out of the water as her pack dragged her back. She unclipped the front strap, pulling it from her shoulders, but when she tried to fling the bag forward so that she wouldn't lose it, the current swept it from her fingers, swallowing it up. She continued to struggle until she finally got herself onto the log, but she didn't dare try to sit up for fear she'd be thrown free again.

"Tristan!" But her voice was consumed by the deafening rain, roaring like an airplane engine.

He had to be close.

And if he wasn't?

She had no answer.

CHAPTER 25

Brynn slowly opened her eyes. Unbelievably, she had fallen asleep. Or maybe she'd been knocked unconscious and hadn't known it.

The rain had stopped, and she was still on the log, which was crammed into an inlet with what looked like fifty other trees all floating on their sides. A misty haze hung in the air, and the cool remnants of the torrential rainstorm lingered.

She sat upright. Where was she? Where was Tristan?

Wary to move too much, she tucked her legs closer. Tristan would be fine. He was far savvier in this environment than she was. She clung to that thought, not letting the alternative drag her into despair.

Her pack was gone, so she now had no gear. No mosquito net, no machete, no water bottle and pills to treat the river water, and no food. No flashlight. No dry clothes. No cellphone with pictures of the glyphs at Innadaltu. The ugly ring from Istanbul was gone too, after so recently rediscovering it. And Gramps's notebook … a sob ripped from her mouth.

She was so stupid. Why had she brought it? It was beyond precious and irreplaceable, and now it was gone.

Her shoulders heaved as the loss ripped through her. But through the haze of her grief, came a tiny voice. *It's just a book.* A very important book, at least it was to Brynn, but still just a book.

She sought a way to snap out of her sadness, her panic. *I'm not thinking clearly. And there can be no doubt that I must.*

She took a deep breath. A calm mind was needed. It was time to start making smart decisions.

She needed to live. Tristan knew she was here, somewhere. He would come back for her. He'd find her. All she had to do was wait. She could survive without food for some time. And water ... well, she could drink from the river. Probably not the best course of action since she could ingest parasites, but at least dehydration wouldn't do her in.

But what if Tristan was hurt? Or worse?

The thought squeezed her chest. Not only would that lessen her chances of someone searching for her, but she couldn't imagine a world where Tristan didn't occupy some small part of it. With determination, she pushed the anguished images aside.

The mist gradually lifted and in the waning light it was obvious that night was coming. As visibility improved, she could see that she was in an enclosed inlet. She must have been pushed down an offshoot, a literal dead-end.

This was bad. It meant that a search party could miss finding her altogether. Because surely someone would come looking for her. If not Tristan, then Shea.

Hit with the finality of her isolation, Brynn tried to keep her rapidly increasing panic at bay.

Okay, think.

She could attempt moving off the log and try to find dry land, but from what she could see, it appeared boggy to her right. There were many creatures that came out in the night, and she had no protection.

But hadn't she been sleeping in the jungle all this time in nothing more than a nylon tent? Had that been protection? She had trusted that it was, but in truth it never would have stopped a jaguar or a tenacious monkey if they had really wanted to attack her. But it at least had held the mosquitos and bugs at bay.

Based on that, she decided that she should stay on the log. If a boat came looking, she would likely be more visible. If she tried to get to land, she could become even more lost. And that was presuming she could even *find* land.

She unzipped her rain jacket, removed it, and shook it out, then she folded it into a makeshift pillow. She unrolled the sleeves of her shirt and buttoned the cuffs to cover her arms. Recalling that she had put an energy bar along with a few hard candies into her pants pocket, she retrieved it and broke off one-third of the bar. Slowly she ate it, savoring every bite, fighting the urge to consume the entire thing. She needed to ration it. And she would save the candies for later too. Thirst wasn't yet an issue, so she delayed taking a big gulp of river water. Although ... her gaze shifted to a collection of rainwater in a shallow cavity of the log a few feet from where she sat. Scooting forward on her butt, she decided to drink half of it and save the other half for later.

No, that was wrong. A bug or a mosquito could lay eggs in it. She needed to drink it all now. Dehydration was the biggest danger she faced, because it would muddle her thoughts and affect her decision-making.

Leaning forward on hands and knees, she slurped the liquid until it was gone. It surprised her how refreshing it was, and for a moment this small treat buoyed her spirits.

She thought of Lindsey Coulson, Ty's new girlfriend, who had nearly perished in August on K2 when she had become separated from her team. She had fought to live in a remarkable feat of endurance.

Brynn's situation wasn't nearly as bad. *I can do this. I can survive.*

She lay on her back with the jacket as a pillow and stared at the swirling clouds above her. Still wet, a shiver ran through her. She hugged her arms across her and sang Barry Manilow songs.

~

FROM THE PERCH of her log, Brynn searched all day for a sign of another human being, but there was no one. As twilight descended, she ate another third of her energy bar, and found two more pockets of water on adjoining logs. Then she settled in for a long night, trying not think about what it would be like with no protection. Sometime later, she slept.

She was running across a lush meadow, in a dress that was far too long and billowy. She stopped and glanced down. The maroon velvet gown appeared almost medieval, offset by gold-spun embroidery of symbols resembling a language of some kind. A closer inspection revealed it to be Gaelic, which she had studied briefly in high school after accompanying her family on a trip to Scotland to explore the history of the Galloways.

Scanning the impossibly green countryside surrounding her, a light wind stirring the trees to life, Brynn felt the chill of the air through her heavy garments. Just beyond was a lake, reminding her of the many lochs they had visited. *Was she in Scotland?*

In the distance, a white horse emerged from the dense forest, a man riding with a confident, almost arrogant demeanor.

She knew instantly it was Magee.

Brynn laughed as he neared. He wore the attire of a knight in shining armor, with a broadsword nestled into a scabbard at his side, as if he'd come straight out of a dramatic film laced with a romantic flair.

He reined the horse to a stop before her, his gaze filled with focus and intention.

"I am Sir Tristan, Seeker of the Truth." He reached out to her. "Will you take my hand?"

Yes.

The scene shifted and she was now with her grandfather in his home.

"You are fine," he said. "I'm dreaming you into the future."

Relief filled her. Gramps knew what was happening. He would make sure it all turned out okay.

He smiled and said, "'Midway to the journey of our life, I came to myself in a dark wood, for the straight way was lost.'"

"I don't understand," she said.

"That's from *Dante's Inferno*." He paused, then said, "Or how about this one from Ovid's *Metamorphosis*: 'Let me sing to you now, about how people turn into other things.'"

"What are you saying?"

"You're shedding your skin. Like a snake. Like one of those anacondas. You're becoming something more than you were. You're becoming yourself."

His words resonated like a long-repressed memory. But she couldn't waste this opportunity for answers. "Why did you create the shorthand?" she blurted.

He chuckled. "Don't you know?"

She had no idea what he was talking about. "I've lost the notebook ...." Despair filled her voice.

"It doesn't matter, Bee. You have everything you need."

"What does that mean?"

"*You* taught *me*. You wrote the shorthand."

WHEN BRYNN AWOKE, her dream of Tristan and Gramps faded as reality set in. Her spirits dropped. It was still night. She was still on a log in the middle of nowhere. Brushing tears from her cheeks, she stared at the most intense display of starlight she had ever witnessed. It was breathtaking, a bucket of glitter spilled across the sky. It seemed impossible that life only existed on Earth with such endless possibilities beyond.

But her awe soon turned to trepidation as she was forced to listen to the jungle in the dark. It hadn't seemed that noisy when she'd been on land, but then she'd always been exhausted and there had always been people around her. For some reason that had made her feel safe.

She became aware of the murderous shrieks and howls first. *Monkeys. It has to be monkeys.* Because if it wasn't, then she didn't want to think what it might actually be. Then came the bumping noises, then the rustling noises. Then the flopping in the water noises, which made her jump more than once.

But it was the growls that made her both tremble and feel hopeful at the same time. Because it meant that dry land couldn't be that far away. As reluctant as she was to leave the log, she knew that come first light she would have to. She couldn't remain floating on this piece of timber for another night.

When black faded to a grayish hue, she stretched her stiff limbs, her muscles aching, and ate the last of her energy bar. Fog blanketed her, and Brynn imagined this place wouldn't have looked much different eons ago, when life had just begun. The lungs of the planet, the womb of Mother Earth. A place filled with ancient wisdom. But also a place of death. And if she didn't want hers added to it, she needed to move.

But her thirst had become a beast in itself. She could no longer hold back and began scooping handful after handful of river water into her mouth, spitting out the twigs and dirt.

Suffering wasn't an unnatural state for her—she'd learned mental fortitude surfing and chasing after her father and brothers. Even her mother had fine-tuned Brynn's skills, since she could be emotionally remote at times.

Galloways compartmentalized, and they were good at it. It helped them excel. Her father, a software engineer by education, had built a thriving consulting firm from the bottom up. Her mother had been a kick-ass mountain climber before becoming a stay-at-home mom, although she continued to maintain multiple hobbies and projects. Her oldest brother Alec had formed his own underwater filmmaking company with his friend Dan "Double D" Donovan, travelling around the world filming the most dangerous shark of all —the great white. Tyler, the middle child between her and Alec, had reached the summit of K2, the second highest mountain in the world.

She had acquired focus and mental perseverance from Gramps, spending many summers learning cuneiform under his tutelage. Later, she'd dealt with the boredom of hours spent translating tablets at the museum in Istanbul.

She dated fringe guys and rebels to keep her on her toes.

Very little rattled her. In fact, she could count unsettling incidences on one hand.

Ty's childhood disappearance.

A surfing accident when she was fourteen and nearly drowned. *You gotta get pounded sometimes, you gotta get drilled,* Alec had told her.

Falling into a crevasse near base camp at K2. *Fuck death,* one of the climbers—Billy Packer—had said to her.

The breath of a wild jaguar against her cheek.

Looking into Magee's soulful and often cynical gaze.

She hung her head as tears burned her eyes. So much for being tough, because if Tristan were dead, she feared she would fall into the abyss and never find her way out.

She was tired and itchy from mosquito bites that had popped up in all crevices of her body. Hunger and thirst taunted her. She was alone in one of the most dangerous jungles on Earth.

No one knew where she was, not even Magee if he were still alive.

She released a scream, a grumbling cry, filled with frustration and anger.

Enough. She squared her shoulders. She could weep buckets later. Now, it was time to go.

A wave of dizziness hit when she stood. Lack of food, to be certain, and her stomach felt a little off, but thankfully it hadn't gotten any worse, especially after ingesting river water. She was weaker than expected, occasionally swaying as she fought to get off the floating tree trunks.

Was it a good idea to leave her logjam home? She didn't know anymore. Her mind felt fuzzy, her senses dulled.

One thing was certain, if she stayed here, she was giving up.

She wanted to live.

Carefully, she began stepping from log to log, going in a direction opposite of the river.

SHE RAN out of logs and with no land appearing she was forced to wade in a marshy bog. Her feet became stuck in mud, and she started to sink. Struggling to escape, her efforts only seemed to get her more entrenched.

Panic set in.

No no no.

What if she was trapped?

She knelt and went into the water, wiggling back and forth until she was able to free her foot. She remained on her stomach and swam through the shallow bog, dodging tall reeds and lily pads, hopefully avoiding snakes, caimans, and piranha. Tristan had said the locals liked to eat the vicious fish.

Trying to keep her cool, her eyes darted back and forth for a sign of anything, but would she actually see a danger coming for her?

An anaconda would likely be completely submerged. Piranha would eat her feet before she could stop them. But a caiman would have its eyes above the water, wouldn't it? She began to search for eyes.

She swore at every horror movie she'd ever seen.

Her hands pushed against the silty bottom—there was only about two to three feet of water—and she could tell that it was still too muddy to stand. She continuously spit water from her mouth as it splashed into her face.

She fought her way through this terrain for what felt like hours, periodically stopping to pant for breath. Her arms ached and she worried that she had no idea what direction she was headed. Finally, there was enough jungle debris to facilitate getting out of the water. She collapsed on thick vegetation, the sounds of the jungle surrounding her, the humidity thick, the unrelenting sun making her sweat profusely despite her lengthy swim.

She lay there, too spent to do anything else, and at some point, she dozed off. A loud plop in the water jolted her awake, and she snapped her head up in time to see the slithering backside of a large snake about ten feet from her. She rapidly shuffled upright as it disappeared into the water.

"It's okay, it's okay," she chanted to herself. "That snake wants nothing to do with you." Saying it aloud had to make it true.

But it didn't escape her notice that she easily could have ended her swim by climbing right onto the creature if she had been a little bit more to the left of her current position.

Rage and frustration boiled over. "I fucking hate the jungle!"

The foliage looked denser up ahead, so she willed herself toward it. At last, she reached sure footing and the blessed canopy overhead blocked the merciless sun.

She took in her surroundings. Now what?

If she went to the right, would she find anyone from their expedition? Shea? Tristan? Conrad and Irene, if they hadn't truly betrayed them?

But if she went left, could she find the Beni? Or a settlement since most were situated along the riverbanks?

Left it was.

With renewed determination, she set off.

CHAPTER 26

The jungle was hell.

Brynn missed her machete. Aside from her ongoing fantasy about a tall glass of ice water, she couldn't stop thinking about the wide blade that would have made all the difference as she fought her way through the dense tangles of vines and trees and plants with huge leaves.

She came face-to-face with spiders the size of her hand, turtles, smaller snakes that she had to assume were poisonous, and obnoxious monkeys she was certain were stalking her.

Anger had become her friend, motivating her to deal with these horrors as if they were nothing more than an imposition. The alternative was to let herself slide into madness.

Not on my watch.

She muttered to herself relentlessly, much of it filled with colorful and blush-inducing cuss words, and she took particular glee in combining them into innovative phrases that would've made the most hardened sailor gasp.

She was so immersed in her wordplay that she didn't see the men until she was right upon them. Stifling a scream, she gaped at four short indigenous males wearing very little clothing, staring at her from round faces with blank expressions.

Two of them held spears, standing upright, in their hands. The other two were squatting before a fire.

She swallowed past the lump in her throat, fearing she had made a fatal mistake. Surely they had heard her coming. Why hadn't they hidden? Had they thought she was a wild animal?

Seconds ticked by as the stare-down continued. Brynn's mind raced. Maybe she should run since one of them could spear her at any minute.

One of the men spoke, and she recognized it as Quechua, although she could hardly understand it.

She raised a palm in greeting and gave a shaky smile. *"Hola."* Her rudimentary Spanish would have to be good enough.

One of the men responded, but it was too rapid for her. The two men who had been squatting now stood.

She stumbled through a smattering of Spanish, telling them she had been lost for two days and could they help her? She motioned for food and water.

The men glared at her, their round faces showing a stern countenance. With only a cloth covering their genitals, the musculature in their stout bodies conveyed a physical prowess that Brynn knew not to underestimate despite that she had at least six inches of height on them. Markings, or tattoos, covered their faces, which were framed with straight, glossy black hair in a bowl cut. And they were barefoot.

Brynn feared she was making a terrible mistake worse by staying and attempting to communicate with them. She should have run away, but she was tired and hungry and thirsty, and as a sudden rush of tears overcame her, she released a humiliating sob. Quickly she covered her mouth to stifle any more of the outburst.

One of the men grabbed a pouch hanging from his body and offered it to her. Her hands trembled as she took it. She removed the stopper on the spout and took a drink. Water. It was blessed water. Closing her eyes, she took several long swallows.

With a grateful smile, she handed it back to the man. He nodded, still grim-faced. But at least they hadn't tried to kill her. Yet.

One of the other men handed her a cloth pouch. Inside she found dried bananas. Her hunger spun outward from her belly like a tornado, and it took great restraint on her part to not inhale the entire pile in one gulp. Carefully, she plucked one up and ate it. Not bananas, plantains. It was the most delectable thing she had ever eaten.

She nodded and gave a wan smile. *"Gracias,"* she whispered.

The man seemed to sense her hunger and indicated that she should keep the entire portion of chips. She scooped the food into her hand, nearly crying, and thanked him repeatedly, then she wolfed it down in less than thirty seconds. So much for restraint.

The man watched her with a palpable air of disgust. They all did. But Brynn couldn't bring herself to care. If they would help her, that was all that mattered.

Collecting their gear, they waved her on to follow. She gratefully obeyed, but apprehension never really left her.

Please don't let this be a mistake.

~

It HAD GOTTEN DARK, but her helpers hadn't stopped. They produced two flaming torches and kept going. Brynn was happy to trail behind, letting them run into whatever animal or snake might be up ahead. But she was careful to keep up, remembering how she'd gone astray while with Tristan, Shea, Dimar, and Freddie. It could happen so easily.

Without warning, the jungle gave way to a clearing surrounded by lit torches, revealing several huts and dark shapes of men, women, and children moving about. A dog barked and approached, and while Brynn loved animals, she hesitated to touch the animal when he came forward to sniff her, unsure of his reaction to a stranger. But he quickly accosted her with sloppy kisses, and she could almost hear Tristan's voice in her head. *Animal whisperer.*

As the group became visible to the villagers, a crowd formed around them. Much discussion ensued, none of which she understood. A Bolivian woman finally stepped forward, middle-aged and dressed in a cotton shirt and pants, and she touched Brynn's arm. Then she waved and yelled until the crowd parted, and led Brynn to a nearby hut, the dog finally departing for entertainment elsewhere.

Once inside, the woman indicated for Brynn to sit, which she did. Exhaustion came quickly. Brynn hadn't realized how much she had strained to keep it away. Now, she struggled to stay awake as the woman brought her a bowl of something warm and aromatic. Using a wooden spoon, Brynn made fast work of the stew-like meal, and drank great gulps of water when it was offered in a gourd.

She wiped her face with the back of her hand. *"Gracias."*

The woman gently pushed Brynn to lie on her back, giving a nod, her gaze filled with compassion, and then she fitted a mosquito net around Brynn, draping it from a hook above.

As Brynn fell asleep, it occurred to her that the tribe must have contact with the outside world, considering the woman's clothing. And how would they have gotten a mosquito net? Brynn hoped in the morning she could ask for help in getting back to Rurrenabaque. Surely, they would have heard of the town. Their supplies had to come from somewhere.

The mat she lay on was far from luxurious, but after that long night on the log, it felt like heaven, and she let her eyes drift shut.

BRYNN AWOKE ALONE in the hut, sensing from the muggy atmosphere that the sun had been up for a while. She had slept deeply, and although stiff and sore and feeling as though she had run a marathon without eating enough food, she felt ten times better than yesterday. Her energy was returning, as if she were once again plugged in and charging her batteries.

She sat up and pushed the netting aside, then combed fingers through her hair, wishing for something to tie it back. Maybe she could ask one of the women. She pulled on her shoes, somewhat drier than they had been the night before. For a moment she indulged a daydream that featured a hot shower, clean clothes, the company of a certain physicist, and fish tacos at her favorite beachside restaurant in Los Angeles. But that prompted a grumbling response from her stomach. She rose and stepped onto the front porch, and a young girl in a colorful dress appeared from around the corner and waved.

"Hello," she said.

"You speak English!"

"Yes."

Brynn realized the girl must have been waiting for her to wake up.

"I learned at school. My mother told me to take care of you and to talk to you."

"Thank you. My name is Brynn."

The girl smiled, her teeth white against smooth dark skin. "I am Kamila."

"I'm very happy to meet you, Kamila," Brynn said with gratitude.

"Are you hungry?"

"Very."

She waved Brynn to follow. "Come with me."

They passed a collection of huts and wooden buildings, then came to an open palapa where Kamila handed her a plate with chicken, rice, and sliced oranges. Brynn sank to the ground, crossed her legs, and quickly gobbled up the food. Kamila sat quietly until Brynn was finished.

"Gustavo said they found you in the wilderness," Kamila said.

"And I'm very grateful. I was lost."

"It is easy to become confused. We are told as children not to go into the jungle alone. But then when we are older, we are sent in."

"Why?"

"The jungle leaves all kinds of clues. You must learn to understand them. I'm sorry you were lost. Were you scared?"

"Yes."

"Do you have other people with you?"

"Yes. I need to go to Rurrenabaque. Can someone help me?"

Kamila nodded. "In two days, Gustavo can take you in his canoe."

"Thank you." Brynn wished it were sooner, but she didn't have much negotiating power.

"How did you get lost?"

"I was floating on a log with a man when a storm came, and we were separated. I got stuck in a side channel of the river and had no idea where I was. I don't suppose you've seen a tall white man with dark hair?"

"You are the only *gringo* to come out of the jungle." Kamila laughed, and Brynn suspected it was over the name she'd called her.

"Maybe he'll be along," Brynn answered. "He probably went much further downriver than me. He's probably already in Rurre." At this point, she was talking only to reassure herself.

Kamila suggested a tour of the village, and Brynn gratefully accepted. It was larger than it had first appeared, with nearly fifty villagers in residence, many of whom came to catch a glimpse of Brynn. Out of the crowd, a young girl stepped forward with a small monkey attached with a leash.

"This is Aracely," Kamila said. "This is her pet monkey."

The girl, her cheeks rounded and her nose flat, smiled shyly up at Brynn. Brynn knelt, wanting to appear friendly, but also watchful of the monkey. He was cute, and he watched Brynn with open curiosity.

"We did not steal the monkey from its mother," Kamila said. "He was found abandoned as a baby in the jungle. Aracely's father brought him back to nurse him to health, and now he is a favorite."

The young girl stepped close and suddenly the monkey climbed up Brynn's arm and perched on her shoulder, its little hands grabbing her cheeks and nose. She laughed, not sure what to do, while the little girl giggled.

Kamila revealed a toothy smile. "He likes you."

"Does he have a name?"

"We call him Kusillu. It means monkey. Or silly monkey. Or stupid monkey."

Kusillu made a snickering sound and climbed atop Brynn's head.

"He won't poop on me, will he?" Brynn asked with a laugh.

Kamila's young face took on an expression of concern. "Why? Do animals always go *caca* on you?"

Aracely tugged on the leash and Kusillu jumped down.

Brynn stood and said, "Something like that."

Kamila gave her a strange look and motioned her forward. "Please come this way."

They walked to a hut that was set farther back from the river, as well as distant from the other villager's homes. Kamila entered first and then indicated for Brynn to follow. Brynn was shocked to see Miss Carla. Beside her was a bright green parrot. His penetrating gaze watched Brynn from below a vibrant tuft of red and blue.

Reluctantly, Brynn dragged her attention from the stunning animal to the female shaman. "Miss Carla? I'm so happy to see you."

Kamila translated as the woman beckoned Brynn to sit. Brynn did as she bade, inordinately happy to find a recognizable face.

"Miss Carla is our medicine healer," Kamila said. "Not many women do this since they cannot marry or have children, and that is very hard for most."

Something in Kamila's voice caught Brynn's attention. "Do you want to be one?"

"I do. But I also want to leave Bolivia. I want to see New York City."

Brynn released a skeptical grunt. "Well, if you do, you'll appreciate this place a thousand times over." And Brynn knew it was true. As hard as it had been in the jungle these past few weeks, there was something deeply compelling about it.

But the sparkle in Kamila's eyes made Brynn realize how serious the girl was, and Brynn could hear her father whispering in her ear. *How can you change the world if you don't know the world?* Her parents had always believed in exposing her and her brothers to other people and cultures. *Don't be self-centered in your viewpoint. The world is a treasure waiting to be discovered.*

Kamila sat cross-legged beside Brynn and said, "Miss Carla wants to know where you are from."

"California."

Miss Carla rocked back and forth and with a laugh said, "Beach Boys."

The uncharacteristic outburst and cultural reference surprised Brynn. "You aren't as isolated as it would seem."

When Kamila stopped giggling, she said again, "Where are you from?"

"I just told you."

Miss Carla was speaking rapidly to Kamila in Quechua, who then said, "No. You are from somewhere much further away, a place that requires the pathway of time."

The intensity in Carla's dark eyes sent a shiver through Brynn.

Brynn sighed, thinking of her time with Ninsun and her dead grandfather. "I don't know. I suppose that might be true."

"She says you opened the portal."

Brynn frowned. "Is she talking about Innadaltu?"

Miss Carla nodded.

"I didn't know it was closed," Brynn replied, but the markings she translated in the cave, the ones that apparently had been written by her grandfather, had said the same thing. She remembered that afternoon when it had been her and Tristan beside the blue granite monolith, when she had been singing and generally goofing off. And then she had sung the tones Gramps had taught her. Was that when the portal opened?

Miss Carla spoke, and Kamila intermittently translated. "It has been closed for two rainy seasons. The light people have had nowhere to go. It has been a most distressing time for everyone here. But you have opened it. She is very happy. She wants to tell you that she is thankful."

"You're welcome." Brynn hesitated before asking the next question. "Can you ask her if the portal is used to travel through time?"

Kamila asked Carla, who nodded. "Sí."

"Has Carla traveled through time?"

The older woman gave a nod.

While Brynn would have liked to learn more details, something in Carla's gaze spoke of secrets to be kept, that Brynn's own journeys were for her and her alone. Brynn couldn't explain it, but it were as if Carla was looking at her like an equal. As if Brynn were a shaman. It greatly humbled her, mostly because she suspected that Carla had spent years honing her skills, and Brynn had all but stumbled into it when she had entered the jungle.

Kamila continued to translate when Carla spoke again, her voice low and the air becoming thick with foreboding.

"She says that while it is good the portal is open, there are those spirits who will use it for personal gain. A type of evil. You must be careful."

Brynn sat up straighter. "What can I do?"

Carla paused, considering Brynn, then said through Kamila, "You are strong, Brynn from California. You have many animals following you but heed the snake. He is of the underworld and very powerful. Earth energy. He can help you."

Miss Carla released a loud burst of laughter, startling Brynn. It triggered the parrot to squawk and start a jig, bobbing up and down and swaying back and forth.

And with that, Brynn's time with Miss Carla was done.

CHAPTER 27

"You mean there's a conservation outpost not far from here?" Brynn asked, incredulous.

It was the following morning, and Kamila had just told her of it. "An American with sunshine hair lives there."

Jack Montgomery. *Thank God.* He would know how to help her.

"Can you take me there?" Brynn asked.

Kamila nodded. "I can."

"Why didn't you tell me this before?" Brynn tried to tamp down her frustration. She liked Kamila and everyone here had been kind to her but getting to Rurre had been proving to be problematic in the extreme. She had been told Gustavo would take her tomorrow, but within a few hours that had changed to three days. And then she had received word that he was going hunting and didn't know when he would return. It had become clear that Gustavo would take her when he damned well felt like it, and there was little Brynn could do about it.

Jungle time appeared to run on a clock all its own. Considering her recent shamanic escapades, Brynn had wondered idly if she could sidestep it and create her own timeline, as ridiculous as it sounded, because worry over Tristan continued to weigh on her. If he were missing, then she would need to mount a search party for him. What if he was wasting away on a log just as she had been? What if he was still there?

"Can we go right now?" Brynn urged.

"Yes."

It took Kamila an hour to return to Brynn with supplies. Everyone in the village showed up to say goodbye, which took at least another forty-five minutes. When at last she and Kamila set off, a sense of urgency and foreboding accompanied Brynn into the wilderness.

AFTER A DUGOUT CANOE trip across the river followed by trekking all day with few breaks—Brynn's insistence, not Kamila, but the girl was in far better shape than Brynn anyway—they reached the conservation outpost by nightfall. Upon entering the main hut, Brynn was greeted by Shea.

She stopped abruptly and demanded, "Why are you here?"

He rose from the chair and engulfed her in a bear hug, then stood back. "Trails aren't as easy to follow as I'd hoped, but I'm about to head out. Where's Magee?"

"You haven't seen him?" Alarm filled her. "He's not here?"

"No. Jack hasn't seen him either. When did you become separated?"

She had to stop and think. "I'm not sure. Four or five days? I was lost. This is Kamila." Brynn stepped aside to introduce the girl. "She and her village helped me."

Jack entered and beamed at the girl. "Kamila, it's good to see you." Then his eyes landed on Brynn. "What's wrong? Where's Magee?"

"Not with me." Brynn's voice sounded hollow even to her.

Jack's dark gaze went soft. "I'm sure he's gone back to Rurre."

Montgomery was probably right. Except ... would Magee truly have abandoned looking for her? Would he have assumed she had gone to Rurre? It felt like a stretch, since she felt in her heart that he cared about her. Or had she simply been in the jungle too long? Had she managed to fall for the wrong guy yet again?

But something in Shea's eyes gave her a bad feeling. "What aren't you telling me?" she asked quietly.

"It's just I don't believe Tristan would abandon you, Brynn," Shea said. "So if you haven't seen him in days, and no one here has heard anything, then ..."

"Then what?" Panic edged her voice.

Shea didn't speak, but his answer was all too clear.

And with that, the wind got knocked clean from her. Her legs buckled and Shea caught her before she hit the wood floor. He helped her to sit on a bench, leaning her back against the wood-planked wall.

Her world was bottoming out, and she was spinning, the rush of her own blood screaming in her ears.

A sob escaped her lips, a grief-stricken howl, the sound inhuman. How had she not noticed the depth of her feelings for Magee? Pain sliced through her, awful and unbearable, and tears poured down her cheeks.

Please stop. Please please please.

She was stumbling in the darkness, her arms flailing ahead of her, searching for something solid to stand upon, a place that could shield her from the chaos that was fast consuming her, pushing her head underwater. She was drowning.

Shea put an arm around her. "Easy, Brynn." His voice echoed in the distance. "I've got you. Just breathe."

But Brynn was somewhere else entirely. Only later did she realize she was searching for him in a place where the dead might go. When she was unable to find him or some essence of him, his spirit, a ghost, anything ... it gave her the tiniest bit of hope that Shea was wrong.

Tristan couldn't be dead. She would know, somehow, if he were. And she was damned certain the stubborn man simply wouldn't allow it.

∼

TRISTAN APPROACHED Jack's station in the dark, completely spent. He'd been in the jungle for days searching for Brynn.

He hadn't found her.

After becoming separated in the storm, he had made it to land and immediately backtracked to look for her. But there had been nothing. Until this afternoon when he'd found her pack caught in a collection of brambles, bobbing in brackish water.

He tried to convince himself that it didn't mean anything, but if she were lost without any supplies .... He didn't want to wrap his mind around that outcome.

He was exhausted, and he needed help. Thank God he'd found his way back to Jack's.

Since it was so late, he decided to crash in the main building and talk to Jack in the morning. There was no reason to wake him. They couldn't mount a search in the dark anyway. But Tristan feared for Brynn, and dread churned in his gut.

He climbed the porch and walked into the main building. No one locked their doors here. Tristan wasn't sure what time it was. He bumped into someone in a hammock and cursed.

It was Shea, who said, "Jack?"

"No, it's Tristan."

Shea bolted out of the hammock, locking Tristan into an embrace, surprising him with its strength. "We thought you were dead," he whispered, then released him.

Shea flipped on a battery-powered lamp, casting the hut in a soft glow, and Tristan sank to a bench.

Tristan wasn't dead, but if Brynn were, a part of him would be.

His cousin sat across from him. "What happened to you?"

"I'll tell you later. Is Jack here? I need to look for Brynn, and I need help and supplies. I want to leave at first light."

Shea's strained expression lessened, and he flashed a fleeting smile. "She's here."

Tristan's body sagged with relief.

Thank God.

Overcome with emotion, he hung his head, not wanting to embarrass himself, but he shook as the tears came.

Shea's hand clasped his shoulder. "She arrived this evening. You two have been through the wringer. She's staying in the guest hut, alone. You should go to her. We can talk in the morning."

Tristan raised his eyes and swiped at the wetness. "Look at me, bawling like a baby. What the hell do you think that means?"

"She did the same earlier. She was devastated when she thought you were dead." He paused. "I think it means you've met your match. There's no turning back now."

"As if I ever could with her." The emotion in his voice shocked him. And despite his bone-deep fatigue, his chest was filling with a hope that he hadn't experienced in days. *She's alive.*

"But a word of advice," Shea said. "You stink like peccary. You should get cleaned up before you tell the love of your life that you're not dead. And let me get you some food."

Tristan nodded. He would give Shea five minutes, and that was it. Then he would find Brynn.

AFTER EATING brazil nuts and dried plantain chips, Tristan gave himself a makeshift bath with a wet rag and changed his shirt with a spare loaned from Shea. He went to the small hut that sat in the back of the compound, a flashlight guiding the way. Quietly stepping into the enclosure, he kept the light to the side and could make out Brynn's sleeping form in the hammock, mosquito netting covering her.

He was so damned glad to see her. He wanted to wake her up and pull her into his arms, but Shea had told him how exhausted she was when she'd arrived earlier. After briefly sharing what had happened to her, Shea decided that she and Tristan must have ended up on opposite sides of the river, which would explain why he hadn't found her. She had remained on a log for a day and a night with no shelter, very little food, and questionable water, and she'd had no protection if a wild animal had decided to prey on her.

She was lucky to be alive.

Gratitude filled Tristan's chest as he watched her.

She appeared serene, but her cheeks looked splotchy, and Tristan wondered if she'd cried herself to sleep. Over him. Shea had said she'd been inconsolable when they all had thought Tristan was lost and possibly dead.

Staying away from her was no longer an option. He couldn't pinpoint the exact moment when he'd fallen for her, but there was no doubt a connection had sparked at Isla del Sol. He'd just refused to acknowledge it. Probably because he'd known on some deep level that if he gave in to it, then Brynn Galloway would irrevocably change his life. And was any man ever ready for that?

But none of it mattered anymore.

It was time to stop dancing around her. Flirting, isn't that what she'd called it? A smile tugged at his lips.

Brynn Galloway was about to get courted the likes of which she had never seen. To hell with any other man she'd ever been with.

There was a pallet on the floor, with mosquito netting. Tristan went to it, lay down, and turned off the flashlight. For the first time in several endless and terrible days, he relaxed and slept.

Brynn came awake with a start.

In the darkness, a strange stillness encompassed the little hut where she slept. She wished she could go back to sleep, because in wakefulness the real world came crashing in. And in the real world, Tristan was gone. She rubbed at her chest and the very real physical pain in her heart, knowing it was futile. It would never disappear.

Something moved on the floor. She froze.

Had an animal found its way into the structure?

She struggled to see into the darkness. The netting didn't help, and she could just make out a dark outline. It looked big.

As her eyes adjusted, a human form materialized.

Someone was asleep on the floor. They must have come in during the night. A little discomfited that she was sharing the space with another person, she wondered if it were Shea. Maybe there hadn't been enough beds—or hammocks—to go around.

But as she continued to stare at the sleeping form, a sliver of hope began to blossom.

Was it …. It couldn't be ….

"Tristan?" she whispered.

The shadowy figure shifted, rolling onto his back. It was definitely a he.

Her heart pounded, but she was afraid to believe it was actually him. Maybe she was dreaming.

"Hi, Lola." His quiet voice reverberated clear through her.

"Am I still asleep?"

"I don't know. Are you?"

"Shea said you were dead."

"Reports of my death have been greatly exaggerated."

She rubbed a hand across her face, making sure she was awake. "Are you real?" Her voice was filled with so much longing it surprised her. If this were a dream, it was both the best and most cruel gift the universe had given her yet.

He pushed aside the netting surrounding him and stood, moving to the edge of her hammock. In her haste to get out of her hammock, she rolled out, her knees hitting the floor. Strong hands gripped her, keeping her from falling on her face.

Her fingers clasped onto hard muscle. He was blessedly solid.

Or else this was the most vivid dream she had ever had.

Could she be on some kind of spirit walkabout? It felt real, but so had her time with Ninsun in ancient Mesopotamia. Brynn really hoped she wasn't losing her mind, but at the moment she didn't care. She clung to Tristan, climbing her way up his body like a monkey on a vine, and pulled his face to hers, kissing him without preamble. His mouth tasted like nuts, his lips chapped and rough, or maybe it was hers from days in the sun with little protection. She didn't care.

Everywhere her hands touched—his rough-hewn cheeks, his damp hair, the smooth texture of the t-shirt that stretched across wide shoulders—her mind reeled from the headiness of it. She had fought this for so long, but now it didn't matter. He was here, now, wherever that now might be, and she gave herself over to the sheer pleasure of it.

His arms came around her, crushing her against him, and she shuddered from the wave of desire that coursed through her. He deepened the kiss, sweeping her mouth with his tongue, and she met him with the same desperate need.

His fingers fumbled with the buttons of her shirt, while she tugged at the hem of his and lifted it upward, tossing it to the floor. In the darkness, she couldn't see much, so she let her hands explore the thin layer of hair across his chest, then slide lower to his flat stomach. His muscles clenched and his breath hissed under her hungry caresses. He was every desire she never knew she had.

He pulled her pants down, which she kicked away, and then he shed his own trousers. Running a finger beneath the rim of her panties, he watched intently as she was bared to him.

"Brynn." His low voice tugged at that place deep in her abdomen as he fixated on her, running both palms along the side of her hips and down her thighs. He kissed her belly, just above the vee between her legs, but didn't go further. It was just as well. Brynn was impatient to feel him inside her.

She pulled her sports bra upward and tossed it aside. Tristan came back to his feet, his head still dipped forward as he continued to gaze at her naked body.

"I can't tell you how many times I thought of this," he murmured.

She splayed her hands into his hair and pulled his face to hers, smiling against his mouth. "I know."

"You just wanted me to suffer?" he teased.

"You had to earn it, Magee." She devoured his mouth, pressing her breasts against his bared chest, the contact drawing a ripple of pleasure in her pelvic region.

She arched, moaning, then slid her palms down his back, his skin slick with sweat. His mouth captured hers again as his hands cupped her buttocks and pressed her against him. He was rock hard, and she was so ready.

His voice was ragged, raspy. "I don't have any protection."

It rather warmed her heart—possibly the only part of her not on fire at the moment—that he wasn't loaded with condoms just waiting to get laid by the next female he might encounter.

"I've got it covered," she whispered. While she hadn't been in a relationship for many months, she had used a more long-lasting form of birth control before traveling to Pakistan over the summer with her brother. It had been her mother who had prompted Brynn to protect herself, not just from an impromptu romance, but from a situation that could place her in danger.

They moved to his pallet on the floor, where he pulled her down to straddle him. She teased and taunted him until they had a good fit, but they still hadn't completely joined.

"You're killin' me, Lola," he hissed.

Looping her arms around his neck, she lifted her hips slightly and slid down him until he was fully inside her. Wrapping her legs around him, she kissed him hard while he bucked. Her body clenched, trying to get as close to him as possible, and then her orgasm slammed into her and she rode the crest for as long as she could, Tristan's embrace holding her locked against him.

As the passion slowly ebbed, they remained together like two puzzle pieces that had finally found their match, the shadows thick with sex and satisfaction.

Her mouth found his, the salt of his sweat coating her tongue, and she kissed him with seduction and hunger, as if they hadn't just satisfied each other. Their limbs slipped against each other, slick with perspiration.

He was still hard inside her, and they began to rock again, this time with less fervor but no less connection. His mouth dropped to one of her breasts, and his teeth lightly grazed a nipple, then he suckled, and she came again, long and languid, his mouth remaining on her breast until she was finished, then he thrust hard, capturing her lips with a rough, primitive kiss, and he gripped her tightly as he took her again.

As they both recovered in a haze of contentment, Brynn felt spent in the best possible way. She leaned her forehead to his and ran her fingers along his lower lip. He captured one, sucking on the tip before releasing it.

"I think," he said, "no more riding logs."

A laugh escaped her. "Now you tell me."

CHAPTER 28

Tristan sipped hot coffee in the main hut with Jack and Shea. It was early—too early—to be up and about, but he had wanted to talk to the men alone.

Brynn was curled up on the pallet on the floor in the guest hut, sleeping soundly. During the night they had talked briefly about what had happened while they had been apart. And then Brynn had slept. She was exhausted, as was Tristan, but his heart was full with her in his arms. Sometime during the night, she had awakened again, and he'd gladly succumbed to her carnal needs once more. After their lusty first encounter, he hadn't thought he would want her again so soon.

When he did sleep, his dreams had been filled with her, his body caught in a state of semi-arousal throughout the night.

Even now, he wanted to expedite this conversation so he could get back to her.

Jack offered Tristan a plate of sliced papaya, the man's blond hair obviously combed back with a quick swipe of his hand. "It's good see you, Magee."

Tristan set the food on the table beside him. "It's good to be seen." He popped a piece of the ripe fruit into his mouth, savoring it much the way he'd savored Galloway's body just hours before. "There were moments I wondered if this was it. If this was where I was going to eat it."

They were all clad in wrinkled T-shirts and shorts and sporting mussed hair, and it would appear they all had stumbled here in search of the panacea of coffee.

Shea grimaced. "It's a good thing you're not dead because there'd be nothing left of you down here. And there'd be nothing left of me because Aunt Eleanor would strip my hide and throw salt on it."

"Aww, c'mon. I could be a mummy like the one Conrad stole and is spiriting away to La Paz as we speak." Tristan polished off the remainder of the fruit. "Speaking of which, why aren't you following him?"

Shea leaned his head back against the wall. "The rain came, as you well know. That's when I lost them. But I'll be leaving shortly. Are you coming?"

Tristan nodded. "Yeah. Brynn too. It's time to get out of the jungle. We'll reassess in La Paz."

Shea looked past Tristan's shoulder and smiled. "Good morning," he said.

Tristan turned and saw Brynn standing in the doorway wearing her pants and shirt from last night, looking sleepy and sexy as hell. The sparkle in her eyes was directed at him, making him want to usher her right back to the hut, but he was also glad she was looking more herself. Shea had said she'd been a wreck the day before.

"Morning." She stepped inside.

Tristan rose from his stool and offered it to her. "Coffee?" he asked.

She nodded. He poured a cup from the side table and brought it to her.

"Thanks."

Shea chuckled. Jack smirked.

"What's so funny?" she asked.

Jack flicked a glance at Shea. "I didn't believe you."

"I told you. He's got it bad."

Brynn's cheeks reddened and Tristan glared at them. "Stop embarrassing the lady."

"Yeah, sorry, Brynn," Shea said. "I just never thought I'd see the day."

She took a sip from her cup. "For what?"

"The fall of Magee. I hope you know what you're in for."

Tristan grabbed a brazil nut from a nearby dish and tossed it at his cousin. Shea leaned to the side and swatted it away.

Brynn smiled and held her coffee cup close to her nose, inhaling the aroma while drinking. "So what's the plan?" she asked.

Tristan grabbed another stool and sat beside her.

"First, Rurre," Shea said. "Then La Paz."

Tristan suddenly remembered her backpack. He retrieved it from the corner of the hut where he'd dropped it last night.

Brynn gasped. "Oh my God. You found it?" She set her coffee down and took the pack, stiff and crusted with dirt. "I thought I'd lost it all—the ring, the notebook, the photos on my phone."

"What notebook?" Shea asked.

Brynn crouched and unzipped the main pouch. She pulled out a clear baggie that held all three items.

"You're lucky you did that," Tristan said.

"I know," she murmured as she removed the contents. The notebook looked intact but there was evidence of water damage, and she was able to turn on her phone. She glanced up at him. "Thank you for finding it."

She stood and placed the notebook on the small table. Shea and Jack gathered beside her. "This belonged to my grandfather. And it contains the truncated glyphs that we found at Innadaltu."

"Your grandfather had been there?" Jack asked.

Brynn shook her head. "No. Not as far as I know. And I thought that he had written the glyphs because I broke the code and translated what was written in the cave."

"You did?" Tristan asked, surprised. "Why didn't you tell me?"

"Because it wasn't anything of importance. In the end it was simply a note to me. Although," —she groaned under her breath as she flipped through several pages—"some of his notes are damaged. Dammit."

"You're saying that somehow your grandfather wrote you an encoded message in a cave in the middle of nowhere Bolivia?" Shea's voice rang with skepticism.

Brynn pulled herself out of her stupor and looked up, her eyes flashing with determination. "Oh, it gets better," she said. "Turns out, he didn't create the shorthand. I did."

Everyone jumped when a disheveled woman burst into the hut.

"Milenka?" Brynn rushed forward and helped her to sit as the woman tried to catch her breath. "Did you run here from your village?"

Jack offered a cup of water, which Milenka gratefully drank in loud gulps. Her sweat-soaked blouse clung to her rounded curves, and sticks and leaves stuck to her black hair.

When she could finally talk, it came out in spurts. "Turtle Village ... Rigo ...." Her brother's name was more of a cry. "He's done something terrible ...."

It didn't take a prophet to know what it was. "He drugged the *chicha*," Tristan said.

Milenka's eyes widened in horror, but Tristan was doubtful of her innocence.

"I didn't know that," she cried, then took another long drink, emptying her cup, which Jack proceeded to refill. "But I heard he's involved again with the Mamani boys."

"The Mamanis search for gold on behalf of outside interests," Jack said. "The rumors are they're a bit ruthless, but in truth I've never heard of any violence. Mostly, they bully and intimidate if anyone sniffs too close. I've no doubt they regularly trespass where they shouldn't and pollute water sources with mercury."

"They've kidnapped Dimar," Milenka wailed.

"What?" Brynn asked, a line creasing her brow. "Why?"

"I don't know!"

"And Freddie?" Brynn added.

"Yes, they have him too."

When Tristan met Brynn's gaze, he understood her questioning frown. It would appear Milenka was more worried about her old boyfriend than her current one. Poor Freddie. He'd never had a chance with her.

Tristan turned back to the hysterical woman. "I'm gonna go out on a limb here and say they have Pico as well?"

"Yes. Pico too. And those *gringos* you were looking for."

Shea swore. "Conrad and Irene."

Milenka's eyes darted from one person to the next. "I heard that Solomon owes the Mamanis money. It's all his fault."

Perfect. "Are they the ones who took my clay tablet from Pico?" Tristan asked.

"I don't know. Probably. They steal stuff all the time, especially artifacts. I need your help to save Dimar."

"And Freddie," Brynn said pointedly.

Milenka nodded, but Tristan guessed she'd agree to anything to get their help.

"All right," he said. "Let's go check it out."

"I'll grab my gear," Jack said. "And I know a shortcut."

CHAPTER 29

B rynn crouched beside Milenka, hidden in the late day shadows of the jungle. Together they peeked at the scene beyond—a large fire with several men on guard, looking haphazard but still dangerous.

Upon cursory contact with Turtle Village, they had quickly learned, thanks to Milenka's language skills, that something was happening in a clearing about a mile northeast, but it seemed separate from the villagers, something they didn't wish to be a part of. Brynn and the rest of them were on their own.

Tristan and Shea had circled to the far side of the encampment, and Jack had blended in somewhere else. They all had guns, as did the apparent ruffians at the campfire, making Brynn nervous. None of this was worth getting shot for.

As some of the guards shifted their stance, the prisoners became visible—Conrad and Irene, Solomon, and Dimar, Freddie, and Pico. Each sat on the ground with their hands tied behind them.

Milenka's distress was becoming palpable, with her rapid breathing and faint whimpers, and Brynn wondered if she'd be forced to muzzle the woman.

Why did the captors—which likely included these Mamani brothers—want so many prisoners? It was almost as if they were waiting for someone. And Rigo was missing.

"Milenka, where's your brother?" Brynn whispered, but when she turned to the woman she was shocked to see she was gone. A commotion just beyond the camp caught her attention, revealing a woman in a colorful skirt walking toward the group of prisoners.

Miss Carla?

The woman certainly seemed to be popping up everywhere.

"Don't move," a strange voice said in a Bolivian accent, and Brynn froze. "Stand up."

Slowly, Brynn complied, raising her hands above her head. As she carefully turned to the guard who pointed a gun at her, Brynn wasn't surprised to see Milenka tucked behind him. Had the distraught woman turned Brynn in? Or had she simply made a run for it and gotten caught? Brynn hoped it was the latter, because then perhaps the presence of Tristan, Shea, and Jack had yet to be detected.

Brynn was ushered to the campfire, concern flashing in Irene's gaze as their eyes met. The guard shoved Brynn to sit beside her, and Milenka too, then their hands were tied behind them.

Miss Carla surveyed the scene with a cool detachment. Words hung on the tip of Brynn's tongue, a plea to the older woman to help them, but something sharp and angry in Carla's eyes made Brynn hold back.

A discussion ensued between one of the captors and Miss Carla, and while Brynn couldn't understand it, she guessed it was about them.

Brynn leaned near Irene and said quietly, "What the hell is going on?"

"They came for us days ago. You were out cold from the *chicha*."

"Why didn't they take us too?"

"They didn't want the dead weight."

"Tristan thinks the *chicha* was drugged. Was it?"

Irene gave an imperceptible nod. "Probably. Conrad and I never drink the stuff."

Brynn shifted her attention to Milenka, but the woman's tearful eyes were fixated on Dimar. *Good grief.* "Milenka," Brynn whispered. "Why is Miss Carla here? What's going on?"

Milenka sought to compose herself. "She asks why are all these people here? She says she only wanted Solomon. That man, he is a Mamani, says they have a mummy and a buyer for it. He thinks she is being hysterical. That has made her angry." Milenka paused and swallowed hard before continuing. "I am shocked by how Miss Carla is speaking to him. We shouldn't ever speak to them that way."

Brynn swung her gaze to Solomon. With his chin raised in defiance and his face hardened, he was obviously angry at Miss Carla. Had Dimar been right all along? Was this a battle of spooks out here in the jungle? Brynn wanted to search the perimeter for Tristan and the others, but she didn't want to give them away. Surely Solomon would know or suspect that Tristan was here. But the question was, would he tell his captors?

Miss Carla approached Solomon, and if the frosty interaction was any indication, they were most definitely not friends. They began conversing in a mish mash of Spanish and Quechua, and Brynn thought she heard *doorway* and something about *stopping this*.

Without warning, a throbbing pain flared inside Brynn's skull and she looked behind her, thinking that someone had hit her. But there was no one. As the ache grew, like a migraine on steroids, she cried out and toppled to the side against Irene, slumping to the ground. The spasm escalated and just when she couldn't bear it any longer, the intense ache suddenly stopped. The jungle disappeared and she slipped into darkness, feeling as she had when she'd gone to Mesopotamia. Was she sliding to a different place? A different time?

She opened her eyes, dizzy and disoriented. Carefully she stood. She was still in the jungle, but it was alive in technicolor, and everyone around the fire was gone. Movement caught her attention, and she jumped back as a giant anaconda revealed itself.

What sweet hell was this? The thing was gigantic. Was this the sixty-footer Tristan had mentioned that Percy Fawcett had witnessed? But this wasn't real, she reminded herself. She was in some kind of alternative shamanic reality. Fawcett must've been trippin' too. Yes, that must have been it.

The snake can't hurt me in this realm.

Right?

A flash of light momentarily blinded her, and then Solomon and Miss Carla were there, facing off as if warriors in a battle. It was the strangest thing Brynn had ever seen.

Carla was speaking in a low voice, chanting, and Solomon held out a hand, palm forward. Suddenly Carla was pushed onto her back, flat on the ground, and gold coils wrapped around her, restraining her. Struggling, she couldn't break free.

Solomon walked over to her. With a hovering hand, he began slicing through parts of Carla's body, starting at her feet, as if he were chopping an onion.

Brynn rushed forward. "Stop!" She knew this wasn't the physical realm, but she was still horrified. Somehow, Solomon was trying to separate the parts of Carla.

He ignored Brynn and continued his assault.

Brynn waved her arms. She put her face directly in front of Solomon's, trying to block him, but it was as if she were invisible to him. Frustration welled up inside her, a fountain of anger spewing from the center of her being.

"Stop!" she roared, pushing at Solomon's ethereal form with both of her hands.

He flew back, stunned, and only then did he look at her.

Good. You can see me.

"What are you doing?" Brynn demanded.

Solomon's face was suspended in shock. "How did you get here?"

"Somehow you brought me here."

Carla's gaze was glassy, and she was surrounded by severed pieces of her feet and lower legs. If she died here, could she die out there?

"Why are you hurting her?" Brynn asked.

"This doesn't concern you."

"Is this about the portal?"

"Of course it is," he yelled. "You opened it after I made sure it was closed."

"Why would you close it?"

"Because my father would not stay on the other side. He kept coming through. He kept clinging to me and taking my life force. I close every portal I can find."

Understanding began to dawn. "Did my grandfather give me the key to open Innadaltu?"

Solomon stood. "That would explain it, since you are certainly not strong enough to do it yourself."

Ignoring his condescension, Brynn looked back at Carla. "Is she dying?"

"She was going to do the same thing to me," he defended. "It separates your spirit. It drives you mad in the real world."

Nice.

"I can't let you." Brynn put herself between them.

"How will you stop me? You may have traveled back in time, but it wasn't you. That woman pulled you back. You have no skills here. Get out of my way."

Brynn hesitated. Somehow, she had ended up in this place, with them. And she doubted that Solomon or Carla had thrown out the welcome mat. What did this mean?

Brynn stood straighter. "You'll have to get through me to harm her."

Solomon stomped forward, determination on his face, and Brynn's body locked into a mode that was more like remembering a long-forgotten skill. A deep memory in her heart. An echo from the past, of her ancestors in Scotland, and further. It was clear now. She was born of the blood of Ninsun, as was Gramps. They were Ninsun's offspring. Her ancestral children. Ninsun had come looking for them, having imbued her skills and her magic directly into the bloodline.

Brynn sang the tones, the ones Gramps had taught her. The ones that Ninsun had taught him. The resonance built in her chest, vibrating, and whatever power it held, it stopped Solomon. He couldn't get past her. Fury filled his eyes.

His gaze shifted from rage to calculation. "You'll pay for this." And with that he was gone.

For a moment, Brynn was elated, and she ceased the sounds, waiting for Solomon to return. But finally, when he seemed truly gone, she turned to Carla, and out of instinct she let her hands hover over the broken pieces of the woman's body, wanting—hoping—to help, to ease her discomfort.

Heat sprang from Brynn's fingertips and a humming began, and the pieces came back together.

Carla opened her eyes, and on a sigh, she whispered, "I knew you were the one, but you must go. Now." This conversation wasn't in English, but Brynn understood her.

"What do you mean?" she asked.

"You must find Solomon before it's too late. To change the present, he must change the past. He means to take him from you."

Magee.

"But I thought Solomon cared about Tristan?"

"Solomon cares about balance. That means more to him than anything else. Or any person."

"How do I find him?"

"The hospital."

CHAPTER 30

Tristan watched the scene unfolding by peeking over the roots of a wide tree trunk. Shea and Jack were also hidden somewhere. Tristan had almost blown his cover when he'd seen Brynn and Milenka brought in by one of the guards, but then Miss Carla had appeared, and by all accounts she looked to be in charge. So Tristan had waited, trying to figure out what the hell was happening. When his gaze landed on a pile of gear off to the side, he was sure he spotted a hard-shelled suitcase. It had to be the case that held his clay tablet.

If he waited, maybe he could get it. And he'd get Brynn. And then they could get out of here.

A rapid tingling formed at the base of his neck, and he rubbed at it. Had something bitten him? The sensation intensified, culminating in a sharp pain deep inside Tristan's brain. He barely contained a strangled groan as every muscle in his body clenched tight. He rolled to the right, cognizant that he needed to hide his location, and then suddenly the heat and the jungle and the incessant buzz of bugs disappeared.

His awareness changed and reformed itself, slowly revealing a different reality. He was in the goddamned hospital room. Again. Fuck!

For a moment, he railed against it, his rage boiling white hot. He was so fucking done with this panic-inducing flashback that he couldn't seem to stop reliving.

Wake up, Tristan. Wake the fuck up!

But a quick glance revealed that this was different than the other flashbacks. Instead of viewing everything *from* the hospital bed, he was now standing beside it, where a younger and much smaller Tristan lay. There was a tube in his child-self's mouth, his youthful skin pasty white in stark contrast to his dark brown hair. This Tristan was so fragile. So alone.

The urge to protect him—to protect himself—flooded him.

And then he sensed them. In the room, just beyond the visible. Anxiety clawed at his chest, but he refused to step back, to hide, to make himself invisible. Someone had to fight for the young boy in the hospital, because what if this time the entities succeeded? What if this time they took him? His dad had interviewed so many alien abductees that Tristan had never doubted that it could happen to him.

A form stepped into the room, and a wave of unease filled him. It looked like a man, but it couldn't be. It was an alien, here to hurt his child-self. Every time before, Tristan had kept his eyes shut. Some part of him had always believed that if he didn't witness whatever the creature was or whatever it did, then maybe what happened hadn't actually occurred. It had always worked before, because despite the numerous encounters that Tristan had relived, he had always come back. Brynn had been right. He needed to stop looking away. He needed to face this.

Thinking about her brought a rush of emotion, sharp and sweet, and he longed for her, to see her again, to hold her and drink in her gasp when she came apart in his arms.

Brynn.

The form coalesced into something denser, and Tristan forced himself to move forward, to stand between this creature and the boy lying in the bed. And then ....

Tristan stopped, stunned.

It was no alien from outer space, with a big head and dark insect-like eyes. It was Solomon.

"What are you doing here?"

"He's not supposed to be here." A female voice echoed from the shadows of the room. Brynn?

Solomon moved so fast that Tristan didn't see him shoot to the other side of the hospital bed. The shaman held a hand, palm down, over young Tristan, and Tristan could feel the power emanating from the man, he could feel the constriction in his child-like chest.

"What the hell are you doing?" Tristan demanded.

Solomon raised his gaze, and fear coursed through Tristan. The shaman always had been dangerous. On some level, Tristan had known, but he hadn't wanted to believe it. He'd wanted desperately to admire the man, in the same way that he had desperately wanted to admire his father.

Solomon turned his head, looking at something behind Tristan. "Tell her to stop. Tell her to close the portal."

Tristan didn't need to look to know who was there. It was Brynn. Somehow, time was folding on itself. Whatever was happening, she had always been a part of it. He'd studied physics, and now he knew it wasn't to debunk his father and his obsessive beliefs, but to understand this woman who had always been tied to him across time.

"Why?" Tristan asked. "Are you going to kill me? The me in the past? Will this erase this timeline? Won't it erase you, too?"

Solomon shook his head in impatience. Tristan knew the man had never liked science. It was too cold. Too impersonal. Shamanism was alive and vibrant and as real as the reality normally occupied in three-dimensional space. "We must close all the portals. We must keep my father out." He flicked his gaze to Brynn. "Do it!"

Brynn appeared beside Tristan, glowing white like an ethereal snowman. "The portal is used by far more beings than just your father, Solomon," she said. "You can't shut down this dimension. It isn't yours to control."

Solomon's eyes flashed with fire. "Do it, or I'll end his life right now." His hand still hovered over the sickly Tristan.

The first sonic wave shoved Solomon back. The second one threw him to the floor. The third one made him disappear altogether.

With the air around them still vibrating, Tristan whispered, "How did you do that?"

"It all begins with music," Brynn said. "I started with John Denver, then moved to Barry Manilow, but the grand finale was the Carpenters. You need to go back into your body, Tristan, but I'll see you soon. In about twenty years."

The fear that had remained a hard, heavy knot in his chest broke apart. And finally, Tristan could breathe.

But his relief was short lived when alarm flashed in Brynn's eyes. "I must go."

TRISTAN'S EYES FLEW OPEN, the jungle canopy filling his vision. He lay on his back on the hard ground, his head still pounding from *whatever* had just happened. Miss Carla's round face slid into view as she bent over him, smiling, which then turned into a boisterous chuckle that revealed all of her discolored teeth.

Somehow, he knew it was going to be okay.

He was helped to his feet by two of the guards. As he was guided to the fire where the prisoners had been kept, every one of them had been released and were now standing around, dazed, as if they'd survived some natural disaster. Shea and Jack had also emerged from their hiding spots. Solomon was no longer shackled but he appeared spent and defeated, sitting a distance apart, his head hanging forward with both hands clasping his forehead.

Tristan locked eyes with Brynn almost immediately. In a few short steps, she was in his arms.

"What the hell was that?" he murmured.

"Apparently, I was caught up in Dimar's spook war." Her words tickled the skin at his throat. Leaning back, she looked directly at him. "Do you remember?"

"Yeah. No aliens. It was you. Singing a Tristan Magee playlist."

She smiled. "I can't even begin to tell you what I did, but I think

Gramps had been prepping me for it. Somehow, he must've known. Maybe Ninsun told him."

"But what happened at the end?"

A crease formed between her brows. "Somehow, Solomon left the hospital and went in search of me. It turns out the day you were in a coma was the same day Tyler went missing in that meadow."

"Solomon went looking for you? You were only five years old in that time period."

"Luckily, I had help."

"Who?"

"Me. I'm wondering now how many 'me's' there are in that meadow."

"Don't worry. I can look past this."

She gave him a pointed glare. "Past what?"

"That you're a multidimensional time traveler. Nobody's perfect."

She gave him a playful shove.

He kissed her. It was much too chaste for his taste, but they had an audience, so he reluctantly held himself in check. "I'm liking this wrinkle in our relationship," he added.

"Why's that?"

"Isn't it obvious? Can you imagine how many artifacts we can track down now? You can hop back in time and locate them in their original hiding place."

"Magee ...."

He held onto her, kissing her again, laughing.

"Can we go now?" Dimar demanded, flashing a nervous look at Tristan. "Before the Mamani brothers change their minds?"

"Miss Carla has given us permission to leave," Irene said, holding the suitcase Tristan had seen earlier.

Tristan reluctantly released Brynn and asked, "Is that for me?"

Uncertainty crossed Irene's face, but she silently agreed. She handed it to him. "Sorry for the misunderstanding."

"Yeah, right." Tristan carefully set the case on the ground and opened it. Nestled inside a foam insert sat a round clay tablet, intact. While he would have liked for Brynn to study it right then and there, it seemed wise to move out as soon as possible. He shut the case and secured it.

"Any chance you'll let me in on the translation?" Irene asked as Tristan stood.

"That's up to Brynn."

Brynn grinned, her genuine gratitude slipping past his natural defenses and landing squarely in his heart. There was no doubt about it. He was gonna have to figure out how to keep her in his life. Permanently.

"I'll get back to you, Irene," Brynn replied, keeping her eyes on him.

"I've a feeling it belongs more to you than me anyway," he added, staying lost in her gaze until Milenka interrupted them, clinging to Dimar like a toddler clutching her mother, tears streaming down her face.

Dimar looked at her like she'd lost her mind.

"I don't want Freddie, I want you!"

"What?" Freddie's voice boomed as he stomped over. With Milenka wailing and Dimar trying to unhook her fingers from his arm, an emotional argument took off between the three of them.

Tristan took Brynn's hand and led her away from the volcano that had just exploded, taking her to where Jack and Shea were speaking with one of the Bolivian men who had held everyone captive. When they neared, the man took one look at Brynn, backed away, and left them.

"What's all that about?" Tristan asked.

"It seems Brynn has garnered a reputation." Jack tugged the strap of his gun higher on his shoulder, the weapon tucked behind him.

The Mamani brothers had let them keep their firearms, speaking to how much influence Miss Carla held in this area. Tristan wondered if Pepito knew how much clout she had. Is that why he'd insisted on that first shamanic ceremony? As some kind of insurance plan?

"What kind of reputation?" she asked.

"The worst kind—you're a gypsy."

Her forehead creased into a frown. "You've lost me."

"They're afraid of you," Shea said. "Miss Carla told them what you did, and that the light people are back, which makes her inordinately happy for some reason. And they can see for themselves what kind of shape Solomon is in." He glanced over to where the shaman still sat, his shoulders sagging, appearing as if his lifeforce had been knocked out of him. "The cause is being laid entirely at your feet. But their fear is giving us the chance to escape, so I suggest we stop dawdling and make use of it."

"You've saved us all, Lola the Gypsy," Tristan murmured.

"I thought she was a showgirl." Her quiet voice held a tinge of regret as they both gazed at Solomon.

Tristan sighed. "Give me a minute."

He walked over to Solomon, who looked up at him with bloodshot eyes rimmed with dark circles.

"You look like hell, old man."

"And you have a fierce protector." Solomon's voice was tired, resigned.

"Were you really gonna do it?" Tristan's voice cracked despite his best effort to hide his disappointment; a chasm as big as the Grand Canyon threatened to engulf him at any moment.

"You know I don't play by the rules. My *papi* taught me that." Bitterness dripped from each word. "The world is a place to survive. I had to stop him. But now, I won't be able to." Solomon looked at Brynn where she stood with Jack and Shea several yards away. "She has skills, but no understanding of what she's done."

Tristan shrugged, exuding a casualness he didn't feel. "The world is what you make of it. Maybe you should face your father's ghost and deal with him instead of running." Brynn had said as much to Tristan when she'd told him to face his terror in that hospital room. And she'd been right. But Tristan guessed that Solomon wasn't that introspective. "Just close the portal yourself. Brynn said you already did it once."

"I tried. I can't. Between her and Carla ... somehow, they've safeguarded it. And I'm injured." He tapped the side of his head. "In here." His gaze slid to Brynn again. "She did it."

"You didn't give her much choice. Maybe you'll heal."

Solomon raised his gaze to him. "Maybe." His expression darkened. "You probably won't believe me, but I am sorry."

"Can't say I do, but take care of yourself, old man. That's what you seem to do best."

"You judge me, but you are the same."

The words stung, hitting their target dead center.

"Then we both need to change," Tristan said, the resolution reverberating through him, an acoustical truth serum penetrating clear to the cellular level.

With great effort, Tristan turned and walked away, wanting more but knowing it was impossible. He had loved Solomon, just as he had loved his father. Time to begin the long journey of forgiving both for their failings. Failings that Tristan no doubt had himself.

Brynn came to him and took his hand. The compassion in her eyes told him she knew of the deep wound he carried. She said nothing as they joined the others and left the jungle.

CHAPTER 31

La Paz

Brynn wrote down the last of her conclusions and closed the notebook. She was alone in the motel room, having shooed Tristan away so she could work, although the mussed sheets reminded her of their early morning romp, still humming through her body, and the faint aroma of sex still lingered in the air.

Carefully and delicately, she placed the tablet back into its cushioned carrying case. She would be transporting it back to the U.S. in the morning. She didn't look forward to telling Magee the results of her first pass at a translation, although there was a certain ironic humor in it. With hope, he would appreciate it.

She found him across the street at a crowded restaurant, sitting in a corner with Shea, both men drinking a dark-colored ale. Dodging patrons and waiters, she made her way to their table. When Tristan caught sight of her, his somber face lit up, causing her heart to bounce in her chest. She was in deep, and she hoped it wasn't written all over her face. Instinct told her that the key to Magee would be an abundance of patience.

He quickly stood and pulled out a chair for her. He waved the attendant over and Brynn ordered a beer, although something far less bitter than what they were drinking.

"Are we eating too?" she asked. "I'm starved."

"Whatever you like," Tristan said.

She ordered a plate of chicken empanadas.

Tristan leaned back in his chair, his eyes filled with excitement. "Give it to me, Galloway."

No reason to drag it out. "It's not the Moon Tablet."

Tristan's face fell, and she wished they were alone so she could coax him back to happiness in the best way she knew.

"You're certain?" Shea asked.

"I am. However, I do believe this tablet was a collaboration between my grandfather and Ninsun."

"How so?" Shea kept the conversation going while Tristan sank into a mood.

Brynn wondered where he was on the spectrum: John Denver sad, Barry Manilow melancholy, or full-blown Carpenters depressed. She laughed to lighten the mood. "They made it easy," she said. "They signed their names."

Tristan released an audible sigh. "What does it say?"

"It's right up your alley. It involves music. Gramps gave her a formula for cymbals. Not groundbreaking, necessarily, since instruments like those do date back as far as the seventh century B.C., but I do believe he gave her a unique alloy to use."

Tristan arched an eyebrow. "You're telling me she traveled forward in time to add some percussion to her band?"

"Something like that. I realize it's not quite as grand as you'd hoped. And it's not the Philosopher's Stone, as Conrad and Irene had hoped. But don't forget, we did establish contact between Mesopotamia and pre-Columbian cultures. That's no small potatoes."

"But it's all shamans and voodoo." Tristan grimaced. "Are you going to put all this in your dissertation?"

Brynn glanced at Shea, who watched her with a questioning look in his eyes. "Well, while Conrad and Irene are headed back to UCLA and their teaching positions," she said, "I've decided not to continue with them."

Such a simple statement, but it carried far more weight than she wanted to delve into at the moment. Her college career had been shaped by the two professors, and she had held genuine affection for both, especially Irene. Unraveling that would take some time. Along with her mixed emotions was the uncertainty about whether she should report them to the university. By all accounts, they were good teachers. And they hadn't technically broken the law in Bolivia. And Tristan was unlikely to press charges regarding his stolen tablet. So for now, Brynn had decided to let it go. Although, there was still the issue of the excavated mummy from Innadaltu.

She turned to Shea and asked, "What happened when you told your government contact about the mummy that was dug up?"

"Since the remains are still in the possession of the Mamanis, they said they'd handle it. But I've heard through back channels that they won't. Someone high up is protecting those thugs, so there's nothing more I can do." He shook his head in disgust. "It's such bullshit. I'm done with it."

"What about Rigo? Any recourse for him poisoning us?"

"He was finally picked up. He claimed it wasn't him. The Mamanis spiked the drink without his knowledge. Again, all he had to do was throw out the Mamani name and the officials quickly caved, sweeping the investigation aside. All I can say is, don't drink any more *chicha* unless you make it yourself. Oh, and by the way, it was Milenka who narced on us two years ago. Dimar must've said something to her."

Tristan arched an eyebrow. "Not Solomon?"

"It would seem not."

"I guess it's time to let go of past grudges." Tristan drained the beer from his glass in one swallow.

The waiter arrived and placed Brynn's food on the table before her. Both the men stole an empanada from the plate.

"Hey," she admonished, waving them off and protecting the remaining two meat pastries.

"You didn't finish telling us about your dissertation," Tristan reminded her, taking a large bite from his.

"Well, I'd been hoping for a position at the British Museum since they have an extensive collection of untranslated cuneiform tablets. But I've been offered something better, I believe."

"What's that?"

She grinned. "A position at Hartigan Archaeology and Consulting."

Tristan cast a surprised look at his cousin, empanada juice dripping between his fingers. "You offered her a job?"

"I think she'd be a good fit for what we do."

Tristan cast a bewildered look at him. "And what is it that you do exactly? Besides riding on my coattails and following me into the jungle."

"And the bullshit still continues," Shea said under his breath, pinning Tristan with a flat stare. "What we do isn't that much different than what you do." He scooped up his empanada and took a large bite.

"Are you offering me employment too?"

Shea scoffed, saying around his food, "You don't do well with having a boss. I'm offering to employ your girlfriend. That's my olive branch to the family."

"Wait," Brynn chimed in, wiping her mouth with a napkin. "I don't want to be a charity case."

"Believe me," Shea said. "You're not. You're highly qualified, and I'm happy you decided to take up my offer." Having finished his food and his drink, he stood. "Time for me to exit. I'll see you both in the morning."

They planned to share a taxi to the airport.

Once they were alone, Brynn said, "You need to tell me if working with Shea is going to be a general problem, or just a problem for *you*."

"What?" He said around a mouthful of food. "No problem." He grabbed a napkin. "You're a big girl."

"And that remark about me being your girlfriend ...." She didn't need Shea ruining her long game with Magee, dammit.

"Are you saying you don't want to be my girlfriend?"

Feigning nonchalance, Brynn said smoothly, "Are you saying you do?" And then she held her breath.

He released a bellowing laugh, which startled her, then tossed the crumpled napkin onto the table. "Of course I want you to be my girlfriend." He grabbed hold of her hand, pulling her close, and brought his face within inches of hers. "I knew you were going to be trouble the first time I saw you about to desecrate that site at Isla del Sol."

"I only *thought* about climbing on it. I didn't actually do it. That's an important point."

"I still want to find the Moon Tablet. And I'd really like you to tell me now if you were the one who wrote it."

"I don't know. I'm still not sure why I wrote that shorthand, or rather *will write*. Since that part of Gramps's notebook was unrecoverable, I'll have to rebuild it from the cave translation. I guess you'll have to stick around to find out."

"I've heard some rumors about possible artifacts."

"Where?" she asked.

"Marrakech. Ever been?"

"No."

"Wanna go?"

She narrowed her eyes. "Maybe. What's in it for me?"

"Good food. Great sex. A chance to find more portals so you can trip the light fantastic of time. You game, Lola?"

A smile spread across her face. "Definitely."

EPILOGUE

Marrakech
Mid-October

Brynn walked along the crowded street in Old Medina in the late afternoon. She was dressed conservatively with khaki trousers hanging loose, an oversized button-down shirt, a turquoise scarf hugging her neck, and a wide-brimmed hat covering hair that was pulled back. As a woman, it boded well not to bring too much attention to herself.

She, Tristan, and Shea had arrived in Marrakech yesterday. They'd come straight from La Paz, deciding it was easier to take the trip now rather than later. Shea had decided to accompany them at the last minute when Tristan had told him he might have a lead on the Moon Tablet.

They had left El Alto International Airport in La Paz in the evening, taking a short flight to the largest airport in Bolivia—Viru Viru International Airport in Santa Cruz de la Sierra—and then it was on to an overnight plane to Madrid, Spain. That had been over eleven hours, and Brynn was surprised that Tristan had booked them into Business Plus, with spacious leg room and lay-down seats. She'd insisted she could pay for her own ticket, which would have put her back in coach—she only flew in the nicer seats when her parents were footing the bill—but Magee had insisted. She couldn't deny that she enjoyed the luxury after the endless days in the jungle. After Madrid, it had been a two-hour flight to Marrakech, arriving the evening of the following day.

Weary and jet-lagged, she'd happily shared a bed with Tristan while Shea went off to his own room, although it was illegal for an unmarried couple to bunk together in a hotel in Morocco. So on paper, Brynn had one reservation while Shea and Tristan had another. But it was impossible for her to stay away from Tristan, and the resulting sheet action had aided a very deep and welcome sleep for her. It was why she was finally starting to feel more herself this morning.

Shea and Tristan walked ahead of her, wearing the laid-back look of the desert with linen trousers and shirts. They were on the lookout for Tristan's antiquities contact, so Brynn was indulging browsing the medina at the center of the city.

They were in a maze of narrow, meandering streets filled with open-fronted *souks* selling everything from leather bags, colorful rugs, pottery, and spice. She was rather enamored with the caftan, wondering if she could translate the fashion back home in America. And she loved the Berber-style necklaces, some bearing a collection of silver amulets with different symbols. She'd never been to Morocco before, and she wondered at the cultural subtext present, and what each symbol meant, for surely they were ancient signs.

They moved along the narrow cobble streets, the aroma of sizzling lamb permeating the air, along with the rich smell of harira soup, a traditional lentil and chickpea dish that Brynn was looking forward to sampling. Street performers played lutes and drums, and herbal remedies warded off the evil eye, a superstition among Moroccan people.

Brynn looked curiously at a giant egg at one display and the saleswoman told her it was ostrich. Hand symbols were everywhere, some decorated with swirling designs of henna, and the same woman told Brynn that these represented Fatima's hand.

Her attention shifted to a snake charmer in the street, and she was roughly pushed closer by someone in the crowd.

"Cobra," the man said, sitting on the ground and waving her forward. "You look. You look."

She watched transfixed as he pulled the snake from a basket and held it as it bobbed its head and slithered around his arm and across his shoulder. He moved the snake to the ground, causing Brynn to jump back, and then he coaxed it to open its hood.

"It's safe," the man said. "No venom."

Brynn guessed they had probably expressed the poisonous substance so they could safely handle the reptiles. But still ….

Without warning, a younger man standing nearby picked up the snake and threw it around Brynn's shoulders.

Holy shit!

She gasped, horrified, as every muscle in her body froze.

"You like?" the man said.

Abject terror filled her, and she hardly dared to breathe. The snake had to be at least eight feet long and hung heavy around her neck like a thick rope. Without moving her head, she angled her eyes downward to watch its head bobbing up and down near her left hip. All it had to do was whip toward her and ….

Without moving her mouth, she said through clenched teeth, "Please take it off."

First an anaconda, now this. She held no ill will toward the slithering critters, but she really didn't want to be this close to them.

The snake was lifted from her, and as she sucked in a long hit of oxygen, she turned to see Tristan holding the reptile. "Leave her alone," he said to the Moroccan as he handed it to the man.

Brynn stumbled forward, readjusting her hat as Tristan took her arm. Supporting her, he ushered her away.

"He put that snake on me before I realized what was happening."

"They do that to make you pay them." He guided her through the crowded marketplace, his hand on her elbow.

"The venom was taken out, right?"

"That's what they say."

～

TRISTAN CAME to a stall in the crowded Jemaa el Fnaa marketplace with a bright blue rug hanging outside. He'd worked through several contacts to get this tip and the rug was the beacon. Shea and Brynn followed behind him.

When he found the shopkeeper, a stooped old man with sunken cheeks and wearing a yellow tunic, he said, "I'm Magee. I'm looking for Nizar."

The man nodded and shuffled to the back of the shop, leading them through a corridor, and then across an enclosed courtyard to a small room with cushions on the floor. He told them to sit and then he left.

After several prolonged minutes of silence, Brynn spoke first. "Who is this Nizar exactly?"

"Witchdoctor," Tristan said.

Shea swore.

"Really?" Her voice was so low that it was barely above a whisper. "Are we back to that?"

Tristan sighed. "Look, I never claimed I use sound contacts. I'll use whatever the hell works."

Brynn frowned. "What does a witchdoctor do exactly?"

"Well, they can help ward off jinns."

"What are those?"

"Spirits. Mostly bad ones. Remember Aladdin?"

Brynn performed a slight eye roll, which only energized Tristan.

"There was a jinn in that story," he said. "Locals believe that jinns are not only fond of the desert but also drains and lavatories."

"So we're here to get protection from our bathroom?"

"Don't knock it," Tristan said. "I might not be able to save you if the shower drain sucks you down."

She snickered.

He pointed to a metal object with a gemstone at the center hanging on the wall. "That's a Hamsa Hand. It represents the Hand of Fatima, the Prophet Mohammed's daughter. It wards off evil spirits, curses, and bad luck. Early Christians used it, and it was eventually linked to the healing hand of the Virgin Mary."

"I'm guessing our witchdoctor will try to sell us one," Brynn murmured.

"Like any good businessman would," Shea said, rising to stand, his body vibrating impatience.

The old man returned with a younger woman wearing a colorful lime green caftan with wide sleeves, her dark hair pulled away from her face in a thick braid. He placed his hands together in prayer and gave a bow. "I am Nizar."

Tristan frowned, wondering why the man hadn't said that in the first place.

"This is Najma," Nizar said. "She is a Shawafa, a fortune-teller. She is able to open treasures that have been hidden for hundreds of years, maybe even thousands. Here is her proof." He gently took her hand and turned it palm up. He pointed to a line down her palm. "Very straight," he said. "That is a sign, as well as that her eyes get crossed from time to time."

Tristan knew of such superstitions and beliefs, but he could feel the doubt coming from Brynn and Shea.

Tristan nodded his approval to Nizar.

"Behold my hjabat, my talismans." Nizar waved at an array of trinkets that filled a side table. "They are filled with magic." He lit incense and the exotic aroma began filling the room. "Now, she will answer your questions."

Tristan suppressed his impatience. He hadn't come to speak with her. Nizar was the one his contact had recommended, but Tristan knew from experience that rudeness would get him nowhere. Still, he didn't like being jerked around, and if Najma proved to be a fake looking to fleece some foreigners, he'd leave.

Tristan described what he knew of the Moon Tablet to her.

Najma sat near them and began to rock, and her voice changed in pitch.

Tristan's perception elongated and he couldn't hear anyone in the room. It were as if he had entered a time warp. Time was normal for him, but Brynn and Shea and the Moroccans were hardly moving.

Images began to play out for him. He could see a boy and his mother. When she turned he saw that it was *his* mother. The boy must be him.

A man approached. His father.

"It's about time you showed up," Tristan said, but the longing in his voice negated the indifference he was going for.

He had never admitted it aloud, but with all of Brynn's time traveling to see her grandfather, Tristan had held a secret hope that somehow, some way, he could see his dad again.

Charlie Hartigan stopped and looked almost happy to see his only child. He was much as Tristan remembered in those early days when Harold Gatty was in his heyday of fringe fame, his gaze clear and determined, his hair dark, his smile a carbon copy of Tristan's.

"You've become a man," Charlie said.

Irritation needled Tristan. He'd been a man when Charlie had passed a year ago. Guess he hadn't noticed.

"Did you get your answers in the great beyond?" Tristan asked.

"About the aliens?"

Tristan nodded, not asking what he really wanted to know. *Do you miss me? Do you miss Mom?*

"I will say this," his dad said. "We're not alone. We live in a multi-dimensional universe that I'm only now beginning to understand. I guess your physics was right." Praise from the old man. Slim but it was a start.

A glow grew behind his dad and a doorway appeared. Charlie turned to leave. "I'll be seeing you around."

"Wait." Tristan didn't want the moment to end.

His father smiled. "I've got so much to see, so much to do. Just remember—life and death are simultaneous. We'll talk again. Oh, and tell Shea that those DNA results were correct. There *were* Europeans in South America. And you're going to have some rowdy kids with that one." His gaze landed on Brynn. "Bye, Tristan."

His father walked through the entryway and disappeared.

"Bye, Dad."

Tristan's phone buzzed, breaking the trance. He was surprised when he saw the text message. Still reeling from having seen his dad, he wondered if the old man had his hand in this too.

❦

BRYNN SAT on the bed while Shea relaxed in the chair across from her. Tristan paced the floor of the hotel room she shared with him.

He'd just told them the most fantastic story about talking to his deceased father. She believed him, but Shea looked a little harder to persuade.

Shea sighed. "I'm still not convinced about the mummy. Apparently, Uncle Charlie is still a zealot even in the afterlife."

Tristan shook his head. "It doesn't matter. We have a new lead on the Moon Tablet."

"You mean your dad didn't tell you where it was?" Shea raised a skeptical brow.

"I think he may have. Marina texted me. She wants us to come to her. Maybe he nudged her from the great beyond."

Shea whistled.

Brynn's female radar went on high alert. "Who's Marina?" she asked, fearing she was an ex-girlfriend. Brynn didn't think she'd have to fight one off so soon after getting involved with Magee.

"An old friend," Tristan said, doing little to quell her concerns.

"Shall I wait at the hotel?" She held back on adding *and for how long?*

"No." Tristan answered without hesitation. "She invited you as well. Better pack up. She'll insist that we stay overnight."

"How far?"

"Not much. It'll take us a few hours."

"Where does she live?"

"In the mountains."

❦

BRYNN SAT in the front seat beside Tristan in the modest-sized rental car. They had left Marrakech and were now headed into the Atlas Mountains. It was a beautiful drive, quite romantic really, if not for Shea's light snoring coming from the back seat.

"So who is this Marina woman?" Brynn asked, her curiosity gnawing at her. Best to know where she stood. "Does she have a last name?"

"Marina Kallis."

"She sounds glamorous. Should I be worried that she might steal you away from me?"

Tristan took a double take, then laughed, startling Shea in the back.

"Keep it down," Shea mumbled, then went back to sleep.

"Marina's not a young woman," Tristan said, still smiling.

"That doesn't change my question." She folded her arms across her chest.

Tristan gave her a wicked grin. "Are you jealous?"

She jammed her eyebrows together. "No."

He reached over and pulled her hand free from her crossed arms and clasped it. Tightly. "Is it time for the talk?"

"What do you mean?"

"The relationship talk. The one where we agree to see only each other."

"I'm not pushing for the talk," she insisted. God, what had she done?

"What if I am?"

She kept her eyes forward, but let her hand relax in his. "We don't have to do this right now," she said quietly.

"I'm in this, Brynn. One hundred percent."

She glanced at him, enjoying his profile, the strong jawline, and the compelling gaze he slanted her way. As usual, her heart skipped a beat in response to the smoldering passion mixed with his devil-may-care attitude.

What the hell. "Me too," she replied.

"That's good, because if the aliens come then I want you to go with me."

"Like at the end of Close Encounters of the Third Kind when Richard Dreyfuss's character abandons his family to live with the little grey people?"

Tristan exhaled on a light chuckle. "When you say it like that, you make him sound like an ass. He was called, compelled if you will. It was out of his hands."

"Fate?"

"Don't you believe in kismet? I think meeting you was exactly that."

She looked out the passenger window so he wouldn't see her happy smile over the new status of their relationship. Fate indeed.

Dusk was upon them. "An in-between place," she murmured.

"What are you mumbling about, Galloway?"

"Many ancient people believed that the gloaming—that moment between day and night—was special. Things that were invisible could be seen. Witches cast their spells, animals did their hunting, doorways opened."

"Watch out, Lola the Gypsy. Your inner shaman is emerging."

"Maybe. Tell me about Marina."

"I met her years ago when I first started hunting antiquities. She's quite the collector. She mentored me for a time."

"Why?"

"Because of my rugged good looks."

"I knew it. Hussy."

He laughed. "I think the word you're looking for is gigolo. And no, I've never been one, no matter how much I wanted an artifact. In the beginning, I didn't know why she helped me, but later I learned she had lost her son in a plane crash. I suppose I reminded her of him in some way."

"Why didn't you make a point to see her as soon as we arrived in Marrakech? Why did you wait for her to contact you first?"

"Well, when Shea and I had our falling out, she was the one I called to clean up our mess with the Bolivian officials. Marina has a lot of ... contacts. But she was a little pissed at how it all went down, and she told me so in no uncertain terms. I hadn't heard from her until today."

"How did she know you were in Morocco?"

Tristan shrugged. "Probably that witchdoctor Nizar."

"You think he contacted her telepathically?"

"No." Tristan laughed. "When he left us that first time, I'm guessing he immediately went to call her."

"Why?"

"Because little happens in Marrakech that Marina doesn't know about."

TRISTAN PARKED the car in front of the large house hugging the hillside. Located not far from the Berber village of Imlil, Marina's home was an extravagance compared to the red-clay buildings in town, but Marina Kallis was as well-known for her privacy as she was for her generosity to the local economy. And although she was of Greek descent, Morocco had been her home for over thirty years.

A certain amount of relief welled up inside Tristan. He'd missed Marina, but he'd accepted her chastisement for the handling of the mummies and had stayed away.

There had been a locked gate at the bottom of the driveway, but when he'd pressed the button it had opened automatically. He knew Marina would have a camera on him. At least she had let him through.

Tristan got out of the car and went to the trunk to pull out the suitcases. Brynn and a sleepy-looking Shea each grabbed their own. Tristan went first up the wide stone stairs to the front door. It opened before he could knock.

Marina stood there, an amused smile on her aging face. She looked much as he remembered, her short hair still gray and fashioned away from her face, her face still wrinkle-free. She'd always had an ethereal quality to her. There were times when Tristan had wondered if she were a fairy or some other creature of the night.

Maybe Marina was an earth-bound alien.

Dressed in slacks and a sweater, she rested a hand on her hip while the other held the door open. She was a petite woman who nevertheless commanded a room. "Tristan," she said, pursing her lips together. "I'm glad you've come."

"It's good to see you, Marina. I wasn't sure if you would ever forgive me."

She narrowed her gaze. "Time heals all wounds." She stepped back to let them enter.

"You remember Shea," he said as his cousin stepped into the foyer. "And this is Brynn Galloway."

Marina nodded and smiled warmly at Shea, then she reached out a hand to Brynn. "I can't tell you how happy I am to finally meet you."

A blush suffused each of Brynn's cheeks. "You know about me?"

"I do. And not just because of him." She jutted her chin toward Tristan, before turning back to Brynn. "I've had my eye on you for a while," she added, her face glowing with reverence.

Brynn's eyes widened. "You've read my paper on the Moon Tablet?"

"Yes, of course. But it's more than that. We'll discuss it once you all are rested from your travels." Marina shifted her focus back to Tristan. "You came to Marrakech and you weren't even going to call me?"

Feeling like a boy rebuked by his mother, Tristan said, "My mistake."

"Spoken like a man who's made many." Marina waved them inside. "Leave your bags. Wassim will take them to your rooms." She led them to a spacious sitting area, and then glanced over her shoulder with a glint in her eyes. "I'm assuming just two rooms?"

"If you're asking if I'm sharing a room with Shea, the answer is no," Tristan said.

Marina laughed. "Are you hungry? I've had my cook prepare a light supper. And then you can retire to your rooms and rest. I'm sure you've had a long day."

Once everyone had washed up, they were soon seated at an elegant table in the dining room. Tristan noticed Brynn's interest in the many artifacts that decorated Marina's house. Her tastes ran to every-thing—the Chinese dynasties, the moors of Spain, the French, the American Southwest, the Maya of Central America, and Mesopotamia.

"You have quite a collection," Brynn said as a young man brought them wine followed with bowls of a fragrant lentil soup.

"It's a passion of mine. It's how I met Tristan, and then later Shea. Good boys, if not distracted at times by a pretty bauble. And how did Tristan find you?"

"In Bolivia. He saved me from falling into the Fountain at Isla del Sol."

"Chivalry." Marina smiled. "I like it. I always told you, Tristan, that heroics would look good on you. It's a shame you never believed me."

"Don't make me into a saint yet." He set his spoon aside, having finished his soup in record time. A woman dressed as a housekeeper appeared and cleared the dish.

"Marina," Shea said. "I'm sure you know why we're in Morocco."

"I do." She leaned back as the cook brought a dinner plate for each of them.

White fish in a light sauce, sautéed vegetables, and a potato gratin. Tristan savored the first bite and then kept going.

"Conrad Fontana isn't the most discreet man, I'm afraid," Marina said. "And neither is his wife. But she didn't acquire the Moon Tablet, did she? Despite her backroom deals?"

"That's about right," Tristan said.

"But she thought she'd stolen it from you."

"She claimed she didn't know."

Marina made a noncommittal sound. "She's not discreet, but she's not stupid either. Still, she was outwitted on this one."

Tristan stopped his fork midair. "Sonofabitch. You have it!"

Marina's face revealed nothing as she shushed him. "Watch your language, Tristan. Perhaps I know how to find it."

"What's the catch?" There always was one with her.

"No catch. But this has nothing to do with you boys."

Tristan frowned. "What are you talking about?"

"I'd like to speak to Brynn once we've eaten. Alone."

AFTER SUPPER, Brynn followed Marina downstairs, feeling full in a way she hadn't in quite some time. It was no doubt the delicious meal, followed by a crème brûlée dessert and a decaf coffee, but she also felt a kinship with this woman. Marina's fondness for Tristan was apparent, their recent rift notwithstanding, and it only warmed Brynn's heart more. Even Shea had relaxed, showing more humor than Brynn would have given him credit. The men had settled in the study with a nightcap, although Brynn could feel Tristan's frustration that he wasn't allowed to be a part of this meeting.

If Brynn had been mesmerized by Marina's collection in her dining room, she was downright astounded when they entered an area Marina opened with a key punch code. She flipped on the lights and revealed a room that was deep and lined with shelves and tables.

"Extraordinary." Brynn couldn't keep the awe from her voice. "Are you an archaeologist?"

"No. But maybe in another life. I'm self-taught. I've always been fascinated by the past, but when I was young my father insisted that I study literature. Another practical pursuit," she added with a soft chuckle.

As Brynn followed Marina to the back of the room—cool and obviously temperature controlled—she stared at the tables filled with archaeological riches. She identified many from Mesopotamia. All were in excellent shape.

Brynn fought the urge to stop several times. Even if she had a month down here, it wouldn't be enough time.

Marina came to another door and punched a code once again on a nearby panel. As they stepped inside, Marina switched on a bright overhead light. This room was much smaller with glass-enclosed shelves on three of the walls.

A chill ran down Brynn's back.

Something about the pieces—and the special care that Marina took with them—told Brynn she was about to witness something she guessed very few did.

Brynn focused on a collection of faded and withering parchment. She recognized the language as Greek.

"The Gospel of Mary Magdalene," Marina said. "It's just a fragment, located sometime at the turn of the nineteenth century. The main apocryphal text is owned by a man in Germany. Some dispute that it's not Mary Magdalene but some other Mary. His mother perhaps? A long-lost sister of Jesus?" Marina smiled. "I'm of a mind that it *was* Mary Magdalene, who was sorely misrepresented among the disciples. Strong women usually are. But that's a debate for another time."

Brynn's attention shifted to a small stone statue of a very voluptuous female figure with a thick round belly and full breasts. It wasn't more than four inches high.

"That's the Willendorf Venus," Marina said. "It was uncovered in Austria and dates back nearly 26,000 years."

"I know," Brynn said, reverence dripping off the words.

"There are, of course, other similar 'Venus figurines' from Europe's Old Stone Age, or Paleolithic period, but I've always been fond of this one. The ultimate symbol of fertility, isn't it?"

Brynn caught a glimpse of a spiral tattoo on the inside of Marina's left forearm. "That's something found around the world," she said, pointing to the marking.

"An ancient symbol often used to mark places of high resonance, places where shamans would conduct their rituals and interdimensional travels. But it's also a symbol of serpent power, representing the life force itself." Marina watched Brynn with speculation in her gaze. "Encompassing the very idea of immortality."

Brynn laughed. "The Philosopher's Stone. A myth."

"Perhaps. Have you had any recent encounters with snakes?"

"A few." *An anaconda. A cobra.* "I wouldn't describe them as pleasant."

"I'd like to hear the details but first this." She indicated another enclosed case and pointed to a stone tablet resting upon a silk green cloth.

Excitement coursed through Brynn. "Does Tristan know you have this?" Her voice was nothing more than a whisper, as if her words might disturb the precious artifacts in the room. She didn't take her gaze from the Moon Tablet of Ur.

"It was never meant for him. It was meant for you."

Brynn raised her eyes and met the warmth and compassion in Marina's. "I suppose you're about to tell me a wild story."

Marina's laugh was filled with pure merriment. "It's so good to see you again."

Again?

~

BRYNN FOUND Tristan sitting on the veranda alone, the invisible cord between them tugging even tighter after her conversation with Marina.

A slight breeze rustled the lush foliage beyond, the leaves just beginning to turn from green to yellow. Brynn breathed deeply and settled into a chair beside the man whose fate was becoming more entwined with her own.

Tristan glanced over and handed her his half-filled glass of clear liquid.

Brynn took a sip. "I'm no connoisseur, but this is some smooth stuff."

"It's called Mahia. It's a brandy made from dates. They grow them here." He indicated the valley with his hand. "Along with walnuts and cherries."

"It reminds me of warm sunshine." She took another drink and set the glass on the mosaic table between them.

Tristan slid his gaze to her. "She has it, doesn't she?"

"Yes."

"And she's had it for some time."

"Yes."

He released a resigned laugh, gazing at the starry night sky. "And she's not gonna give it to me, is she?"

"No. But if it's any consolation, she gave me a fast and dirty translation, courtesy of me."

"Now you've lost me, Lola."

"It would seem your fate and mine have been wrapped up with Marina for a while. She knew my grandfather."

Tristan gave her his full attention.

"It was many years ago. They were introduced through her companion, a man named Michail, who Gramps had met during a trip to Moscow. Through a love of the Sumerian culture, they remained friends."

Tristan frowned. "Marina has a Russian boyfriend?"

"I gather she's a very private person, even with her closest friends. Anyway, over the years, Gramps told her about me."

"About Brynn the child."

"And Brynn the adult," she added quietly. "You see, the Moon Tablet *is* about travel. But not space travel. It's about the kind of travel that Ninsun did with me in the jungle."

"Time travel."

Brynn nodded. "Marina acquired the Moon Tablet nearly ten years ago and set about deciphering it."

"Did your grandfather know she had it?"

Brynn tucked her legs beneath her and turned toward Tristan. "Well, here's where it gets interesting. He told her about my visit from the future. She told him she had the tablet. After exchanging copies of the glyphs, they were able to make a cursory translation. Enough so that Marina tried it."

"She time traveled?"

"Yes." Brynn laughed. "She went to the future. She came to see *me*."

"No shit?" Tristan's voice held both humor and disbelief. "Then why don't you remember it?"

"Because it hasn't happened yet. C'mon, Magee. Keep up. You're a physicist, after all."

"I think I'm going to change my discipline to philosophy."

She continued, "It gets better, and so circular it makes your head hurt. Marina learned the contents of the Moon Tablet from me in the future, so in this time I now need to decipher it. She won't give me the actual piece, which is fine, but she's given me photos. She shared all of this with Gramps, so that would explain his fascination with the tablet and why he was always talking to me about it. But he and Marina decided to keep their knowledge of the future to themselves for fear it would somehow muck up the timeline."

"And the cuneiform shorthand?"

Brynn shrugged. "I created that as well. Not yet, but eventually, I guess. And I'll go back and give it to Gramps."

"What came first, the chicken or the egg?" Tristan muttered.

"I'm not sure we'll ever know." A fluffy Persian cat jumped into her lap.

"Who's that?"

"This is Sean Connery." Brynn cooed at the animal as he rubbed affectionately against her. As the crease in Tristan's forehead deepened, she added, "Marina seems to have a special regard for Scottish boys."

"I guess that explains why she likes me."

"And who wouldn't like you?" Brynn teased.

"I don't think you did. At least, not in the beginning."

"That's not true. I thought you were quite compelling that day at the fountain. I was just playing it cool. But there's something else. When Marina visited me in the future, I told her about you. And she—"

"Befriended me on your advice," he finished for her.

"I didn't tell her to exactly, but essentially yes."

He chuckled. "It would seem you've had a hand in more than one life-changing moment in my life."

Doubt churned in her gut. "Are you angry?"

"No, just ... surprised. This didn't go how I thought it would."

"In what way?"

"The search for the Moon Tablet. Proving the existence of alien technology." His gaze landed on her, dark and full of intention. "Meeting you."

"Fate."

"Fate, my ass. You, Marina, and Ninsun have shown that female intervention exceeds it all. You've shown that time isn't linear, that human progress hasn't been helped by outside forces but rather by other humans." He reached over and clasped her hand, using it to pull her to him. "And I'm not sharing you with Sean Connery."

She carefully scooped the cat from her lap with her free hand and settled him on her seat, then she came to Tristan and straddled him, looping her arms around his neck.

"So I'm still around in the future?" he said against her lips. "Give me the lowdown, Lola. Are we married with 2.5 kids?"

"You'll have to wait and find out."

"Well, according to my dad, the answer is yes." He kissed her, a light, feathery touch.

She leaned back to look at him. "Really?"

"He said, and I quote, our children will be 'rowdy.'"

She leaned her forehead against his. "Sounds about right. Are you worried?"

"About our unruly kids?"

"No. About knowing." She shrugged. "The future."

"Nah." His hands teased her body with gentle caresses. "We're temporary gatherings of stardust anyway, so best not to waste our time. I'm happy to focus on you right now, right here, in the present."

His fingers slipped beneath the edge of her pants and his palms were soon cupping the bare skin of her buttocks. His mouth captured hers in a heated and thoroughly carnal kiss that had her squirming to get closer to him. When it became too intense, they reluctantly stopped and moved with great haste back to their room, shifting Sean Connery to a sofa in the den.

Later, she lay in his arms on the soft bed, her backside nestled against him, his steady breath tickling the back of her neck. Moonlight slanted through the gauzy curtains decorating the bedroom window, shimmering, ethereal, otherworldly.

And she began humming *We've Only Just Begun.*

THE END

If you enjoyed *Ancient Winds,* would you consider posting a review at your favorite book site? Not only does this help other readers discover a book, but it also aids an author in pursuing promotional opportunities. My heartfelt thanks. ~ Kristy

SIGN-UP FOR KRISTY'S newsletter to receive the latest Pathway series news at kmccaffrey.com/subscribe/.

Read about Brynn's college roommate, Audrey Driggs,
in the long novella
Blue Sage

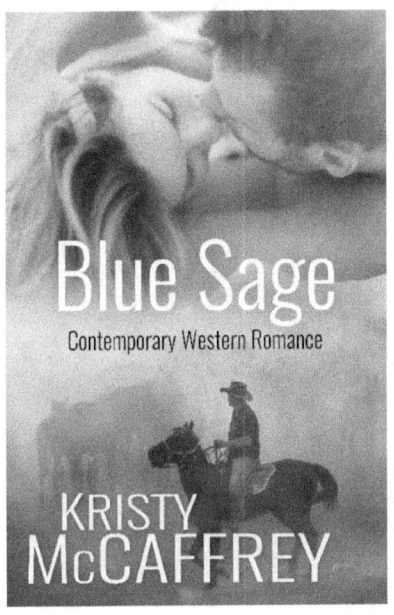

What do you do when a woman literally lands at your feet?

Braden Delaney has taken over the family cattle business after the death of his father, but faced with difficult financial decisions, he contemplates selling a portion of the massive Delaney ranch holdings known as Whisper Rock, a place of unusual occurrences. The sudden appearance of a pretty relic-hunter while he's collecting his livestock, however, is about to change his mind.

Archaeologist Audrey Driggs arrives in the remote wilderness of Northern Arizona looking for clues to a life-altering experience from her childhood. When she rolls off a mountain and lands at the feet of rugged cowboy Braden Delaney, it's clear she needs his knowledge of the area to complete her quest. But if she tells him the truth, will he think she's crazy?

Together, they'll uncover a long-lost secret.

Learn more about Blue Sage
at
https://kmccaffrey.com/blue-sage/

Don't miss *DEEP BLUE*
The Pathway Series Book 1

Dr. Grace Mann knows great white sharks. As the daughter of an obsessed shark researcher, Grace spent her childhood in the company of these elegant and massive creatures. Now, finally, she's testing a prototype shark array that may lead to a reliable alert system for swimmers and sharks to coexist. All that stands in her way are two men—her ex, Brad Michaels, fellow shark researcher and the man trying to steal her work, and Alec Galloway, an underwater filmmaker hired to produce a documentary about Grace's project. Grace mixed her work and love life before and it was a disaster. No matter how sexy Galloway is, she won't make that mistake again …

Alec Galloway prides himself on being the best in the business, so he's baffled when Dr. Mann rejects his application to capture her work on film. When her boss overrules her decision and gives Alec the job, he learns that winning over Grace won't come easy. But Alec is accustomed to dealing with unpredictable creatures, and Grace's passionate focus on great whites puts her in a class of danger all her own. As his fan-boy crush on the woman quickly turns into something more, his greatest competition turns out to be the sharks themselves.

Learn more about Deep Blue
at
https://kmccaffrey.com/deep-blue/

After reading the novel DEEP BLUE, don't miss three exciting short stories featuring shark researcher Dr. Grace Mann, her boyfriend, underwater filmmaker Alec Galloway, and Double D.

DEEP BLUE AUSTRALIA
Grace and Alec travel to Western Australia for a commercial shoot with great white sharks.

DEEP BLUE REUNION ISLAND
Grace joins Alec on a trip to the French island of Réunion to document efforts in relocating aggressive bull sharks from the coastline.

DEEP BLUE COCOS ISLAND

Alec is hired to film Grace and several distinguished female marine scientists in the waters off Cocos Island.

Learn more about this collection
at
https://kmccaffrey.com/pathway-shorts-collection-one/

Cold Horizon
The Pathway Series Book 2

Lindsey Coulson likes to scale mountains. With her sister, Alison, she has made a name for herself climbing the tallest and most treacherous peaks in the world. But when Alison dies on a K2 expedition—the second highest mountain on earth—Lindsey stops climbing. Unable to shed her heartache, it becomes clear she must return to the wilderness and only one place will do—K2, the Savage Mountain. And to get there, she'll need handsome, enigmatic Tyler Galloway.

Ty Galloway welcomes Lindsey to his small crew with one hitch—to help with funding he wants to write about her for a magazine feature. In climbing circles, Lindsey and her sister had been famous for their mountain exploits, and her comeback story would be compelling. But he didn't account for how captivating the woman herself would be.

Tackling K2 will test Ty's limits, but Lindsey Coulson will test his heart.

2021 National Excellence in Romance Fiction Winner

Learn more about Cold Horizon
at
https://kmccaffrey.com/cold-horizon/

The Pathway Series Reading Order

Each novel can be enjoyed as a stand-alone, but for those interested here is the chronological reading order:

Deep Blue (A Pathway Novel)
Shark Reef*
Deep Blue Australia*
Deep Blue Réunion Island*
Cold Horizon (A Pathway Novel)
Deep Blue Cocos Island*
Ancient Winds (A Pathway Novel)
Blue Sage (Related Novella)
Cold Horizon Telluride*
Sapphire Waves (A Pathway Novella)
Deep Blue Hawai'i*

*Short stories in the Pathway universe

ACKNOWLEDGMENTS

N ormally, I pen an Author's Note with background information on the writing of a book, but I didn't feel a great need to do this with *Ancient Winds*. While I did immerse myself in research of the Bolivian jungle, shamanic time travel, and ancient Mesopotamia, along with lurking in online forums that supported ancient alien theories, this novel was borne mostly from my imagination. My goal was to entertain, and I sincerely hope I succeeded.

My first round of thanks must go to the stories of my youth, absorbed mostly via films, for inspiring me with adventure, romance, and the outrageous. They include *Raiders of the Lost Ark, Romancing the Stone, The Mummy* (with Brendan Fraser and Rachel Weisz), and *High Road To China* (Remember that one? It starred Tom Selleck and Bess Armstrong.). I always envisioned myself on those journeys alongside the characters, and without question I wanted to write such a tale one day.

I must thank my beta readers: Becky Humphreys, Corie Carson, Vicki Huskey, Cindy Nelson, Heather Chargualaf, Bob Dickerson, and Michelle Davis for their wonderful comments and enthusiasm for the story. A special thanks to Debby Fields for proofing one of the final copies. Thank you to author Ann Charles for her read-through and for bouncing around ideas. The book is better for it. Diane Garland performs many jobs for me: beta reader, proofreader, and tracker of story details. As always, I value her input and appreciate her time spent in my world, as well as her eleventh-hour corrections.

A big thank you to my editor, Mimi Munk. When she offers a critique, she does it with such kindness that it soothes my quaking fragile author-ego, making me feel that, yes, I *will* attempt to write another book despite the lingering madness from the last one.

And finally, a big hug and round of applause to my husband, Kevin. If you've read any of my other novels, you know I frequently thank him, but I can't pass up another opportunity to express my gratitude. He's the first person I turn to when my plot inevitably, and more regularly than I would like, crumbles into pieces. If you had a magnifying glass, you'd find his fingerprints all over my stories.

Thank you, dear reader, for trusting me with your precious time. I don't take your attention lightly, and please know that I worked my butt off to make this an adventure to remember. Be cool, and I hope you'll join me in my next book.

ABOUT THE AUTHOR

Kristy McCaffrey has been writing since she was very young, but it wasn't until she was a stay-at-home mom that she considered becoming published. A fascination with science led her to earn two mechanical engineering degrees—she did her undergraduate work at Arizona State University and her graduate studies at the University of Pittsburgh—but storytelling has always been her passion. She writes both contemporary adventures and award-winning historical western romances.

An Arizona native, Kristy and her husband reside in the desert where they frequently remove (rescue) rattlesnakes from their property, go for runs among the cactus, and plan trips to far-off places like the Orkney Islands or Machu Picchu. But mostly, she works 12-hour days and enjoys at-home date nights with her sweetheart, which usually include Will Ferrell movies and sci-fi flicks. Her four children have all flown the nest, so she lavishes her maternal instincts on Jeb, an American Bulldog her family rescued in 2021. He has his own Instagram account at @jeb_therescue.

"Be in love with your life." – Jack Kerouac

Connect with Kristy
Website: kmccaffrey.com
Newsletter: kmccaffrey.com/subscribe
Facebook: facebook.com/AuthorKristyMcCaffrey
Instagram: instagram.com/kristymccaffreybooks/
BookBub: bookbub.com/authors/kristy-mccaffrey
TikTok: tiktok.com/@kristymccaffrey